THE
EYE COLLECTORS

A STORY OF HER MAJESTY'S
OFFICE OF THE WITCHFINDER GENERAL

PROTECTING THE PUBLIC FROM THE UNNATURAL SINCE 1645

Nihil obstat: Dorothy Aphrodite Coldwater
Imprimatur: Campbell Percy Hardknott-Lewis KCB DL,
Lord High Witchfinder of All Wales

THE EYE COLLECTORS

A STORY OF HER MAJESTY'S OFFICE OF THE WITCHFINDER GENERAL

PROTECTING THE PUBLIC FROM THE UNNATURAL SINCE 1645

SIMON KEWIN

Elsewhen Press

The Eye Collectors

First published in Great Britain by Elsewhen Press, 2020
An imprint of Alnpete Limited

Quotes are included from *Dracula*, Bram Stoker, London, Archibald Constable and
Company 1897; *The Mabinogion*, from the translation by Lady Charlotte Guest,
London: Longman, Brown, Green and Longmans, 1848; *Malleus Maleficarum*,
Henricus Institoris, 1487, from the translation by Rev Montague Summers,
London: John Rodker, 1928; *Le Morte d'Arthur*, Sir Thomas Malory, c. 1469, from
the modern rendering edited by Pollard, A. W., New York: Macmillan, 1903; *The
Picture of Dorian Gray*, Oscar Wilde, from *Lippincott's Monthly Magazine*, London:
Ward, Lock and Company, 1890. Quotes from documents in the internal archives
of Her Majesty's Office of the Witchfinder General that are no longer, or have
never been, in the public domain, are used with permission.

Elsewhen Press, PO Box 757, Dartford, Kent DA2 7TQ
www.elsewhen.press

British Library Cataloguing in Publication Data.
A catalogue record for this book is available from the British Library.

ISBN 978-1-911409-64-9 Print edition
ISBN 978-1-911409-74-8 eBook edition

Condition of Sale
This book is sold subject to the condition that it shall not, by way of trade
or otherwise, be lent, re-sold, hired out or otherwise circulated in any form
of binding or cover other than that in which it is published and without a
similar condition including this condition being imposed on the
subsequent purchaser.

Designed and formatted by Elsewhen Press

This book is a work of fiction. All names, characters, organisations, places,
and events are either a product of the author's fertile imagination or are used
fictitiously. Any resemblance to actual events, villages, cities, magical cults,
or people (living, dead or in Oblivion) is purely coincidental.

CONTENTS

For Andrew Walton – thanks for all the gigs

1 – The First Victim

Many have attempted to trace the deep roots of true English Magick. Does it flow with the pure waters that spring spontaneously from our fair hills and mountain uplands? Does it rise with the very sap of our ancient oak woods? Has there perhaps, over time, been a certain *intermingling* between the people of these isles and creatures of a more ineffable, less visible nature? Whatever the truth of it, the primacy of English wizardry in the catalogues of the eldritch arts can scarcely be contradicted.

–Samuel Bedfellowes, *The Old Ways*, 1847

The killer had extracted the victim's eyes. That got my attention. Also, the pentagram daubed around the body in what I doubted was red paint.

I'd been summoned to the crime scene without much expectation of finding anything significant. You'd be surprised how often it happens: a murder with hints of *ritual*, a few bizarre or inexplicable circumstances, and some investigating officer in the know will murmur, "What do you think, one for the witchfinders?" And another investigating officer in the know will purse their lips, pause, then nod, only too happy to have a potentially troublesome case handed over. And then I'll discover the victim's jealous spouse buried that knife in the victim's neck because they'd been unfaithful, or abusive, or just plain irritating, and that's all there is to it. Nothing arcane, no forbidden arts perverting the natural order, nothing.

That's basically how it always goes. Except, occasionally, it doesn't.

I crouched beside the body, feeling ridiculous in my white crime-scene onesie. Not clothing that would normally be much use or protection to me. Still, I was careful not to touch anything, in case the investigation did turn out to be a simple matter of hair follicles and fingerprints and mere criminal laws.

The complete lack of blood spatter intrigued me. Murder is a messy business, but there was no blood anywhere apart from in that spell-circle. Whoever carried out this mutilation knew what they were doing. At the very least it had to be the work of a surgeon or someone else used to taking a scalpel to the soft tissues of the human body. Which, okay, didn't mean anything unnatural was involved. Maybe the victim had particularly beautiful eyes and some crazy wanted them for their private collection. Or maybe the victim had witnessed something they shouldn't have, and the murderer wanted to *really* emphasise the point.

I don't know. People kill people for all sorts of reasons. But the removal of both eyes reminded me of something. I resisted the temptation to call it *instinct*. That was magical thinking, within shouting distance of superstition; it was what we in the Office existed to stamp out. No, it was some half-remembered case from the archives, or some investigation I wasn't privileged enough to have full access to.

It didn't help that I hadn't slept much and that thinking straight was like trying to see through a fog rolling in off the Bristol Channel. I haven't told you the date. Let me tell you the date: 31st October. All Hallows' Eve. Samhain. Hallowe'en. The date when the veils between the worlds weaken and all leave in the Office is cancelled. I had my own reasons for dreading the date on top of all that: it was my birthday, and that was bad because it meant it would have been my brother's birthday too.

I forced my attention back to the body. The victim was a thirtyish guy, handsome if you excused his lack of eyes. He lay on his back, hands by his sides, as if he'd made himself comfortable and nodded off. It was hard not to read an expression of wide-eyed amazement upon his ruined face. Disbelief at how his day had gone. He wasn't clean-shaven, but his stubble was trimmed, deliberate. His suit was tailored, fashionably skinny, and his new leather shoes shone. All of which was odd in itself: the house was a boarded-up hovel in a row of boarded-up hovels, in a part of Cardiff where most of the terraces had been demolished in the 1960s and 1970s to make room for tower blocks. So, a pimp or a drug-dealer, maybe. Perhaps he'd walked right into some rival street-gang's ambush.

"This thing with the eyes," I said. "Is that the calling-card of any of the local mobsters?"

A uniformed officer squatted beside me. He was no one I knew. From what I could see of his features, he looked like he was maybe only a few years out of university – so about my age. Chances were he wasn't on the inside, and he thought I was from some specialist police unit rather than a completely separate arm of government not subject to *Heddlu* lines of command. The misunderstanding often came in handy.

"Never seen anything like this," he said, voice muffled through his mask. "When the local bastards want to make a point, they don't go in for delicate surgery, they go in for as much gore as possible. Right bloody animals they are."

I leaned in closer to examine the eye-sockets, picking up the faint tang of a caustic chemical even through my mask. The eyeballs had been removed recently. The only blood was a dried trickle of watery red down the left side of the man's head. Someone had gone to the trouble of cleaning up as they went along, just as a surgeon would. Most likely, there'd been more than one of them: one to cut, one to swab.

"Who alerted you to the crime?"

"It was sheer luck. They're planning to knock this terrace down, and someone from the company came in to make sure no one was squatting."

"That's quite a coincidence."

"I suppose it is."

Then there was the pentagram. The victim lay in its exact centre, head to the south. Either he'd been placed within or it had been drawn around him. The former seemed more likely. I'd only seen a few mystic circles in my three years with the Office, but that was enough to tell the difference between a fake and one humming with real power. This was the genuine article, emblazoned with sigils conveying screams of torment when glimpsed from the corner of your eye. I was too lowly to be trusted with full knowledge of the forbidden alphabets, but I had some inkling of what I was looking at. The pentagram sent a chill shivering through me, made my testicles contract walnut-tight.

Something malign had taken place in this room.

The other person crouching beside the body was a forensics officer, currently photographing the corpse from every conceivable angle. Strictly speaking, if she took any shots of the pentagram, she was committing a serious magus law offence. Reproducing proscribed symbols of power with intent could be punishable by immediate dispatch to Oblivion. I was pretty sure she had no clue about the significance of the runes; she would probably comb them for fingerprints or stray hairs, utterly oblivious to the howling agonies they hinted at, but I instructed her not to reproduce the symbols in any way, and to delete any pictures she had taken.

Her response was a raised eyebrow. Lines of command between the Office and other law-enforcement bodies can be hazy, but in such matters, we absolutely have the final say. I directed her to discuss the matter with her commanding officer if she had any concerns. To which she shrugged and returned to her work.

"He was killed recently?" I asked.

She at least managed to keep her voice civil. "This morning, maybe late last night."

"Too soon to work out a cause of death?"

"Hard to say without turning him over or opening him up. Apart from the eyes, there are no wounds or marks visible. I'd guess he was poisoned before *that* was done to him."

"You think he was dead when his eyes were removed?"

"I'd say that's likely. It would have been impossible to make such neat incisions with a struggling victim."

"He might have been unconscious."

"He'd have bled heavily from such wounds with his heart still pumping. My guess is that the murderer incapacitated him, extracted his blood to paint the magic circle, *then* took the eyes. By which time he was probably dead from blood loss."

"Have you found a puncture hole?"

"Not so far."

She hadn't mentioned the most likely explanation of what had happened: that the victim had been slain by some ritual of death-sorcery. Or merely paralysed. Perhaps he'd been conscious throughout, aware but unable to move even as the scalpel approached and his tormentor began the work of cutting away his eyelids, severing the muscles wrapping around his eyeballs. Still seeing, maybe, even as his eyes were pulled from his skull attached only by their optic nerves. It was the sort of grim detail the deviants we pursue revel in. Some essential component of the sorcery – or, simply, the arrogant sadism of those who don't feel bound by normal human laws. Blood collection for ritual purposes is a common enough feature of such crimes, and I'd studied three or four cases where magic was used to carefully drain a victim of their blood so that runes could be drawn.

I kept these thoughts to myself.

"Do you know who he is? *Was*, I mean?"

"Not at this point. We might get something from his fingerprints if he's been a bad lad."

"Thanks for your help."

"It's been an absolute pleasure."

I took out my phone and took pictures of my own, making sure to capture each rune in close up. At my level, I just about had clearance to reproduce the marks so long as the shots remained upon authorised Office equipment and I used them only for the purposes of investigation. I had to be very careful. If they got into the public domain, it would be me never seeing the light of day again.

The forensics officer looked baffled at my actions but said nothing.

I looked around the room to see if there was anything I'd missed. The smallest details could be significant, and they might well be things a police officer would overlook.

It was a sad, shabby little place. My mask almost kept out the mouldy smell. Square lines of light filtered in through metal sheeting screwed to the window frames. The floorboards were bare, and there was no furniture apart from a yellow armchair, worn and peppered with cigarette burns. It was a grim place for your whole life to lead to, a sad end. The walls were bare plaster, and someone had made soot marks upon them with a cigarette lighter or a candle. They didn't look like anything relevant – it was hard to know how long they'd been there – but I photographed them, just in case.

There was a small pile of grubby, stained bedding in one corner. At some point someone had slept in that room, although probably not, I guessed, the sharply dressed man lying on the floor. Nevertheless, the police had marked the bedding off in chalk, drawing a circle – a circle with a different sort of power – around it.

It was then – turning to look around the room – that I had one of my episodes. Let me tell you about them. I don't know if they're migraines or epileptic fits, or some sort of mild psychotic episode. So far, medicine hasn't found a good explanation. The attacks usually hit me at times of stress or when I've witnessed something traumatic. Or when I haven't slept well. They're like this: the world around me goes dark, but the shadows get brighter, dancing and lurching and laughing. Sometimes there are voices – blaring, disjointed cries – and sometimes there are faces looming from the gloom to shout into my face. There are words, but I don't understand them: garbled syllables of a confused tongue. The words carry with them a weight of nausea, sometimes enough to make me retch and vomit.

Pretty insane stuff. The first few times it happened I was terrified, thinking I was going crazy. These days I'm calmer; I know it'll pass. The episodes can last for ten or twenty minutes, but quite often only a few seconds go by. The people I'm with might not even notice: they'll just think I'm not paying attention, my thoughts wandering for a moment. I've got used to covering my affliction up.

The visions this time were unsettling. There's a nightmare quality to the scenes my brain conjures up, a twisted version of reality. Dizziness whirled through me. The victim on the floor was still alive. He was pinned to the ground by his hands and feet, white-sleeved arms restraining him. He screamed and writhed to escape but could not. There was a deep-throated terror to his ragged cries. There was also a knife: I saw it in sudden close-up, filling my vision, the ornately carved handle and the shining keenness of its blade. Then the weapon was held over the victim, letting him see. He stopped struggling, like he was paralysed, as the blade was brought towards his body, his face, his eyes…

As soon as it came, the episode dissipated and I was back in the room, left only with a sickness in my stomach and blood thundering in my head. I panted like I'd been running. And Detective Inspector Nikola Zubrasky, the investigating officer who'd called me in, was watching me from the doorway with an intrigued look on her face.

I forced myself to breathe slowly and stepped towards her. Zubrasky *was* on the inside and knew at least something about the workings of the Office. Knew we existed, at any rate. We'd cooperated on a couple of cases over the past year, neither of them amounting to much. Also, although she didn't know it, I'd thoroughly investigated her background as one of my first assignments in the Office. She'd had a string of striking successes, made impressive arrests, and alarm bells had rung. She wouldn't have been the first to use the forbidden arts to cheat her way to professional success. There were plenty of rumours on that score about every politician you could name.

But Zubrasky had been clean; she was simply good at her job. There was Irish blood in her parentage as well as Eastern European, explaining her autumnal red hair, her green eyes. That, in turn, may have explained our suspicions. Three hundred years ago, such characteristics might have spelled *witch* to those too ignorant to know better. I was fairly sure we'd moved on since then – although sometimes I wondered. We were supposed to be as inclusive and meritocratic as any modern organisation, yet the Office was still largely run by old white guys. I mean, okay, I had my Indian ancestry, but I'd never been any farther east than Great Yarmouth. And to be honest, Norfolk seems pretty foreign to me.

I only hoped Zubrasky hadn't found out I'd investigated her. Our techniques are thorough, and I knew everything – everything – there was to know about her: partners, medical records, affiliations. Creepy, yeah. I was actively trying to forget as much of it as I could before I made some slip and gave away the truth.

She raised a questioning eyebrow as I approached. She had a way of unleashing a frank gaze that no doubt served her well with suspects. It unsettled me, too, however hard I tried to pretend it didn't.

"Are you okay?" she asked. "You look drained."

Not a great turn of phrase given what had been done to the victim. "Is there somewhere we can talk more privately?"

"It's that bad?"

"I think it might be, but obviously I can't discuss it if you need to make notes of our conversation."

She looked amused. I guess I always said the same thing at this point. "Just between you and me, then."

Zubrasky led me into a rundown, bay-windowed room that might, once, have held a dining table and chairs. Hideous, flowery wallpaper from the 1970s, all mustard and brown, covered the walls. It looked like the infestation of some malign creature, a mass of tentacles and watching eyes. Or maybe it was time I took a week or two off and did some walking in the Welsh hills to clear my head.

"So, Acolyte Shahzan," said Zubrasky, "you believe this is a case of interest to Her Majesty's Office of the Witchfinder General?"

"We will be investigating it further, yes," I said. "There are signs that evil and forbidden powers have been employed in that room."

"Well, I'm only a simple police officer, but I did rather get that impression."

She was playing with me. Our conversations often went like this, unsettling. I tried to ignore it. She was so … together, and just then I wasn't.

"Some of the runes on that pentagram are quite disturbing," I said.

"Oh, they are?" She obviously had no conception of the demonic forces besieging us. She doubtless thought the Office was a bit of a joke. Fine; that was better than knowing the truth.

"Will the pentagram be part of the evidence you gather?" I asked.

"Of course, it's clearly material."

"I'd like it to be erased as soon as possible. The fewer people who see it, the better."

"The *pentagram* is your main concern here?"

"Without it, this looks like a simple enough case of aggravated murder."

"You've been watching too much television. There is no such crime in this country."

So much for trying to pretend I knew what I was talking about. "I just mean, maybe you could mention the circle in evidence without including images of it?"

She hesitated for a moment, then conceded. A modern

British judge or jury didn't need to know the details of magical runes. "Very well."

"Good. I'll arrange for a team from the Office to come along and destroy the sigils later today."

"The what?"

"The markings on the floor."

She nodded. "Regardless of that, a crime has been committed. I have a duty to pursue it; I can't simply hand it over to you and walk away, not at this stage."

It was the usual problem in these cases. There was no statute in British criminal or civil law outlawing the practice of the magical arts, at least not anymore. It was best for the public not to be aware such things existed. Her Majesty's Office of the Witchfinder General was, if anyone asked, an interesting historical anomaly, a ridiculous piece of quasi-mediaeval pageantry, like so much of the British governmental and judicial systems: the sombre men in wigs and tights, the archaic rituals at the opening of parliament, the monarchy, the marble and gold palaces. It was a distraction, a cheap magician's misdirection.

It was just a good job people didn't know the size of the Office's annual budget, or the number of people working for us up and down the country. We'd watched in amusement as MI5 and MI6 stepped out of the shadows to reassure the public by their presence. That wasn't our way at all. If the public suspected the tiniest amount of what we protected them from, they would be ... whatever the opposite of *reassured* was.

"I understand," I said. "Can we at least agree to cooperate? Share information as our respective investigations unfold?" She knew I was privileged, had the legal right to view all information uncovered by the police. Still, I preferred to maintain friendly relations if I could. It was surprising how disgruntled officers could lose vital information or forget to inform you of key details. And I very much wanted her to remain gruntled. The Crow had taught me well: contacts in the force could often do things we could not, or at least do them more easily. Knocking on someone's door and showing them an *Office of the Witchfinder General* card rarely got you very far with the Great British Public. Most likely it got you laughed at or sworn at. Or both.

"Just as long as it cuts both ways," she said. "If you learn anything relevant to our investigation, I get to hear it, yes?"

The operative word there was, of course, *relevant*. There were lots of things I could decide were *not* relevant to the comfortable world of evidence and trials. Things I would never, ever be allowed to tell her. Still, the more I could help her, the more she might help me. We were more or less on the same side; there was considerable overlap between criminal and magus law. A ritual murder upset us both. Plus, I needed all the help I could get at All Hallows'. "You have my word. There'll be an autopsy?"

"I'm pretty sure we expect foul play, given the circumstances."

"We'll want to carry out our own... equivalent investigation upon the body within the next few hours."

"I'm sure that can be arranged, as long as he isn't mutilated or tampered with any further. Arrange it through the usual channels. Can you tell me anything about the users now?"

Users. Magic users. People like Zubrasky know enough about the Office to pick up on our slang. "I'd prefer not to speculate. I have no insight into who might have done this, or why."

"But you have seen something similar before? This thing with the eyes makes sense to you?"

It's common for people who know about the Office to mix up what we do with the things those we pursue do, as if we are somehow complicit. In fact, the two are total opposites – the practice of evil and the attempt to stamp out that evil – but somehow the distinction eludes people. They think we routinely employ unnatural powers ourselves, as if that would ever be allowed. Or maybe they just think that some of the shit we wade through sticks to us.

"It doesn't *make sense*," I said, "but we would like to investigate further."

Her eyes sparkled with amusement as she listened. She was smart; she was winding me up with her insinuations. I let it happen every time. "Well," she said. "If you do hear any useful whispers from beyond the veil, you will let me know about it straight away, won't you?"

I tried to come up with a suitable reply, but before I could she turned and left the room.

2 – The Crow

He is a seemingly arbitrary man, but this is because he knows what he is talking about better than any one else. He is a philosopher and a metaphysician, and one of the most advanced scientists of his day; and he has, I believe, an absolutely open mind. This, with an iron nerve, a temper of the ice-brook, an indomitable resolution, self-command, and toleration exalted from virtues to blessings, and the kindliest and truest heart that beats—these form his equipment for the noble work that he is doing for mankind—work both in theory and practice, for his views are as wide as his all-embracing sympathy.

–Professor Van Helsing described by Bram Stoker,
Dracula, 1897

I was weaving my way through the crowds of shoppers in Cardiff city centre, heading for my debrief with the Crow, when my phone rang. My mother. A call I needed to take: she'd want to speak to me on my birthday, and lately she'd struggled with the technology. I'd give her my number and she'd scribble it down on a scrap of paper that she'd immediately lose. I was near St John's Churchyard Gardens, an odd little fenced-off square of greenery in the retail heart of Cardiff, so I climbed the steps to sit on one of the benches in there to talk.

"Hello, ma," I said.

"Azad? Is that you?"

I'd grown used to questions like that. They still pricked, even after all this time.

"No, ma," I said. "It's Danesh."

"Of course. It's just I haven't heard from your brother in such a long time."

She'd never recovered from what happened to Az. You don't of course: when such things happen you merely carry on existing. I have clear memories of what she was like when I was a boy: loud, large, lighting up any room she entered. Now her voice was quavering, a fragile thing. I thought at the time it was worse for me, the loss of a twin, but I don't know. I'd got on with my life, turned it into a purpose even, but she'd never been the same again. My mother's memories came in and went out like a bleak winter tide upon a deserted beach. Her life in our London family home consisted of moments of lucidity interspersed with long periods of fogged confusion. In grimmer moments I thought it wasn't so far removed from my life as a witchfinder.

"How are you, ma?"

"Oh, don't worry about me, it's your birthday, isn't it? Are you having a good day? Will you be letting your hair down later?"

Of course, I couldn't tell her what I did. Couldn't tell anyone not officially in the know. So far as she was concerned, I was a civil servant in the Welsh government, working in the sphere of public health. It was more or less accurate, I supposed.

"There might be drinking later," I said. "There might even be singing and dancing." Actually, I doubted if my co-workers even knew it was my birthday, but I didn't want her to know that.

"Well, don't do anything I wouldn't do."

"I'll try not to."

"Oh, I meant to tell you," she said, sounding animated for the moment. "I remembered something he told me."

"Az?"

"No, the man who was there that day, when the accident happened."

That threw me. My memories were vague; I'd only been eight. But no one had ever mentioned the presence of another adult, and I certainly recalled none. "What man? What are you talking about, ma?"

"I saw him. He spoke to me."

I couldn't make sense of what she was saying. "You've never mentioned this before."

"No, well, my memory isn't what it was. Something reminded me of him the other day."

Her revelations sent a shiver of anxiety through me even

though I knew that, in all likelihood, she was getting real life and fantasy mixed up again. She was probably thinking of some scene from a film she'd seen.

"What did the man say?"

"Which man?"

"The man who was there when Az died."

There was silence from the other end. I could almost hear the cogs in her brain struggling and failing to mesh. "I don't … I'm not sure."

Sometimes it was hard work not to get frustrated with her, although she obviously wasn't doing it on purpose.

"Can you remember what he looked like, what he said?"

"My brain's like a sieve these days! It'll come to me."

I was already late for my meeting with the Crow; there was nothing I could do but wait for the whirligig dance of my mother's thoughts to line themselves up again.

"Listen, ma, I need to understand what you're saying. I'll give you a ring tonight so we can talk properly, but if anything occurs to you in the meantime, write it down. Can you do that?" It was a system we used more and more: reminders written on whiteboards in her kitchen telling her to take pills or turn off appliances. Notebooks dotted around her house so she could scribble down any stray thoughts that came to her.

"Of course."

"I'm going to come down at the weekend, too. We can go through it all then."

"Oh, that would be lovely," she said, her voice bright. "Will Azad be coming too?"

I never knew if it was kinder to let her live in her delusions or to correct her. I think I probably just said what was easier most of the time.

"No, ma," I said. "It will just be me."

'The Crow' was just my name for him.

Campbell Hardknott-Lewis, the Lord High Witchfinder of All Wales, sat in his customary position behind an oak desk in his dusty, book-lined office at the top of the Black Tower of Cardiff Castle. He was an old man, scrawny like some plucked bird. His gaze through his half-moon glasses was piercing. Portraits of former Lord High Witchfinders were arrayed on the walls behind him. They, too, appeared to gaze at me with scowls of disapproval.

The painting of Isaac Shackleton looked particularly angry, as it always did. Shackleton was Lord High Witchfinder in mid-Victorian times, an age when Britain was plagued with vampirism. Office legend had him as the basis for Bram Stoker's Van Helsing in *Dracula*. Shackleton, though, was ruthlessly effective in comparison to his fictional *alter ego*. He devoted his life to ridding the empire of vampires – as well as anyone he considered to be at risk of the taint. At his worst, he killed with the gleeful abandon of one chopping down healthy trees in order to halt the spread of a forest fire.

Hardknott-Lewis was a little more civilised, but he still terrified me. He didn't drink, didn't smoke, didn't eat meat, and he stuck obsessively to a punishing fitness regime that shamed everyone else in the Office. He'd boxed for his university and fenced for his country as a younger man – and still practised both disciplines. There were plenty of stories in the Welsh Office about his deeds in former days, the covens he'd disbanded, the sorcerers he'd hunted down, the demons he'd destroyed. At the age of twenty-five, when he was merely Acolyte Hardknott-Lewis, he'd led a group of witchfinders into the crypt of an abandoned Aberystwyth church to break up a summoning ring only to find that he was a minute too late: the writhing, keening horror dragged through the veils was already material. Hardknott-Lewis's three companions were ripped to shreds in the ensuing fight, but Hardknott-Lewis destroyed the demon before it could escape to terrorise the good – and bad – people of the town. When Hardknott-Lewis ran out of bullets he used his knife, and when that was dashed from him, he used his bare hands to choke the creature. It was said his back still bore the scars of the imp's raking claws.

He was also a member of the Star Chamber, the inner circle made up of the Office heads of the various British countries, regions and islands. That meant his word was gospel, in Wales at least. Magus law does not admit juries; it was decreed long ago that normal people could be too easily swayed, their judgements befuddled by the evil eye or some other magic. Individuals like Hardknott-Lewis were considered strong-minded enough to be immune.

Consequently, he could decide to banish anyone to Oblivion and only one person could override his order: the Witchfinder General himself, Earl Grey, watching over the whole country from his hidden office in No. 13 Downing Street.

As a result, Hardknott-Lewis had only to wish me a "Good morning" to send me into loops of anxiety over everything I'd said or done in case I'd crossed a line. Being summoned to his eyrie to report on the killing did nothing for my peace of mind, especially given the date. There'd be pressure to get the matter resolved urgently. He was scrupulously fair-minded, but when he decided someone had contravened magus law, his decision was swift and terrible, and I lived in fear of his judgement.

"You believe you have uncovered something of interest, Danesh?" His voice was dry, as if he were reading his words from old parchment.

"I think so. A man with his eyes very carefully removed, lying inside a potent pentagram. I've heard of something similar before but I thought it might mean more to you."

Hardknott-Lewis peered at me for a few moments, unmoving, in a way he often did. It was hard to escape the troubling thought that he was reading my mind. Although, obviously, that was a seditious thought. I tried not to think it just in case he *was* reading my mind. The grandfather clock against the wall behind him ticked slowly through a few seconds, filling in the silence while he considered me.

"I don't believe I'm familiar with any such case," Hardknott-Lewis said finally. "Both eyes, you say?"

"Yes."

"And the arcane letters daubed around it were genuine? Did you recognise them?"

"Some. I recorded them before ensuring they were obliterated."

"Did you now?"

"I … yes." My heart pounded as he considered me. I held out the camera I'd used, trying not to feel like an errant child caught in the act of something. He took the device and flicked through the images. He paused on each one, his frown deepening.

"Such evil," he said, his revulsion at the images clear on his features. "It is, of course, All Hallows' tonight. The alignments would make sense."

"The runes tell you something?"

"Only that we are dealing with someone wielding deep arcane knowledge. It seems my assumption that all such individuals had been rooted out of Wales might have been premature."

"The eyes, though? Why do that?"

His gaze returned to mine, and it was hard to escape the impression that his look of disapproval was now meant for me. "That is something new to us, in the Principality at least. What makes you think you know of these magics?"

My throat was sandpaper. "I … thought I'd heard of something similar."

"Hmm."

I was an Acolyte now, two or three years more senior than a Neophyte in the hierarchy of the Office, but it gave me scant job security. By the nature of our jobs, we came into contact with the forbidden arts again and again, and many stories were whispered about the witchfinders who'd gone bad, who'd succumbed to temptation and dabbled in magic without authority, often with the best of intentions. None were ever seen again. Hardknott-Lewis had impressed upon me many times that his watchword was *semper vigilans* – always vigilant. Of course, I dared not reply that no one had watchwords anymore, if they ever had. I certainly didn't tell him that was two words, not one.

He returned his attention to the images on the camera. He stopped at one and studied it, twisting his head from side to side as if trying to make it out, then zoomed in with a pinch of his fingers.

"Interesting," he said.

"One of the runes?"

"No, not that. It's this candle mark on the wall." He held the image out to show me. I could make nothing from the black smudges and squiggles.

"You recognise it?" I asked.

"I'm not sure. What does it portray, do you think?"

The markings looked random. "Is that a cloud? Or it might be some kind of single-legged beast? Perhaps a mushroom."

"And these smudges above it?"

"They're just smudges, aren't they?"

"I'm not certain. This reminds *me* of something, but I may be seeing patterns where there are none. I'll have to look into it."

"So, you want me to pursue the case?" I asked.

He set down the camera and placed his fingertips together to consider me. "We are stretched thin, far too thin for my liking. The timing of this isn't ideal. You may have heard that there's a particularly virulent outbreak of lycanthropy around Rhyl consuming a lot of our numbers in the north, and then there's the presence of something in the Swansea water supply, the way the taps keep running with blood. There are the links we are uncovering between far-right groups and diabolists attempting to summon nameless horrors from the Endless Depths. And let's not even mention the continuing situation at Caerlech. We must protect the public but, as you know, Government cutbacks are seriously affecting our ability to repel malign forces."

He sighed, staring out of his window into the Cardiff sky. "Yet, yes, this very much needs looking into. I'm afraid you are going to have to pursue the case alone. But I want to know the moment you uncover anything. And I want to know if you fail to uncover anything, as well, yes?"

"I understand. Will you authorise an Assay of the body?"

"Do you really feel that's necessary?"

"I'd like to be absolutely sure sorcery was involved in this."

"That's perfectly clear from the sigils."

"Still, an Assay might reveal something of interest, give me a clue."

He didn't like it, inevitably, but he relented after a moment's frowning. "Very well, I'll authorise you to take that creature Gilroy along with you."

"Is there no one else we could use? Gilroy is weak, and I'm told he's a difficult man to deal with." I took a wild stab in the dark. "There's no chance we could persuade Earl Grey to send the Sorceress over?"

I could see from the look of distaste washing over Hardknott-Lewis's features that using the nickname *Sorceress* had been a mistake. I needed to be more careful. To Hardknott-Lewis, any sort of humour about users, any attempt to reduce them to a joke, was perilous. I think he probably disapproved of the simple frivolity of it, too. It was just a good job he didn't know I called him the Crow.

I really, *really* hoped he didn't know that.

"Evangelina Mormont is no longer available to anyone. I've been informed by Earl Grey that it was decided she posed too great a risk to the Office. You know she never accepted our strictures and rebelled against them constantly. It proved to be simply too difficult to ensure that she was contained. She was sent to Oblivion some weeks ago."

That was news to me. Evangelina Mormont – the Sorceress – was by far the most powerful Assayist the Office had ever encountered. It was said she could find out obscure details about people who were weeks dead, but there was very much more to her than that. Necromancy, summoning, alchemy, weatherworking – you name it, she was adept in it. Her capture back in the nineties had been very costly. The word was that over thirty officers had died in the operation that eventually neutralised her powers long enough for her to be contained. For her interrogations, a dedicated facility had been built at the disused Aldwych underground in London, one of the so-called ghost stations.

Apparently, it hadn't been enough. It was a relief she was in Oblivion, but she would certainly have been the best chance we had of finding anything useful from what remained of our eyeless man. It was theoretically possible to converse with people trapped in Oblivion, waking them briefly from their torpor to extract a few words from them. Supposedly, with the right magics, the victims could even be released from those frozen waters and returned to the world. As far as I knew, neither rite was now performed, as they tended to be fatal to everyone involved. Oblivion was as close to a death sentence as we were allowed. Mormont was lost to us.

"Just make sure Gilroy returns safely to our custody afterwards," Hardknott-Lewis continued. "I doubt he'll make a run for it, but if he does, he is to be stopped."

Stopped. He meant, of course, killed.

"I understand. Will I also be given access to any details on the runes?"

"Are you asking because you hope to discover their meaning?"

Maybe I only imagined the look of suspicion on his face at my request. I hoped that was it. "I simply thought they might be of help."

"They will not. They are sigils of twisted cruelty, but I don't believe they'll lead you to any particular individual or location. The fewer who know them, the better. Find out what you can about the victim instead."

"I'll need access to deeper levels of the Book Vault to research the magics employed."

He shook his head as he spoke, his words quiet. "I think the books on the ground floor will suffice for now."

"But if they reveal nothing, surely I will need to study the volumes on the lower floors?"

Hardknott-Lewis frowned again, eyes narrowing behind his glasses. He was torn. He clearly did not want to grant me access. "You seem very keen to learn what you can of the forbidden arts."

"Only to help with the case, of course."

After a moment he relented with a sigh. "Very well, I'll allow you temporary admittance to the next level down, but no farther. I'll send a memo to the Librarian to inform her."

"Thank you, Lord High Witchfinder."

He returned to his papers, and I rose to get out of there as quickly as I could.

3 – A Glimpse through the Eyes of the Dead

While the greater demonic presences represent the most fearsome threats to human society, it is the array of lesser entities that are likely to cause the greatest day-to-day harm, simply because such beings are more numerous, and because they are easier to summon and bind. The daemons, imps and other visitants that may be pulled through the veils to trouble our world vary enormously in their power, but it is the sly, quiet creatures of the shadows that are likely to wreak the most havoc rather than some fearsome member of the demonic aristocracy. That said, the risk remains that one of these greater beings might be successfully summoned by chance – or that they may choose to encroach upon our plane for purposes of their own.

–The Reverend Jebediah Snow,
A True Study of Imps and Daemons, 1836

Outside, I paused to suck in the cold, autumnal air. Rain was gathering itself to hit us, a grey slab of cloud hanging over the city. The cloud didn't quite fit the sky properly, a circle of bright blue running around the horizon, glimpsed behind the castle walls and Cardiff's shops and office-blocks. Everything looked mundane. It was hard to believe there were powers and horrors lurking in the Beyond that could threaten it all. That the undead could walk those streets; that demonic possession was a *thing*; that curses and hauntings were real; and that people could be hunted by slavering creatures we didn't even have names for.

One or two late tourists, muffled up in coats, picked their way about the grounds of the castle, reading the noticeboards and trying to imagine what it must have been like there in mediaeval times. The Black Tower loomed overhead. Much of the castle was an affectation, Victorian Gothic, but buildings like the tower were much older. It was a pretty impractical place for an office, but I had to admit it looked the part. It wasn't so high in modern city terms. Office blocks, church spires, even the shops overtopped it. It was dwarfed by the high stands of the nearby Principality Stadium, settled across the city like a landed UFO. Still, wherever I was in Cardiff, I imagined Hardknott-Lewis up there, his gaze upon me. Upon all of us. The rest of us huddled in a set of shabby offices at the back of the Town Hall, but the Lord High Witchfinder of all Wales had inhabited the Black Tower of Cardiff Castle for hundreds of years.

No flags flew from the tower. There were Welsh dragon flags all around the castle walls, and up and down the main shopping streets too, but Hardknott-Lewis didn't approve of a flag depicting a magical beast, even if it was (so far as I knew) mythical. He was a born-and-bred Welshman, but that didn't stop him scowling at the sight of his own national flag. I'd never met the Lord High Witchfinder of All Scotland, but I imagined he had a similar problem with the Scottish national animal which, for reasons that escaped me, was a unicorn. At least the English only had lions. No less odd as a national symbol, but natural at least.

The Town Hall is on the opposite side of the castle, past the law courts and next to the National Museum. The Vault is there, too, well-hidden behind the Town Hall's baroque walls. It was said that the deeper floors of the library extended far out beneath Alexandra Gardens, making it one of the most significant magical libraries in the western world, built up over the centuries.

I planned to find out the truth about that for myself one day.

My phone buzzed again as I crossed the little bridge over the canal on the northern edge of the castle. Zubrasky. I allowed myself a single, deep breath before slotting back into keen-eyed witchfinder mode.

"DI Zubrasky."

"I thought you should know we have an ID for the victim," she said.

I resumed walking. I needed to get back to the office. "You

had his DNA on record?"

"He had his driving licence in his jacket pocket. Evan Cornwallis. Does the name mean anything to you?"

"No, but I'll consult our archives. Is he a known underworld figure?"

"I would have thought that was more a question for you."

She couldn't resist, could she? "I clearly mean the criminal underworld, not the underworld underworld."

"He's not known to us. So far as we can tell, he's an accountant from Chepstow without even a speeding offence to his name."

"What was he doing in Cardiff?"

"Come to see the lights of the big city? Rugby match and a few pints? Hard to say, he's refusing to answer any of our questions; I thought maybe you could persuade him to talk."

"We can try. Are we able to carry out the examination this afternoon?"

"I can give you half an hour at two. The police surgeon knows enough not to be there."

"I'll be bringing one other."

"Let me know when you're here, and I'll send someone to let you in."

Gilroy was a good example of the fine line we walked. There'd been practitioners of one sort or another in the Office from its earliest days, the time of Matthew Hopkins, the original Witchfinder General in the seventeenth century. Since the Assizes of Suffolk at the start of the eighteenth century, the Office had been granted the right to employ demonic powers if it allowed some greater evil to be defeated. The original declaration, inevitably, concerned itself solely with witchcraft, but, in these less misogynistic days, that was taken to refer to any supernatural threat. Still, there was great wariness about using Assizes-granted powers. Both Hardknott-Lewis and Earl Grey did all they could to avoid employing them. In the more liberal 1960's, their use had become almost commonplace, and the line between demon and demon hunter had blurred. Perhaps that explained the attitude of people like Zubrasky. Now the powers were used only *in extremis*.

We kept Gilroy locked in a cell in our hidden subbasement. It wasn't as bad as it sounded. His rooms were clean, comfortable and well-equipped. He had TV and radio, privacy, but obviously no internet or phone. His few relatives thought he was long-dead. He was fed, and he was given proper treatment if he was ill. He had books and paper and pretty much anything that he asked for. He could do whatever he wanted – except leave.

It was a lot better than the frozen limbo of Oblivion.

"What the hell do you want?" he shouted as I rang the bell on his locked door. He did not appreciate our hospitality. "Come to beg for help with another problem you're too fuckwitted to solve yourselves?"

"I need you to come with me," I said through the speaker grille.

The inner door shot open to reveal his lined face and grey hair. "Come where?"

"To carry out an Assay."

Gilroy grunted. "Who's died now?" he asked, as if he were personally keeping track of everyone.

"You'll find out if you perform the Assay well enough. You will be tagged with a GPS device. Try to escape and we'll hunt you down, send you immediately to Oblivion. Do you understand?"

"Yes, yes, course I understand. Been hearing the same bullshit for twenty years. Be a good little slave and I get to keep my prison cell for another month, yes?"

He peered through the reinforced glass window in the outer door. There was a flicker of surprise in his eyes as he saw me properly. "What's your name, boy?"

I ignored the *boy*. "Acolyte Danesh Shahzan."

"Shahzan?"

I was pretty sure I knew what was going through Gilroy's mind. "*Acolyte* Shahzan," I said. "I amuse you somehow?"

"As a matter of fact, yes, you amuse me very much. *Witchfinder Shahzan.* What is the world coming to?"

I'd come across similar reactions often enough. They claimed it wasn't prejudice, that they merely wanted to protect their own culture. They ranted against the pollution of British magic, as if it were something that had arisen spontaneously among the oak woods and hadn't evolved from the deeper roots of Middle Eastern and African spellcraft. They ranted and they raved, and you knew they hated you just because you were standing before them. Because you existed. And they hated you especially if you were telling them what to do.

But, fuck him. The look in his eye made me feel better about using him. I spared him the lecture; you couldn't argue with people like him. He was part of the old world: the superstitious, mediaeval world we were stamping out.

"I'm opening the door now, Gilroy. Once you're tagged, you'll follow me outside. You will do exactly as I say at all times or this will be your last day on this world, understood?"

He looked amused at my words. "Oh, I understand, boy. I understand perfectly."

"So, can I call you Danny?"

We were making our way to the police station where Cornwallis's body had been taken for the post-mortem. I'd told Gilroy to walk a pace ahead of me. I doubted he'd get far if he did try to run: he was getting on in years, and, by the look of him, he hadn't made much use of the fitness equipment that we'd thoughtfully provided. Still, I wasn't taking any chances. I scowled at his back as he ogled every woman we passed, his gaze up and down their bodies. He gave me the creeps in just about every way it was possible to do so.

"Don't call me anything," I said, trying to sound as gruff as I could. "We are not out for a pleasant stroll here."

He grunted in amusement over his shoulder, like he'd scored a point. "Shitty weather, though. Next time could you arrange for someone to die on a warm sunny day?"

I didn't reply.

The police morgue was precisely what you'd expect: a wall of stainless-steel doors for the bodies to slide in and out of; the tang of bleach; clinical white walls; a hard cold air. And, in the centre of the room, a shroud-covered body on a dissecting table. My mind did the thing everyone's always did: imagine the prone figure beneath the sheet slowly rising. It probably didn't help that I'd seen it happen on two separate occasions.

Gilroy pulled back the sheet to reveal Cornwallis's blue-white body. He hadn't yet been cut open for his post-mortem.

I was slowly becoming used to the sight of corpses. In my experience, they weren't the problem; it was the living you had to look out for. Okay, the living and the reanimated, but fortunately Cornwallis appeared to be neither. It didn't stop us questing into his fading mind to ask him what had happened to him. Under magus law, the phrase *habeas corpus* was often used quite literally.

"He doesn't have any eyes," said Gilroy. I was watching his reaction carefully. So far as I could tell he was as puzzled as I was over the mutilation.

"No."

"What happened to them?"

"That's what you're here to tell me. I want to know who killed him, and why."

"I should have been called in earlier. There's probably not a lot left of him now."

"Just find out what you can."

Gilroy placed one hand on the body's forehead and another on his chest. "Are you sure you want to watch? I don't want you to run away crying while the nasty magic user does your work for you."

"Just get on with it."

Gilroy bared his teeth in either a grimace or a smile – I couldn't tell which – and closed his eyes. Nothing happened for a moment. He frowned, as if he were trying to hear a faint sound or had a twinge of pain somewhere. Then his body went rigid, the muscles in his arms and neck standing proud like old rope. His head jerked around alarmingly, and low guttural sounds emerged from his throat.

His voice was rough, snarling, but there were words in there. "This creature is mine, mortal. Leave him in my clutches and be gone."

The coldness in the room deepened. There was something in the bestial tones that set off primal reactions in my hindbrain, made me want to flee. Instead, heart thundering, I made myself step closer. But only one step.

"Who are you?" I called out in as clear a voice as I could manage. "Tell me your name."

The creature speaking through Gilroy laughed. "I do not obey the orders of a worm like you, mortal, but I will give you my name. I am Beelzebub, Prince of All Torments."

For a moment I was too stunned to speak. I had no idea how to deal with such an entity. Neither Hardknott-Lewis nor Earl Grey himself could hope to face so demonic a force. There were strictures and boundaries built into the fabric of reality that made such a manifestation almost impossible to achieve, even if there were people willing to devote their lives to trying.

"Gilroy, leave him," I shouted. "Let his soul go!"

The voice coming from Gilroy's throat grew louder, deeper. It made my muscles creep beneath my flesh. "Live your little life, Danesh Shahzan. An eternity of searing agony awaits when you die."

"Gilroy!"

Gilroy stepped back and shivered, as if some great hand were shaking him. But then I saw that his movement wasn't because he was possessed, that he wasn't being animated by malign forces.

He was laughing.

He opened his eyes and the delight on his features was clear. His voice was completely normal as he spoke. "You should see your face, boy. That look of terror has made my whole day. Pissed yourself in fear, have you?"

"You bastard."

"Do you really think Beelzebub would be walking the streets of Cardiff? Do you really think he would even notice someone like you?"

I tried to regain some semblance of authority. I didn't sound convincing even to me. "Do your job, Gilroy. If you're no use to us, I'll tell Hardknott-Lewis it's time you were sent to Oblivion."

Gilroy shook his head and, still clearly delighted at his prank, placed his hands back on the body. He closed his eyes once more. He didn't speak again for several minutes. Occasionally he narrowed his eyes, as if trying to understand whispered words. He didn't shake or writhe in any way.

Finally, he stepped back from the body and opened his eyes. That was all there was to it.

"You made contact?" I said. "You found something?"

"A little. He is far-gone. I told you, I should have been brought in much earlier."

"What did you find?"

"He was murdered by two people."

"Why did they kill him?"

"I have no idea; they didn't bother to explain their motive to their victim like they do in films."

"Can you tell who they were?"

"He got a good look at them. Some of the images were confusing, swirling, almost as if he was still alive as his eyes were cut from him. Is that what happened?"

"We don't know. So, he got a look at the two attackers?"

"Yes, but it won't help you much. A man and a woman I'd say, but they both wore masks. Most likely they knew someone might carry out an Assay on the corpse."

"What sort of masks?"

"Ridiculous Hallowe'en masks. A red demon and a green witch."

"Can you tell me anything else? How tall they were, the way they walked, anything?"

"The woman was taller, that's all I could tell."

"Did they speak?"

"I got very few words. That's how it goes. It was hard to hear much over the screaming."

"You saw the weapon they used?"

"A dagger with an ornate handle. There may have been other implements lying around on the floor, but they were only in peripheral vision."

"You must have got *something* from the victim's thoughts and memories."

"Everything was blotted out by the pain of what he was going through."

"So, you can't tell me a single useful fact. Makes me wonder why we bother with you, Gilroy."

He didn't look worried. "I can tell you three other things. One, they both wore white robes, head to toe. Matching robes, like priests or something. The robes had matching symbols on them."

"What symbol?"

"A tree with stars above it."

Interesting. The death was looking more and more like a twisted rite, the victim a sacrifice.

"What does the symbol mean?" I asked.

"You don't know?"

"No."

He shook his head in disbelief at the stupidity of the young. "Then you'd better go learn your fucking history."

I let his comment slide – partly because he was right; I clearly did need to do some research. "Okay, what else?"

"I did get a few words, right at the end, after the cutting was done and before he succumbed to his injuries. A snatch of conversation from one of the attackers. The woman."

"Go on."

"She said, 'Now we have the eyes, we can see for ourselves'."

"What does that mean?"

"No idea."

"And the other thing?"

Gilroy glanced back down at the body. His voice became quieter, almost a whisper. "This unfortunate was one of ours."

"What do you mean?"

"He was a magic user. You should be happy – whoever those two were, they were doing your job for you, ridding the world of the deviants you snowflakes are too terrified to pursue."

"Cornwallis was a sorcerer?"

"Weak, yes, but there's no doubt. He was a user killed by other users. You lot are losing your grip. Looks like you've got a wizard war on your hands."

4 – The Vault

Watch for the signs that those around you have succumbed to the temptations of the unnatural arts. Colleagues, friends, family, lovers – all are at risk, and it is your sworn duty to act upon any suspicions. By doing so, you may be saving them. Remember, those practising forbidden magics are always devious and will do their utmost to hide their degeneracy.

–Earl Grey, Witchfinder General,
Office of the Witchfinder General Handbook, 1999

Back at the office, I returned Gilroy to his subterranean hotel. He was still amused at scaring me with the Beelzebub thing. It was, he assured me more than once, the funniest thing he'd seen in a long time.

Then, as I closed his cell door, he looked back at me, all humour suddenly drained from his expression.

"You look like him, you know," he said.

I didn't know who he meant. He probably thought people from all across the vast continent of Asia looked the same. Still, I just couldn't resist asking, could I?

"Like who?"

"Only met him once. Well, hardly *met*. It was a few words exchanged across a crowded dark chapel. Things were pretty frantic; we were both preoccupied with the creatures being summoned through the fell gateway. But I knew him. I'd fought with him before."

"Who?" I asked again.

"Amoor Shahzan. Your grandfather, right? *Bi Bi* Shahzan."

I didn't reply. The grin spreading across Gilroy's features made my guts twist within me. He hadn't been sure, but he knew as he watched me that he'd struck home.

Gilroy chuckled to himself. "You're going to have to get a whole lot better at concealing your emotions if you're going to survive in this game, boy."

Five or ten different responses flashed through my mind. I decided not to use any of them. He was just trying to get under my skin. I slammed the outer door shut and locked it as loudly as I could.

Gilroy's repeated taunt followed me as I headed for the stairs. "Witchfinder Shahzan! What is the world coming to?"

Back at my desk, I sat with a black coffee to think about things. The drink was bitter and slightly treacly. Just as I liked it. Gilroy had simply done his research about me or had heard the name Amoor from someone. My grandfather had been nothing to do with the world people like Gilroy waded through. I'd barely known him; he'd been an architect, with no time whatsoever for anything he considered *not normal*. The man had worn *slippers*.

"You alright, Danny? You look like you've seen a ghost."

It was Kerrigan, one of the Office old-timers, giving me the standard witty welcome of witchfinders everywhere.

"Yeah, something like that."

Kerrigan was okay. He was fiercely loyal to Hardknott-Lewis on account of something the Lord High Witchfinder of all Wales had once saved him from, and he looked ferocious, his straggly hair and gym-bulked muscles right out of the Viking Chieftain collection, but he was a team player. If something was wrong with any of us, he'd be the first to spot it, the first to ask us idly if there was anything we needed to talk about. He could have gone much higher in the organisation, but I think he valued keeping his feet on the ground, hitting the streets with the team.

"Just put Gilroy back in his box."

"Ah, right. That scum. Time we sent him to Oblivion if you ask me. Bastard troublemaker. He said something that got you?"

"He tried to."

Kerrigan considered me more closely. He dropped his voice a few decibels, so no one would overhear. "Something bad?"

I thought about telling him. I knew I could trust him; knew I could trust all my colleagues with my life. I'd done exactly that on numerous occasions.

"It's nothing," I said. "He makes my skin crawl, that's all."

I could see Kerrigan didn't believe me, but after a moment

he let it drop. "Hey, I hear it's your birthday, though."

"Yeah."

"Excellent. You don't have any kind of religious or cultural objection to hitting the pubs of Cardiff and getting rat-arsed with your mates, do you?"

"I don't believe I was warned about that particular sin, no."

"Excellent. I'll go and inform the others that they've decided they'd really like to come out for an evening on the lash."

I had to smile as Kerrigan strode away. I knew what he was doing: a few pints and maybe I'd be ready to tell him what was troubling me. That was how his mind worked.

I wasn't going to, though. Wasn't going to let on that my grandfather's first name had, indeed, been Amoor. Or that his close friends (although certainly never his children or his grandchildren) had called him by another name.

Bi Bi.

I filled the rest of the day finding out what I could about Evan Cornwallis. We had good IT systems in the Office, perhaps surprisingly for such an ancient (you might say anachronistic) organisation. The reasoning was that, as soldiers in the fight against the unnatural, we loved anything scientific or technological. It didn't always work out well. Somewhere beneath the streets of London, there was a laboratory where very clever people beetled away on our behalf, producing science-y weapons and detectors with flashing lights for us to deploy in the fight against the denizens of other dimensions. To date, they'd created little that was useful.

Still, our computer systems were top notch. The Police had HOLMES – the *Home Office Large Major Enquiry System* – to assist them with controlling and cross-checking evidence gathered anywhere in the country. We had our own system which gave us full access to HOLMES through an encrypted backdoor. As well as being able to add notes and research on our side, we could amend what they'd recorded on theirs. Obviously, we only did that very rarely, when they'd written down some dangerous scrap of an incantation or something. No one in the police, so far as I knew, was aware of our presence, and they certainly had no visibility of *our* data.

Whoever had designed our system had thought it amusing to name it MORIARTY. I'd read that the letters stood for *Multiagency Operational Research, Investigation And Redaction Tracking sYstem*, but that sounded so horribly contrived it was most likely a backronym, reverse-engineered after the fact.

Still, good as MORIARTY was, I found nothing on Cornwallis. No association with any contravention of magus law. I ran facial recognition searches on him – using his passport picture from HOLMES, taken at a phase in his life when he still had eyes – but didn't even get any fuzzy matches. No one who even looked like him had ever been photographed doing anything the Office was interested in. According to HOLMES, Zubrasky had turned up nothing, either; I was pleased – maybe also a little disappointed – that there was no mention of me in her report. Cornwallis was either good at not getting caught – or he was simply the innocent victim in a game he had no connection with. If he were a user, as Gilroy claimed, it was possible his powers were latent; unknown even to him. A simple case of wrong place, wrong time – bad for him, clearly, but bad for us, too. Most likely, we weren't going to get very far following up on him.

I logged some reports of what I'd found, taking care to include the detail of the tree with the stars. I made sure to tag Hardknott-Lewis so that the notes came to his attention. If anyone knew what the symbol meant, it was the Crow.

I was on the point of pinging an email to Zubrasky, to see if she had any leads or ideas, when a message from her arrived in my inbox. She was going to Chepstow the following morning to look around the victim's house. Did I want to come?

I understood what she was thinking. She wanted to be damn sure I held to my promise of sharing anything useful with her and was giving me every opportunity to be as helpful as I could. I told her I'd be there. She might think she needed me, but the truth was I needed her a hell of a lot more.

The thing with the eyes was still bugging me. My unhelpful subconscious had so far failed to relent and tell me what connection it had made, where I'd heard about something similar before. I decided to spend the last few hours before putting myself into Kerrigan's hands seeing if I could turn up anything useful in the Vault.

Hardknott-Lewis was as good as his word. My Office badge normally refused to open the stairwell doors leading down to the Vault. This time as I swiped, there was a reluctant pause before the mechanism conceded defeat. The door lock made a soft *click*, and the usually red LED glowed green.

I'd been granted access to level -1.

I'd spent twenty minutes wandering the familiar labyrinth of shelves on the ground floor before trying my pass. I'd figured it might have been something among those familiar books that the eye removal thing was reminding me of. I probably spent too much time down there, perusing the volumes, fascinated and appalled in equal measure. The books on the ground floor were the ones the Office considered essentially harmless: encyclopaedias and journals and other works in the public domain, although many were out of print and unavailable in most libraries in the world.

There was a good selection of tomes from the 17th, 18th and 19th centuries, with lurid titles like *A True Study of Imps and Daemons*, *Ghost Houses of Britain* and *Reading the Signs of Satan*. There were numerous bestiaries depicting arrays of fantastical and magical creatures in luxurious detail, their illustrations rendered with such loving, twisted intricacy that you could only conclude the artists were in some way pathological.

There were even two reproductions of the infamous fifteenth century *Malleus Maleficarum* – the Hammer of Witches – said to have been one of the main influences on Matthew Hopkins, Earl Grey's forerunner. I'd leafed through the book more than once, basically out of historical interest. The author was, clearly, a misogynistic nut.

One or two books – like the *Maleficarum* – were on that floor because they were widely available elsewhere. There was, for example, an original copy of John Dee's *De Heptarchia Mystica* (detailing the formulae used in the summoning of angels), as well as some of Sir Isaac Newton's more speculative works. Most books there were simply considered harmless because they were wildly inaccurate or fanciful, saying more about the delusions or prejudices of their authors than they did about the real threats we faced. Quite a lot of them were actively laughable. Still, I figured there might be some useful scrap of information in them, some passing reference to a victim having their eyes carefully and skilfully removed.

Also, I had to admit, I was putting off going down a floor and facing the Librarian. Eventually, unable to find any useful clue, I'd steeled myself and tried my pass on the stairwell door.

Level -1 was very different to the familiar floor above my head. Steel book shelving gave way to antique oak running from floor to ceiling. There were a *lot* of books down there: the passageways between the bookcases stretched away into a dimly lit gloom. The word from Kerrigan and other long-standing members of staff was that this floor actually housed more volumes than any other. Here were the esoteric tomes with a hint of truth in them, perhaps a garbled glimpse of truly dangerous arcane knowledge. It was said that there were at least three lower levels, with fewer and fewer books on each, the more and more accurate ones, down to those spelling out in crystal detail the rites and symbols necessary for raising the dead, or for blighting the living with cruel curses, or for summoning your actual slavering horrors from the netherworlds, your *Necronomicons* and *Shadow Grimoires*, your *Bestiaries of Hell* and *Books of the Dead*.

It was also whispered that the very bottom level of the Vault housed a single, terrible volume of forbidden lore: magics capable of bringing about the cataclysmic destruction of all human civilisation. It was kept there for the same reason that a few smallpox samples were kept in secure labs in the USA and Russia: in the unlikely case that some unforeseen calamity struck, and the dangerous knowledge was needed. I wasn't at all convinced that either risk was worth taking. I hoped never to have to open the book's pages, or even go near it. At the same time, I had to admit that the thought of doing so sent a thrill through me. More than once I'd wondered what the book looked like, how big it was.

What was written on its pages...

I shook these thoughts from my head, looking around to get my bearings. I had to be on the same level as Gilroy's quarters, although the library and the accommodation block were reached by separate staircases, with their own security in place. I wondered if there was any passageway between the two; whether I could reach Gilroy's furnished dungeon without going up to ground-level and back down.

I scanned the shelves, looking for something that might set off an association with a dark ritual in which the victim's eyes were carefully cut from their head and taken away. Despite my efforts to make no noise, my footsteps echoed loudly on the hard wooden floor as I worked my way through *Summoning and Reanimation Magicks*, then on into *General Diabolism*.

I was too busy murmuring the title of each tome, rubbing my fingers along their spines, to notice my assailant. The first I knew was the cold tip of a steel knife pressing against the side of my neck.

The Librarian had found me.

Lady Coldwater was perhaps the only librarian in the world who habitually carried two shotguns and an array of well-honed slashing knives with her at all times. She knew how to use them, too. She rarely left the Vault, but on the rare occasions she was called upon to assist in some street operation, she demonstrated very clearly that her weaponry wasn't just for show. She was adept in a wide variety of combat arts and could turn a dazzling array of mundane or innocent objects into deadly weapons by using them in imaginative ways. More than one bad guy had made the mistake of thinking she was the weakest link in the team: a slight, grey-haired lady who looked like she might blow over in a strong wind. It generally only took three or four seconds for them to realise the depth of their miscalculation.

The role of most librarians is to help people find the books they're interested in. Lady Coldwater – no one knew if she actually was a lady, but no one dared check with her – saw her job as more or less the exact opposite. She was there to defend the books from people who might want to take them away, something she achieved with ruthless efficiency. There were all sorts of technological and physical barriers protecting the books of the Vault, but the most formidable defence of all was the Lady. I was pretty sure she lived down there; that, unlike Gilroy and the few others we held captive who had no choice in the matter, she simply chose not to leave.

Hardknott-Lewis was under the clear impression that she was under his command and followed his orders. She, on the other hand, was under the clear impression that Hardknott-Lewis had no idea what the hell he was talking about. The Librarians weren't originally part of the Office; they were part of a separate sect up until the mid-seventeenth century, doing all they could to keep dangerous books out of the hands of those too cruel or too ignorant to have access to them. *The Pale Sisters* they'd been called – a mystical mediaeval order about which little was known. She was, perhaps, the only one of us who wasn't terrified of the Lord High Witchfinder. Hardknott-Lewis had been in office for nearly ten years, but the Lady had been there for more than twice that.

All of which meant that, just because Hardknott-Lewis had granted me access to the lower level, it did not for a moment mean she would be happy about it. There was at least a chance she would make use of one of those knives or shotguns first and worry about the paperwork and the niceties of line-of-command later.

"Please, Lady Coldwater, it's me, Acolyte Danesh Shahzan. I'm allowed to be here. There was a memo."

She twisted the tip of the knife a fraction – expertly so, enough for it to dig into the soft skin of my neck. The pain was sharp, and I felt a trickle of warm blood running down my neck. I tried not to move. I was very conscious how close the blade was to my carotid artery.

She really wasn't like most other librarians at all.

Her voice was like fine bone china. Chipped china, exposing sharp edges. "Are you now?"

I tried really, really hard to speak without actually moving my throat or jaw in any way. A feat ventriloquists could manage but which, it turned out, I could not. There was a fresh prick of pain as I pronounced each syllable. "I've been granted access to this floor for a case."

"It sounds to me like you've got your alibi all straight in case I found you sneaking around in here."

"Can I turn around now?"

The knife withdrew from my neck, but she made sure I

heard the click of the safety catch being released on one of those shotguns. "Tell me exactly what you're doing down here, Acolyte."

She appeared to recognise who I was. That was good. Keeping my hands raised, I turned slowly to address her, putting my best disarming grin on my face. She was dressed all in grey: long skirts and a woollen top with leather belts diagonally across it to hold her guns and knives. Her silver hair was kept in place by two long pins, and I knew fully well that, in her hands, they weren't merely decorative.

They were weaponry.

"I'm working a case and Hardknott-Lewis granted me access to follow up a lead."

"Did he now?"

She didn't seem remotely convinced, but, so far, she hadn't fired the shotgun. That was an encouraging sign. I also knew what her weakness was. She was fiercely defensive of the books in her ward, but she also prided herself on her knowledge of them.

"I'm looking for a ritual with a particular physical component," I said. "I'm sure I read about it somewhere, but I can't put my finger on it."

The tip of the shotgun may have lowered a little. "What component?"

"It's ... to do with eyes," I said, and explained everything I'd learned.

When I was done, she looked thoughtful for a moment, scowling as if she were scanning through the library's index in her mind.

"Does it mean anything to you?" I asked.

Her look was distant, as if she was trying to recall some elusive detail. She appeared to have forgotten about the deadly weapon she was holding for the moment.

"Why don't you digitise all these books?" I continued, trying to engage with her in a friendly way. "Then you could scan their contents in a few seconds."

It was the wrong thing to say. Her hands clutched her shotgun more tightly again. "Idiot! You have no idea what you're talking about. They're magic books. The clue is in the name. They're vile, evil, live; the text mutates, moves around, fades in and out depending on who you are and where you are. *When* you are sometimes. You can't just scan that in and capture it on a computer, can you? You need the original books if you want to know what you're dealing with out there. Always, the books."

She stepped a pace nearer, the gun held up to point at my chest once more. "Or were you looking for an easy way to get access to all this knowledge without me standing in your way?"

"No, I…"

"And what's your plan then? To upload the texts to your dark web and let all the world's freaks and sadists use them for their own twisted ends? Is that it? Unleash the end days?"

"No! I just thought it might make your life easier. I don't want to take anything out of the Vault."

"Nothing apart from this one piece of vile magick that you're suddenly so interested in." The way she pronounced the word *magick* definitely put the hard *k* on the end.

"I told you, it's for this case. I thought you might be able to help." I'd thought no such thing; I'd hoped to avoid her completely.

She considered me for a moment, eyes narrowed, then stepped back. She'd made her point. "If I get the chance, I'll look into what you described, see if I can discover anything useful, but you're leaving, understood? You're leaving now."

I didn't need any more prompting. The thought of a few drinks with Kerrigan and the others was suddenly hugely appealing.

"Thank you, Lady Coldwater. I'll be on my way out of the Vault."

"You do that, Acolyte. You do just exactly that."

5 – Inter-agency Cooperation

Many aspects of Magus law may be traced back to mediaeval times, and the struggles against witchcraft and demonic possession. The dark arts were less well-understood in those days, which explains why so many magus law statutes and remedies are – to our modern minds – so extreme and uncompromising.

–Mirabelle Glee, *Magus Law*, 1982

The following morning, I took an early train to Chepstow. At Cardiff Central Station, I had to battle my way through the streams of commuters pouring into the city. The blaring station announcements did nothing to help my throbbing head. I'd ended up consuming more than a few pints of finest Welsh beer, along with – I was fairly sure – numerous shorter and more potent drinks.

It had been a good evening. I knew, because I could remember almost nothing about it.

The train was quiet heading out of the city, and thankfully I was able to find a seat. I drained the weak station coffee I'd bought, then sat with my eyes shut, the cold window buzzing and rattling against my temples. We hurtled eastwards at, I don't know, thirty miles per hour, or maybe even more.

The address Zubrasky had given me was on Bridge Street, a narrow canyon of a road lined with old terrace houses in greys, blues and pinks. It fell steeply past the mediaeval castle and over the river Wye via an ironwork Regency bridge.

If I hadn't been so hung over, it would probably all have been lovely.

The house whose number Zubrasky had given me was easy to spot: it was the only one on the quiet road with a uniformed police officer standing on guard outside. He watched me suspiciously as I approached. I had the usual problem of how to announce myself: I could use my official title and say I was *WA Shahzan*, but I knew from experience that wasn't going to get me very far. Most people know that, say, *DI* stands for Detective Inspector, but their response is generally confusion or downright hostility if I explain that WA denotes *Witchfinder Acolyte*.

"I'm here to see DI Zubrasky," I said, trying to sound as if I had every right to be there. "I'm Shahzan."

Fortunately, Zubrasky had primed the uniformed officer. With a nod of recognition, but no word, the officer stepped aside and knocked on the door with its stylised black dragon iron knocker to grant me access.

I wasn't sure what I'd expected to find inside. Maybe not your full-on necromancer's lair, all blood-stained walls, tallow candles dripping wax down skulls, and the odd raven – but perhaps something along those lines. What I saw was a modern, clean, well-maintained hallway, with tasteful artwork on the walls and a well-watered pot plant beside an Ikea shoe rack. It looked more and more like Gilroy had been wrong about him: Cornwallis had been just a regular guy.

DI Zubrasky appeared through a doorway. She cast an appraising eye over me, no doubt instantly detecting all sorts of insightful things. She focused on the cut on my neck. I'd meant to cover it with a plaster but had forgotten in the morning rush.

"Have you hurt yourself? Or has someone done that to you?" Perhaps she couldn't help being the police officer.

"Cut myself shaving."

She knew I was lying but didn't pursue it. "Right."

"Can I come in?" I asked.

"Do I have to invite you? I thought that was vampires."

"Just don't want to destroy any vital evidence."

"You're okay. Forensics have been and gone; it's just you and me."

She wasn't coming on to me; she was saying we could talk freely. I closed the front door behind me. "Did you find much?"

She looked amused at my question. I got it: she wasn't going to give me all her information without getting something in return. "A little."

I nodded. My brain was still throbbing too much, my thoughts too sluggish, to spar with her properly.

Trying to look as if I was finding all sorts of subtle and significant clues, I searched each room. The house was clean and tidy – almost obsessively so – with everything in its place. There was a pile of console games stacked near the TV, but it was neat, all the names on the spines facing outwards. I checked, and each case had the correct disc inside. Who even did that?

In the kitchen there was a single mug and plate left out for washing; everything else was put away, every surface wiped clean. The food in the fridge were arranged so neatly it looked like it had been *filed*. There were no pictures anywhere of another person, a loved one or a friend.

"He lived alone?" I asked.

"Very good," she said, in the way a teacher might praise a child for spelling their own name correctly.

"Well, we witchfinders have our ways. Did he rent this place?"

That appeared to be a more sensible question. "No, it was his. Mortgaged, anyway. I guess he lived like this because he was just a naturally tidy person, or else he was away a lot. Now, come upstairs to the bedroom."

"The bedroom?"

She looked amused at my discomfort, just as she'd intended. "It might be of interest. It's a little more lived in."

She was right. The bedroom was still neat by normal standards, but it looked like maybe Cornwallis had got ready in a hurry. Scattered clothes from the night before lay strewn on the carpet. The double bed was unmade, creases in the vague shape of a body still visible. There was only one set of pillows.

There were a lot of bookshelves, covering two of the walls, and there was also a teetering stack of books beside the bed, waiting for Cornwallis to read them. He never would, now. They were almost all fantasy and sci-fi, lots of titles I recognised. There were some in the Office – including Hardknott-Lewis – who found such literature distasteful. Books about made-up wizards and undead horrors were part-way to the real thing in their view. I was more relaxed. Such books knew they were fiction, didn't claim to be anything else. Only someone with a poor grasp of what was real and what wasn't could find them offensive. There were quite a few books among Cornwallis's collection that I'd enjoyed myself.

On his bedside table was the book he was currently reading: the *Mabinogion*, those root myths originally set down in Middle Welsh in the 12th and 13th centuries. It was a fascinating book. His copy was a recent edition, but there were much older ones on the ground floor of the Vault.

DI Zubrasky said, "He was into *Dungeons and Dragons* and *Game of Thrones* and all that. You wouldn't have known it from looking at him, but he was a real geek. My brother's the same. It turns out Cornwallis spent a lot of his weekends travelling to Comic-Cons and anime conventions."

"You're suggesting this is significant?"

"I don't know," said Zubrasky. "You tell me."

I waved my hand to the room in general. "This is all perfectly harmless. Lots of people are into this stuff."

"Not all of them get themselves murdered inside an actual runic circle."

She had a fair point. And I was impressed she knew the word *runic*. Still, I could see nothing significant about his taste in books. After all, I didn't know for sure Cornwallis had been a user. It was entirely possible our tame necromancer had simply been trying to wind me up.

"I'm sorry, I don't see how it helps us," I said. "These conventions, he went with groups of friends?"

"We think so. He had no social media footprint to speak of, and his computer is locked down, but we recovered some photographs from a camera we're currently studying."

"You're chasing his contacts up, looking for possible leads? People he may have fallen out with?"

She gave me the standard police version of *no comment*. "We are pursuing several lines of enquiry in that area. Obviously."

A little light came suddenly on in my mind. My brain was finally sputtering into life. I spoke before I could really think about what the idea meant. "Was there anyone in the pictures wearing a red demon mask? Or a green witch?"

"Okay, you're going to have to explain why you're asking me that question very carefully."

"I will, I promise," I said. I was still trying to decide if Cornwallis had been a regular person – one of us, not one of *them* – or something else. Maybe the whole thing was just a case of jealousy boiling over. Maybe someone among his fantasy-loving friends had stumbled across genuine incantations and runes and used them to extract their revenge. "Was there anyone in the pictures he was clearly close to? A lover, I mean?"

Zubrasky considered, no doubt deciding how much she should let on, what to keep back. "In most of the pictures he was clearly having fun with a group of friends, nothing more. Although there was one in which he had his arms around someone, taken around a year ago. I'd say the way they held each other certainly suggested they were comfortable with one another, intimate even, although they're only in the one shot."

"Man or woman?"

Zubrasky shrugged. "Wood Elf, I'd say. I don't recall observing any demons or witches. Why is this significant to you?"

The little light in my brain flickered off. It suddenly seemed unlikely; from Hardknott-Lewis's reaction, the magical sigils had been rare and potent. They were not the sort of thing you'd learn from playing too many fantasy role-playing games. "I don't know. I'm just trying to make sense of things."

She then said something that demonstrated just how insightful a detective she truly was. "You know, you really look like you need a coffee. There's a place up the street in the centre of town. Why don't I buy you a cappuccino before we continue this?"

"Call it a double espresso and you're on," I said.

We sat in the window of the chain coffee shop that was, indeed, up the street. This being Wales, there was a light drizzle in the air, making the paving stones of the pedestrianised area outside shine. Office and retail workers trudged by on their way to their daily grinds. The coffee shop was fairly crowded, but we were safe to talk; the hubbub of murmured conversations and the angry hiss of the coffee machines venting steam made it impossible for anyone to overhear us.

"So," she said, "rough night chasing demons?"

I shook my head. "Worse than that. Birthday pub crawl."

"Ah, of course. With your brother or just you?"

I sipped at the hot espresso while I tried to form a response to her unexpected words. Galaxies of white bubbles swirled in my cup. So, she'd done some research on me, looked me up, found out I'd been born a twin. I could hardly complain, given how much I knew about her. And she obviously wouldn't have been able to look too thoroughly into my past: the Office goes to a *lot* of trouble to remove details about its operatives from the public realm.

When I looked back up at her it was obvious she knew she'd said the wrong thing. "What is it?" She put a hand on my arm. I wondered if that was the trained response of a police officer or simply the action of a concerned friend. Maybe it was both; maybe the two aspects of her were inseparable.

Trying not to sound like I was angry with her, I said, "My brother died when we were eight."

"Oh, I'm so sorry. It was stupid of me to say what I did."

"You weren't to know. It wasn't a police matter. Natural causes." Although, since the slightly weird conversation with my mother, I'd been wondering about that. In truth, it would have been good to tell Zubrasky everything: the odd things that had happened that day, what my mother had said. Zubrasky was probably used to dealing with such things, and there weren't really many other people I could talk to. I had friends in the Office, good friends, but we tended to steer clear of personal stuff. That wasn't just professionalism, it was because it was drummed into us from day one to be on the lookout for anyone being tempted over to the dark side. Which meant any innocent question about family life or friends or *how was your weekend* ended up sounding intrusive.

We tended to stick to talking about football.

Despite my words, Zubrasky could clearly see my hesitancy. "You can tell me. Whatever it is, I'll bet I hear worse things just about every day."

I very nearly did, too. Instead, I found myself saying, "There isn't really much more to say."

Let's be honest, I would have welcomed a closer friendship with Zubrasky. That, or something more. She was smart, witty, and took no shit from anyone. Plus, I was pretty sure you could never tire of staring into those green eyes. She was also, I knew from my researches, essentially straight, which meant I was at least in the right half of the population. Still, that was for the future. One possible distant future. I had no idea if she was in a relationship now. Let's face it, she probably was. Plus, it would have felt weird using Az as a way of getting closer to her.

"Really," I said, "it's nothing. Birthdays can be hard, that's all."

"Hence the heavy drinking?"

"Hence the heavy drinking."

She let it drop. She knew I wasn't saying everything, but she also knew when not to question any further. "So, after my clumsy attempts at small talk, I'll move on to the sharing of inter-agency intelligence, shall I? We're still running tests on the samples taken at the murder scene, but we do know some things already. For one, we're pretty sure Cornwallis was lured to Cardiff to be murdered."

I sipped at the coffee. The bitterness cut through the fog in my brain, and, dimly, thoughts and ideas began to show up, like the lights of a city slowly coming on at dusk. "Why do you say that?"

"We haven't been able to find his phone – it's probably at the bottom of the Taff by now – but we can see from his provider's logs he'd had several calls from the same number in the week before his death. Calls made from Cardiff."

"But you don't know who made the calls."

"It was your typical unregistered pay-as-you-go SIM that's since dropped off the network."

"That might be perfectly innocent, a mate calling him. That's hardly *lured*."

"Agreed, except we found one more call from that phone before it was switched off. You probably thought it was an odd coincidence that a recently-murdered man should be found so quickly inside an abandoned house?"

"Yeah."

"So did we. It turns out, it wasn't a coincidence. There was a call to the demolition company from the phone just before it went dark. According to the company's receptionist, the call was to tell them to check inside the very house where the body was found."

Okay, that was definitely *lured*. "Someone wanted to be sure the body was found."

"It obviously would have been, eventually. The perpetrator wanted Cornwallis to be found *in situ*, inside the spell-circle and without the rubble of a Cardiff semi on top of him."

"Or maybe they got cold feet and phoned in hoping there would still be time to save him."

"After the trouble they went to, I think that's pretty unlikely, don't you?"

I conceded the point with a nod. I tried to step back in my mind and survey the facts we had. Maybe from the right distance, the right angle, their shape would become clear. Like stepping back from a cubist work of art and suddenly seeing a figure.

"So?" she prompted.

"So?"

"So, this is where you tell me why the perpetrator did what they did. That's how this works, remember? We, obviously, are following up on known associates of Cornwallis, but what we're lacking is any sort of motive. Why was Cornwallis murdered like that, and why did his killer then make sure that we, and therefore you, found out about it? The Sergeant told me you came to the station, you and one other. What did you uncover?"

I drained my coffee cup, down to the sludgy bitter dregs. "We didn't get a lot."

"Tell me you got *something*, though. Otherwise I'm going to send the invoice for that double espresso and this cappuccino directly through to your boss."

"I can tell you he was killed by two people. It's possible there were more but, if there were, Cornwallis didn't see them."

"What do you know about the two?"

"Not much. We're pretty sure one was a man and one was a woman."

"Age, appearance?"

"They made sure they were unidentifiable, with long robes from head to toe."

"And a red demon and a green witch mask, right?"

"You've got it."

"What colour were the robes?"

"White."

"Pretty weird colour to choose if you're engaging in butchery. Was there any evidence of blood splatter? Do we know for sure it was them?"

"The impressions we recovered were from before the cutting began, but it had to be them. I imagine there are some heavily blood-stained robes around somewhere."

"Which have almost certainly been destroyed. They haven't turned up, in any case. Can you tell me anything else? Any detail, however small, is useful. What about the weapon?"

I'd decided not to tell her about the tree symbol thing until Hardknott-Lewis had had a chance to look into it. Nor about the fact that Cornwallis was probably a user. I wasn't clear how that fitted into things at all. "It was a dagger-like weapon with an ornamented handle."

"You're saying it was a ceremonial thing? A ritual weapon?"

"Quite possibly."

Zubrasky looked thoughtful. "That's consistent with what we thought. Whoever these two were, they were putting on a show, telling the world. They wanted to send a clear message, but they didn't want their identities to be revealed. That's interesting in itself, isn't it?"

"It's understandable they'd want to hide who they were," I said.

"I suppose."

"You don't seem sure. Why would they endanger themselves by showing us their faces?"

"It's just, cases like this, killers are often on a power trip. They make a show of hiding their identity, but they deliberately don't do it that well. Like in the videos terrorists make. Assuming these two aren't in our databases and we couldn't get anything from facial recognition, it's like they feared being recognised, either by someone from your side, or someone from ours."

That sounded like a stretch to me. Were the police struggling so badly to get anywhere? "Why do you think they're not known to you? Did you recover any DNA?"

"We did, but from quite a few different people. You saw

the bedding; we're pretty sure there have been squatters sleeping there recently. We haven't been able to match any of the sequences we recovered to known criminals. Whoever they were, they don't have records." She sipped at her coffee, frowning in thought. "What about the runes you were so weird about?"

"Definitely powerful. Again, we're still looking into them, but most likely they were there to amplify the effect of some heavyweight incantation." I was totally making that up; it was complete guesswork. I guess I didn't want her to know just how junior I was.

"Couldn't you have, I don't know, got something more from his aura?"

"His aura?"

"Sure. That's a thing, isn't it?"

"No, that's not a thing. Now *you've* been watching too much television."

"Anything else you can tell me?"

"That's it so far."

She drained her coffee and stood up. "I have to go. Let's keep each other informed if anything turns up, yes?"

"Absolutely."

She was about to leave, then she stopped. "Oh, and Danesh?"

"Yeah?"

"The next time someone cuts you with a knife, even if it's only a flesh wound, and even if it wasn't intended to properly harm you, like it was a joke or a warning or something, you report it to the police, okay?"

"Of course," I lied.

6 – English Wizardry

Beware the temptations of the seemingly innocent. Books, films, games – even if ridiculous and poorly informed – may all act as a sort of gateway drug to the true perils that surround us. They may be the first siren call that lures the curious to cross the line and enter the spell circle for the first time.

–Earl Grey, Witchfinder General,
Office of the Witchfinder General Handbook, 1999

Back in Cardiff, I stepped out of *Caerdydd Canolog* to find there was a weird bright light in the sky: a blinding circle shining down on the city making everything positively warm. More than that, each person hurrying across the concourse was dogged by a shifting black form in the shape of a body sliding along the floor beside them. No one else appeared to have noticed. Odd. What had happened to the familiar, comforting blanket of cloud I'd so grown to love? Where was the drizzle?

My plan was to head back to the office and spend a little more time with MORIARTY. As well as logging what I'd found (admittedly, not a whole lot) I wanted to pick through the updates on HOLMES to see if there was anything Zubrasky wasn't telling me – or anything that had just come to light. The police had clearly been busy, examining Cornwallis's house with impressive efficiency. They'd be running a battery of forensic tests, meaning updates of interest could arrive at any time.

I was also hoping there might be a handwritten note on my desk from the Lady – that was her preferred mode of communication – explaining why the two users had gone to such trouble to remove the eyes of their victim, and why they needed to carry out their surgery inside a potent runic circle. And then if that wasn't enough fun for one afternoon, I thought I might pay another visit to Gilroy to try and find out how much of his story was actually true and how much was the result of his fevered imagination.

I also needed to make some travel arrangements. It was Friday, and it looked like most of my Saturday was probably going to be taken up with the case, but I hoped to get a late train and spend Sunday in *Llundain* with my mother.

I wove my way through the labyrinth of Victorian shopping arcades that are maybe my favourite thing about Cardiff. I hadn't properly got my head around how they're laid out in the eighteen months I'd been in the Welsh capital. Whenever I meandered through them, taking a short-cut between the straight city streets, it seemed the shops and cafes inside had moved around, coming at me from unexpected angles. Sometimes, still, I entered one of them and emerged a few minutes later on a completely unexpected road.

I was idly looking in the window of one of my favourite shops in Castle Arcade – a board game emporium that was a treasure cave of delights – when my phone vibrated with a message. A glance at the screen told me I should pay attention. *The Crow*. A text from Hardknott-Lewis was rare; it wasn't going to be some polite enquiry about how my hangover was doing. *Could you possibly drop into the tower to see me when you're in the area?* The grammar of it was unmistakable. Hardknott-Lewis was one of those people who would never dream of using a txtspeak abbreviation, or even of missing out a punctuation mark. He simply wouldn't be able to bring himself to do it. He texted using the same language as he used for everything else: formal and considered. Anything else would be the thin end of some dangerous wedge. Of course, he couldn't see me, hidden away as I was in the maze of tunnels, but it was hard to escape the notion that his gaze was upon me: that, up there in his tower, he'd watched me arrive back in the city and was now calling me to his side.

I replied that I'd be there soon, finding myself using the same well-constructed syntax he'd employed instead of my normal *kk 5 mins* approach. As I tapped out my reply, I couldn't stop myself thinking back over all the events of the past day. Had I overstepped the mark somewhere, missed something? My heart wasn't exactly racing, but it was certainly cantering. An unexpected summons from

Hardknott-Lewis had that effect on me. He was on my side, obviously, but it was hard to forget that one word from him could have me consigned to Oblivion, with no hope of appeal and definitely no early release for good behaviour.

The door to his office at the top of the tower stairs stood ajar as I reached it – a sign that I was allowed to enter. I knocked politely anyway, before stepping inside.

"Danesh, thank you for coming. Please sit down." This time, Hardknott-Lewis rose to greet me. His handshake was as firm and no-nonsense as ever: *up, down, up.* While I sat, he closed the door behind me then returned to his own seat. His desk was normally tidy, everything on it set out with deliberation, but just then it was strewn with books and files and sheets of paper. The shelves around the walls were also in some disarray: numerous tomes pulled out halfway to mark them as items of interest, gaps where volumes had been removed for study. I wondered whether there were any books there of which the Librarian would disapprove.

Silence gathered expectantly in the room. There was a definite frown on Hardknott-Lewis's face as he considered where to start. It was an expression that meant trouble for someone; I just hoped it wasn't me. As well as the books and papers there was a blue and cream china tea set on his desk, steam rising from the cup that Hardknott-Lewis had poured for himself.

"May I offer you tea?" he ventured.

Despite my English mother and Indian father – basically making me genetically wired to love tea – I'd never liked the stuff. Give my coffee any time. "I won't, thank you."

Hardknott-Lewis sipped from his cup. "You can't beat a properly brewed cup of loose-leaf Earl Grey. Only distantly related to our own Earl Grey, I believe. Did you know that we in the Office were responsible for the widespread introduction of teabags in the early twentieth century? It was for the best of reasons, but I sometimes regret it."

He was circling the issue he'd called me to discuss. I didn't know whether to be flattered or terrified.

"Tea-bags?" I said, genuinely thrown off-balance for a moment. "Why did we do that?"

"Well, you see, when people make tea with loose leaves, they have the unfortunate habit of trying to divine the future from the patterns in the bottom of their cups afterwards. Quite unacceptable. It isn't just by returning revenants to their graves and dispelling mass hauntings that we keep the public safe. There are also the little things people must be protected from. Something like divining the future from tea-leaves can lead you into deep waters."

"Yes," I said. "Of course."

"I read your reports," he said. Now he was getting to it. "Most interesting."

"It's still early days in the investigation. I'm not convinced Gilroy gave us the truth when he said the victim was a supernaturalist."

Hardknott-Lewis nodded. "On balance, I suspect he wasn't lying, for once. I think this really may be a case of groups of users warring with other. It's a situation that can only bring torment and bloodshed, one that can't be allowed to spiral out of control."

"You mean, like a turf war between rival gangs?"

"In a sense. I've unearthed some details from what you found that genuinely trouble me."

"To do with the runes?"

"Those are troubling, but mainly to do with the symbols you spotted smudged on the wall, and then with Gilroy's description of the robes worn by Cornwallis's murderers. It's possible I'm seeing patterns where there are none, and that Gilroy was simply making trouble, but I suspect not."

I thought about that. "You think the candle smudges on the wall depicted an oak tree and stars, the same as the symbol on the robes."

"I suspect so, yes."

It was a bit of a stretch, to be honest. "What does the symbol mean? Have you identified it?"

By way of reply, Hardknott-Lewis steepled his fingers together and appeared to change the subject. "Tell me, Danesh, do you know why I recruited you into the Office?"

His question threw me. It was beginning to look like I had done something wrong. Was it possible I'd said something I shouldn't while out on the town the night before? Let something slip that should have been kept hidden? I mean, *that* wasn't impossible.

I tried to keep my voice calm. "You told me you saw

potential in me. I did well at university, got a First in maths, I boxed and climbed and skied, and you said you thought I might have what it takes if I didn't want to spend my years working for a merchant bank or a hedge fund."

Hardknott-Lewis nodded as if considering this description for the first time. "That was all true. We'd watched you from afar, as we watch a number of graduates who are on our radar, and you seemed to fit the bill. You're resourceful and you're clever. You have a strong moral compass, and you come from a good family who taught you right from wrong, even if there are – if you'll forgive me – certain factors there that are a cause for concern."

My stomach sank within me like a stone in a pond. This really wasn't going well. I trusted Hardknott-Lewis completely. I maybe didn't like him much, but I certainly respected him. Could it really be he was calling me into question because of my cultural background? Because my father's parents had come from India? I'd thought better of him. Much better.

"What factors?" I said.

"You don't know?"

"You mean, because I'm Asian?"

To his credit, it took Hardknott-Lewis a full second to grasp the meaning of my words. A second that told me basically everything I needed to know. Whatever it was he meant, it had nothing to do with race. A look of mortified horror crept across his features. I'd seen the expression before, often enough. It was the look decent, unprejudiced people assumed when they realised they'd said something that might be misconstrued.

"Danesh, I assure you I did not mean that. This has nothing to do with ethnicity. If I gave you that impression, then I apologise unreservedly."

That was good. And also, bad. I was in some kind of trouble, but now I couldn't for the life of me see what it was.

"Then I have no idea what you mean," I said.

Hardknott-Lewis removed his half-moon glasses and began to polish them on his red silk handkerchief. He spoke quietly, as if his words were of no great consequence. "Tell me, Danesh, can I trust you?"

Oh, crap. "Of course."

"But you would say that even if I couldn't." It was a statement, not a question.

"If you couldn't trust me, Lord High Witchfinder, we wouldn't be here having this conversation."

Hardknott-Lewis conceded the point with a dip of his head. "Still, things can change. We find ourselves in a delicate situation, and we face risks whichever way we look. You, especially, face risks. I'm afraid you will be sorely tested by what is to come. There are the obvious physical dangers on the one hand; dangers from the forces and creatures we face, as well as from those who attempt to control them. Then, on the other hand, there are the whispered voices of temptation."

I was struggling to understand where the conversation was leading. "I don't... I'm sorry, what does that have to do with the oak tree symbol? What things in my past trouble you?"

"I will explain all, I promise you. But I warn you at the start not to underestimate the siren lure of that which we face. I have seen too many succumb to the prospect of easy power. I saw great potential in you when we recruited you, but I admit now I was also worried about what you might become without a guiding hand upon your shoulder. Partly you were recruited because I wished that hand to be mine. It may well be that we are now approaching the time when we find out who you really are."

I was floundering badly. This whole conversation hadn't gone anything like I'd imagined. "What do you mean, *what I might become*?"

Hardknott-Lewis balanced his polished glasses back on the bridge of his nose and considered me for a moment. "Well, it is possible you don't see it, possible you have no idea what I'm talking about. Or perhaps, deep down, barely even admitted to yourself, you do understand."

"I really don't think I do."

"I'm talking about your potential in the unnatural arts. It is clearly there in you. Your love of puzzle-solving, of unearthing pleasing patterns within the unknown, demonstrates it. As does your empathy for people, I'd say. Your love of left-field popular culture, fantasy literature and so forth, is yet another indicator. Also, it is a well-established fact that the potential for magic use has a clear genetic component." He held up a hand, palm open. "Again, I assure you this has nothing whatsoever to do with your ethnic background *per se*. I refer, simply, to your family."

Gilroy's taunts about my grandfather came flooding back to me. I started to object, but Hardknott-Lewis waved my words away. "I am not saying you have succumbed, only that you could. The ability for magic use is within you. Our investigations originally suggested any abilities would be completely latent, but I've started to believe otherwise. I suspect it would not be out of malice should you succumb; at the start, at least, it would perhaps be mere intellectual curiosity. You would not be the first. But if you resist the temptation and leave your potential *in potentia* as it were, then you could use that capacity to do good. The best witchfinders over the centuries have often been those who might have walked a path on the other side if their lives had run differently. It gives you a certain ability to understand what is taking place without taking part.

"I saw that clearly when you thought you were familiar with the spells used upon Cornwallis. As I told you at the time, the magic was nothing I had seen before, but you weren't convinced. The pentagram was a part of it, of course, but it doesn't explain your conviction. You knew instinctively this was some dark and troubling death magic. It *reminded* you of something. And I suspect you were right, which means I was also right. I was correct to recruit you where I could keep a watchful eye on you, just in case you ever showed signs of succumbing."

"I am not showing any signs of *succumbing*."

"Good, good. But tell me, have there been any moments when something, let us say, inexplicable and transcendent has happened to you? A moment of genuine foresight, for example, or an instant when you felt that you could make something miraculous happen simply by willing it to be so? A sort of rage to rearrange the world and its broken, irksome ways?"

These were dangerous waters. I had only to say *yes* to put myself in the gravest danger. Fortunately, I could answer with absolute certainty. "No, nothing like that."

"I ask you not to catch you out, genuinely, but to offer you help if there have been... urges."

"No, I assure you. There is nothing."

Hardknott-Lewis's eyes bored into me for a few moments. Long, long moments. Eventually, he dropped his stare and nodded in appreciation, as he might if, say, he were sipping a fine brandy. Not that he drank brandy. "Good, good. Then we will proceed. Let me explain to you about English Wizardry. And then we can discuss your grandfather."

He picked a piece of paper from one of the folders on his desk and slid it across to me. It looked like a photocopy of the title page of an old book. From the lettering it appeared typeset, mass-produced, but the layout and decorative title suggested the book was antique. Flower-like smudges mottled the surface of the paper in photocopier grey.

It said:

The Old Ways

BEING AN ACCOUNT OF

THE ANCIENT AND TRUE WONDERS OF

ENGLISH WIZARDRY

COLLECTED AND CATALOGUED BY

SAMUEL BEDFELLOWES

Published by the author

SUSSEX

MDCCCXLVII

And there in the space between the first and second lines was a stylised illustration I recognised: a drawing of an oak tree crowned by seven stars.

"This is the image that your photo of the candle smudges at the murder scene reminded me of," said Hardknott-Lewis. "*The Old Ways* was published in Sussex in 1847. So far as we know, only twelve copies were printed. The Office holds seven of them, all in London. I had this scan of the first page emailed to me last night. We have done what we can to remove the work from general circulation over the years, either by hiding away the copies we track down – or destroying them."

"I've never heard of it," I said.

"Well, no. There you are. Really, the book is only mildly dangerous. It contains scraps of incantation and ritual that could, given the right alignments and a bit of luck, summon something regrettable into our world. Most of what it says is nonsense, a collection of misguided delusions and half-forgotten rhymes. Bedfellowes was a clergyman with too much time on his hands. He travelled far and wide across England, collecting folk stories and spells. This book was the result."

"Then I don't see why it is so significant."

Hardknott-Lewis slipped another sheet of paper across the desk. Another black-and-white printout. "This is from 1935. A very different age. This is a photograph of a march by Oswald Mosley's Blackshirts through the East End of London. I assume you are familiar with this chapter of history?"

I knew about it from school – and from the tales passed down within my own family. "Mosley was a fascist, acquiring some support in the years before the Second World War," I said. "There was also widespread revulsion at his activities, coming to a head at the so-called Battle of Cable Street. His significance diminished as the war began and people saw for themselves what fascism meant."

"Quite so. Do you see this banner here, among the Union Jacks and the Blackshirts' flash and circle flags?"

I peered closely to where he was pointing. There could be no mistaking it: someone in that crowd was holding aloft a banner depicting an oak tree surrounded by stars.

"Sometime around the turn of the century, Bedfellowes' book acquired a cult following within certain aristocratic circles," explained Hardknott-Lewis. "We have scant details, but a secretive group of adepts began to meet to read from and discuss the book. They took their symbol from it – and also their name. They began to refer to themselves as *English Wizardry*."

"They aligned themselves with the fascists?"

"If you'll excuse the pun, they were natural bedfellows. Their particular delusion was that their notion of magic use was pure and true, whereas others were degenerate."

"By *others* you mean foreign traditions."

"I do. English Wizardry were fiercely nationalistic and considered other nations and peoples as simply inferior. In their view, the origins of all magic use lay in the mists of English history; the spellcraft carried out by other nations was a bastardised mockery of the high original."

"They were genuine supernaturalists?"

"Some of them, at least. They ably demonstrated to history the dangers of letting people employ powers that no mortal should wield. Their activities crop up several times in the record. There is an account from the First World War, for instance, of one of their number proposing the creation of wide-area incantations across the whole of no-man's land, with the intention of reanimating the corpses of the fallen and making them march against German lines. Then again, in the Second World War, when their political allegiances had switched around somewhat, it was claimed that Neville Chamberlain was under a spell of their design when he meekly accepted German assurances of non-aggression. London's pea-souper fogs were supposed to be their doing too, cover for some city-wide necromancy with which they hoped to terrorise or enslave vast numbers of the population. As you can imagine, the Office opposed them at every turn, fought many battles. Eventually, in the late 1950s, we succeeded in destroying their organisation."

"And now we're seeing their symbol again."

"It appears English Wizardry has been reborn. There are sometimes cycles to these things. The lessons of the past are forgotten, and old ways become new again. Perhaps the group never really went away, or perhaps someone in the modern age read about them and decided to emulate them. Whatever the explanation, I believe it was they who were responsible for Cornwallis's murder – or, at least, someone who wants us to believe that."

"So, maybe Cornwallis was one of them, and an argument broke out? A schism within the group?"

Hardknott-Lewis weighed up my words with a side-to-side movement of his head. "It could be; it certainly appears that the killers hated Cornwallis passionately. Equally, it could be that they have resumed some of their old activities, seeking out and exterminating those they disapprove of as well as those who stand in their way. That means us in the Office, and it means other supernaturalists. English Wizardry were merciless, ruthless people. That is why I talked about the dangers to you. And that is also why I mentioned your grandfather."

I had that sensation of things clicking into place in my mind. Certain words Hardknott-Lewis had said – *potential, background, bloodshed* – spun around and formed an orderly line in my mind. The taunts of Gilroy echoed through my mind, as well.

"You're saying my grandfather was involved in the fight against English Wizardry?"

"I know this piece of family history has been kept from you, Danesh. Your parents knew of it, and I was sworn to secrecy unless I felt the time was right to tell you. What Gilroy said makes sense. Your grandfather was a practitioner of Indian folk sorcery. He fought English Wizardry with all the magical powers he could summon. Or possibly they came for him and he was forced to defend himself; it makes little difference in the end. You see, this is about your background, after all. There is a chance English Wizardry will recognise you. They will hate you as an agent of this Office, and they will despise you because of what else you represent: a foreign culture that they regard as inferior. But they will also hate you because you are a Shahzan, the grandson of your grandfather."

I had the sensation of pits opening up in the once-solid ground. "I had no idea."

"That is all one danger," Hardknott-Lewis continued relentlessly. "Then there is another. Those opposed to

English Wizardry are, I believe, disorganised, but *they* may see you as a potential ally. They may try and bring you over to their cause. In the end, that may even be the greater threat to you. Given the xenophobia of English Wizardry, given what they did to your grandfather, it would not be completely impossible to understand the temptation. English Wizardry and their opponents are equally malign, threatening life and limb and possibly even civilisation itself with their dabblings. Sometimes, when it comes to a fight, it is easy to think you have to choose sides, rather than oppose all those who are fighting. The fact is, both sides are capable of unleashing terrible cruelty upon the innocents caught in the middle."

"What did they do to my grandfather?" So far as I knew, he had died peacefully at a relatively young age; some problem with his heart.

"Details are scarce, but we believe he was deliberately trapped within a runic circle. It was a favourite form of English Wizardry execution. Their adepts sealed those they wished to be rid of inside a circle, then summoned some nightmare creature from one of the shadow realms. There was no escape for those trapped inside. The English Wizardry adepts would stand and watch as their screaming victims were ripped to shreds and devoured."

My mind was reeling from it all. Hardknott-Lewis saw it on my face. "I could assign someone else to the case if you prefer. Kerrigan perhaps. Or Digbeth or McLeland. This is a clear lead that needs to be pursued, but it would be perfectly understandable if you didn't want to expose yourself to it."

I thought about Az and my mother. All manner of sinister thoughts trickled through me as I remembered her words. *The man who was there that day.* Was it possible that Az's death was somehow tied up with all this? Was I in danger? Was my mother? I would sit her down and talk to her that weekend.

"No," I found myself saying. "I can do this. I want to do this."

"Despite the dangers?"

"Yes."

"I imagine you'd like to visit your mother. Given that it's just been your birthday, I mean."

Sometimes, I swear he *can* read minds. "I would like that," I said.

"Go tonight. I will arrange for someone from the London Office to meet you and give you everything they have on English Wizardry. They were never particularly active here in Wales, so most of our records about them are in Whitehall. Spend the day there tomorrow, making what sense of this you can. Again, I wish I could send more bodies to accompany you, but it's simply impossible."

"Thank you, Witchfinder General. I'll leave right away."

"Just promise me you'll be careful, Danesh."

"I will."

I stopped off at the office to sort out my travel arrangements. As I finished booking my train tickets, Kerrigan wandered over to my desk, holding a white envelope. It was sealed and had my name handwritten upon it.

"Lady Coldheart left this for you. Bit of a shock to see her up here, frankly. She looked pretty unhappy about leaving her lair."

I thanked him and put the letter in my pocket for later. I had to hurry if I wanted to get to my flat to pack a few essentials before catching my train. Half an hour later, I was running down Queen Street *en route* to the station. As I wove through the crowd, I found myself casting a glance over each person in the street, wondering who they were, where they were going.

Whether they were watching me.

Whether any was one of those robed figures from Gilroy's vision, an English Wizardry adept pursuing their quarry.

7 – Whitehall

Her Majesty's Office of the Witchfinder General is one
of those quaint anachronisms so beloved of the British
state. It obviously no longer serves any serious function
in the modern lives of the people, but it has been
preserved to appeal to a sense of history and tradition
enjoyed by citizens and visitors alike. In fact, there is
still a Lord High Witchfinder, but these days his is a
strictly honorary role, a title bestowed upon a trusted
civil servant or an ex-politician. Fortunately,
witchfinders are no longer called upon to deal with
malign magic use or the incursions of the unliving.
Their position is entirely ceremonial.

    –Miranda Oglethorpe, *The State We Are In:
Politics and Power in Modern Britain*, 1985

I made it onto the platform exactly one minute late.
Fortunately, the train was running exactly ten minutes late, so
it all worked out fine. Nobody tried to sacrifice me or subject
me to any sort of vile blood magic at any point. I even had
time to grab another cup of the same station coffee I'd bought
that morning. It hadn't got any stronger.

Once on the train, I phoned my mother to tell her I'd be
home that evening. She sounded genuinely delighted at the
prospect, something like her old self.

"What time will you be here?"

"Around 10:30, assuming no delays or replacement bus
services."

"You'll be hungry. I'll cook some food for you to eat."

"There's no need, I'll grab a sandwich on the train." I
knew, even as I said it, that she'd ignore my words. She'd
spend the rest of the evening in the kitchen, chopping and
frying and boiling. I wasn't going to complain. My mother
loved to cook. More than that, although she was Manchester
born and raised, from English working-class stock, she was

one of the best cooks of Indian food I knew. She'd learned from *the* best: her mother-in-law, my grandmother, who'd arrived from Jaipur just after the war with all the clothes she owned, her pan, and a treasure trove of hand-mixed spice sachets. I knew all this because it was family legend. As a boy I'd had visions of my grandmother walking up the steamer gangway in Calcutta, peacock-blue saree flapping in the wind, her pan held aloft as if she were a marauding pirate. I guess it probably wasn't really like that. Still, my grandmother had put that pan and those spices to good use, and there'd surely been no finer food on the planet – although my mother's came close.

She'd even inherited the famous family pan.

Once everything was arranged for my stay, I turned my attention to the Librarian's letter. I slit the top of the envelope open with my thumb. Inside was a single sheet of folded paper, and written upon that in the Lady's flowery, calligraphic style was a single word, drawn out in the very middle of the sheet. It said:

Optograms

I turned the sheet over looking for more writing, a further explanation, but there was nothing. This one word was the sum total of the Librarian's communication. I had no idea what it meant. *Opto-* suggested eyes, so that seemed to fit, but *-gram* suggested, so far as I could recall, a drawing, which didn't make a great deal of sense. Was she suggesting I create a drawing of Cornwallis's eyes? What was that going to achieve? The letter was maddening. She *had* to know more than she was telling me. Getting knowledge from her and her precious books was like trying to wring blood out of a stone. It wasn't like I was asking her to transcribe illegal incantations or anything.

I spent the next half hour hitting the internet to find out if *optogram* was even a word, and if so, what it might mean. I was constantly hampered by the completely useless data signal I got on my phone as we whisked through the English countryside. I was hampered even more by the train's onboard WiFi, which put a series of unnecessarily complicated forms in my way – and then also failed to give me any more than a few dribbles of bandwidth. Again and again, pages loaded a few words and then froze – typically just before the bit where they told me anything useful.

Sometimes, you have to wonder whether Britain is comfortable with the modern world, or whether it secretly longs for its mediaeval past.

Still, by Reading, I'd ascertained a few scant details. An optogram was a thing. Some people in Victorian times believed that the retina preserves the last image projected onto it at the moment of a person's death, and the thinking was that, by removing and dissecting someone's eyes, you could work out what they'd witnessed in their final moments. There was some talk of the technique having been tried in the Jack the Ripper murder investigations. Most commentators agreed the whole thing was complete nonsense, although apparently there was a case where someone had successfully identified an image upon the retina of a rabbit – a rabbit deliberately placed in front of a bright, barred window for a while, then beheaded and dissected so that its eyes could be examined.

Lovely.

The connections to my case were obvious – but baffling. Surely Lady Coldwater didn't really believe such pseudoscience could be of any material use? Even if she was suggesting the two robed figures had carried out their crime because they believed in optograms, it didn't explain the runic circle, or the English Wizardry angle. Information on optograms was in the public domain, and not in any way a contravention of magus law – so why the secrecy? Why the cryptic single word? Weren't we on the same side?

I sat looking out of the window as the dark fields and lit towns of Berkshire slipped by to the train's clatter and rumble. She had to have found something in the Vault that was relevant but, clearly, she was too protective of her tomes and scrolls to tell me what it was. Which, okay, maybe meant it was dangerous magic she could only allude to, that she didn't want me to properly understand. Maybe I was being unfair to her.

I tried to grasp what she might have found by what she'd told me – and what she hadn't. Lots of echoes of genuine spellcraft leaked across into common knowledge – usually in a misunderstood, garbled fashion. People fear bats and cats and spiders without understanding the notion of familiars and personal daemons or knowing that some adepts can assume those forms if they choose to. Similarly, a few mispronounced syllables of genuinely devastating curses have made it into common parlance as playground rhymes or swear words. Perhaps something similar was going on here: the supposed science of optograms was an echo of real sorcery, magic that required those strong runes to function. If so, it would make sense that more and more potent magic was needed the further you wanted to trawl backwards through someone's visual memories.

It suggested that whoever had removed Cornwallis's eyes intended to retrieve something he'd witnessed. A face, an action – or maybe something mundane like a password or a PIN. Was that possible? The idea led me onto another track completely. What if the whole thing was little more than common criminality, a case for Zubrasky rather than the Office? Perhaps the whole thing with English Wizardry was misdirection, an attempt to throw us off the trail. They'd made their phone call, worn their ridiculous robes, smudged the candle marks on the wall, knowing it would send us off down the wrong path.

The killers might be little more than magically adept criminals intent on retrieving, say, banking log-on details used by Cornwallis. In his line of work, he may have had control over significant amounts of money and therefore might know the security credentials necessary to administer them. Did that work? Most sites didn't show you your password as you typed, so the characters wouldn't have been emblazoned on his retinas, but some did, and maybe Cornwallis had been one of those people who wrote their passwords down. He would have had to read his passwords, and so the images of them might be recorded on his eyes.

That was all guesswork, but a lot of what we did in the

Office was tackling users who committed criminal acts using their forbidden powers: theft, blackmail, extortion, you name it. It wasn't all unnamed horrors breaking through the walls. There'd been at least three recorded cases that year of people using illegal clairvoyance to foresee the National Lottery results. We had AI routines running that monitored for such things. I recalled, also, the case of a gangland assassin who, it turned out, had used a particularly vicious summoned creature called a *Shadow of Vengeance* rather than a gun or a knife to despatch his luckless victims. He would summon the entity, turn it on his target, then sit back and let it do its work, knowing that no barrier or obstacle would prevent it seeking out its prey. Such cases were difficult to prosecute. The problem was that magus law evidence was inadmissible in a criminal court – and no jury was going to believe much of it anyway. The police and the Crown Prosecution Service were generally reduced to building a case based on what non-magical evidence they could muster, or else we in the Office took charge and acted under magus law, and the courts and the public never heard anything about it.

I had to run all this by Zubrasky, see what leads the police had found on Cornwallis's recent movements: where he'd been, who he'd seen, what he'd been up to. Problem was, I had no idea how far back into his visual impressions an adept could reach – even assuming the whole thing was possible, and I hadn't jumped to the wrong conclusions completely as a result of the Lady's unnecessarily cryptic message.

I had Zubrasky on a chat app so I could communicate with her without using anything as insecure as email. It was a useful backchannel, far removed from the official logs of both HOLMES and MORIARTY. I fired over a few questions and suggested it was a possibility the criminals might have been able to recover details of whatever Cornwallis had witnessed in the recent past. *Possible motive?* I wrote. I left it vague, because vague was all I had. She might see connections I knew nothing about. The message didn't send immediately because the internet connection inevitably chose that moment to dematerialise again, but the message would reach her as soon as I neared some approximation of civilisation.

I reached my childhood home in good time. The smells of my mother's cooking were unmistakable as I walked the last few steps of my journey up the familiar checkerboard mosaic pathway to the red front door of our Dulwich house. Frying onions, cumin, garlic and coriander filled my nostrils: the scents of my boyhood. My mother would sometimes recall, a fragile smile on her lips, how my father would tease her that she, a white Mancunian woman, was more Indian than he was. I hadn't been home for six months or more. I shouldn't have left it so long.

She greeted me with a strong embrace – a *cwtch* I would probably have called it now, although she wouldn't have known the word – then stepped back to examine me.

"You've lost weight. Are they looking after you out there in Wales?"

I wasn't sure who *they* were. "I'm fine, really. I'm busy but it's… interesting work."

She considered me for a moment more. I sometimes suspected she knew more about what I did than she let on. At some point over the weekend I had to sit her down and have a proper conversation with her.

"Come and eat," she said. "I've made a few things in case you were hungry."

By *a few things* she meant a table full of curries, dals, breads, chutneys, two types of rice, a jug of sweet lassi and even some kulfi for dessert. My favourite dessert in the whole world was her chocolate kulfi – not a recipe my grandmother would have recognised. The whole spread was enough to feed everyone in the Welsh Office even when they were all in town.

"You shouldn't have gone to so much trouble."

She said what I knew she'd say. It was reassuring simply to hear the familiar response: "What you don't eat will freeze. Now sit down."

She sat with me, sipping tea and occasionally nibbling at naan bread dipped into one of the sauces. She watched me eating – I'd starved myself knowing what would happen – with a look of the greatest satisfaction on her face. She looked well. A little greyer, a few more worry-lines apostrophising her eyes, but well.

Behind her head, on the mantlepiece, the gold carriage-clock that had whirred throughout the years of my childhood had stopped. "I have to work tomorrow," I said, "but I'll be back in the evening and we'll have all of Sunday together."

"That sounds lovely. Oh, I forgot your birthday present."

She stood and went to a drawer to remove a present wrapped in silver and festooned with curling decorative bows. She'd gone to a lot of trouble with it. Inside was a really nice watch, a mechanical one with all sorts of additional dials and functions, the sort that lets you dive fifty metres into the sea and still know the time, date, day and phase of the moon. Because those are obviously all really important things to know when you're deep in the ocean. It had to have been very expensive – so expensive it was probably called a *timepiece* or even a *chronograph*. I'd always gone for cheap watches – they kept the same time – but I had to admit my new one looked great.

"This is wonderful. You shouldn't have."

"Oh, nonsense. It suits you. You have to look the part."

She beamed at me, and she was my old mother again. There'd been no mention of Az still being alive, no hint of her confusions and delusions. She was a fine lady, getting on in years a little, proud of one son and sad for the loss of her other.

But when she stood again to shut the drawer from which she'd pulled my gift, I noticed there was another one still in there, identical. She'd wrapped a present for my dead brother, too.

Later, when I had my new watch on my wrist and got it all adjusted, I took my chance to ask her. "That conversation we had the other day. Did you write down what you'd remembered? You said something about seeing a man."

She shifted a little in her seat, as if avoiding uncomfortable truths. "Did I say that? I don't recall."

"But you would have written what you remembered down?"

"Yes, yes of course, I'm sure I would have done."

"Could I look at what you wrote at some point this weekend?"

"I'll find my notepad." She looked around the room, a look of confusion on her face. The room hovered somewhere between a lived-in clutter and a not-coping mess. There was only her in the house now, and I often thought when I returned that the disorder of her home was like some kind of map of her mind. Most things were in their right place, but quite often they weren't at all. I had no idea, for instance, why there was a muddy garden spade leaning against the dining room wall.

"Do you know where it is?" I asked.

"Well, it'll be here somewhere. Things turn up eventually, don't they?"

I set off for the London Office early the following morning. Hardknott-Lewis had set up a meeting with a colleague called Peter Warder, the resident expert on English Wizardry. I'd chatted with him once or twice at office parties and team-building exorcisms. He was tall, bookish, his expression one of permanent startlement, like that of an owl. A leggy, flamingo-bodied, white-boy owl. His background was the familiar story of public-school education and an Oxbridge degree – Art History in his case. He was the sort of person about whom people said *he comes from a good family*, by which they meant *his family have been rich for many generations*. Still, my experience with people like him – at least with those recruited by the Office – is that they generally are impressive: bright, brave and with all the unflappability of the genetically entitled.

As I sat in the swaying tube carriage on the way to Whitehall, I caught up on the messages my phone had pulled in before losing signal in the underground network. Zubrasky had replied to thank me for the angle I'd suggested. *No sign of theft at any of C's clients. All advised to change passwords. Also checking whether he had access to sensitive information in case stock market fraud or industrial espionage.*

I guessed the latter was a possibility – except Cornwallis seemed like a pretty small-scale local accountant, not some city high-flyer. Would he really have access to the sort of information that could send share prices soaring or crashing? It was always possible he was part of some sort of network that did have such access. And the fact that the police hadn't identified an act of fraud or corporate theft didn't at all mean one hadn't taken place. Companies, wary of their share prices, were very sensitive about such things and often preferred to keep such losses in the dark – even if it meant not telling the authorities. *Especially* if it meant not telling the authorities.

Still, Zubrasky and her colleagues would be well aware of that. I could leave it to them to pursue all the possible channels pertaining to mere criminality.

As in Cardiff, most of our staff in London operated out of a set of perfectly normal-looking offices. Apart from some of the odder notices on the noticeboard they might have been the home of any government department or private company. Earl Grey kept his authoritative distance by working from his office at No. 13 Downing Street, just as Hardknott-Lewis kept himself aloof in the Black Tower. Just as, I believed, the Lord High Witchfinder of All Scotland looked down upon the world from the battlements of Edinburgh Castle.

The plaque on the wall outside the impressive Whitehall building – visible to the whole world as it was – made no mention of my department. Inside, a grey-haired man in a smart blue uniform stood behind a reception desk. He had the upright bearing of an ex-soldier. He probably knew thirteen different ways to kill me with his bare hands should I prove to be a troublemaker.

Warily, I held out my acolyte's badge for him to see. "I'm looking for the Office of the Witchfinder General."

The old boy didn't bat an eye lid. "You want the Basement. There's a lift over there. Put your finger on the scanner next to the door and it will give you access."

The Basement. Of course. "Thank you."

"You're welcome, sir," he said, in a way that suggested he didn't consider himself in any way subservient to me. Which, to be honest, I approved of.

Somewhat to my surprise the electronic fingerprint scanner on the lift recognised me immediately. Once I was inside and the doors had slid shut, the lift descended without me even having to choose a floor. Clearly my dactylogram (not a word I really knew; I'd come across it while reading about optograms on the train) only gave me access to the basement level, so that was where the lift was going to take me.

Another set of security doors greeted me down there.

Hidden out of the sight of impressionable eyes, there was another brass plaque. This one read:

Her Majesty's Office of the Witchfinder General
Protecting the public from the unnatural since 1645

The subtitle had been added in the 90s, when government departments were going through yet another reorganisation and someone figured we needed a mission statement. It had been the subject of a certain amount of satire among the rank and file over the years: the *unsociable*, the *uneducated*, the *unthinkable* and so on. The Office, incidentally, had been made an arm of the British state in 1645 because of Parliamentarian fears that their Royalist opponents in the English Civil War were employing the arcane arts to gain the upper hand on the battlefield. We were empowered then to stamp out all such devilry, and even to this day there is a strong Puritan streak to people like Hardknott-Lewis.

I had to admit the plaque looked pretty good, too. Maybe I'd talk to the Crow about getting one in Cardiff.

I was thinking these thoughts, my fingers on the handle of the door next to the plaque, when another episode of nausea overwhelmed me.

The room lurched and the floor – unreasonably I thought – tilted to throw me sideways. Booming metallic voices blared at me from nowhere, their misshapen words as incomprehensible as ever – as if they were shouting in a language I didn't know, or as if their tongues and mouths were crippled by some withering malady. Sickness washed through me and my stomach heaved. I was aware of something monstrous approaching: a vast presence I couldn't identify. It reached for me, *longed* for me. I think it wanted to devour me. It lumbered slowly, but also flew at me with great speed, in the illogical way things do in a dream. I tried to scramble away but couldn't get any traction on the smooth floor.

The scene changed, became overlaid by another vision, lurching past my eyes. Four figures sat in a darkened room, a single candle burning between them. They were hooded, their faces completely concealed. They, too, were making incomprehensible sounds. The sense of threat in the room was palpable, as if some great weight was thundering down upon them.

Then the four figures disappeared, and a face appeared in my vision: the oversized visage of a savage beast, all teeth, jaws wide enough to swallow my head whole. It roared more half-formed syllables. The stench of its breath on my face was oily and cloying, as if it were some machine exhaling steam. The jaws snapped shut…

…and the delusion dissipated, leaving me curled upon the floor, arms around my head.

I may have whimpered.

I uncoiled myself and stood shakily. My tongue hurt sharply where I'd bitten it. I was still alone in the corridor; no one had noticed my attack. The vision had seemed so real it was hard to believe the impossible beast I'd seen wasn't behind me, about to leap. I found myself turning around and around, just to be sure.

I looked at my new watch to see that only a few moments had passed. I really had to get these episodes under control. If one struck at the wrong moment, when I faced some supernatural hostile for instance, I'd be done for. I waited a moment for my breathing to calm then, warily, as if it were to blame, grasped the door handle again. This time, nothing happened except the handle turned and the door opened.

Inside, I was met by the Office's receptionist sitting behind another desk. She didn't appear to be aware of the attack I'd just suffered. Behind her was a frosted glass wall through which I could see, dimly, the shapes of my London colleagues flitting backwards and forwards as they went about their work of protecting the country from the ineffable. Occasionally, a distorted face loomed through the mists as someone walked nearer, but I could hear nothing save the low hum of computers and quiet conversations. The large letters *OWG* were frosted onto the glass in a stylishly corporate way.

The receptionist regarded me through her spectacles as she

might a stray dog wandering in off the street. I imagine she heard all sorts working where she did. "Can I help you?" she asked, in a tone that implied she wanted to do nothing of the sort.

I showed her my card and tried to sound unruffled. "Acolyte Danesh Shahzan from the Welsh Office. I'm here to see Peter Warder." I'd resisted the urge to say *I'm here on important business*. She looked like she would decide what constituted important and what didn't, thank you very much.

She tapped at her keyboard a few times, frowning at the screen that was presumably visible to her beneath the lip of the desk.

"I'm afraid he's been out on urgent calls all night," she said. "It looked like he was expecting you as there's a message to pass on if you turn up."

"May I ask what it says?"

She read some more from the screen. "He says he's gone to investigate some sounds heard from our warehouse."

"Your warehouse?"

"You don't have a warehouse in Cardiff?"

"No, I… no. I'm afraid I don't know what that is."

"The Possessed Statue Warehouse," she said. "Do you let yours roam the streets in Wales?"

Possessed statues were a rare problem in Cardiff; I guessed they had a lot more of them to worry about in London. They could be troublesome. People freaked out when a statue randomly spouted pompous nonsense at them, but the real problems started when one moved. Being grabbed by the bronze hand of a Victorian general was the least of it: sometimes, when the possession was strong, the figure wrenched itself free of its pedestal and walked. Sometimes they hunted in packs; it had happened a lot during London's pea-soupers I believed, and I now wondered whether English Wizardry had been involved in that. I'd heard of a more recent case where the nature of the possessing entity meant that the statue's touch turned anyone coming into contact to stone. There'd been a case of a human statue performer who'd done a roaring trade collecting impressive amounts of money – until it was discovered he'd been petrified by the touch of a rogue statue and had become, ironically, the very thing he was impersonating.

Hardknott-Lewis took a very hard line against all possessed objects. He had them immediately destroyed, which tended to break the incantation very effectively. It seemed they had a different practice in London.

"Do you know how long he'll be out?" I asked.

"He didn't say. Is there anyone else you could talk to instead?"

I needed to speak to Warder. No one else knew so much about English Wizardry.

"Is he contactable?"

She shook her head. It was the answer I expected. Standard procedure was to turn phones off before going into any sort of delicate situation. Even the buzzing of a silent device could attract the attention of something you'd really prefer left you alone, and there was a theory that certain disembodied entities were attracted to the electromagnetic fields put out by mobiles.

I came to a decision. I wasn't going to sit around waiting all day. "Can you tell me where this warehouse is?"

"Are you sure you want to go?" the receptionist enquired. "If there is something going on, it'll be dangerous. We've lost officers before now."

How tough could statues be? I could run pretty fast when I needed to. Besides, I was perfectly within my rights to operate within London. Unlike the police forces, the Office doesn't have regional boundaries. Arbitrary geographical borders don't make much sense given the pan-dimensional nature of many of our enemies. "I'll be careful."

She thought about things for a moment, and then conceded my request was probably acceptable to her. "I'll give you some directions."

Forty-five minutes later I was standing outside the high, razor-wire fence that surrounded a brick-built Victorian warehouse on the southern bank of the Thames. There was no plaque or sign to identify the building, other than the name and number of the security company who were, supposedly, monitoring the premises twenty-four hours a day. The place looked dilapidated, water weeping from the gutters to stain the walls with Christmas trees of green slime. The faint aroma of burning plastic ghosted through the air. There was no sound save the rattle of a passing train somewhere and, underneath that, the constant hum of the living city. The shabby chic of the place was, I figured, partly an act: a gleaming construction of glass and steel would have looked far more suspicious than this crumbling cathedral to commerce.

The fences barring my way were anything but rusty and broken, though: they were heavyweight, buttressed barriers that would repel any lorry or bulldozer attempting to smash them down. Only we in the Office knew that they were there to keep things in as much as to keep them out. The surveillance cameras, also, looked top-notch. I could see at least three trained on me, tracking me as I moved. I must have looked very suspicious there in front of the gates. Facial recognition software had probably already identified me. I hoped so, in any case. The security systems probably didn't react with overwhelming kindness to strangers.

Once again, somewhat to my surprise, my Office card and my thumbprint granted me access. The claustrophobic full-body turnstile clunked when I pushed it, but it admitted me to the no-man's land between the two sets of fences. The second turnstile also recognised me, and I was in.

There was no sign of Warder or anyone else. The tiny windows of the warehouse were all dark; I could see nothing at all of what lay inside the building. The heavy steel doors barring the entrance to the interior were new and serious-looking, blast-resistant and battering ram-proof. Once again, my credentials checked out and I was admitted.

I turned off my phone – the one thing I could use to summon help if I really, really needed it – and stepped inside.

8 – Possessed Objects

The thick, choking London fog severely limited our ability to react to the incursion. We chased a fleeing figure, thought to be the necromancer responsible, through the back-alleys of the East End, but soon lost them in the maze. The creature that they had summoned, or fashioned, or hexed to carry out their crimes also disappeared. All we had were the seven victims – their bodies and limbs horribly crushed and elongated – laid out in a crude approximation of a summoning circe [sic].

–Acolyte Rodney Merryweather,
Office of the Witchfinder General, *Case notes*, 1952

A grey light slanted down from the high windows, outlining looming shapes in front of me without properly illuminating them. Fortunately, as this wasn't a horror film, there was a perfectly functional set of lights. I flicked them on, wondering why Warder hadn't done so. Perhaps he had, and the lights turned off if no motion was detected after a while – which I had to hope was basically *all* the time, given the warehouse's occupants.

As white light flooded the cavernous room, I had the sensation that all the statues had been stepping towards me the split second before I could see them properly and had then frozen, like they were playing some kid's game. I ignored the thought. We are trained to recognise and ignore the tricks our brains play on us.

There were a *lot* of statues: hundreds laid out in regimented rows like a stone and bronze army ready to march. I guessed London had so many figures of historical importance that the English Office had no choice but to keep the capital's possessed statuary warehoused out of harm's way. Some of them were familiar; I could only assume that when a famous or well-loved statue become irretrievably possessed, they made another cast of it and replaced the original. Some sites would be more prone than others; it depended what had taken place there over the years or whether there was a nearby portal between the worlds. Judging by the fact that some of the statues I could see were identical, some had clearly been replaced more than once.

Most of the statues were single figures and most were men: able-bodied, larger-than-life, dead white guys commemorated for their contributions to war, or politics, or social progress, or whatever it was. Some simply stood looking impressive, while others gazed or pointed towards an imaginary future or distance. They came from any time in the last two hundred years. One or two were giants, from atop plinths or columns maybe. There were some women among them – I could see a couple of Queen Victorias – but really not many. There didn't appear to be any individuals of colour, which was ironic given that their stone or metal faces were actually grey, beige, black, brass-brown – or green. One or two figures sat astride horses and there were also some riderless steeds, as if the statue-people on their backs had climbed down and shambled away at some point.

On every one of them, a blue light blinked from a silvery disc about the size of a medal. I'd never seen so many Armitage Hobbles – devices used to stop possessed objects moving – in use at any one time before. The hobbles were more or less fool proof, but we rarely used them in Cardiff. We might deploy one temporarily during a retrieval operation or a fight, but that was it. Their name was a lie, designed to sound like a technological device, something similar to a Faraday Cage maybe. They were nothing of the sort; they were ensorcelled talismans, akin to a miniature runic circle in function and constructed to keep the item they were in contact with locked in Oblivion-like stasis.

They were another of our troublesome grey areas, just like Gilroy and the banned books in the Vault, and here were hundreds of them, blinking innocently away. Each one would have to be re-enchanted regularly. Who did they use to do that? The effort of it had to be huge. I knew the London Office made more extensive use of Assizes powers than we did, but I hadn't appreciated how much more. I wondered how much Hardknott-Lewis knew of this – and what his reaction would be when I told him.

There was no sign of Warder among the statuary. I resisted the urge to shout out; if he was in some sort of delicate situation, he wouldn't be able to reply. I made my way between two of the lines of statues, trying my best to shake off the feeling that each one was watching me warily with its blank eyes. My footsteps were loud in the hollow space, hard *clacks* echoing off the stone and metal objects around me.

The warehouse was split into several chambers. Through a doorway, I found a landing with stone steps leading upwards and downwards and, beyond, another chamber of similar size to the first, this one containing a lot of pointing figures, as if they'd been frozen in the middle of some angry argument. There was also a charioteer pulled by two horses, several kings and clerics and, in one corner, a collection of animals: dogs, bulls, sheep, goats and a cat. Glancing up, I could see the tops of the walls were ringed with an impressive array of gargoyles, grotesques and carved imps, captured from the battlements of London's cathedrals or other ornate buildings. The room didn't only hold statuary: in one corner an area had been caged off, and a sign on the door read *Beware: Highly Possessed Objects, Totems and Touchstones*. Through the grating I could see lines of shelves holding an assortment of odd and broken objects, swords and televisions and toys, each also hobbled.

None of the statues so much as blinked a stone eyelid or murmured a mournful syllable. Everything in the warehouse appeared to be under control. Warder had been called out to a false alarm. Maybe he'd been and gone and was now back in Whitehall, wondering where the Welsh boy had got to.

But then I heard the hefty *thud* of something on the floor above me. Then another. Then another. Something large and weighty – made of solid stone, say – was lumbering around up there. Curtains of dust showered down from the impacts.

The time for stealth was over. I reached for my phone to switch it back on; I could at least summon heavyweight firepower if things got out of hand. Then I ran for the stairs. I had little antimagical equipment with me, technological or sorcerous; I'd come for an academic discussion, not a fight with some unnatural conjuration. I had no weaponry other than my discreet Office handgun and the *clothcutter* blade we all carried on operations. The gun might pulp the head of a lumbering revenant satisfactorily, or even stop the relevant necromancer dead in their tracks, but it wasn't going to be much use against statuary. Similarly, we carried the blades in case we came face to face with an extra-dimensional horror and needed to puncture a tear through reality to suck it back into the shadow realm from which it had come. I could feel the dagger's malevolent power humming in its sheath against my ankle. Again, it wasn't going to trouble a statue possessed by a spirit from this world.

There *was* a rack of unused hobbles on the wall beside the stairs, powered up and ready to be used by the look of their flashing lights. I grabbed one and twisted the ring on top of it – a motion curiously like opening a jam jar – to prime it. Maybe it would be useful. With hindsight – I thought as I bounded up the stairs three at a time – I probably should have checked out something more assertive from the London Office before coming to the warehouse.

It was too late now.

If one of the possessed statues had somehow shaken off its shackles it could cause huge damage. If it started to attack the other statues – or even to barge mindlessly into them – it could dislodge *their* hobbles. The touch of some possessed objects was enough to infect other objects, as if the magic were a contagion. The whole thing could snowball, and before we knew it, we'd have the whole place alive with demonically-possessed effigies. And no one wanted that.

A sign next to the door at the top of the stairs read:

Warning: Plague Pit room

High unquiet soul concentrations

I knew that areas built upon plague pits – sited all over London – were some of the most spectrally active in the city, which meant that the statues placed upon them would be particularly susceptible to possession. Malevolent, seething-rage possession. Yay. I paused for a moment to steel myself, then turned the handle to push the door open.

There was a moment when the animated statue twenty metres away and I stood completely frozen – you could say statuesque – as we took in each other. The creature making all the noise was a treacle-black metal lion the height and bulk of a fair-sized Indian elephant. I recognised it immediately as one of those from Nelson's Column in Trafalgar Square. Clearly, at some point over the years, the original had become possessed and been replaced.

The beast rose from its sitting position, eyes intent on me, mouth pulled wide in a grimace that was the start of a snarl. I could see no other statues moving. That was something. I reached into my pocket for the hobble. Maybe I could get close enough to the lion to incapacitate it without becoming permanently incapacitated myself. It was all I had. I decided not to bother with the handgun. Bullets weren't going to do any harm to this creature, but a ricochet might do quite a lot of harm to me.

I was pretty sure that the trick with real lions – it's actually lionesses that do all the damage, but I wasn't banking on this sculpted creature knowing that – was to maintain eye-contact and back away slowly. I decided to try it. It didn't work out well. As soon as I moved, the spell that had held us in place was broken. The creature charged, its iron roar like a jet engine at full throttle, the floor shaking to its thundering surge. I threw myself backwards into the doorway, hoping the creature was too big to fit through the frame. Given its wrecking-ball momentum, however, there was also a very good chance it would demolish the door and the wall completely. And me along with them.

Oddly, as this went through my mind, I also found myself thinking how beautiful the creature was. Huge, but so vivid with fluid life. The four frozen statues in Trafalgar Square were of course familiar, but there was something glorious in the cat-like, predator's grace of the moving version. Possessed statues tended to take on the characteristics of the people and objects they represented, and clearly that was happening here. *Sculptural determinism* we called it, in the jargon.

My appreciation was cut short as the giant black beast leapt to devour me. A thing like that can knock you out of an aesthetic reverie. I fell through the doorway, sprawling to the hard floor of the landing, the impact jarring the hobble free from my hand.

The possessed metal lion crashed into the door frame, splintering it to shards, but the stonework of the walls slowed it for a moment. Its great head lashed as it tried to force its shoulders and body through the narrow gap, its carved muscles bunching and knotting.

I made full use of the moment. Scrambling to my feet I grabbed the hobble where it had rolled across the floor. If I could slap it on the lion's nose while it was trying to force its way through the doorway, I could freeze the beast, return it to dead metal.

The lion, however, became only more furious as I stepped closer. I got to within two feet. My proximity seemed to send the beast into new heights of fury. It forced itself forwards, bringing down one of the walls that held the door frame and buckling the other alarmingly. Another lunge and half its body was through. The sound of its roar shuddered the building around me.

I turned and raced for the next flight of stairs before it could bite my head from my shoulders. I didn't want to lure the lion down to the ground floor and risk all the statues there coming to life. Maybe the upper floor was more deserted.

It wasn't, but at least there were no top predators ready to roar into life. The next floor was where they kept the abstract sculptures: twisted, bulbous forms I'd probably have taken time to consider if I weren't moments from death. What would they be like if the lion breathed on them and brought them to animation? What lumpen, hulking forms would pursue me then? Perhaps they'd only stand there confused, gyrating elegantly. I didn't want to find out either way.

There were no other exits from the room apart from the windows, and I certainly didn't fancy leaping down to ground level. From the sound of it, the lion had finally succeeded in smashing through the doorway down below and was now forcing its way up the narrow stairwell, roaring in its fury and frustration.

Avoiding the beast seemed like my best option. Change of plan: I had to get away, phone for help, and just hope the lion was occupied long enough by the strange objects on the second floor not to notice. There was no sign of Warder; either he'd never made it to the warehouse, or the beast had killed him. I stood with my back to the wall five yards from the door, thinking that once it had forced its way through and leapt into the room, I could slip back out behind it and make my escape. In its mindless rage it might not notice me.

The crashing and bellowing from the stairwell stopped abruptly. I stood there not breathing or moving. Three, four, five seconds went by. Was it possible the creature's magical hobble had reactivated? Was Warder there after all, in pursuit of the lion? I stood and listened, trying and failing not to breathe. From somewhere in the distance an alarm wailed. Underneath, there was only the constant rumble of the city humming to itself. Could the beast smell me? I didn't know enough about the nature of its possession. It seemed unlikely, but I didn't want to test the theory out.

I waited unmoving for maybe two minutes. If Warder had hobbled the creature, why hadn't he shown himself? But then, perhaps he was on the other side of the wall wondering exactly the same about me. I edged along the wall to the doorway. Everything was quiet. I crouched down so my eyes were at an unexpected height and peeped around the corner of the doorway.

The furious lunge of the lion nearly took my head off. It had been waiting for me to appear all along, as patient a hunter as any domestic cat, its feline form directing its behaviour. Once again, I fell backwards from its onslaught. Once again, the lion managed to get its magnificently maned head through but was pinned back by its shoulders.

But I was prone on the floor and within reach of those dagger teeth. The creature stood over me in triumph and roared again. It looked down at me for a moment, considering which chunk to chew off first. I took my opportunity to act. In a single movement, I tossed the hobble I carried into its maw and back-pedalled desperately away.

9 – Hidden Histories

In all honesty, the soiree with Lord Beaumaris and his odd little group of supernaturalists left me feeling more troubled than entertained. There was a distinct undercurrent of threat to the whole affair. I might even say, of *malevolence*.

–Sir Anthony Deville,
private diary (unpublished), 1906

There was a sound like an explosion happening in reverse: a white noise crash of sound becoming quieter, harmonic, cohering into a single tone until it resolved to a gentle *ting*. I crouched to one side, watching to see what was going to happen. The blue light blinked on the hobble in the lion's mouth and the creature froze, bunched muscles slowing to become lifeless metal. The hunger went from its eyes as its legs folded up beneath it to adopt the familiar sitting pose it had been carved into.

A moment later, as gravity chimed in to have its say, the lion smashed to the floor in an explosion of dust and splintered woodwork, halfway into the room and halfway out. The floor skipped at the impact but mercifully didn't collapse.

I was very, very glad I had pushed myself away from underneath it.

A face appeared from behind the lion then, a man, hair wild and dusty, his expression one of alarm. "Danesh. What are you doing here? We were supposed to meet back in Whitehall."

Warder looked shocked to see me, his wide eyes exaggerated by his round glasses. He'd clearly been in a battle, cuts scarring his face.

"I came to help," I said.

Warder clambered over the back of the lion statue. He wiped his face with the back of his hand, smearing blood across his cheek. He had a makeshift bandage wrapped around the palm of his left hand but looked to be in one piece. "Damn beast had me cornered. I couldn't move until you came along to distract it. In hindsight, it was probably a mistake to put the creature in the plague pit room. Good job Landseer carved guard lions – seeing no threat, the beast simply sat and waited. Things would have been a whole lot worse if it was Boadicea in her war-chariot that got free."

"You should have phoned for help," I said. "In fact, I'm pretty sure you shouldn't have come here alone in the first place." Standard protocol was always to approach unknown and potentially dangerous situations in pairs.

Warder grinned in a way that conceded his own foolishness. "Fair point. My phone had no charge left, but I thought I'd chance it. Stupid of me. It's been a long night." He slid to the ground to sit beside me, gasping with the pain from some injury.

He could obviously hear the Dulwich in my voice. "I'd forgotten you're a Londoner."

"I went to Cardiff University, and Hardknott-Lewis recruited me from there."

Warder considered that for a moment, as if it was a revelation of particular interest to him. "Well, I'm very glad you came along. I'd have had to make a run for it at some point, and I didn't fancy my chances, to be honest. That thing is vicious when it's awake."

"How did it even come alive?"

Warder scratched the side of his face thoughtfully. "Hard to say. Maybe a pigeon got in and pecked at the hobble. Or a magpie, they like shiny things. Or a mouse. Or, I don't know, it was shaken loose by a train rumbling past or something. The device was on the floor when I got here. I thought I could sneak up to the creature and slap it back in place, but the lion must have been watching me all the way. It jumped from the pedestal when I was a few yards off and went for me, caught me a glancing blow. Then it cornered me behind Winston Churchill and sat there watching me like a cat toying with an injured bird, waiting for me to move."

"It seems insanely dangerous to keep them in here. In Wales we melt them down."

Warder conceded the wisdom of the point with a nod of his

head. "We used to put two hobbles on each statue, just to be sure, but there are so many now there aren't enough of the devices to go around." He pushed himself back to his feet. "Come on. I need to make a circuit of the whole building and make sure all the other occupants are sleeping peacefully."

"What about the lion? We can't leave it here blocking the doorway."

"We use a mobile crane to hoist the statues in. There are goods doors on the exterior of every floor; it's one reason the building was chosen. I'll arrange to have the lion put back on its plinth on Monday. We usually move them in at the dead of night, but we can make an exception here."

"It's a wonder people don't realise the statues are being replaced."

"Generally, we put out a press release saying a statue is being temporarily removed for renovation or cleaning, and people believe it. I get what you say about breaking them up or melting them down when they're possessed, but Earl Grey prefers not to destroy objects of historical or artistic merit if he can help it. There are one or two selected academics who know the truth of the situation, and they get to come in and study the collection from time to time."

That was interesting. Was it possible someone had deliberately ambushed Warder, set the whole thing with the lion up to get rid of the Office's resident English Wizardry expert?

"Have any been in recently to study the statues?" I asked.

"Not that I'm aware of, but we could look in the logs."

I took Warder's hand to lever myself up and walked to the lion lying askew in the broken doorway. It didn't move. I touched it on the nose, half-expecting it to be warm, a quarter-expecting those jaws to snap my hand off. But the cold metal remained impassive.

"Let's check around," said Warder from behind me, "then we can lock up and get back to base."

We found no more out of place hobbles, no more creatures intent on rending us to tasty gobbets of flesh. The statues of London were as stationary as their sculptors had intended, which was just how I liked them. When the warehouse doors were locked behind us, we passed back through the double metal gates and into the relative safety of London's post-industrial hinterland. Warder's silver BMW was parked on the street nearby, at least one of the warehouse cameras trained sniper-like upon it. The car was a recent model, top-spec, arrow-sleek. It had to cost more, surely, than any Office salary could pay for.

I sank back gratefully into the passenger seat as the engine purred into life. I closed my eyes for a few moments; I was feeling a little shaken up by the attack and it was good to feel cocooned within so much expensive German engineering. Warder didn't appear to be at all affected by his experiences, as though he was attacked by outsized metal lions every day. We moved off, surging into the traffic, the note of the car's engine rising only slightly to a gentle growl.

"Are you sure you can drive with that hand?" I asked. A stigma of blood was soaking through Warder's makeshift bandage as he steered. I'd caught him grimacing more than once.

"It's only a flesh wound, really. I'll get it cleaned up at HQ. The car more or less drives itself anyway."

"The receptionist said there had been problems in the warehouse before."

"It's pretty rare."

"It still doesn't seem worth the risk."

Warder didn't reply for a while as he negotiated the car onto a series of busier roads, forcing his way through the ruthless traffic of the capital.

When he'd got into the right line of vehicles, he replied. "I get what you mean, I do. But London isn't like Cardiff. You know both of them; you must know what I mean."

I did and I didn't. Despite being a Londoner, I was surprised at how defensive about the Welsh capital Warder's words made me feel. I guess Cardiff was home now, too.

"There are differences," I said, "but the threats we protect the public from are the same. Magus law is the same."

Warder glanced aside at me, then back to the road. He looked a bit sheepish. "Sure. I don't mean there's anything special about London. It's just bigger, I guess. We get so many things coming at us from all angles we have to make tough choices. Do you know where I was last night, for example?"

"Where?"

"Out in the Thames Estuary, forty miles from here, on a deserted stretch of mud flat which you might think wouldn't see very much to upset the natural order of the world. Except, the shifting sands had revealed the hulk of an old mortuary ship, plague-era maybe, piled high with bodies to bury away from the capital. Some of those entombed in the mud for hundreds of years were pretty pissed off when they finally made it back into the light. They'd had a long time to think about the precise details of the revenge they wanted.

"Then, a few days ago, on Wednesday, I was investigating credible reports of witchcraft in the leafy suburbs and woo-woo crystal shops of Richmond. I barely got out of *that* little episode uncursed. On both occasions I had to go in alone because there was no one to partner with me, despite what the regulations say. I know you guys in Wales are stretched thin, too. I'm not trying to come over all metropolitan elite; I just mean we have a lot on our plates, and we have to choose our battles."

"I take your point, but if you destroyed all the statues, you'd have one less battle."

"Fewer."

"Pardon?"

"Never mind. You're right. But I think Earl Grey may be keeping them for other reasons, too. This is basically guesswork on my part, as he obviously never tells me anything, but I do wonder if he's got people working on some kind of modification to the hobbles. Don't mention to anyone I said this."

"What sort of modification?"

Warder shifted in his seat slightly, glancing in his mirrors before he cut into the next lane to manoeuvre around a red London bus. "Well, it's occurred to me before that if you could alter the embedded sorcery in the devices, you might be able to let the statues keep their mobility while also directing them. I mean, I'm no expert, but maybe. That was presumably the idea behind some of the illegal magic use in the first place, right? Take control of your own pre-made golems and direct them to commit whatever outrage you fancied."

I thought about that. "You mean, like a remote-controlled statue you could direct? A remote-controlled *army* of statues?"

"Well, perhaps you could assemble a small task force kind of thing, but yes. Who knows? If that were possible it could be really useful. Next time we faced some gibbering nightmare from the seventh circle of Hades we could send *them* in to face it rather than us. Makes a lot of sense to me. We've lost too many people over the past couple of years. As I'm sure you have, too."

I didn't like it. Sure, we were making compromises all the time, fighting fire with fire, but that felt like a step too far. Too easy for something to go wrong, for some enchanted stone soldier to get out of control and run amok. And then we were no better than those we were supposed to be stopping. We operated in the shadows so the people of Britain could walk around in the light, oblivious.

"You're not convinced," said Warder. We were crossing the Thames now, stopped at the lights on Westminster Bridge. He could obviously see the doubt on my face.

"I'll be honest with you, I'm not," I said.

"I understand. I came here from Oxfordshire five years ago; it took a bit of getting used to. Perhaps we're a bit more liberal here about all sorts of things, including our attitude to the forbidden powers. I think, sometimes, the ends can justify the means. Does it matter *how* we turn back an incursion of the undead or the never living, just as long as we do? You came to find out about English Wizardry, and I feel something similar about them. To all intents and purposes, they're history, truly, but even if they or people like them did become active again, should they be our top priority? I mean, they're evil, yes, but they're also doing our work for us, aren't they?"

Gilroy had said something similar, although from a very different viewpoint. Day by day, the simple certainties of right and wrong, of good guys and bad guys, were being eroded. Was the world always so complicated and I hadn't noticed? I'd joined the Office to protect people from the unnatural, like it said on the plaque, but more and more I seemed to be using the unnatural to protect people. It made me feel bad. The sort of bad you feel when you've swallowed something that doesn't agree with you.

We pulled into the private car park underneath the Whitehall offices I'd visited earlier, the barrier recognising

Warder's car in some way and flipping up automatically as we approached. At the same time, a line of lights came on in the garage floor, directing us to a free space like a plane being directed to its standing at an airport. It was all a lot more impressive than Cardiff.

"Come on up," said Warder. "Let's get cleaned up and then I'll show you what we have on English Wizardry."

An hour later, we sat together in an alcove of the London Office's library. There was no sign anywhere of an armed librarian intent on defending her books to the death. Which, after the lion, I was glad of. When I commented on it, Warder said, "Ah yes, the famous Lady Coldwater. To be honest, I'd be uncomfortable with an individual having that amount of control over the forbidden books."

"You don't trust her?"

"I don't mean that. I don't really know her, except by reputation. She has her own agenda, and I'd rather rely on technological safeguards. We have rooms with different levels of access, but we employ electronic locks and book tagging and so forth to protect them, not the vagaries and prejudices of one person."

Their approach probably made for less bloodshed in the whole book-borrowing process, but it also seemed a bit soulless. At least their library wasn't buried away beneath the ground: it was up on the fifth floor of their impressive, neoclassical, grey stoned building. From where we sat, I could gaze through sash windows across the rooftops of Whitehall and down to the Thames. The curve of the London Eye rose above the skyline, an eye peeping over the parapet at me.

"Just about everything we know about English Wizardry is on these shelves," said Warder. He sat in one of the green leather reading chairs, dabbing at the wounds on his palm with antiseptic and occasionally wincing from the sting. "It's actually because of this room that I ended up working for the Office."

"How so?" He was good company, keen to talk. It was hard not to like him.

He continued with his tale. "I studied Art History at Oxford, and I came across mention of the group when I was researching the iconography of the British Union of Fascists for my BA. It was a fleeting allusion, but I was sufficiently intrigued to dig deeper. I couldn't make any sense of the name, but they seemed important as the ringleaders of the group were known to Mosley. Of course, I now know that the Office has worked hard over the years to suppress information about them. I was fortunate, however, that they hadn't destroyed all the papers stored in the book vault of my college. I unearthed a few facts and decided to research the group for my PhD. Luckily, my supervisor knew someone who knew someone and managed to wangle me temporary access to this room. Of course, I had to agree that the Office had the right to veto anything I produced, under pain of death. Probably *literally* death."

I ran the tips of my fingers along lines of journals and leather-bound volumes, the binders and box files that contained, according to their labels, letters from and to the various individuals involved in the group. The shelves were full; the Office had done a good job of expunging English Wizardry from history. The seven copies of *The Old Ways* that Hardknott-Lewis had mentioned were all there, lined up next to each other on one of the top shelves.

"If you weren't going to be allowed to publish your PhD, why write it?"

Warder looked rueful. "The plan was to publish only to the shadow academia, the researchers who operate outside the purview of mainstream historians. Like those we let into the warehouse to study the statues. As it happens, it wasn't an issue because I didn't complete my researches."

I'd opened one of the volumes at random, a book claiming to be a true history of the legends of King Arthur and the wizard known to us as Merlin. Somewhat surprisingly – perhaps I'd missed the detail of the argument – Merlin was characterised as an enemy of English magic; a representative of a debased and barbaric Druidic tradition that led Arthur astray. Was that relevant? Was Cornwallis part of some Celtic tradition that English Wizardry disapproved of? It was an angle that probably wouldn't have occurred to me before I moved to Cardiff, but now it made some kind of sense. Tension and mistrust between England and Wales were sublimated, historic – but still very definitely real. Walk around the streets of Cardiff when England are in town for a game of rugby and you'll see that very clearly. As someone born in England but living in Wales I was immersed in that tension – although as a British Asian I was also removed from it, able to see it for what it was.

"You didn't find enough evidence to back up your arguments?" It seemed unlikely, given how many books the Office had collected.

Warder scratched his chin, looking around the room as if he knew every book in there. Perhaps he did. "It wasn't that; I simply became more and more intrigued by this room, this library. What was it here for? Who ran it, paid for it? Inevitably I came across references to the Office, bumped into people who worked here. Of course, none of them could tell me what they did, how they spent their days. What they *were*. I'm afraid I rather lost interest in my researches as I became more and more intrigued. Eventually, I managed to arrange an internship, and within six months I was a Neophyte in the Office of the Witchfinder General."

It was a familiar enough story. The Office doesn't publish job adverts like any normal organisation. People arrive by a process of osmosis, by knowing the right people, or simply by chance. It partly explains why there are ten Warders for every Shahzan. Perhaps that's how all the British secret services operate.

"Okay, so tell me about English Wizardry," I said. "I believe they date back to the start of the twentieth century?"

"There's actually evidence the tradition goes well back into Victorian times. Something I discovered while I was doing my researches. The British Empire was in its ascendancy, and it was perhaps only natural for the supernaturalists of the day to assume their magical tradition was the one true original. By the time Queen Victoria died and the new century began, there was an established group, made up of aristocratic spell users and their devotees, which was intent on restoring what it saw as the natural order upon the magical world."

"Was Samuel Bedfellowes ever one of them?"

"He died in 1882, but he was involved in the early years. He was always peripheral, in truth. He catalogued and codified a lot of the group's beliefs, but he did so mainly out of a pathetic desire to be accepted by them. It's ironic that the oak tree symbol he used became intimately identified with the group, when most of them saw him as an irritating populariser."

"Did he come up with the name *English Wizardry*, too?"

"I don't believe he did. There are few written records before Bedfellowes' book, but there are some letters from the early decades of the nineteenth century which use the phrase. I think probably it was just a name for all users, like we would now say *supernaturalists*."

"So, the users of the time were a pretty xenophobic bunch."

Warder considered that for a moment. "That's obviously a modern viewpoint; I think they thought they were attempting to restore the natural order of things."

"Did everyone think like that at the time?"

"Interesting question. Then, as now, supernaturalists tended to be united by the common threat of the Office's attempts to eliminate them. There were arguments and disagreements, but a common enemy tends to make a disparate group see its similarities rather than its differences. But a strident opposing voice did emerge, centred around a user called Arthur Stonewall."

"This was, what, the middle of the twentieth century? The blackshirts and so on?"

Warder's enthusiasm for his subject was clear by the way he emphasised his words with an expressive set of hand movements. "No, no, long before that. Turn of the century, World War One. Stonewall and his followers were a renegade group of users who disliked mainstream English Wizardry thinking and espoused a more inclusive world view. They were fascinated by overseas magical traditions. Conflict between the factions became an open schism, just as you see in any religious or political movement. Eventually the whole thing degenerated into open warfare. There was a great deal of suffering and bloodshed, and many people died, some of them quite horribly. In my view, the divide weakened British magic so much it allowed the Office to achieve its current position of dominance. It's not a popular thing to say in these parts, but in the Victorian era the Office of the Witchfinder General was considered a joke; an embarrassing anachronism. We were nearly disbanded several times. Half of the people who worked here were under a curse or a *geas* imposed upon them by some controlling user. The other half were simply incompetent or corrupt, allowing all manner of supernatural threats to trouble Victorian Britain. The conflicts between English Wizardry and those who opposed them changed all that. All those wizards coming out of the woodwork and unleashing spells and summoning horrors onto each other focused politicians' minds. They saw the need for a strong and well-funded organisation, and the modern Office we know and love was born. At the same time, the dangers we had to face were reduced because users were too busy killing each other to unite against us."

"Am I right in thinking you just gave me the central thesis of your PhD?"

"It was something along those lines, yes."

"This Stonewall was an aristocrat too?"

"He was actually from a humble background in the north of England. He was in the British Army, spent a lot of time in India and elsewhere, and through that he moved in what you might call aristocratic circles for a time, even became a trusted friend of some of the higher English Wizardry adepts. I know it's tempting to see people like him as colonial oppressors, but – forgive me if this is offensive in any way – it's not always that simple, is it? I think his time in the East opened his eyes to other magical traditions, and when he came back he went renegade and turned against his peers. As the conflicts engulfed British magic, Stonewall became known as *Abaddon*, the Destroyer, because of the damage he unleashed upon them all."

"What happened to him?"

"He died, like so many around him, torn to shreds of flesh by imps, if the accounts are to be believed. The name they gave him turned out to be prescient; as I say, magic use in Britain suffered a fatal blow as wizard fought wizard. Their loss was our gain."

"And now? You really think English Wizardry are history?"

Warder considered for a moment. "I think I do. The conflicts were so long ago and there are few if any organised groups of underground magicians left. I read your case notes on MORIARTY and they were intriguing, but they're the first evidence we have of any activity from anyone associated with the group for many decades. There is no one left alive who is known to have been involved. Evangelina Mormont was the last of them."

"*She* was a member of English Wizardry?"

"She was part of the group's leadership in the 1930s and 1940s."

That threw me. The dates were completely wrong. "I've seen recent images of Mormont. She was only a decade or two older than us."

Warder shook his head. "She was old, she simply looked young. It was a part of the reason Earl Grey eventually took the decision to consign her to Oblivion. Somehow, despite being locked away in isolation in Aldwych, she was able to continue working the sorcery that gave her apparently eternal youth. We could never work out how she did it. Which meant we could never be completely sure she wasn't up to other things as well."

I was gladder than ever that the Sorceress was out of the picture. The country was a safer place without her.

"And by this time English Wizardry were an extremist, far-right organisation allied to the British fascists of the inter-war period."

"Well, that's how others saw them. They described themselves as patriots and followers of an oppressed tradition of ancient English magic."

"What did you make of the use of the English Wizardry iconography I discovered?"

"I've been thinking about it. I believe it's likely it was an attempt to lead us astray. Or, it could just be that the murderers approve of the symbolism without being involved in any sort of real movement. Like people putting Che Guevera posters on their wall."

"I can't understand why they would make the candle marks on the wall so vague. If you want people to see the symbol, why not draw it big and clear?"

"Perhaps it was an attempt to be intriguing, have us missing other leads while we obsess over a few marks on a wall. Or perhaps they were interrupted before they could finish their artwork. It's also possible we're seeing patterns in random marks, just as it's possible Gilroy's testimony is unreliable and there is no English Wizardry angle at all to this crime. If I'm honest, I think that's the most likely explanation. I suspect that whoever carried out this magically aggravated murder had no connection with the group whatsoever, either in its original incarnation or in some sort of modern reboot."

I must have looked disappointed at hitting a dead end.

"Sorry," said Warder. "That doesn't help you much with your investigations. Your other leads aren't getting you very far?"

"The local police are investigating Cornwallis, chasing up his contacts. That might reveal something." I wasn't too hopeful. From what Zubrasky had told me so far, Cornwallis was law-abiding, normal – even dull. To further complicate matters, we were under pressure from the building company to allow the house where we'd found his body to be demolished to make way for their new construction. Every day we insisted they hold off cost them serious money. If I wasn't careful, I'd have no murder scene, no suspects, no motive – and no case. I could already imagine the look of disappointment on Hardknott-Lewis's face when I reported back to him.

All I could do was to keep picking away at the knot.

"Tell me," I said. "In your researches did you ever come across any mention of an Amoor Shahzan?"

A frown of puzzlement passed across Warder's features. "A relative? He's connected with the case?"

"He's not connected, but he was my grandfather. Hardknott-Lewis told me he'd been involved in the struggle against English Wizardry, years and years ago. I thought, maybe, you'd come across mention of him, that's all. Gilroy also claimed to have encountered him as a young man."

"You didn't mention any of this in your case notes."

"It's not significant, a family matter. The circumstances of my grandfather's death are unclear, and I'd like to know more." There was another thought in my mind, but it was perhaps too crazy to share even with a trusted colleague. Was it possible I was being targeted by some rump of English Wizardry? Hardknott-Lewis had explained why they might hate me, and it seemed the fact that I was from the Welsh Office was only going to add to their prejudice. Was it remotely possible that the murder of Cornwallis was part of some scheme to get to me – or to discredit me? Like I said, I couldn't decide if the notion was brilliant or insane. It was hard to believe I was that important, for one thing.

Warder was shaking his head. "I can't recall any mention of a Shahzan in the records, I'm sorry. There are certainly plenty of accounts of the battles between English Wizardry adepts and those who opposed them. If you like, I'll look through the archives and see if I can turn anything up."

"Thanks, I'd appreciate it." I stood. There didn't appear to be much more I could uncover, and Warder looked done in. He'd been out on operations all night and didn't need me interrogating him further. Plus, it was time to go and talk to my mother.

"Just sorry I couldn't be of more help," said Warder. "If I find anything, I'll let you know."

We shook hands in the lobby of the building, watched over by the blue-uniformed security guard I'd encountered earlier. The old boy nodded his head slightly as I left, a slight smile playing about his features, as if he knew secrets about me that he couldn't, or wouldn't, divulge.

10 – The Family Curse

It is no longer considered safe to hold the supernaturalist Evangelina Mormont within her specially-constructed prison. It is unlikely any useful information can be extracted from her. For the safety of us all, she is to be removed to Oblivion with immediate effect.

–Earl Grey, Witchfinder General presiding,
Rulings of the Star Chamber, 2020

I picked up some flowers for my mother at the train station – pink, white and red roses – before repeating the twenty-minute walk back to my childhood home. The sky had clouded over, and devilish gusts of wind whipped down the streets, throwing handfuls of autumn leaves at me. The day was already fading into a grey tea-time gloom, lights in house windows springing up to dispel the gathering darkness. I was lost in thought about the case. There had to be something I'd missed, some loose end of thread I could tease free to make everything unravel, but I couldn't see what it was. I wanted to sit down with Hardknott-Lewis and talk everything over, but I also dreaded doing so. We were only a few days into the case, but I hadn't made much progress at all.

"What happened to your face?"

The moment my mother saw me she detected the microscopic abrasions to my cheek that I'd picked up during the tussle with the possessed metal lion. They were nothing compared to Warder's injuries and certainly weren't worth seeking treatment for. But, of course, it would be hard to explain how I'd got them at all being (so she believed) an office-based civil servant.

I heard myself resorting to a stupid cliché. "It's nothing, just a scratch."

Her eyes narrowed imperceptibly – possibly only one of her children would have been aware of the subtle change –

and she looked like she was going to pursue the matter. But then she seemed to think better of it and let it drop.

"Come on," she said. "Get yourself cleaned up; we're eating out."

Despite the mountain ranges of food that she'd prepared the evening before, she had arranged for us to dine at one of the local Asian restaurants. It was a tradition. We were soon walking arm-in-arm along familiar avenues towards the high street, my mother babbling away merrily about people I'd known when I was growing up. Who had gone off the rails and become, as she put it, a *hippy*. Who was doing very well for themselves as a financier or a doctor. Who was married and who was in the market. Who had children. There was no ulterior motive to any of her words, no insinuation. My mother had supported me completely in my choice of career, and never wistfully asked whether I was seeing anyone and whether, therefore, there might be grandchildren one day. No doubt she would have liked that, but I think she was basically happy if I was happy, whatever I did.

The closest she'd got to getting on my case was a year previously, on another trip home, when she'd mentioned, as if in passing, that if I was gay, I was to feel absolutely welcome to bring my *young man* home with me. She'd looked almost disappointed when I told her I was straight, but (a) unlucky and (b) stupidly busy. I obviously didn't mention I felt my work was too dangerous to allow me to commit to any sort of long-term relationship. In the first six months of my working life at the Office I'd lost three colleagues. Two of them metaphorically – they'd been killed in the line of duty – and one literally. A guy called Jamie Tavish, ten years my senior. He'd gone out to tackle a haunting and had simply never been heard from again. *Lost in the mirrors*, someone had explained to me, as if I might know what that meant, and no one had said any more.

I walked in silence, happy to let my mother talk. Each gatepost and garden and front door of the streets was completely familiar to me, but they were slowly changing, too, as the residents built extensions and redecorated and moved things around. Strange how I expected everything to stay the same in my absence; I felt almost annoyed that people were altering the familiar landmarks of my boyhood. I guessed that was how it went.

Once the waiter had bustled off with our scribbled order, I took the plunge. I really wanted to ask about Az, of course, and her words on the phone, but this seemed like a gentler introduction to a difficult conversation: "I was thinking about grandad," I said. "Dad's dad, I mean."

A pinpoint of wariness sharpened deep in her eyes. She'd been talking almost non-stop since leaving the house, but now she took a moment or two to reply. "Really? What made you think about him?"

I thought about telling her some version of the truth but bailed out. "Maybe because it was my birthday. Talking to you on the phone made me think about the family."

She nodded but didn't speak. Her forehead was furrowed with a frown, as if I'd said something troubling. There was an uncomfortable moment of silence. Fortunately, the poppadums and pickles arrived at that moment, and we busied ourselves spooning chutney and chilli onto broken triangles of fried crispy snack.

"What were you thinking about him?" she asked eventually.

"Just that I never knew him. I obviously never met him."

"Oh, you did, actually. He was alive when the two of you were babies. He loved to come and see you. He would charge around with one of you under each arm and you'd giggle until you were sick."

"I didn't know that."

"Well, you obviously wouldn't remember. He was great fun."

"Still, I'm surprised you never said."

We were suddenly treading on difficult ground. It was a familiar pattern; we could talk about anything and not feel awkward or embarrassed, but somehow, any attempt to delve into family history made things uncomfortable.

"I didn't *not* tell you, love," she said. "It must have slipped my mind."

It would have been easiest to change the subject, talk about life in Cardiff or friends – or cricket, something both my parents, from their respective cultures, had shared a deep love for. I decided to plough on. "He died of a heart attack?"

A flash of something like alarm passed across her features.

For a moment she looked… hunted.

"Yes," she said, although it sounded like she was recalling an indistinct rumour rather than a key moment in her family's history. "A heart attack. So sad for someone so young. But it was nothing congenital, nothing to worry about."

"You had no warning it was going to happen?"

"Nothing, no. It was a terrible shock to everyone, especially my mother-in-law as you can imagine. He was so young at the time, and very fit."

"What was he like?"

This was safer ground. "Oh, he was a lovely man. He could be stern, or at least appear so if you didn't know him. I was a little bit frightened of him at first, but I grew to love him dearly. He would do anything for his family or his friends. He was intelligent, one of those people who could hold a conversation on any subject you could mention. He also had a very strong sense of right and wrong. They were different days, of course, and there was a lot more overt racism, but he refused to make any concessions or let some passing comment in the street go by. He would challenge anyone if they said something vile." She smiled to herself, seeing memories in her mind I would never be a part of. "He was hilarious when he let his hair down, too. He had a very sly sense of humour."

I felt weirdly like I was interviewing my own mother. It was an uncomfortable sensation. I tried to make my next question sound as if it was just a passing idea that had occurred to me just then. "Was what happened related to his work in some way?"

She took a long time to reply this time. The frown returned to her features. "Why would it be? He was a marine architect; he spent his days drawing up plans for freight vessels. He didn't do any of the building."

"Maybe there was, I don't know, some extra-curricular activity or hobby that put him at risk."

She shook her head. "No. He looked after himself, didn't smoke even though most people did in those days. What happened to him was nothing congenital, nothing to worry about. Sometimes things just happen, for no reason."

It was the second time she'd used the phrase *nothing to worry about*. It was hard to escape the impression she was repeating words she'd learned somewhere. But she wasn't one to keep anything from me, to lie for the sake of an easy life. That wasn't how the family worked, especially now there were only the two of us.

Our bhunas and mixed grills and pilau rices had arrived and we sat in silence for a time while we ate. I wanted to say, *you weren't aware he was killed by a sect of xenophobic magic users?* but somehow couldn't bring myself to utter the words. Maybe she genuinely didn't know any of it. It seemed unkind to draw her any further into that world, family honesty and openness notwithstanding. It wasn't an offence under magus law to know or suspect the truth about the supernatural dominions and powers – just to spread knowledge of them, use them, or incite others to use them. The less she knew, the better.

Warder had said he'd see what he could discover about my grandfather from the London archive, and I resolved to do the same from the Cardiff end. There was unlikely to be anything on HOLMES about such an old case, but a direct request to Zubrasky might yield something – if I could suggest it might be related to the murder and not simply a personal matter. The Shahzans had had little to do with Wales until my arrival, but it was just possible there was something in the Vault that might shed some light on the matter. I'd also brave the Lady's knives again and go and ask her. Then there was Hardknott-Lewis: he clearly knew something of my family's history. I needed to quiz him further.

As I ran through these thoughts, I had one of those moments when an idea hits you unexpectedly – and knocks you sideways. Adrenaline trickled through my stomach as I gave the thought full consideration. My grandfather had died young, and my twin brother had died young, too.

Then there was my father.

He, also, had died long before he should have – some twelve years earlier, when I was old enough to know and understand what was happening. In many ways, the loss of my father had been a much more terrible blow than the loss of my own twin. They were grim times, days I think we really only got through because our extended Asian and northern families rallied around. A succession of aunties and uncles I barely recognised came to stay with us, be there for us. It was bothersome, at the time, to have to provide room for them, to have to talk to them. But perhaps there'd been wisdom in their actions. Keeping busy, having to run around after others, had somehow made the whole thing a little more bearable.

My father had been forty. He, too, was fit and healthy. He drank a little and smoked not at all. He played squash and golf. He wasn't a fitness fanatic, but he liked to walk up the sorts of mountains that had well-beaten tourist paths to their summits. It wasn't his heart that got him but a London bus, knocking him from his bicycle on his evening commute, dealing him injuries from which he never recovered.

Or so I'd understood, in any case. I chewed my bhuna slowly, trying to think clearly, barely noticing the chilli tingle filling my mouth. Was it possible three generations of Shahzan men had been killed? Was there a pattern there? What if all three were secretly magical adepts – my grandfather certainly was – and English Wizardry had come looking for them? Az's powers, if he'd even had any, would only have been nascent, a mere potential, but perhaps that had been identified and they'd come for him. Had the truths about all three deaths been kept from me? Maybe I'd only been spared because, despite Hardknott-Lewis's assertion, I had no magical powers.

These were troubling thoughts, deep waters. Perhaps I was also seeing patterns where there were none, and we'd simply been unlucky as a family. My mother surely had to know something; she'd been closely involved with all three of the dead: father-in-law, husband and son.

But as I lifted my gaze to my mother, thinking of some delicate way to ask the questions I wanted to ask, I saw a change had come over her while I'd been lost in my thoughts. Her face was white, by which I mean sheet-white, milk-white, not simple Caucasian pinky-white. She had a migraine coming on. She suffered with them a lot and it was always the same: visual disturbance, the ghastly appearance and then, later, the searing agony. I'd often thought my attacks might be some condition inherited from her. She hadn't eaten any of her food. She pushed chunks of grilled meat around her plate, as if hoping to make it look like she wasn't leaving so much.

"Your head?" I asked quietly, reaching out to her.

Her voice was barely above a whisper. "Yes."

My questions about our family history would have to wait. "Come on, let's get you home. Do you have your pills with you?"

She shook her head almost imperceptibly, as if any greater motion would make her brain clang agonisingly against her skull.

I summoned a waiter over and explained. We settled the bill and he took our food away to be parcelled up. We were soon retracing our steps back home; this time my mother leaning on my arm, her eyes half-shut as I guided her.

"I'm sorry, Danny," she whispered.

For some reason I felt like I was to blame for her attack. "Don't worry. We have all of tomorrow. Let's get you home and lie you down in a darkened room."

I helped her up the stairs and drew the curtains while she lay on her bed fully clothed. I told her I'd fetch her pills and a glass of water but she didn't reply, one hand over her forehead and eyes.

It took me several minutes to find her migraine pills: they were in a tea-caddy rather than the medicine box where she normally kept plasters and painkillers and the like. When I went back upstairs, she was asleep, breathing slowly and deeply. I placed water and pill beside her bed but didn't wake her.

I don't know what made me try the thaumometer on her. A hunch, a moment of intuition at her sudden change of mood in the restaurant. Or maybe some part of my brain was still trying to work through the things it had come up with as we ate.

Such devices, inevitably, are imperfect. They operate by identifying patterns of disruption in the electromagnetic fields of the brains of those unfortunate enough to have been cursed, bewitched, jinxed or magically afflicted in some other way. I knew for a fact phones held too close to the contraptions made them incorrectly register the presence of a magical field, and that leaking microwave ovens made them ping like all the hordes of hell had been unleashed.

Still, they sometimes gave a useful reading. I took the pen-like device from my inside pocket and flicked it on. My mother lay oblivious, her breathing peaceful and slow. She would feel nothing. I passed the device around the top of her head and across her face in slow spirals, following the pattern we'd been instructed to use. After ten seconds, the little LCD screen on the device gave me its reading.

For once, the numbers on the display were unequivocal. All five bars on the stylised graph were solid. It meant only one thing: my mother was under the influence of a strong magical affliction, powerful enough to significantly disrupt the functioning of her mind. At some point, possibly years earlier, she'd been exposed to a powerful hex.

The revelation struck me like a punch to the abdomen. How could I not have known this? I was a trained operative in the Office of the Witchfinder General, fully versed in the arcane threats society faced. How could I not have seen? There was no way of knowing the nature of the curse – the thaumometer was crude and could give no clue about the affliction – but it was surely something bad. My mother slept on, oblivious to the revelation, a beatific expression playing about her lips as if she were lost in some dream of delights. I let her sleep while I thought.

I'd assumed – everyone had assumed – that the changes in her state of mind at the time of Az's death were the understandable product of her maternal grief. She'd become worse when her husband had died, but that was perfectly understandable, too. They'd been absolutely devoted to each other, and she was already emotionally wounded.

Now I was having doubts about the whole story. Most of the time, people moved on from grief, or learned to live with it at least. She hadn't. Was it possible she'd been tainted with this magical affliction all along? Was that why her memory had become so patchy, her grasp of reality so precarious? Why she'd never said anything to me about my grandfather? Curses cast on a vulnerable mind could be hugely destructive to that person's emotional and psychological wellbeing. Anxiety, delusions, obsessive thoughts, depression and – yes – migraines were all common by-products, something the general public were blissfully unaware of. Had someone done that terrible thing to my mother when her resistance was at its lowest? Precisely *because* her resistance was low?

She might have been fighting the spell all these years,

repeatedly gaining and losing her grasp on reality as the battle-lines in her mind inched forwards and backwards. And I'd just watched her, letting it happen, even making stupid little jokes about her forgetfulness, her confusion.

And if all that was true, the obvious question was: who had unleashed such a destructive hex upon her traumatised mind? Who, and why? The effect on her memory suggested the spell was intended to disrupt her recollections in some way, make her forget a thing she knew or had witnessed. And that led me, inevitably, to her description of Az's death, the indistinct man whose existence I had doubted and who she'd never previously mentioned. Perhaps his presence was ghostly, ethereal, because the incantation was attempting to make it so, constantly veiling and erasing her true memories. Was that why she'd looked so confused, so troubled, when I'd pressed her about her father-in-law in the restaurant? Had an enemy like English Wizardry attacked my family again and again across the generations, wiping us out and covering their tracks with mind-altering spells? They'd spared my mother simply because she was white, maybe. A Shahzan only by marriage. They'd spared *me* because I posed no threat to them, or they'd simply missed me out. Except, now I was very visible, wasn't I? Now I was an acolyte in the Office, and the danger was clear. Just as Hardknott-Lewis had feared.

I wanted to hold my mother tight, tell her I was sorry, sorry for everything. I didn't move. Better she slept. She looked happy asleep.

Darkness gathered in the little room, the night noises of the city creeping in at the window to remind me, distantly, that life went on. Whatever personal horrors and traumas there were in the world, life went on, because there was nothing else it could do. And what was *I* to do? The hex threatened my mother's life. Even if it didn't kill her in the end, there was the simple fact of my sworn duty to the Office. I was under an obligation to report the situation to Hardknott-Lewis immediately. That was standard protocol, and there were no exceptions. The Office would take control of her. If she could be cured, she could be left to live, but otherwise the danger to her and to others was too great. She was a victim, yes, but we couldn't risk the curse spilling over, tainting others around her, as happened too often. Then there was the fact that such a deep-seated incantation, twining through her brain for years, would be both difficult and dangerous to remove – both for the victim and for the person attempting the counter-spell. In most previous cases I was aware of, the cursed individual had eventually been placed into the near-death, near-life limbo of Oblivion rather than run that risk. It was the kindest, or the least cruel, thing we could do.

I sat unmoving for the best part of an hour, thoughts thundering through my brain. I had to turn her in. There could be no debate.

Throughout it all, my mother slumbered on, unaware.

11 – The Second Victim

Potential recruit Danesh Appleby Shahzan exhibits many of the intellectual, emotional and physical traits required of an acolyte in the Office of the Witchfinder General. He is young and raw, but cuts an impressive figure. Nevertheless, he requires careful handling. While he exhibits no tendency to deploy any unnatural powers, the possibility of him being able to do so remains a concern. It may be preferable to have him on the inside where he can be guided rather than on the outside. His family background, especially his father's side but also (more distantly) his mother's, suggests the clear possibility of latent abilities within him. Then there is the fate of his deceased twin Azad, the circumstances of whose death remain a significant...
(further details redacted)

–Campbell Hardknott-Lewis, Lord High Witchfinder of All Wales, *private journal*, 2016

Eventually, I slipped out of my mother's room and went downstairs. The food from the restaurant in its collection of plastic tubs was still lukewarm, but I zapped half of it in the microwave and sat to chew things over.

Match of the Day came on, and I paid enough attention to allow me to participate in office banter about team performances the coming Monday. I drank one beer, then another, and then a third while I streamed a horror movie. Its premise and monsters were so ridiculous I doubted even Hardknott-Lewis could have found anything much to object to.

There was still no sound from my mother. I crept upstairs again to my own room, hearing the creaks of the floorboards as I placed each foot down. As a wayward – waywardish – youth, I'd often come home late the worse for drink, trying not to wake my mother. Each groan from the house was a familiar old friend.

I lay in bed for some time, watching lights playing across the ceiling as cars cruised by on the street outside. This had once been the room I'd shared with Az, and it was still occasionally referred to as *the twins' room* by my mother, but it had been exclusively mine for most of my life. Everything about it was utterly familiar: the silhouette of the corner of the wardrobe against the curtains, the square of light around the door, the mattress moulded to the contours of my back. Much of my teenage clutter – posters, books, DVDs, games I hadn't played for years – were still there, just where I'd left them.

In the darkness, I found myself listening once again to the sounds of the city outside: the roaring cars and rumbling trains, the occasional banshee wail of an alarm. I found I was also listening for the sounds of intruders, either in the house or snuffling around in the bushes outside. I was finding it hard to shake off the troubling thought that someone was out to destroy my family, a war quietly waged over three generations. And, given recent events, perhaps they – whoever *they* were – were out there now, preparing to slaughter the remaining Shahzan male as he lay unprotected in bed. The Shahzan who had started asking such awkward questions.

After a while, I convinced myself I was being ridiculous, and that I needed to sleep. But before I closed my eyes, I slipped my Office handgun under my pillow, just like they do in the movies. Then, when it proved to be incredibly uncomfortable, and I found myself worrying that some night-time movement of my head would somehow manage to discharge it, I pushed it between the mattress and the bed-frame, from where I hoped to grab it if some assassin did creep into my room.

I slept fitfully, perhaps as a result of such thoughts. It was one of those nights where you swear you haven't slept at all but somehow the hours go by. I was in the midst of a repeated, vivid dream – relentless animated statues pursuing me through the streets of a city that was London and Cardiff combined – when a repeated buzzing sound, like an angry hornet trapped in a box, woke me up.

It took me a few moments to disentangle nightmare from

reality and work out what the sound was. Someone was ringing me.

I fumbled for my phone, checking the screen to see who was calling, as well as what time it was. The screen said *Zubrasky* and *6:15am*. I had survived the night without being slaughtered in my bed. So that was a good thing.

"Hi," I said, trying my damnedest to sound like I was completely used to being awake and functioning at such an ungodly hour.

"Hi, Danesh," came the familiar voice of DI Zubrasky. "I'm not interrupting a stakeout at a graveyard or anything, am I?"

My fuddled brain was taking a little time to kick into gear. There had to be something significant for her to ring me at all, let alone so early in the morning. Had she unearthed some imminent threat to me and my mother? While I floundered, my default sarcasm kicked in. "No, you're good, I'm not on vampires this week. Have you found out something about Cornwallis?"

"Actually, yes, a little. But that isn't why I'm calling you."

"What is it?"

There was a rustling and fumbling sound from the other end, as if Zubrasky was juggling several things in her hands. Her voice was more muffled when it came back on the line, her phone maybe wedged under her ear. "I'm in Ross-on-Wye. Do you know it?"

I'd driven past it on the way into Wales a few times, but I'd never stopped. "What are you doing there? That's over the border."

"We cooperate with our colleagues in West Mercia when related crimes have taken place in both regions. Besides, in the Welsh Marches it isn't always clear which side of the border you're on, especially when you're driving around on such little roads. The boundary's often more of a vague idea rather than a hard line."

"You're saying you have another victim?"

"I'm standing over her now."

I swung my legs out of bed, her words cutting through the fuzziness in my head. "The same set-up as before? The body laid out inside a runic circle with the eyes surgically removed?"

"It all looks identical. Of course, I'm not an expert in magical symbols."

"Try not to look at them, Zubrasky. Seriously. Make sure no one copies them or touches them in any way."

"I've already issued orders to that effect, given how weird you got last time."

"Good. Who's the victim?"

"Unknown. She's in her thirties, black British, but we don't have an ID yet."

"So, about the same age as Cornwallis."

"She is. Do you think that's significant?"

"Not from any kind of supernatural perspective. I just meant they were contemporaries; they might have moved in the same circles. Can you leave everything intact until I get there?"

"Can you be here in an hour?"

"Actually, no, I'm in London."

"I'm not going to be able to keep the body lying here all that time. The local force is stretched thin enough as it is. They have to cover a huge area with insufficient numbers."

I knew how that went. "If I can arrange for someone from the Office to get over there from Cardiff, can you leave everything untouched until then?"

"I can try, but I'm not the ranking officer, I'm here strictly in an advisory capacity."

"Is there anyone there from West Mercia in the know?"

"There's a DI who looks gullible enough to believe your insane nonsense. I'll talk to him. He currently has Forensics doing their thing. Once they're finished, I'll try and make sure the place is sealed up. When will you get here?"

It didn't look like I was going to be able to spend the day with my mother after all. We clearly weren't looking at a one-off isolated murder, something personal. If we weren't careful this could become a *spree*. A magical-killing spree.

I tried to recall a few details of Ross. It stood majestically above a loop of the River Wye, every inch the ancient English market town. So it looked from the modern bypass, anyway. "There's a train station there, right?"

"Nope. Gloucester's your best bet, or Newport. You're going to need a car in any case; we're a few miles out of the town. It's very picturesque, very beautiful."

"Apart from the mutilated corpse and the vile death magic."

"Apart from that, yes. Look, I'm going to be here for a few hours talking to the indigenous population and striding around looking thoughtful. Try and get here while I'm still around, yes? I really need to understand what's going on with these killings. My superiors are not going to be happy."

I knew how that felt, too. "I'll be there as soon as I can. Message me the address."

"Already did. It probably came through while you were still asleep."

She rang off before I could come up with a stinging retort.

My mother surfaced as I sat downstairs in the kitchen sipping my second cup of strong black coffee and booking train tickets on my phone. She looked a little better. Her greying hair looked like it had been blown around in a particularly vicious gale, but she was a healthier colour. I could tell from her smile she was no longer in pain. I really had to explain to her what I'd discovered the night before. But how did you even begin a conversation like that?

Instead I said, "You look better."

"A good night's sleep often helps. Sorry about last night."

I put the kettle on to make her a cup of tea. "Don't worry. Your food is in the fridge; you could heat it up for lunch, maybe."

"Oh, we should go out somewhere. I'm not going to get two migraines in two days."

"The thing is, I need to get back to Wales. Something's come up at work."

"On a Sunday?"

"That's the way it is when you're a public servant. I'm really sorry."

She hid it, but I could tell she was disappointed. She'd been looking forwards to having me over. She put her hand to my cheek. "Ah, Danesh. Always so driven. Sometimes you act like there's a horde of demons with whips at your heels."

It seemed an odd thing to say. I really needed to do something to sort out her condition, help her. I desperately wanted her to be herself so we could talk properly.

"I was thinking," I said, "I might look into transferring back to London, see if there are any openings. I could even move back in here if you'd have me." One way or another, whatever happened with the Office and her magical affliction, she needed me to be around. For a time at least.

She saw straight through the white lie immediately. "You work for the Welsh government. How can you transfer to London? So far as I'm aware there isn't an embassy."

I gave her the tea, no sugar and a splash of milk, just as she liked it. "I just meant, there are lots of ties between us and our English colleagues. We co-ordinate all the time, and I could find out if there are any openings. If you'd like."

She sat at the table, one hand clutching her dressing gown shut at her neck while she sipped at her tea. "I think you should do what you want to do. You have your life in Cardiff now. You're happy there."

"I am, but I'd like to be here more often, too."

"I'm not some sad, lonely old woman, you know. I'm perfectly happy."

"It would be nice to be back home. I like Cardiff, but London is London. Coming back would open up lots of opportunities." I was thinking of my experiences with the statues, of everything Warder had said. It sounded like life in the English capital was a lot more varied than it was in Wales. And it didn't have to be a permanent move. I could maybe set up a secondment until whatever was going to happen to my mother had been sorted out.

As I was thinking all this, I wondered at myself, too. I'd contacted the Office requesting someone attend the address Zubrasky had sent me, but I noticeably hadn't reported the deep curse I'd uncovered in my mother. Which I absolutely should have done.

She patted my arm in a maternal way. "It would be lovely to see more of you, of course, but you must do what's right for you. That was what your father and I always wanted. His parents came all the way from India seeking a better life, you know."

It was an old family joke, repeated often whenever we faced some difficulty or obstacle. *My parents came all the way from India, you know. I'm sure you can manage to complete your homework.*

"I'll look into it," I said. "I'd like to look into it."

"Well. Perhaps you can get back down in a week or two

and we can have that day together."

I rose to head off for the shower, kissing her on the top of her head first. She smelled of comfort and reassurance.

"Yes," I said. "I'll arrange something, definitely."

Half an hour later, I was hugging her on the doorstep, huddled up in my coat against the dreary grey cold of the South London morning. "Take care of yourself, mum. Ring me if you need anything, yes?"

She smiled in a way that said, *Look at you, I'm the parent and you're the child and now you're the one fretting about me.*

She didn't give voice to her thoughts. Instead she said, "Oh, I meant to give you this. I found it while you were getting ready." She pulled a child's exercise book from her dressing-gown pocket and held it out. "It's the notebook you wanted. See, I said it would turn up."

The taxi from Gloucester dropped me at the edge of a random scattering of buildings and farmhouses that apparently constituted the village whose name Zubrasky had sent me.

"Do you know which house it is?" asked the driver. His Satnav had brought us as close as it could and was now suggesting that a field containing two bored-looking horses and a lean-to shelter was our destination. "Satnav's never much use round places like this."

I had the name of the house but little else. "Drop me here and I'll find it."

"You sure?" The driver sounded unconvinced. A silver Ganesha on a chain dangled from his rear-view mirror. The elephant-headed god turned to face me. I resisted the impulse to consider it a good omen.

"Yes. There are only a few places it could be."

My belief turned out to be wildly optimistic, as it took me the best part of half an hour to find the right address. Whoever had laid out the village had apparently gone to a great deal of trouble to hide houses behind rises in the ground, in the middle of clumps of trees or down rough farm tracks. Some didn't appear to have any road access at all, just pathways across green fields, with sheep eyeing me suspiciously as I passed them by. It was hard to escape the thought the whole thing had been set up to confuse a city boy on a day trip into England's green and pleasant land.

I found myself wandering down a track – judging by the signs I'd seen it was technically a road – between high hedges that prevented me from seeing anything of the surrounding area. The hedges were heavy with blackberries and other red, marble-sized fruits that I couldn't identify but which screamed *poison*. Two birds circled overhead, soaring on thermals like vultures in the Wild West. Occasionally their forlorn, mewing cries split the air. They were, clearly, waiting for me to keel over so they could feast upon my parched corpse. The sun wasn't actually shining, but the high clouds were glowing in a promising sort of way, as if an hour or so of weak, autumnal sun wasn't completely out of the question. To my left, the fields sloped upwards to a long line of trees crowning the hillside. Something like crows croaked and cursed at me from up there – their harsh calls indignant, offended at me for invading their ancient domain.

Mostly, it was eerily quiet; the only sounds apart from the birds were the occasional strangled bellow of a bovine and the rustle of something unseeable in the hedgerow near at hand. A rodent? A bird? Some malevolent spirit of the greenery? I had no idea. I could walk the mean streets of London or Cardiff late on a Saturday evening and feel completely at my ease. I understood rowdy, drunken revellers, but the quietness of these surroundings spooked me. I found my gaze darting to each whisper and rustle in the bushes. At one point I glimpsed a single huge eye, peering back at me from the tangle of brambles and twigs. A cow, most likely, standing on the other side of the hedge, curious about what strange creature was passing by. Later, a cry like someone suffering hideous torture echoed through the air from a distant clump of trees. I had no idea who or what had made the sound.

Hardknott-Lewis's warnings about the dangers I faced whirled around in my mind. I was in an environment I clearly didn't understand, a place where, it seemed, English Wizardry had recently carried out another magic-fuelled act of slaughter. I felt vulnerable. I pulled out my phone, looking for some connection to the modern world, but there was no signal. I was cut off.

The road curved ahead of me making it difficult to be sure I was even heading in the direction I'd intended. I walked around one turn and caught a glimpse of two figures disappearing around the next bend. A woman and a man, I thought, walking side-by-side. Another sensation of oddness, of nausea, washed through me, but for once it passed as quickly as it had come, and fortunately, given the circling birds of prey, I didn't pass out in the road. Instead, I stepped up my pace, hoping the two might be locals out for a stroll.

The bend I'd seen them pass round opened onto a long straight, but there was no sign of them. I stepped forwards more warily, expecting to come across the gate to some house they'd gone inside, or some track leading off across the fields, but there was nothing. They'd completely vanished. The realisation sent an involuntary shudder through me. Perhaps I'd imagined them, a trick of the shifting rural shadows and my own creeping anxiety. Or they were the product of another brief episode of delusion. That was probably it.

Continuing on, I did, finally, see signs of human habitation. At the far end of the straight, a police car with its blue and yellow checkerboard markings was parked by the side of the road. The chimney of a house peeped over the top of the hedgerow nearby.

It was certainly the right house: as I approached, I could see crime scene police streamers festooning the gates. The stone cottage looked to be a converted farm outbuilding of some description, but I couldn't begin to work out what its original function might have been. There were in fact two cars parked outside: the Welsh police vehicle and, pulled up on a gravelled driveway, a black jaguar saloon with no marking upon it of any sort.

The sight of that car took me very much by surprise.

Two people were waiting for me inside. Seeing them together threw me for a moment; they were from completely different compartments of my life. DI Zubrasky and Hardknott-Lewis had clearly been engaged in some conversation, standing over a runic circle painted on the stone-flagged floor. They stopped conversing as I entered, and it was hard to avoid the notion they'd been talking about me – which was no doubt just perfectly normal self-centred paranoia. They were probably both wondering why I was breathing heavily from my long and uneasy trek through the badlands of Herefordshire.

Zubrasky nodded at the Lord High Witchfinder of All Wales. "I'll go and complete my house-to-house calls. There are a few neighbours I still need to interview." She smiled at me in a knowing sort of way as she passed, although I had no idea what it was she knew.

Hardknott-Lewis watched her from the window as she made her way up the short garden path, making sure we were alone. He was as immaculately dressed as he would be on any weekday, his finely-tailored three-piece suit set off by his red tie and his polished black leather shoes.

"I didn't expect you to be here, sir," I said.

He considered me through his spectacles. "I didn't want to pull anyone else off their current assignments. Besides, it does me good to get out and about from time to time, remind myself what it's like at the sharp end. There's only so much you can do pulling the strings from the Black Tower. And this case is troubling."

He paused for a moment, then said. "You appear to have accumulated minor abrasions to the side of your face. Did you have adventures in London?"

Nothing got past him. He was as bad as my mother. "It was unrelated to the case. A brief battle with a possessed statue."

"Ah yes, Earl Grey's warehouse. Between you and me, we have disagreed about his policy towards possessed statuary many times. And you have a new watch, I see. I assume it was a birthday gift?"

How did he know things like that? "Yes."

"Tell me, how is she faring?"

I hesitated for just a moment, then heard myself saying, "She's as well as ever. Good days and bad days."

He nodded, pausing for a moment as if expecting me to say more. "Were you able to uncover anything of interest as regards English Wizardry?"

I hadn't updated my case notes on MORIARTY since Friday afternoon – something I really needed to get to. "I'll file a proper case report, but the London expert on them basically said they don't exist anymore, haven't mattered for decades."

"Ah," said Hardknott-Lewis. He looked puzzled, as if that

also wasn't what he'd expected to hear. He stepped around the runic circle on the floor, regarding each symbol with clear disdain. He squatted once to study a particular sigil, turning his head as he interpreted what he was seeing. Finally, he stood, wiping his fingers on his silk handkerchief.

"They took the body away, then?" I asked. It was clearly a stupid question.

"I persuaded them to take her to Cardiff. I suppose it's inevitable that we attempt another Assay, although it will reveal even less than the last one, I fear. This victim had been dead for twenty-four hours longer when she was discovered."

I counted back. "She was killed on Friday?"

"Late Friday or early Saturday is their best guess. Obviously, we'll know more when we get the detailed forensic report."

"Who was she?"

"Her name was Martha Ndidi, we believe, although there's been no formal identification yet. Does that name mean anything to you?"

I shook my head. I had never heard it before. "She was killed in the same way?"

"We don't know how she or Cornwallis were killed, I believe, but her eyes were surgically cut from her head if that's what you mean. It looks like the work of the same perpetrators."

"Do we know if she was another supernaturalist?"

"Not at this stage, although it seems likely, wouldn't you say?"

"The runes in the spell-circle look similar." I was trying hard not to look at them too closely, aware of Hardknott-Lewis's eye upon me.

"They are identical to those used in Cardiff. Potent magics were employed in this room."

"So, more optograms," I said. I'd at least completed my notes on the Librarian's findings – if that was what they were – as well as my speculations about their meaning.

Hardknott-Lewis nodded. "I believe so. I concur with your conclusions about Lady Coldwater's findings, although I concede it might have been helpful had she been a little more fulsome. The sorcery employed here and in Cardiff does appear to be a thaumaturgical equivalent of optography. After

I read your case notes, I did a little research of my own into the subject. As I think I mentioned, it's an area of sorcery with which I was unfamiliar, but it does appear to be real. The magic involved is something like an Assay, but using the eyes in this way makes it possible to retrieve extremely vivid and detailed images if it's done properly. Apparently, the spells were often used in mediaeval times to allow rival kingdoms to spy upon each other."

"How did that work?"

"If you wanted to know what your neighbouring Baron was planning, you sent in a few peasants or merchants or appealing young women to look around, see what they could see. They didn't have to be particularly intelligent or resourceful, didn't have to be armed with hidden blades or anything of that sort. They were basically just walking biological cameras. When they came back thinking they had only to report what they'd witnessed, you slaughtered them, took their eyes, and you had full access to what they'd seen. Given a powerful enough sorcerer, you could go back weeks or even months. You could keep the eyes from decaying, too, go back through what they'd witnessed at your leisure. Embed someone in the enemy camp for long enough – someone beyond suspicion because they were so insignificant – and you knew everything going on behind the walls of the next castle along."

"You're convinced something like that is happening here?"

"Someone is harvesting these victims' eyes, collecting them, and using powerful magic to extract recent optical memories from them. The two victims saw something very important to the killers. Do you have any inkling yet of what that might be?"

"Not at this stage, no." It clearly wasn't a simple case of Cornwallis and Ndidi having seen something incriminating to the killers. If that was it, why take their eyes? The killers weren't killing their victims so much as finding out something they'd seen. The murders might have been irrelevant in that sense, a way of gaining access to optical memories without all the inconvenience of having to take away the rest of the victims' bodies.

"There's one useful thing I can tell you that the Librarian didn't," said Hardknott-Lewis. "When the images are magically extracted from the eyes, they have to be relived at the same speed at which they were experienced. You can't rewind or fast-forward. It's one reason the sorcerers of old devised ways to keep the corruption from the eyes they'd harvested."

Maybe that was significant. It looked like the two murders had been carried out two or three days apart, so perhaps Cornwallis's very recent experiences were significant in some way. "What do we know about the victim?" I asked, trying to look like pieces of a jigsaw were slotting into place in my mind.

"Not a great deal, alas. She was originally from Walsall but had lived here for a couple of years. She was a vet by training, specialising in horses and other equines, I believe."

"She lived alone?" It felt very weird to be questioning Hardknott-Lewis, but I was trying really hard to be the professional investigator.

"I'm told she lived here with her boyfriend," said Hardknott-Lewis, something in his tone suggesting he disapproved of such an arrangement. "One Oliver Auchter. There is no sign of him; I believe our friends in the police force are actively trying to ascertain his whereabouts."

"He's a suspect?"

"What do they say in these situations? He needs to be eliminated from enquiries. Your DI Zubrasky seems to be an extremely capable officer; I'm sure she could fill you in on the more routine aspects of the investigation."

I looked around. The decor was quaint in a rustic sort of way, the walls at odd angles, the beamed ceilings low, but it had all been brought up to date, too, a good-looking stereo and cinema system complementing all the oak and stone. It was a comfortable, well looked-after home. Cushions were scattered at artful angles on a deep sofa in front of the log-burning stove. There were framed photographs on the walls of, seemingly, a series of overseas trips: the Eiffel Tower, Manhattan by night, a black woman and a white man astride a camel in front of the great Pyramid. Martha, it appeared, had loved to travel. I noticed, also, that there were no faces visible in any of the shots.

"There's no sign of any English Wizardry iconography," I said. "That's a difference."

"So I thought at first. But there was no haste to this killing; there would have been plenty of time to do something a little better than produce a few carbon smudges with a candle flame. I looked a little more closely and found this."

He took out a leather wallet from his inside jacket pocket. It contained an array of useful implements: tweezers, knives, a thaumometer, a voltmeter, a mini hobble. A handy witchfinder kit for the busy executive. He selected a pen-sized torch with a purple tip to it. With it he shone ultra-violet light onto one of the bare, plastered walls. A large representation of an oak tree sprang out. Hardknott-Lewis moved the light around, revealing more of the drawing. It was maybe a metre across, beautifully worked. Above the stylised oak tree were seven stars arranged in an arc. Underneath, the lettering like a woodcut, were the letters *E* and *W*.

"Someone went to a great deal of time and trouble to draw this," said Hardknott-Lewis.

I peered closer at the wall. Without the ultraviolet light the painting was utterly invisible. "Do we know if this is a recent drawing? If Ndidi put it there, maybe *she* was an English Wizardry adept, and whoever killed her was a member of a group opposed in some way."

"Are you aware of any such group?"

"Not at this point, although it appears they did exist in the forties and fifties. It doesn't seem impossible there's a long-running magical feud rumbling on that we simply haven't been aware of. Maybe this was a reprisal killing for Cornwallis."

"Perhaps," said Hardknott-Lewis. "It seems unlikely that someone who is ethnically West African would be a member of English Wizardry, though – even a modern reconstitution of it."

"Agreed, but it isn't impossible," I said. "Maybe the modern incarnation decided to drop the racism and concentrate on following their *True English Magic* agenda."

"There's another feature of the drawing, which, in fairness, you couldn't have known about," said Hardknott-Lewis. He stepped to the wall and brushed a finger across the trunk of the oak tree, then held the UV light up to his digit. The tip of his finger glowed. "It's still wet. It's a recent addition. I think once again we have to face the conclusion that English

Wizardry – or someone who wishes us to think they are English Wizardry – are responsible for a crime that is severe under both criminal and magus law."

We were back to a magic-fuelled killing spree. "Are there any fingerprints on it?" I asked.

"Only my own, now that I've touched it."

"I think an Assay of the second victim is essential," I said. "Will you authorise it, sir?"

"I suppose I must. Can you organise it? Once I've finished here, I have an unrelated matter to attend to in the area that might take up my time for a day or two."

"If only there was someone other than Gilroy. We need corroborating evidence, and I don't think we're going to get it from him. If he's lying to us, he's going to keep on doing it. It's probably the only fun he gets."

"He's all we have. He may not be a particularly impressive human being, but he is capable. Study his responses closely and look for any inconsistencies; he may tell us something without meaning to."

"Sir."

"Now, Danesh, if you will excuse me, I'll erase this painting and then begin the process of disarming and destroying the runes. Some of them appear to be trapped and all of them are malevolent. It's best I tackle them alone."

I really wanted to know what that meant, and how Hardknott-Lewis would undertake his task, but I knew an order when I heard one. "I'd like to take a look around the rest of the house while you're working," I said.

"Please, be my guest. The police forensic experts have taken all they need to take."

It is always strange nosing around someone else's house, peering into their cupboards and drawers. It felt intrusive, although I knew the police would already have done exactly the same thing. And it wasn't as though Martha Ndidi was going to object.

She clearly was a vet, as Hardknott-Lewis had indicated. A room at the back of the house, overlooking rolling green fields lined with trees, was evidently used as a study. Books and periodicals dedicated to the care of animals filled the shelves. I noted that many of the volumes were dedicated to animal surgery.

There was a well-appointed kitchen, including a coffee machine I approved of, and a dining room opening out onto a patio that had to be a delight in the summer.

Upstairs was mainly given over to a large, airy bedroom, skylights and tall windows admitting the autumnal sun. The bed was king-sized but judging by the look of the duvet cover had been slept in by only one person. There were no piles of fantasy and science fiction books as in Cornwallis's house; everything was tidy, elegant, a symphony of tasteful creams and lilacs. Somehow, there was a connection between the two victims, but it was hard to see what it might be. They'd been about the same age and had lived maybe fifty miles from each other; apart from the manner of their deaths, there wasn't a lot to go on.

There was an immaculately clean en suite bathroom leading off the bedroom. It was clearly used; there were towels and a half-empty soap dispenser, but oddly there was no toothbrush. Perhaps there was another bathroom that she preferred to use.

I was on the point of leaving when I spotted the book on the bedside table, next to a little stand for bracelets and a phone charging cable. The book was edge-on to me, obscured by a dislodged pillow, but something made me go back into the room to see what she'd been reading.

I recognised it immediately. It was a copy of the very same edition of the *Mabinogion* that Cornwallis had been reading. For some reason I picked it up warily, as if more of Hardknott-Lewis's runes would explode in my face, but it was just a book. There was a bookmark in it, a used train ticket to London, indicating she'd been two-thirds of the way through. I ruffled through all the pages, hoping some other scrap of paper would fall out that might give me a clue, but nothing did.

There was one thing of interest, though. At the front of the book, on the title page, someone had written, in purple-inked calligraphy, *Borderland Reading Group*. I hadn't checked Cornwallis's copy, but I reckoned there was a good chance his edition had been similarly labelled. I took a picture of the inscription, then placed the book back on the table.

Through one of the floor-length windows, I could see Zubrasky was making her way back down the road towards the house. No doubt she'd be heading back to Cardiff at some point, and she looked like my only option if I wasn't going to walk all the way. In truth, it was a relief that Hardknott-Lewis wasn't heading home immediately. The thought of sharing a car journey with Zubrasky was more appealing on many levels.

I made my way back downstairs, making sure to tread heavily on the stairs to give Hardknott-Lewis warning I was approaching. I didn't want to be under any suspicion of having witnessed something I shouldn't. I knocked on the door of the room in which he was labouring.

"Come in, Danesh. Everything is stable at this point."

Maybe half the runes had been removed, the paint excised completely as if the sigils had never been there. Hardknott-Lewis wasn't simply scrubbing away the marks with chemicals; there was something altogether more thaumaturgical going on. He'd removed his jacket and looked a little flushed as if some physical effort was involved in what he was doing.

"If there's nothing else, I'll head back to base with DI Zubrasky," I said. "It will give us chance to exchange intelligence about the case."

Hardknott-Lewis nodded his approval. "Very good. Find out as much as you can as quickly as you can, Danesh. I want this nipped in the bud before it gets out of hand."

Zubrasky was waiting for me in the police car, talking on her phone to somebody. She ended the call and her window slid down as I approached.

"Acolyte Shahzan."

"DI Zubrasky. I don't suppose you're heading back to Cardiff, are you?"

"As a matter of fact, yes. Should have been off duty an hour ago. There's a hot bath and several glasses of red wine waiting for me. You don't get to drive a nice black Jag like your boss?"

"Afraid not."

"Well, we can spend the journey filling each other in on developments."

"That's what I was hoping," I said.

We were soon speeding past fields and woods as we headed across country for Monmouth and the A40. Twice, we had to squeeze against the hedgerow to avoid the spikes and blades of a giant killing machine thundering down the lane towards us. I guess combine harvesters are common in those parts at that time of year.

We were a good ten minutes into our journey before it occurred to me that I hadn't said anything to Hardknott-Lewis about the curse upon my mother.

12 – Ultra Judice

Hauntings are among the most serious threats faced by the Office, especially in long-abandoned locations and out-of-the-way houses, where the resentments of unquiet spirits can fester and grow unchecked.

–Earl Grey, Witchfinder General,
Office of the Witchfinder General Handbook, 1999

"So, what do you know?" Zubrasky asked, between her manoeuvres to escape the jaws of the first and second death machines. "I presume you've had time to consult with the spirit world by now?"

"Spirits are refusing to cooperate," I said. "We're going to have to rely on evidence and logic."

"That's just damned inconsiderate of them," she said. She sounded suddenly tired. She'd probably been on duty all night. "Although somehow I don't think your boss is back in that house using *logic* on those runes. He was as weird about them as you were in Cardiff."

"Like I said, they're pretty heavyweight sigils."

"Sigils, right. Not a word we use often in the police force, if I'm honest. So, he's, what, dispelling them somehow?"

I didn't feel in the mood for an ethical debate about the use of Assizes powers in the fight against the supernatural. "Something like that. He's one of very few people capable of doing so."

"I got that. I thought some of my superiors were scary, but he almost made me feel sorry for you. He's, what, the Grand Wizard of Wales or something?"

"Seriously, don't ever let him hear you call him that. You probably just contravened several magus law strictures by even thinking such a thing. Hardknott-Lewis is the Lord High Witchfinder. That basically means he's the exact opposite of a wizard. He's the Welsh antiwizard."

I think she was probably genuinely intrigued about how we

operated. If she wasn't police, I might have been suspicious.

"But he's in there using forbidden powers to tidy up that magic circle?"

"Like I say, it's what we have to do. It's a grey area. It's like you striking plea bargains with criminals in exchange for evidence about worse criminals or using force to prevent the outbreak of greater violence. It's a lesser of two evils thing."

"Well, wherever you're getting your information from, I could really do with knowing about it. Because, I'll be honest with you, I'd be a lot happier if I could simply treat this as a normal police investigation without having to involve, forgive me here, the spooks."

Spooks. Police slang for people like me. I let it pass.

"There have been some developments I can share with you."

"You mentioned about the eyes and what Cornwallis might have witnessed before his death. I assumed from that you meant it was possible his recent optical impressions were being magically collected in some way?"

She'd effortlessly worked out the implications of what I'd left deliberately vague in my messages. Not a lot got past her.

"The fact that two people have now been killed and mutilated in the same way makes that more and more likely," I said.

"Isn't it possible the murderers simply took the eyes to make sure they weren't identified? Sometimes the most obvious explanations are the right ones."

"But, why go to so much trouble? If you simply burned the bodies, say, it would be impossible to retrieve any useful information from the eyes. In fact, why go to the trouble of all the magical paraphernalia at all? If the police just found two bodies with nothing weird about them, you presumably wouldn't have thought to even call us."

"Which suggests the killers either wanted us to know magical ritual was involved – or they didn't care if we found out. And also that there's something Cornwallis and Ndidi saw which the killer really, really wants to know about."

I'd been thinking along similar lines. "Perhaps they were together somewhere and each saw one aspect of the same event. Like the pieces of a picture the killers are trying to slot together."

She didn't reply for a moment as she manoeuvred the car onto the A40. She probably didn't notice, but it was amusing to watch how other drivers behaved when they saw a police car. They suddenly became extremely polite, and very, very attentive to speed limits.

"It seems to me more like a trail," said Zubrasky eventually. "These mysterious killers of yours found Cornwallis, and by extracting his visual memories they found out about Ndidi. For all we know, Cornwallis wasn't the first link in the chain; this might have been going on for some time. Maybe Ndidi met someone else and now the killers will be trying to identify them."

"You mean like a trail of spies, who only meet face to face?"

"I realise it sounds pretty unlikely, but everything you've said to me sounds pretty unlikely. I presume you don't get sound with these recovered memories?"

"No, but a competent lip-reader could work out what people are saying easily enough."

"Right. But, whatever the setup, it's pretty clear the two victims were connected. And if we want to prevent more deaths, we need to work out whether there's a next link in the chain or find someone else who saw what they saw."

"Did you find anything from Ndidi's social media posts?" I asked.

"That's another connection between them. Neither she nor Cornwallis used any social media platform that we've been able to identify. I mean, not everyone does, but they're right in the correct age group to be using Facebook or Twitter or *something* at least. It's almost like the two of them were deliberately keeping a low profile. Which might mean they simply valued their privacy, and I absolutely get that, but it might also mean they were worried someone might identify them. Like, say, a group of insane magical killers intent on ritually slaughtering them."

She had a point. No one in the Office was allowed to use any form of social media: no posts, no comments, nothing. One or two of my colleagues claimed to use anonymous accounts to find out what was going on in the world, but they were obviously extremely careful.

"Did you get anything from their computers? Pictures, emails?"

"A laptop was recovered from both murder scenes. They're being looked at, but we've got nowhere so far. I'll be honest with you: this thing with the eyes and the magic circles, I'm beginning to think the case should be declared *ultra judice*."

Ultra judice, meaning something like beyond judicial consideration, is the term used when the regular institutions of law and order decide that a case is beyond the reach of the normal criminal law and has to be handled by the brightest and best at the Office of the Witchfinder General. It allows the regulars to wash their hands of a troublesome case while also – and here's the crucial bit – counting it as a solved case in their all-important targets. There's a whole unwritten process involved, by which the criminal courts and the Coroner's Office and the Crown Prosecution Service quietly disentangle themselves from a case and pretend it never happened. Many police officers I've worked with love to have cases marked *ultra judice* – although the more conscientious ones like Zubrasky are less willing than others.

Taking that step also meant that the police wouldn't be obliged to offer us any help or resources in the ongoing investigation, and, understaffed as we were, we needed them. I had another reason to hesitate, too. If the case was declared *ultra,* then that would be the end of my contact with Zubrasky until the next murder with a hint of weirdness or ritual came along. I clung to the belief that her sarcastic humour meant that she cared about me, really.

Plus, putting my professional head on for a moment, I wasn't yet convinced it was the right road to go down.

"It still seems to me regular crimes have been committed here," I said. "Magus law crimes too, clearly, but the magery seems to me to be a means to commit a crime, rather than the reason behind the whole thing. There's something bigger going on. Like I say, it could all be a huge misdirection to put the police off the trail."

She glanced across at me, slipping the action into her regular cycle of checking her dashboard and her mirrors. Always the police driver. "You still think this is a financial crime? Some sort of vet insurance scam maybe?" Her tone made it perfectly clear how ridiculous she thought that was.

"Maybe not that, but something Cornwallis and Ndidi and who-knows-who each knew a small part of. Perhaps they were both at some secretive meeting and each saw glimpses of the other people present. The killers might be building up a complete picture of who was there from scraps of information. Or maybe each person was given a part of a code or a password, and the killers are piecing it together."

"A secretive meeting about what?"

"Money. Or maybe factional infighting. Or some sort of corporate espionage situation."

"Okay, you're going to have to explain how you ended up there from a couple of victims with their eyes removed."

As we sped down the A40, I filled her in on everything I knew about English Wizardry: the smudge marks on the wall in Cardiff, the much more impressive artwork back on the wall in Martha Ndidi's house, Hardknott-Lewis's warnings and Warder's history lessons. Even Gilroy's claims about the two killers. I didn't mention my concerns about my own family history.

We were nearly at Newport by the time I'd summed it all up. "So far as I can tell, there is no English Wizardry anymore, in the original sense of a white supremacist sect of magic users. I think maybe we're seeing some remnant of the original organisation. The reason I think money might be involved is that the original English Wizardry would have been rich. They were founded by a group of land-owning aristocrats. They were closely involved with some of the most significant events of the twentieth century. With some sensible investments, there could be a *lot* of money washing around in their coffers by now, hidden away somewhere. Maybe the two victims knew where the money had been stashed and the killers were pursuing them for it."

She exhaled, puffing out her cheeks. "This is all turning into a much bigger deal than I'd imagined. I can see how this oak tree symbol could be a sort of taunt or a warning, like a gang sign when two rival groups are warring over territory. Do you have any idea who the two suspects might be?"

"A few ideas, nothing concrete enough to pass on. Like I say, I'm not convinced our witness is even telling us the truth. Plus, compared to the optogram magic, an Assay gives only indistinct images, although there are sounds, too."

"We need more to go on," said Zubrasky. "We have lots of wild speculation but little solid evidence. Whatever the truth of it, we need to understand what the connection between the two victims is."

"It's a shame Ndidi has been dead so long; there might be nothing left of her memories to recover."

"You can do this Assay tonight?"

"I'll get it set up when we're back in Cardiff. Any news on the boyfriend yet?"

"Nothing. We're actively pursuing him."

"But you suspect him."

"It's interesting he's disappeared. Maybe this whole thing comes down to jealousy. Maybe Cornwallis and Ndidi were having an affair and Auchter killed them both. He's also a vet; he'd have had access to sedatives and medical implements."

"That's your preferred hypothesis?"

"If this were a normal case it would be," said Zubrasky. "But this is not a normal case. Forgive me, but you being here makes it not normal. From what you've told me there's a lot more going on."

"Which doesn't mean a simple love triangle isn't part of the picture," I said.

"Or a love *pentangle*."

"What?"

"Never mind," she said. "Go on."

"I'm just saying it's possible things got out of hand and went as far as they did because of all the fighting and feuding in the background."

Zubrasky sighed in a way that suggested she needed a good night's sleep before things would start to make sense. "Maybe. I don't know."

"Have you got anything from the second scene that might be useful?"

"Not a whole lot, yet. The science takes time and it's a Sunday. We do have a report from a dwelling on the other side of the valley from Ndidi's house that two people were seen walking along the road up to the house late on Friday afternoon."

The same two I'd seen? Except, of course, I wasn't sure I had seen them. I chose not to mention any of that to Zubrasky. "Did your witness know who the two were?"

"People they didn't recognise. Not from the village."

Two people walking along a country lane surely wasn't that unusual or uncommon. "If it was the perpetrators, why did they walk? Why not drive?"

"I wondered about that," she said, "but it makes sense. A strange car parked outside a house for several hours might attract attention. People in places like that know each other's business and habits; they keep an eye out for each other. But two strangers simply passing through on a walk would be much less likely to appear unusual. The perpetrators must have parked some distance away, parked their car out of sight of the road or any houses, then walked the rest of the way."

"What time on Friday was this?"

"Evening. We don't know if they stopped, or, if they did, when they left."

"They could have been there all night for all we know," I said.

"Could be. Presumably what they did to Ndidi would have taken quite a bit of time. The markings, the delicate surgery, the whatever-the-hell-it-is. That would take hours, right?"

"It would. I don't suppose there are any CCTV images from anywhere?"

Despite keeping her eyes on the road and the traffic and her instruments at all times, she managed to fit in a sideways glance in my direction. The disdain in her look was clear. It was fair enough; you didn't get great CCTV coverage in scattered villages in the middle of nowhere.

"What do you know about the Borderland Reading Group?" I asked, trying to ask a more sensible question.

"Nothing at all. Are they another of your shadowy groups of sorcerers?"

"As far as I know they're a reading group. I presume you saw both victims were reading the same book? The same edition of the *Mabinogion*?"

"Very good. Perhaps if the ghostbusting work ever dries up, we could find you a junior position in the real police. Tell me about this group."

"Ndidi's copy of the book was inscribed to the group. Did you seize the copy Cornwallis had by any chance?"

"We didn't, but we will now."

We were on the M4 now, the point where it went down to two lanes through the Brynglas tunnel. Even though it was a

Sunday evening there was a traffic jam. We crawled to a halt and Zubrasky pulled on the car's handbrake.

"You're not going to put your blue lights on and push through the traffic?" I asked.

"Contrary to popular belief, we never do that."

"Don't tell me you're not tempted sometimes."

"I'm shocked you would suggest it; the thought never occurred to me. Besides, how are the cars in front of us going to get out of the way, exactly?"

"Fair point."

Her phone made a series of musical notes as we sat waiting for the traffic to move. I listened to a one-sided conversation with someone from her station for several minutes. When she was done, she studied her phone's screen for a while. By the symphony of further musical notes, I gathered she was receiving a series of messages. One in particular she studied for a time. A slight frown crossed her features.

"Something interesting?" I asked.

"Definitely. It's taken the techs a bit of time to brute-force the encryption, but we now have some pictures."

"From Ndidi's laptop?"

"Cornwallis's. It seems like our idea of a trail of contacts has some truth to it."

She held out her phone for me to see. It showed a photo of a black woman I didn't know. She was in a pub by the look of it, grinning and pulling a stupid face for the camera while holding up a half-empty wine glass.

"That's Martha Ndidi?"

"It is. We were right. Cornwallis and Ndidi knew each other."

13 – The World Went Grey

It has come to my attention that WA Marieta Greensward is showing clear signs of having succumbed to the evils that we live our lives trying to defeat. Twice I have witnessed her carry out actions that are as abhorrent as they are unnatural. It is my recommendation that she be brought before the Star Chamber with immediate effect.

Acolyte Campbell Hardknott-Lewis,
internal Office of the Witchfinder General memo, 1979

Once we'd finally battled our way through the tunnel and I had a signal once more, I phoned the office to make urgent arrangements for an Assay on the body of Martha Ndidi. Every hour lost meant that the memories Gilroy could recover would be weaker. I'd meant to sort it all out as soon as we left, but hadn't been able to get a reliable connection from the backwoods of Herefordshire.

That evening, the duty officer was Olwen Evans, one of the newest recruits into the Office. She was a slight, five-foot-nothing woman, and one of the most ferocious operatives we had. Like me, she'd been recruited from Cardiff University by Hardknott-Lewis. Apparently, three years of studying English Literature had persuaded her of the wisdom of doing something completely different for a career. As the youngest member of staff, she tended to get lumbered with the graveyard shifts in the evenings and at weekends. I sympathised – that had been me a couple of years previously – but not quite enough to volunteer to take over her slots in the roster.

"Hi, Danesh," she said when she picked up. "Did you get that picture I sent you?"

"I did. You were right; that hairstyle should never have been seen in public."

It was a piece of nonsense; a pre-agreed exchange to prove

that I was who I said I was, and not some malevolent voice-thrower who had acquired my phone. Which, yeah, has happened.

"What can I do for you?" asked Olwen.

"I need to sort out an Assay of a body the Cardiff police are currently holding for post-mortem. I have authority from Hardknott-Lewis. Is there anyone there who can take Gilroy over now?" I cast a glance at Zubrasky to see if such an arrangement would suit. She assented with the slightest nod of her head.

"Kerrigan is around," said Evans, "and Hardknott-Lewis sent through his authority for your request. But I'm afraid Gilroy isn't here."

"What? Where is he?"

"Out on another assignment."

"With who?"

There was a pause, and then the clatter of keys being pressed. She sounded puzzled when she replied. "The log doesn't say. He was taken out early this morning and hasn't been returned yet, that's all I can tell."

"We must know where he is; someone like Gilroy can't be allowed to wander free."

"He'll obviously be with an officer; it just hasn't been recorded in the log."

"Damn." I couldn't complain, because I very often forgot to complete my records in good time and had to catch up on things after the fact. Still, it was incredibly bad timing. Almost suspiciously bad. "You've no idea at all where he's been taken or when he'll be back?"

"I can go down to the basement to double check he's not there if you like."

"Is there anything on the heat sensors?" We didn't have cameras inside Gilroy's apartment – *we* weren't the monsters – but we did check constantly for a heat signature to ensure he was in his rooms somewhere.

"There's nothing; the place is cold."

"Who's been in today?"

"Sorry, Danesh, I'm not sure. I only came on duty a couple of hours ago."

"Okay, thanks. We need to get the Assay sorted out as soon as Gilroy is returned. Can you phone me the moment he's brought in?"

"Of course. Sorry about that."

"It's not your fault."

I hung up. I probably made a little grunt of frustration.

"Problem?" asked Zubrasky.

"We're currently unable to carry out the Assay on Martha. The relevant expert is otherwise engaged."

"You can't use someone else?"

"There is no one else. It's a rare skill, unfortunately."

"So, we might not be able to get anything from her?"

"We still might, but it will be vague. Our best bet is to chase up the more mundane lines of enquiry."

"By *mundane*, you mean me?"

I knew she was joking, but I couldn't keep the note of horror from my voice. "You know I didn't mean that."

"Well, for the sake of good inter-agency relations, I'm very pleased to hear it."

By the time we reached the city centre it was already late afternoon. In my imagination, Zubrasky would accept my invitation to come inside my flat for a coffee. We'd talk, all our usual spikiness and sarcasm dropped as we finally opened up to each other: two colleagues from different arms of the state, with much in common and many stories to share. We'd compare notes and theories about what we were facing in our double murder case. She'd then tell me all about herself, who she was, what she wanted. What her dreams were. I'd explain about my background, what it was I really did in the Office, my hopes and fears. We'd laugh and talk as the light outside faded into spellbook-black night.

In reality, none of that happened. She stopped at the side of the road near where I lived and dismissed me with a weary wave. Then she sped off into the Sunday afternoon traffic. I threw the backpack I'd taken to London over my shoulder and headed inside to my lonely flat.

Inside, I checked my emails and messages while heating up some food in the *popty ping*. Zubrasky had left instructions with the police techs that any more images of interest were to be sent over to me before they went onto HOLMES. Nothing else had come through, although there was a copy of Cornwallis's shot of Martha Ndidi. I studied it in more detail, hoping to discern some clue about the location, but got nothing. There was some metadata attached to the image, but it didn't contain anything useful like a geotag, just unimportant details about resolutions and shutter speeds.

I spent a bit of time searching for any mention of the Borderland Reading Group on the web, but got nothing. Which was interesting in itself – any group like that would surely go out of its way to establish a presence on the internet to attract new members. There was a passing mention of a Borderland *Writing* Group, but that appeared to be unrelated, dedicated to creating rather than reading fiction. I briefly entertained the notion that the two murders might have been committed by a disgruntled fantasy author angry at the reading group's review of their work, but soon dismissed the notion.

I thought about going into the office and seeing what I could glean from MORIARTY while I awaited the return of Gilroy. In the end, I decided to make the most of what little remained of my weekend. Besides, I'd so far failed to study the notebook my mother had given me. Partly that was because I'd been so busy with the case – but mainly I'd been putting it off. I'd assumed for years that those long-ago events were safely locked away in my past. While they could still return to barb me at unexpected moments, it was an old hurt, one I knew the taste and shape of. Revisiting those events, perhaps altering my understanding of them, felt like well-healed wounds being cut open afresh.

My mother's handwriting was precise, elegant, each word beautifully formed, but the phrases and snatches of language she'd written down refused to form coherent, clear sentences. I read what she'd written again and again. She'd clearly started a new notebook recently – the first page had notes about a previous notebook *losing itself*, and there were only five pages filled in in the whole book. I reckoned they covered a period of a few weeks, no more. There was a note about my visit, jotted down after our phone conversation, I assumed. *Danesh visiting weekend* it said. *Wrap presents*. The latter had been underlined twice.

After that was the paragraph she'd written at my request about her memories, and the man she'd seen the day Az died. This is what it said:

Short man, long coat, his face invisible. Too late, too late. Danesh hiding in trees, terrified, but Azad was gone. My poor, beautiful boy. I failed you, failed you, failed you. I held you but you were gone. Man filled with fury, demon eyes, face invisible. Danesh hiding, so small, out of sight. Don't move, don't breathe. I run in the other direction to lead him away, but I'm caught, still holding Azad. His little body lifeless and limp.

The man did something to me. The world went grey and the colour has never come back. I walk through the mists shouting your names but there is never a reply. Only him, laughing from a mouth I cannot see.

I failed you, failed you, failed you.

The man's face is gone.

It was almost unbearable to read – and hard to know what to make of it. I recalled Az and I playing in the woods near our home often: we'd lived somewhere farther out of town then, a house we moved away from after Az's death. The events of that day were vague to me; I guess I'd blotted them out. I recalled only something overwhelmingly terrifying, old moments that wake me with a terrified gasp in the middle of the night even now. I remembered staying hidden for a long time, until eventually my mother and a policewoman came for me. I didn't recall the faceless man my mother had described.

Reading between the lines, it appeared he'd come for both of us, but the attacker had missed me, perhaps because of my mother's actions. It was possible Az and I had been playing some child's game of hide and seek, and that had saved me. Whoever our attacker was, he'd let my mother live. Because she was a white Englishwoman and his twisted morality meant she could survive? Or was it because she wasn't a magical adept, and therefore no part of his feud?

Because he, this short man in his long coat, was a user, too, if I read it right. He'd placed the curse on my mother there and then, wiped the memories from her mind so that his identity would be safe. Even with snatches of her memory returning, the man's face remained invisible in my mother's mind's eye. The user had clearly gone to a lot of trouble to make sure that detail was expunged. Because he was known to her? Unlikely, I thought. Because he knew he'd be pursued. Because he feared and hated my family and he knew we'd come for him – we or others.

I made myself read the words again and again, hoping to wring some fresh meaning from them. Then I closed the book and slipped it onto a bookshelf. I had to keep it, but I doubted I could ever bring myself to open it again.

My mother walked in the mists and my twin brother's body had been lifeless and limp.

I lounged away the rest of the evening with studied lethargy, sipping at cold beer and keeping one bored eye on some ridiculous reality TV show that went on for hours. Despite my best efforts, my mind kept returning to what I'd just read, as well as the Eye case. I tried to see through the veils to something I'd missed, some fresh angle, in either. Recent events had thrown the two things together in my head. Were they, in fact, part of some greater pattern, some long-unfolding series of events? If anything, English Wizardry were the connection – but I'd pretty much concluded that they no longer existed. Or, if some modern version of them was now active, that they hadn't existed for a long time. Was I only seeing connections because some part of my brain craved answers to the mystery of Az's death? Maybe my subconscious figured that if I solved the Eye case, everything else would fall into place, too.

Well, maybe. I sat, and drank, and thought, while the

overexcited TV burbled away to itself in the corner. A moment of dazzling insight completely failed to strike me at any point in the evening.

I got into the office early on Monday morning. I stopped by my desk and checked for any messages left for me: another cryptic note from the Librarian, perhaps. There was nothing. Olwen had gone off duty, but Kerrigan had been there all night, catching up on his paperwork and manning the phones in case the undead apocalypse struck Cardiff. Which, fortunately, it hadn't.

He came over to speak as I logged into MORIARTY. "Danny, boy. How was your weekend in the land of our English oppressors?"

I explained how it hadn't been quite as relaxing as I'd hoped. I obviously missed out several details, but I filled him in on events surrounding Martha Ndidi.

Kerrigan looked troubled. "You're into deep waters there, very deep waters. Be careful they don't drown you." It was one of his favourite sayings. When he wasn't around, Olwen did a very good impression of him, even though his voice was a booming baritone.

"I'll do my best."

"How was your mother?" She and Kerrigan had met once, when I'd first come to the Office. He'd pretended to flirt with her, and she'd been secretly delighted. His question was also another point at which I could have reported what I'd discovered about her: the long-standing curse, the danger to her and others around her. Once again, however, I found myself saying nothing.

"Is there any sign of Gilroy?" I asked.

"According to the logs, he was brought back in early this morning."

"Brought in by whom?"

"No one I saw, but I was called out for an hour to a suspected haunting on the dockside. Turned out to be a drunken lass who'd fallen off the quay and who was lying there moaning."

I opened the relevant page of our office portal and checked for myself. Sure enough, there was a record of Gilroy's return, but no mention of who had brought him in.

"How is that possible?" I asked.

"The system registered him returning because of the tag on his ankle, but the officer with him didn't log in to put their name to it. It's a very, very serious offence." His words send a jolt of alarm through me, but his eye twinkled as he spoke. He was joking; he was notoriously poor at record keeping and following procedures.

Zubrasky was off duty that day, but she'd given me the name of another officer to contact, another Cardiff police officer in the know. I sent a message stating that I planned to visit within the hour to carry out an investigation upon the remains of Martha Ndidi. Gilroy wasn't going to be happy, but then he was never happy.

As I worked, a message arrived for me from one of the police techs investigating the two murder scenes. Zubrasky had done a good job of priming them to keep me in the loop. The message contained another photograph, and the note attached to it said it was from Ndidi, not Cornwallis. The encryption on her machine had proved tougher to crack, but they'd managed to uncover a lightly encrypted spreadsheet of passwords and grab some images from a cloud backup.

This picture showed a group of four people, arms around each other, posing for the camera in that familiar, overexuberant way people use when they're letting their hair down.

Two of the people I recognised: there was Cornwallis, complete with his eyes, and there was Martha Ndidi next to him. Martha looked a year or two younger than she had in the other picture, suggesting that the group had known each other for a while. A taller man stood behind Martha, his arms draped across her shoulders in a way that suggested easy intimacy. The AWOL partner, Oliver Auchter, I guessed. He certainly looked like the figure photographed in long-shot in the travel photos on the walls of Martha's home. He didn't look like a crazed, racist sorcerer; but then maybe you don't.

The fourth individual was a woman I didn't recognise. She was definitely one of the group, laughing along with the rest of them. She wore heavy black eyeliner and quite a bit of silver jewellery, a Queen of the Goths look with her long black hair. She stared squarely at the camera with a knowing smile that suggested she knew things about the person taking the picture. The image certainly wasn't a selfie: all eight hands were clearly visible in the frame. Maybe facial recognition could get an ID for the woman. I studied the picture for several minutes, going over each detail, looking for any clue about the location. Again, nothing was obvious. Unfortunately, there were no panes of glass or anything similar behind the group from which I could see a reflection of the photographer.

I was about to close the image viewing software on my laptop when one detail did catch my eye. The unknown woman held something in her hand, cradling it as if it was something delicate or precious. I zoomed in, already suspecting what it would be.

I was right: she held a book, its name visible along its spine. It was a third copy of the *Mabinogion*. They'd clearly been reading the book for a long time, which suggested that they were either very slow readers – which I doubted – or else that they weren't actually reading the book at all, but using it for some other purpose.

Kerrigan, passing by my desk again on the way back from the water cooler, stopped to consider the image on my screen. "Who are they?"

"I think they might be the members of the Borderland Reading Group," I replied.

"Never heard of them."

"No, they seem to have gone to a lot of trouble to keep themselves a secret."

"Ah, you suspect they're more than just a book club."

"I think that's clear by now."

"Two of them are the victims?"

"These two."

"So, who are the others? The woman and the guy standing behind them all?"

"Her I don't know, but I think that's Oliver Auchter."

"And what part do they play in all this?"

"They might just be the killers we're looking for."

A reply came back then from Zubrasky's tame officer telling me I could gain access to Ndidi's body as soon as I was ready. It was time to rouse Gilroy from his lair once again.

On my way down to the basement, I passed the fell portal to Oblivion. In fact, most of the time it wasn't a gateway to the dimension of death. Most of the time it was a broom cupboard. But when the alignments are right and certain chthonic syllables are uttered, the little square room becomes a doorway to a particularly unpleasant elsewhere. Other Offices had more auspicious entrances to the realm, but space is at a premium in Cardiff.

Oblivion is yet another of the Office's grey areas. Magus law specifically allows us to maintain the magical pathway, because it provides the only absolutely guaranteed secure containment for the most powerful adepts. More secure, even, than death, which more than one has chosen to see as little more than an inconvenience. However strong they are, they can do nothing but exist when frozen into the ice of Oblivion. It's a grim eternity. As Hardknott-Lewis puts it, always with a wry smile, sometimes you have to fight fire with fire.

There was only one Oblivion realm so far as I knew, with multiple entranceways – which meant Evangelina Mormont was through there somewhere, along with a whole rogue's gallery of evil sorcerers and diabolists from the long history of the Office. I'd never stepped foot inside – so far as I knew, only Hardknott-Lewis knew the relevant passwords to gain access – but sometimes officers ventured within under his control to waken someone and extract a few slow words of memory.

Gilroy took an age to emerge from his rooms. In the end, I had to hold my finger on the bell to annoy him enough to make him appear. He lumbered into view wearing a threadbare dressing gown and a puffy-eyed glare of pure hatred. His lined face was scribbled with grey stubble.

"What the fuck do you want now? Can't you leave me alone?"

"I need you to perform another Assay."

"Now?"

"That's why I'm here now, yes."

"I only just got in from the last one."

I needed to talk to him about that, find out where he'd been, and with whom, but that could keep. The pressing matter was to get him to the body so he could do his evil work. "Time is short; the victim has already been dead for a few days. Can you be ready in ten minutes?"

"Do I have any choice?"

He liked to rail against us. It was the only shred of control he had over his existence. "You can choose not to cooperate, of course. And then we can choose not to employ your services anymore."

He leaned in closer to the crack in his open door. I could smell his unwashed stench.

"You know," he said, "I'm beginning to think you're attracted to me with all these excuses you find for coming down here."

An actual shiver ran through my body at his words. "Trust me, you're not my type. In so many ways. Now be ready in ten minutes."

I filled the time checking up on a few more details of the case, reading through the police case notes on HOLMES. Auchter was still on the run, his whereabouts unknown. They hadn't yet identified the other woman in the photograph. They'd recovered no unexpected DNA or fingerprints from either murder scene – something that struck me as odd. Maybe it was because all the results weren't in yet. There were no updates from Hardknott-Lewis. Presumably he'd completed the work of tidying up the murder scene and had moved on to his other business in the area.

Twenty minutes later, Gilroy and I were again striding along the streets of Cardiff, he slightly ahead of me once more so I could keep an eye on him. A light morning drizzle coated the roads and pavements of the city in a film of water. At least with people bundled up in raincoats, Gilroy's inclination to ogle every female we passed was reduced.

I stepped a little closer to him so we wouldn't be overheard. Over the rhythmic *swish* of our waterproofs, his breathing was a little laboured.

"Tell me where you were last night," I said. It was hard not to sound like a parent questioning a wayward child.

Gilroy sounded hugely amused. "You don't know, Danny boy?"

"I want to hear your version of events."

"You don't know, do you?" he repeated. "Sounds like there's trouble in the Office to me. Two magical murders and now dissent and confusion in the ranks." He was annoyingly sharp, despite his lack of sleep.

"There is no dissent or confusion."

"Yet you don't know where I was or who I was with. Seems to me you're having doubts about some of your colleagues, otherwise you'd just ask them. Perhaps you're thinking I was with Hardknott-Lewis on some secret mission that he didn't want anyone to know about."

Was he saying that had happened? It was surely unlikely. "I know you weren't, and if you were, he'd hardly have let you out into my custody, would he?"

"Now it sounds like you're trying to persuade me the Office isn't rotten. I think you're really trying to persuade yourself, aren't you?"

"Are you going to tell me what you were doing yesterday?"

"Why don't you guess, and I'll tell you how close you are?"

I ignored his little game. He was enjoying himself far too much. "Do you often get taken outside?" So far as I knew, Assays were rarely sanctioned.

"What do you think?"

"I think I can look in the logs to see exactly when you've been allowed out of your cage. It's hardly a great secret you're keeping from me."

"And yet you're still asking. It's almost like you believe the logs have been tampered with."

He left that little thought to sit with me and, satisfied with his work, began to hum to himself. I gave up on the questioning. He clearly wasn't to be trusted.

We were shown to the same morgue as before, the same clinical bright light whiteness, the same acrid tang of bleach. The assistant who'd accompanied us wordlessly from the front desk selected one of the doors in the body filing cabinet filling one wall. She slid the remains of Martha out and left us to it.

"Let's get this done," I said to Gilroy. "There's no time for any more of your humour."

Gilroy pulled back the sheet from Martha's head. She looked calm in death, peaceful, and if it weren't for the voids where her eyes should have been, she might almost have been asleep. Her hair was intricately woven into fine dreadlocks. Older hands in the Office, people like Kerrigan, said they got used to seeing death, but I was a long way from that yet. Martha had been a person like me, full of desires and ideas and questions. Joys and sorrows. A lot of life lived, a lot more ahead of her. Except, now she hadn't.

Did she have any idea of the fate coming her way? Had she lived her life in fear of her doom, or had she been blissfully unaware of it? If our theory was correct, someone had found images of her in Cornwallis's visual memories, worked out who she was, and come looking. Now her own recollections were being sifted through, until the next person in the chain, the next victim, was identified. The process was as intrusive as it was gruesome. Everything Martha had witnessed, however private or intimate or embarrassing, would be the killers' to linger over, consider; maybe, even, enjoy. It was hard to separate my distaste for that from my distaste for Gilroy. In his own weak way, he was essentially doing the same thing.

Which I guess meant I was, too.

With a gasp of effort Gilroy took his hands from Martha's head and stepped back. His skin looked greyer than it had been, from the effort of working his magic. He was breathing heavily. Without saying anything he crossed the room to the sink to scrub his hands.

"Well?" I said. "Anything?"

His voice was hoarse as he replied. "Indistinct scraps. I should have been brought in a lot sooner."

"Tell me what you saw."

"Two figures like before, hooded and cloaked."

"Did you get any new details about them? Anything at all?"

"The memories were too degraded. There's not a lot of her left."

"But a man and a woman?"

"I think so, impossible to be sure."

It didn't get me any further forwards. No new clues, but also no proof Gilroy was even telling me the truth. "Could you make out any details of where she was killed?"

"I thought you were at the murder scene."

"We don't know for sure she was killed where the body was found."

He shook his head "White walls, grey floor. Shapes that

might have been pictures or windows on the walls."

It might have been the room she'd been found in, but it might also have been a million others.

"Did you hear any words?"

"Some screaming and sobbing."

"And she was a supernaturalist like the other you assayed?"

"She was a user, too, yes. More powerful than the last one. She put up quite a fight, but she was no match for them. For one of them, anyway. I'd say only one of her attackers was a user."

Interesting. "You didn't tell me that last time."

"I didn't know it last time. This isn't an exact science."

"Can you tell me any more?"

"There's nothing."

I nodded. I could see from his face how much the effort of his magicworking had cost him. "Thanks for trying, at least."

"I didn't have any choice, did I?"

"No, not really."

He paused for a moment as he dried his hands on a paper towel, eyes focused into the middle distance.

"What is it?" I asked.

"Probably nothing."

"Tell me."

"While it was going on, one of the figures was standing by the wall for a long time. The one who doesn't have powers. I couldn't tell what he was doing but I think, maybe, he had his back to the room. It seemed odd."

"Which wall?"

"From her perspective, the one on the right."

The wall where Hardknott-Lewis had shown me the painting. We obviously hadn't told Gilroy any details of the murder scene.

"Have you any idea at all what the person was doing?"

"There was a light flashing again and again, like they were illuminating something on the wall repeatedly. It didn't make a lot of sense."

"But you think it was the man?"

"Probably. It's hard to be sure."

"Anything else at all?"

"Nothing. That's all you're going to get."

Interesting. He'd more or less identified the presence of the picture on the wall. There was no way he could have known about that – which meant he was telling us at least some of the truth.

On the way back to the office, though, he finally answered one of my earlier questions. Clearly, he'd decided it would cause more mischief to let me know. "You may not be able to trust your logs, but you can check the CCTV footage from the camera you have trained on my front door. You might as well know who I was with yesterday."

He was probably playing another game with me, but I asked him anyway. "Who?"

"Lady Coldwater herself booked me out for a little road trip."

"You were with the Librarian? Come on."

"Check the footage yourself."

His words threw me; I slowed to a stop for a step. Was he now suggesting that the two figures he'd just described at the murder scene were himself and Lady Coldwater? Was there some arrangement between the two of them that I hadn't considered? Some secretive magical crusade against factions or people they opposed? Perhaps they were both English Wizardry sympathisers, slowly picking off those they despised. It might explain her hostility to me. The Lady had access to all the intelligence they'd need in their operations, and Gilroy was an adept, if a weak one. Had she been quietly freeing Gilroy all this time so they could pursue their vendetta? If that were the case, it would explain how he knew about the oak tree painting, but it would also mean that I had it all wrong about Auchter and the unknown woman.

But if he and the Librarian were the killers, why would he relay the memories he'd recovered from the victims? Why take that risk? Or had he made it all up and struck lucky? Or pretended that the details were so vague so as not to incriminate himself? But, in that case, why tell me anything at all? Perhaps he was simply gloating, enjoying the power trip, relishing my confusion.

I resumed walking as these thoughts chased around my mind. The Librarian would be able to get to Gilroy without any of us noticing if there were a doorway from the library through to the basement accommodation. Gilroy glanced back to watch the confusion on my face, making sure his words had struck home. He was having fun with me. Except, I caught something else in his eye, too. A weariness, a resignation. Perhaps it was just his lack of sleep and the effort of performing the Assay, but there was something else there. Was it possible he was so weary of his imprisonment he longed for the release of Oblivion – but couldn't bring himself to say it? Perhaps he couldn't even admit it to himself, and he was playing a sad little game of self-incrimination.

In that moment I almost – almost – felt sorry for him. "And where did you and the Librarian go?"

"Ah, well," he said, "you'd have to talk to her about that, wouldn't you?"

"Has she taken you out before? When did she last employ you?"

But Gilroy would say no more.

14 – Malevolent Spirit

Today we concluded the unfortunate episode of the possessed children at the Tiger Bay orphanage, a series of events I hope never to see repeated. I remain unclear as to the precise nature of the victims' ensorcellment, but it seems likely that some foreign sorcery arrived upon one of the cargo ships putting into Cardiff docks. In the end, there was nothing we could do for the tainted wretches; they became utterly bestial, attacking anyone daring to go near them. In order to stop the spread of the contagion, we put the children out of their misery with our pistols, burned the bodies, then buried the bones in an unmarked grave on waste ground half a mile from the docks. The screams of the children as we acted, the frank stare of their unblinking, milky-white eyes, will stay with me for a long time.

–Isaac Shackleton, Lord High Witchfinder,
Personal Journal (written in private cipher), 1888

Back at my desk, I called up the footage from the CCTV camera that we did, indeed, have monitoring Gilroy's door. I scanned backwards, instructing the system to stop at any time it detected movement. It soon found the pictures, just recorded, of Gilroy being returned to his lair. I resumed the scan as the two of us, moving with comic speed, left the frame, walking backwards to the stairwell we'd descended. A few seconds later, we were there again as we the hit the moment I'd picked him up to take him outside in the first place.

There was a longer pause, nothing changing apart from the clock counting in the corner of the screen. Then Lady Coldwater shimmered into view, reversing as the images rewound. She stopped at Gilroy's door, there was a long conversation about something, and then Gilroy appeared. Then both moved backwards out of the frame. Seen in reverse, this was the Librarian returning Gilroy to his rooms. The clock read SUNDAY 19:27 – the previous evening.

I went back further and found the footage of Gilroy being roused in the first place. There was another long conversation at the door, the two of them apparently arguing about something. This time the clock on the screen gave the time as 06:15 of the previous morning – so around the time Zubrasky was phoning me from the second crime scene.

I scanned further. If Gilroy was involved in Ndidi's murder, then he'd have needed to be outside on Friday evening and into Saturday morning. There were, however, no visitations in that period. The system kept a week's images available for immediate retrieval, and, apart from my appearances on Thursday for the Assay of Evan Cornwallis, Gilroy's door remained locked throughout. There were definitely no other exits by which Gilroy could have left. Wherever the Librarian had taken him, it wasn't to murder Martha Ndidi.

Back upstairs, deep in thought, I sought out Kerrigan. I jumped straight in with the ideas running around in my head. "Kerrigan, do you think it would be possible to tamper with the images from the CCTV on Gilroy's door?"

Kerrigan scrunched up his face. "It's possible, sure, but it would be bloody difficult. And a hell of a lot of bother to go to. Tamper with them how?"

"Like, maybe to cut out a section, or erase part of the images."

"The clock would make it too obvious there'd been a jump. Editing someone or something out of a whole sequence of thousands and thousands of images and leaving the clock untouched would be possible, but time-consuming to achieve. Besides, I think the system is secure, everything checksummed and encrypted. You'd have to really know what you were doing."

I nodded. It was about what I'd assumed.

"What's your thinking?" he asked.

I told him about everything that Gilroy had said, and about the footage of the Librarian taking him from his cell the previous day.

"Interesting," said Kerrigan. "You were thinking those two might be the killers you're after?"

"It was a possibility I was considering, although it's obviously starting to look unlikely now. I suspect the idea was just Gilroy playing games with me."

"He does like to screw with us."

"What do you really know about Lady Coldwater, though?"

"In truth, not a lot. She was here when I came, and she keeps herself to herself."

"But you think she's truly on our side? She never seems much of a team player."

"She keeps careful watch over the books, and, so far as I know, she does so with absolute efficiency. She's crazy, sure, the mad woman in the attic – only in the cellar – but she's our sort of crazy. She hates the cruelty and randomness of magic use."

"Well, something's going on with those two. It looks like my only option is to go down there and ask her what it is." I'd intended to do so anyway, to check on my understanding of her one-word clue to the eye magic. Plus, I wanted to know if she could unearth anything in her archives about my family history. Now it seemed we'd have lots and lots to talk about.

Kerrigan stood and, with exaggerated emotion, engulfed me in a bear hug. "Danny boy, it's been so good knowing you. Are there any messages you want me to pass onto your loved ones if you don't return?"

"Just tell them I died doing the thing I loved."

It turned out Kerrigan needn't have worried. My badge no longer granted me access to the Vault, even though Hardknott-Lewis had given me privileges for the duration of the case. I tried six or seven times, tried banging on the doors, tried shouting, but it was no use. Someone had barred me from re-entering the Vault.

I gave up and went back to my desk. Kerrigan was gone now, leaving the place weirdly quiet apart from the sound of computers humming to themselves. Olwen was about somewhere: we had a statutory duty to have someone on the end of a phone 24/7, and she'd drawn the short straw once again. The 999 operators were able to route calls through to us if a member of the public was faced with something falling into our domain – not that they knew who or what we were, just that things that were unsettling or weird were to come through to us.

I dashed off a message to Hardknott-Lewis requesting that my access to the Vault be reinstated, but I didn't expect an immediate response. He hadn't yet reappeared from whatever it was he was up to in the Herefordshire countryside.

I checked across on HOLMES for any updates on the two murder scenes. There were, at last, some forensics in, but they weren't a huge amount of help. Several sets of fingerprints had been identified at Cornwallis's house, but, apart from those of the victim himself (taken to exclude him from the results), none were known, either to the Office or the police. Ndidi's house was the same: only the victim could be identified as having been there although, again, several unknown individuals had been present at some point – one of them, presumably, Oliver Auchter.

I spent the next few hours trying to find out what I could about Lady Coldwater and Gilroy, hoping maybe to unearth some connection between them, some hold one might have over the other. I got nothing; there was scant information on either individual, in MORIARTY or anywhere else, and certainly nothing to connect them. I'd hoped for some moment of revelation, some clue they'd once been lovers, say, or had been seen together years earlier on some English Wizardry escapade. But there was nothing.

I did track down the archives of the CCTV images from Gilroy's basement and configured the software to scan backwards a full year, looking for any occasion Gilroy had been let out. Like I said, our technology was good. I found seven over the course of that time; Gilroy saw the light of day roughly once every two months. I was pretty sure it wouldn't have been allowed in a normal criminal prison.

The seven occasions were with Hardknott-Lewis, once back in February, Kerrigan, once in May, and Lady Coldwater five times, at various points throughout the year. Something was definitely going on with those two.

I also ran facial recognition scans on the missing Oliver Auchter, just in case we had alternative IDs for him. He was still on the run, no sightings at all reported by the regulars. I got no hits on our database; apart from the image I'd added to MORIARTY myself, he was unknown to us. Then I ran the unknown woman from the photo through our routines – and somewhat unexpectedly found a match. It was a strong one, too, eighty-five percent likelihood of a genuine positive. There was no name or ID associated, but a woman looking very much like her had been photographed three years earlier at a Winter Solstice gathering – by which I mean a proper *summoning of forbidden beings* type of gathering, as opposed to some people in a field doing a bit of swaying and singing on Midwinter's Day. Apparently, we'd run a surveillance operation to see who turned up. Whoever she was, she appeared to be a user – just like Cornwallis, Ndidi and, presumably, Auchter – although the undercover team hadn't identified any specific magus law offence she'd committed.

I really, really needed to know what they got up to in that so-called reading group of theirs. That prompted me to check on HOLMES for the question I'd asked Zubrasky, and sure enough, the answer was there. Cornwallis's copy of the book had indeed been inscribed, just as Ndidi's had. Thinking that there might be something significant about that specific edition of the book, I went back down to the library, to the ground floor level where the harmless books were housed. It turned out we had three copies of the *Mabinogion*, but none were the same edition as the one Cornwallis and Ndidi had been reading. I decided to try the shops later; surely any bookstore in the Welsh capital would be well-stocked with the work.

While I was down there, I tried the door to Level -1 one more time in case my access had magically sorted itself out, but the little LED remained resolutely red. The day wasn't going well.

Back upstairs, I made a note of my findings on MORIARTY and was getting myself together to venture out to the bookshop when my phone rang. Peter Warder was calling me.

"Hi Peter."

"Hi, Danesh. Did you make it back to Wales safe and sound?"

"There was a bit of a diversion in border country, but I got back eventually."

"Excellent. Are you busy?"

"Investigating leads on my murders, not a whole lot more."

"Are you in the office? I don't want to distract you from anything pressing."

"You're okay; there's not a lot going on here, to be honest. Everyone else is out on a call."

"I saw you had two victims now. Are they definitely linked?"

"Definitely."

"Any solid leads?"

"Nothing worth mentioning. Looks to me like whoever did this knew how to cover their tracks, which is interesting in itself."

"I saw Hardknott-Lewis himself attended the crime scene. I can't imagine Earl Grey getting his hands dirty like that."

"He mainly went to remove more runes from the forbidden alphabets," I said. "Plus, there was English Wizardry iconography he wanted to destroy."

Peter absorbed that for a moment. "We're definitely looking at someone trying to make a point, tell the supernaturalist world they're there."

"I think so."

"Is Hardknott-Lewis still pursuing the matter?"

"No, he's off doing other things. There's basically just me."

"Well, good luck with it. I rang because I've been trawling through the records here in London for any mention of your grandfather. We have lots of accounts from both sides of the war, and quite a few of them digitised so we can scan them quickly, but I'm afraid I couldn't find any mention of a Shahzan."

I felt strangely disappointed. I'd fondly imagined my grandfather being a key member of the fight against English Wizardry, even if that confirmed he was a user. "Does that mean he wasn't involved, or that you simply don't have a reference to him?"

"Could be either, but I'd say we'd have picked up *something* if he'd been there. The most likely explanation is that he simply wasn't involved. Sorry, that doesn't help you much, does it?"

"It's useful in a negative way. I can rule that out at least, and obviously it's good that he wasn't a user. So, you said there was no mention of a Shahzan – not even my brother?"

Warder sounded momentarily confused. "Your brother? Do you suspect him of being involved in all this too?"

"No, he died when we were both small. I just came across something that suggested he might have been targeted."

"Targeted by whom?"

"I truly don't know. Possibly no one; my source is not the most reliable."

"But you believe there's a pattern? A vendetta against your family?"

"Vendetta's a strong word. I just thought there might be a connection between the two deaths. In fact, possibly three. My father died young, too, and I wondered if there might be something going on."

"Well, there might be for all I know, but so far as I can tell it doesn't involve English Wizardry. Sorry."

"Okay, thanks, I appreciate you going to all that trouble."

"No problem. Always happy to do my bit for cross-border relations. Give me a shout next time you're in town."

"I will. Oh, Peter, one more thing. This is a bit of a longshot, but I was giving some thought to moving back to London. Are you recruiting at all?"

"You know how it is: we're always looking out for the right people. Drop an email to Earl Grey's secretary, I'm sure we'd love to talk to you."

"Thanks."

He rang off, and I sat for a moment thinking about what he'd uncovered – or hadn't uncovered. It was tempting to march down to the basement and threaten Gilroy, demand to know the truth of what he claimed to know about my grandfather. I soon gave up on the idea. I wouldn't be able to gain anything useful, and making a scene was probably exactly what Gilroy wanted.

"Danesh." Olwen was poking her head over her monitors, breaking me from my reverie about my troubled family history. "Sorry to interrupt you; I know you're working on your Eye case."

"It's okay, I'm awaiting developments as they say. Has something happened?" I'd been aware of her talking quietly into her headset, answering a call.

"Something came in and there's no one else to take it. I think we need to attend."

"What is it?"

"It's a Code 17." Code 17: a malevolent spirit, presence or other manifestation. Cases ranged from the insubstantial and transient through to the gut-wrenchingly gruesome.

"Shit. Where is it?"

"St John's Churchyard Gardens."

Bang in the city centre; the very spot where I'd sat to talk to my mother four days previously. It wasn't an auspicious location for a Code 17: we'd had lots of problems with the little park, as had the regular police. It was a focus for all manner of antisocial behaviour and troublemaking. The police put that down to alcohol consumption, but we knew better. The little square of greenery between Working Street and Trinity Street might seem like a welcome oasis of greenery in the heart of the pedestrianised shopping district, or little more than a pleasant shortcut, but it was in fact a repurposed graveyard attached to the nearby church. It was old ground, surrounded by modern buildings but never touched. It was a fine place to sit for a while and watch the city hurry by, but it had always struck me as incongruous to see the low line of old gravestones running beside the path marking off one boundary.

The graves accounted for much unquiet soul activity, but they weren't the only reason. Convicted witches had once been burned nearby, events the Office of the Witchfinder General had had a hand in. Our punishments were at least more humane these days.

"Sure it's genuine?" All too often, Code 17s turned out to be delusions reported by people with psychological problems or the worse for drink or drugs. They might need help, but not the sort the Office could provide.

"Looks genuine, sorry. It's been passed onto us by a police officer who knows the codes." Officers like Zubrasky, on the inside about the existence and workings of the Office, are given a set of secret codes to use when they need to pass a case onto us. We find that the public tends to react a lot more calmly to overhearing, say, 'Code 6' rather than 'Incursion by major demonic being'. There really is a Code 666, too. To my certain knowledge, it has never yet been used.

"I'll attend the scene and see what I can do," I said.

"Assess the situation, but don't go in on your own. I'll send

Kerrigan when he's free."

"Thanks." She was right: a Code 17 was definitely a case where the *two operatives* rule applied.

"Is there anything I can do on your case while you're out?" Olwen asked.

"My access to the Vault has stopped working; I could really do with chasing that up with the Crow." She knew my private name for Hardknott-Lewis, admitted to her one evening over too many glasses of beer. And wine. And some fiery spirit the name of which I couldn't now recall.

"I'll see what I can do."

I was about to leave when another idea occurred to me. "And, if you get time, there is something else I was planning to look into. Something discreet."

She knew what that meant: I was researching a colleague. It was a wonder we ever trusted each other with anything.

"Go on."

"I'd like to find out all I can about the Lady's background."

"You suspect the Librarian of something?"

"Let's just say I'm interested in her and what she gets up to. Her background, her motivation. I'd also like to know more about this mediaeval order the librarians originally came from, The Pale Sisters, but there's nothing on the internet. Perhaps there's background in MORIARTY or one of our other computerised systems. Obviously, I can't go down to the Vault to see what's recorded down there about her."

"And obviously you wouldn't dare simply confront her."

"Obviously," I said. "Not unless I really, really have to."

The short walk down to St John's Churchyard Gardens was hampered by a small demonstration grinding its noisy way along Duke Street, right underneath the gaze of the Black Tower. A rabble of far-right nationalists and racists festooned in Union Jacks and Welsh dragons had managed briefly to hold up the traffic in the city centre. I'd seen similar scenes more and more, on the TV and social media. Memories of the black-and-white photograph Hardknott-Lewis had shown me flashed through my mind; it was tempting to think the 1930s were repeating themselves in some way. I found myself looking for English Wizardry symbols among the flags and

Nazi salutes, but I saw none.

One overweight thug in his forties saw me studying them and shouted at me, in an English accent, northern, to go back to where I came from. I guessed an original line was too much to ask for. When I explained that meant London, he charged at me, all beery bravado, red fury on his face. One of the police officers shepherding the march put herself between us. I wondered if she felt as conflicted as I did; we were both sworn to protect the public, even these members of it. The man's threats were frankly laughable; I faced far worse things than him most days in the Office. Still, it was a sign of the times. Maybe this shit and the resurgence of English Wizardry were one and the same thing.

The man shouted more abuse at me as he moved away, struggling against the police officer's grip, his face shading from red to purple. He probably still thought he was white, and I was the coloured one. "We know where you live! We'll come and find you!" An empty threat or something more sinister? Probably the former. The rabble soon passed by – there were maybe only forty of them – and I pushed on to sort out the Code 17.

St John's Churchyard Gardens were fenced around with black iron railings, a fact that had made it considerably easier for the police to seal the area off from public access. They'd done a good job keeping everything low-key: there were permanent signs on the gates saying the park would close at 5pm, and an additional sign had been added simply telling people the doors had been closed early that day. A uniformed police officer stood at each entrance in case anyone tried to storm the barricades, but the officers were adopting a relaxed humour that gave passing members of the public no clue about the malevolent spirit manifesting within. Quite possibly, the uniforms didn't know anything about it themselves.

I approached the DI in the know, who was deep in conversation with a clergyman – presumably from the nearby church. The vicar appeared to know something about who I was: he eyed me with a clear stare of mistrust as I approached. The Office and the Church often have a troubled relationship in modern times. Once we'd been on their side, soldiers in the fight against witchcraft and demonic evil, but now we tended to regard them with suspicion. They might be the good guys, but they were still supernaturalists. Technically, we were supposed to be battling them just as avidly as we battled diabolists, but in practice we tended to be a little more relaxed towards the mainstream religions.

The DI came to meet me. "You're Shahzan?"

"WA Shahzan, yes."

The DI hesitated only briefly before acknowledging my correction of my title. He was a little older than Zubrasky, his buzzcut hair and a nose that had clearly been broken at some point giving him a tough-guy, prop-forward appearance. The musical lilt of his soft Welsh voice was unexpected. "DI Zubrasky told me about you."

"Really, what did she say?"

"She said you were good, said I should trust you."

That threw me a little. I'd expected some sarcastic quip, not a statement amounting to a compliment. I covered my embarrassment by being all professional. "There's a malevolent inside the park?"

"A malevolent?"

"Sorry, a Code 17."

He nodded, glancing warily through the iron railings into the now-deserted patch of greenery. "Bunch of pissed-up lads taking a short-cut were attacked. I think they were here for the counterdemonstration against the weekend Nazis. Up for a bit of a scrap, like. One of them said their dog had been killed, although whether that's true isn't completely clear at this stage."

"Tell me what they reported seeing."

"They weren't completely coherent if I'm honest. One said there'd been an electrical shock from an exposed cable, and another claimed they'd seen a plume of, like, freezing smoke that screamed at them in an incomprehensible accent. Another said there was a figure there, but indistinct, things visible through it. And the biggest and toughest looking of the gang said nothing at all, just shook his head and stared into the distance when I asked him what he'd seen. At least that all makes it easier to cover the story up, persuade them they were seeing things."

Covering up the truth was a constant problem for the Office. However hard you tried to persuade people that they'd imagined it, or been the victim of some prank, rumours inevitably spread about a glimpsed manifestation or creeping horror. Popular fiction was full of garbled versions of that reality. We found it best not to engage, not to even grace the stories with a denial. Like the security services, we had exemption from the Freedom of Information Act, which helped. Plus, to the chagrin of Hardknott-Lewis, we did sometimes encourage the spread of speculative fiction, films and games, as they allowed us to liken actual events to nothing more than *something seen in a film.*

"How did you get involved?" I asked.

"The drunk lads reported what happened to a uniform who was clued up enough to know what might be going on. She patrols this area often, so she's learned to be wary about the park. She contacted me, and I went in to check out the situation."

"There's definitely something there?"

He looked like the sort of guy who could handle anything life and work threw at him, but he was struggling a little to describe what he'd seen. He was, quite literally, spooked. "There's something in the middle of the line of grave markers. Didn't go too close, but it looked like, well, a cold fire burning from the ground, I suppose. I thought I could see the form of a person dancing in the flame or smoke or whatever it is. Or maybe the flame and smoke *was* the figure. Sometimes there was a face there and also a voice, sobbing and crying like a child."

Something had triggered the malevolent into activity. Maybe some anniversary had been reached, or its remains had been disturbed, and it had awoken to trouble the inhabitants of the modern-day city. There was a chance its predominant emotion was confusion rather than malevolence.

"Have you heard it making any utterances?" I asked.

"Like, speaking?"

"Yes, like that."

"There was a voice, but it was hard to make out any words. I thought it might be babbling something in English, but Christ knows what."

"Okay, I'll go in and take a look. Be sure to keep everyone else out while I'm in there. Don't want anyone in the way if it flares up or gets angry."

The DI looked hugely relieved that I wasn't asking him to accompany me. "No problem. Understood."

The black iron gates squealed discordantly as they swung open, setting my nerves on edge.

"Shall I lock them after you?" the DI asked.

"Best not," I replied. "If the entity comes for me, I'll need to get out, and gates aren't going to stop it escaping."

"I was told iron had, you know, magical properties, making them a barrier. That's why the railings are here."

There was a note of hopefulness in his voice. I had to disappoint him. "Afraid not. Iron is a protection against some creatures – but probably not a malevolent."

"Okay. Well, good luck."

"I'll call if I need you to come and restrain the entity, shall I?"

There was a moment of purest horror in his eyes before he got I was joking. You had to take your pleasures where you could.

I climbed the stone steps and crept into the park. I could hear a tinny muttering sound coming from the undergrowth near the headstones, like someone had dropped a radio there. Nothing untoward was visible. I took a couple more steps forwards. I wasn't supposed to go in on my own, but I could get a little nearer and assess the situation while I waited for Kerrigan.

As with the possessed statuary, neither my gun nor my clothcutter knife were going to be much help. Insubstantial entities laughed at bullets – again, often quite literally – and the blade wasn't going to harm a presence if it was originally from our plane of existence. I had some more specialised tools with me, checked out from Supplies as I left. One was a device from the London research lab, designed to emanate a three-dimensional electromagnetic snare to entrap malevolents. They were great – apart from the slight disadvantage that they didn't work in the least. In fact, in my experience they tended to enrage their targets hugely, whip them up into fresh fury. But official policy was to field-trial them, so I'd checked one out.

I also had a few pieces of what we euphemistically called m/tech – which meant not tech at all, but contraptions magical in nature. The hobbles (one of which I'd brought) were an example, but devices called *glimmers* were generally more useful when it came to malevolents. A glimmer looked fairly unimpressive; a shard of glass or crystal, sparkling faintly with an inner glow, like an LED Christmas tree decoration. But malevolents didn't walk exclusively in our plane of reality. To them, ethereal and insubstantial, straddling two planes of existence, spectres perceiving reality with eyes that responded to different spectra, a glimmer was a bright beacon flame. It was beautiful and enthralling, and they were drawn to one like moths to a candle flame or the unreachable glow of the moon.

I also had my knowledge of the forbidden alphabets. Not, of course, the sorts of runes employed in the circles used to kill Cornwallis and Ndidi. They were strictly Greater Arcana, and I knew only a few symbols from the Lesser Arcana – runes mainly dedicated to protection or containment. I could inscribe a runic circle around the malevolent and, if it wasn't too powerful or too furious, it might be contained for a time.

It was peaceful in the little park. Roads and pedestrianised streets, with all the hubbub of traffic and commerce, were only yards away, but there was a hush about the little patch of land. An unnatural hush, perhaps. I took another step forwards, and another. Then I saw it. Just as the DI had described, it looked like a silver-grey fire burning from the ground. There was a form to it, darker lines among the flame that constantly hinted at, without ever reaching, the outline of a body or the features of a face. It was maybe two feet high.

I edged a little closer still. Despite all the devices we used, I generally found malevolents were best addressed by deploying what the police probably called *soft skills* – which meant attempting to communicate with it and find out what it wanted. Often it was a little thing, so easily resolved. A reassurance they could rest, for instance, or that some ancient personal trauma was long over. Usually there was little to the entities other than a few shreds of memory lashed together with bonds of anxiety. Most of the time they weren't malevolent, but simply lost.

I began to mark out my rough circle, thinking to contain the entity without having to get too close to it. When Kerrigan arrived, we could decide between us how best to handle the situation; who would attempt to converse with it while the other readied glimmers to distract it. The circle would be far from perfect, squashed on one side by the edge of the park, but that didn't matter. Runic circles don't really need to be perfectly round – that's simply a matter of style, a necromancer's professional pride. What they need to be is unbroken, so that whatever is held within can't find a way to seep or rage out.

I was maybe ten feet from the manifestation as I set to work. I could hear its words now: a stream of syllables like a confused drunk babbling from the gutter. Or, I thought, like the sound someone might make to reassure themselves when they were wandering lost in the darkness: a wordless flow of sound in a familiar voice. There was a childlike quality to it, a nursery-rhyme singsong. Someone who'd died young maybe, unquiet in their grave because of the terrible injustices of their short life. I'd seen that before. While I couldn't discern any coherent phrases, the words definitely sounded English – maybe even cockney if my ears were right.

The entity didn't appear to have noticed me. I drew my line, spraying it onto the ground over flagstone and earth with the little tin of aerosol paint we carried for just such a purpose. It was low tech, but effective. As I went, I marked out the runes that would hopefully be strong enough to act as a barrier once the circle was complete. I took meticulous care to get each sigil perfectly formed. Any flaw might render the circle ineffective.

I was a third of my way round the ring, pressed up against the fence, when I noticed the glint of something bone-white on the ground at the foot of the billowing column of ethereal fire. There was something there, an object dropped in the undergrowth among the headstones. There could be no doubt: the entity flowed from the object like a flame flickering from the wick of a candle.

It looked very much like a *touchstone*. I'd assumed I was dealing with the spirit of one of those buried beneath the ground of the little Cardiff park, but that wasn't it at all. Malevolents were often tied to material objects: totems of their earthly existence anchoring them to our world, allowing them, or forcing them, to linger. The objects could be something seemingly inconsequential, or ridiculous, a *memento vita* of a lost life as opposed to a *memento mori* troubling someone alive. I couldn't see what this one was. But if it was an object I could easily destroy, I might be able to break the haunting there and then, bring peace to the restless spirit and the innocent locals of the Welsh capital.

I stood and looked around. There was still no sign of Kerrigan. For all I knew, he might be held up for hours, and sometimes malevolents grew in power the longer they were allowed to manifest, like a swarm of angry bees swelling as each moment passed. And I really needed to get back to pursuing my eye harvesters.

I came to a decision.

Precautions first: I completed the circle and the runic inscriptions, taking my time with both. Protect the public from the unnatural and all that. When I was done, I stepped over the line and entered the wonky runic circle, feeling a little like I was stepping into the cage of a lion.

It was just me and the malevolent.

I placed a glimmer on the ground, then stepped around the edge of the little circle to approach the malevolent from the opposite direction. With luck, it would be so fascinated by the light that it would pay me no attention.

I took a few wary steps forwards, close enough to discern what sort of touchstone I was dealing with. The objects tend to be something small and personal, a thing that meant a lot to someone in life. I'd read about dead writers haunting the pens they'd used to invent their worlds, and I'd seen a case of a CD being the focus of a lingering spirit, an album the dead person had loved so much in life that they'd refused to let it go. Sometimes the touchstone was less permanent: a photograph of a loved one, or an actual person. Such spirits didn't linger for a long time. Once their touchstone died or crumbled or rotted away, so did they.

This one appeared to be a child's toy: a hand-sized china doll consisting of a froth of drab, tattered clothes beneath a brightly painted white head. It looked battered and old: Victorian, maybe. The blue eyes of the little doll stared blankly at me, taking note as I dropped to my knees to creep a little closer. It lay nestled among the grass, and I wondered how it had got there. It had to have been placed there recently; perhaps it had been dropped by someone sitting on one of the benches – or maybe placed deliberately as a memorial to a lost loved one. The flickering manifestation was definitely coming from the doll, twining out of the tangle of blonde hair.

The glimmer was doing its job: the stream of words coming from the manifestation remained calm and constant as I made another movement forwards. There was no note of rising alarm or fury as there might have been if the manifestation had felt under attack. If I could smash the head of the doll, there was a good chance it would be enough to make the malevolent dissipate. There might be a moment of fury, but it would soon pass.

I found a stone on the ground beside my knee, heavy enough to smash the rose-coloured cheeks of the doll and stop its frank blue eyes staring at me. I thought about throwing the rock but decided against it. If I missed, I might alert the entity to my presence, and they tended to be extremely protective of their touchstones. I decided against taking a crack with my pistol for the same reason, and also because a shot from even a silenced gun can be loud enough to alarm and enrage a malevolent. I crept closer until I was within arm's length of the tattered doll. I'd get one blow and I had to make it count. Distantly, I heard a motorbike revving angrily somewhere out in the city, but it roared away and the expectant quiet returned.

I reached out to shatter the head of the doll.

There was an instant when the full extent of my miscalculation hit me. The malevolent spirit tethered to the doll tore its attention from the fascinating light of the glimmer and swivelled its gaze fully upon me. It was, or had been, a little girl, her life full of magic and happiness until some old tragedy tore it away from her and she died. The seething fury contained within the lingering presence struck at me. I was attacking her, just as others had attacked her and taken everything from her; now she would have her revenge.

I recoiled an inch from the raging light of the malevolent, but I couldn't move quickly enough. Searing pain lit up my eyes, burning through my nerves, my body becoming fire.

The spirit raged out of control in her fury, and I was lost in the flames.

15 – The Mabinogion

…he who will be chief, let him be a bridge.

                           –The Mabinogion

Hardknott-Lewis's face came into focus as I blinked my eyes into life. Only the briefest moment had passed, yet events in the Cardiff park also felt distant, like things that had taken place days earlier. Also, there was the curious fact that I was lying in a bed, a pillow beneath my head and the white walls of a room around me.

The Crow spoke. "Ah, Danesh. You are with us again."

I said what people always say in that situation, although my parched tongue was welded to the roof of my mouth and it took a few goes for me to get the words out: "Where am I?"

"You're in the Sanatorium."

He meant the little two-bed ward we maintained at the Office, useful if anyone needed to recover from an affliction that modern medicine could do little to help with. Unable to think of anything more original to say, I hit him with the next question people always ask.

"How long have I been here?"

"It's been four days now since the malevolent spirit possessed you. I'll be honest with you, I wasn't sure whether we'd get you back at first. For a time, I thought Oblivion was the only option. The spirit that attacked you was dreadfully powerful, and we could do little to contain it."

I kept on with the clichés, my brain refusing to think of anything original to say. "What happened?"

"We did what we could, used what magery we had available to us to keep you alive. We had little choice; a battle was raging inside you, your spirit fighting your attacker for possession of your body. In truth, we could do little to help. I placed you inside a runic circle, employed Greater Arcana binding runes to contain the malevolent if it prevailed, and watched on. I can only guess what seething injustice tore at the dead spirit of that little girl, but someone had done something brutally cruel to her. We smashed the little doll, of course, ground it to pieces and burned it, but it wasn't enough. I think she simply left her touchstone behind and jumped to you. She was consumed by her need for revenge."

"You came to help at the Park?"

"Kerrigan came to help, too late to stop you attempting to tackle that horror on your own. What were you thinking? Didn't I warn you about the risks you faced?"

"This wasn't anything to do with the case. It was just another call-out and I got unlucky."

Hardknott-Lewis's eyes narrowed as he considered me. "Is that what you think? It doesn't strike you as a coincidence you were attacked at precisely this moment?"

"I wasn't attacked. I attended an incident and miscalculated. Any other day I'd have been fine."

"Someone placed that touchstone there, in all likelihood knowing you would be the officer sent to attend to it when it was discovered. It seems to me highly likely that someone was trying to kill you. Do you have any inkling who that might be?"

I worked myself up to a sitting position and took a sip of water from the glass beside my bed. It trickled cold down inside me. "There are a few possibilities, but I can't name anyone yet."

"But you have suspects? This can't be allowed to get out of hand. Two deaths and, quite possibly, an officer nearly murdered as well: perhaps it's time I took the case over and handled it myself."

Was that a suspicious thing to say? Once again, I was struggling to think clearly. "If they're trying to kill me, it shows I'm getting close. I want to pursue the case."

The Crow eyed me for long moments. Several times he looked as if he was about to say something, but stopped himself. Finally, he did speak. "Very well. Pursue your leads. If we weren't so stretched, I might have reassigned you, for your sake as well as that of any potential new victims, but right now I think you're the best person for this. Just please try not to get killed. We're short-staffed enough as it is."

It was about as close as Hardknott-Lewis gets to actual

humour. "Thank you," I said.

"Is there anything I can do to help? I've made sure your access to the Vault is working again. I believe you wanted to speak to the Librarian?"

"Do you know why my badge stopped working?"

"Lady Coldwater rescinded it."

"Why did she do that?"

He considered me again before replying. He sounded wary. "She's protective of her books, perhaps over-protective. Do I get the impression you suspect the Librarian of something?"

I didn't want to spell out any of my suspicions, not even to him – because there *was* another possibility to consider, one I barely liked to admit to myself. Something he'd said at the Ndidi murder scene had whirled around in my brain; perhaps some part of my subconscious had been dwelling on it while I was dead to the world. It was when I'd asked him about fingerprints, and he said *Only my own, now that I've touched it.* Was that too convenient? A crude cover-up? Was it possible, somehow, that *he* was one of the figures in the images Gilroy had recovered?

He might have put me on the case expecting me to get nowhere with it, then making doubly sure of my failure by refusing to grant me access to the runes and magics employed, and insisting that I had to operate alone. He'd gone out of his way to warn me of the dangers I'd face, perhaps hoping I wouldn't push the case too hard. He might then have been forced to intervene when he deemed it necessary, getting to Herefordshire before I could and deliberately providing me with scant information. But, if I couldn't trust Hardknott-Lewis, then there was no one I could trust: he was the absolute guardian of everything we stood for. We were trained to suspect everyone, no matter how high up, but it had been he who'd provided that training.

He was still watching me, standing over me, waiting for my response. I said, "There are some questions I'd like to ask her. I was wondering, do you trust her?"

"Well, now," he said, "that rather depends upon what you want to trust her about. You are familiar with the history of the Pale Sisterhood?"

"I know the name, nothing more. Further detail is hard to track down."

"Deliberately so. They no longer exist as a distinct body of people, you understand, but they remain a philosophy, a way of thinking. In many ways their views coincide perfectly with those of the Office, but in some significant ways they do not. But, yes, when it comes to the sort of malign sorcery we've seen with these murders, I trust her completely and absolutely. You've been on missions with her; you know she despises the use of magic to harm or endanger anyone."

I had; it was true. She was ferocious when it came to bringing users to justice. Sometimes we had to hold her back from the poor, terrified necromancer. "You're not telling me the whole story, though."

The Crow perched on the hard plastic chair beside my bed. "If you're up to it, I'll give you a brief history lesson. Much of this isn't widely known, but it may be of use to you."

"Please, go on."

"The sect were originally users, of a sort. As with so many such groups, they thought it was possible to differentiate between *good* and *bad* magic use, like seeing a distinction between good and bad murder, say. They summoned creatures of their own to fight the demons and imps brought into our world by the users they opposed. They met curses and incantations with stronger curses and crueller incantations. Much of their magic use was to do with healing rather than harming, it is true, but they couldn't see that by accepting magic use as normal they were lifting aside the veils to no end of horror. Opening the doors. Early in the seventeenth century, they came to the attention of the Office of the Witchfinder General. Over a period of twenty years we very nearly destroyed them, but in the end, rather than doing so, we came to an understanding with them. Historians of our organisation see that as a turning point, the moment when we accepted that sometimes we had to loosen our grip a little and fight fire with fire. If we're honest, it was because we were waging a losing battle against the forces assaulting us. But from there flowed the use of Assizes powers and all the many ways we turn the forbidden arts of our enemies against them."

"You're saying Lady Coldwater is a user."

He picked through his words carefully. "She has certain potentials, but she is strictly forbidden from employing them other than in very special circumstances. She is also allowed to make use of approved Office items and incantations if the situation warrants it and if there are absolutely no alternatives – just as you and I are. The nature of the compromise was to allow them to continue their work so long as they accepted the controlling hand of the Office. It has been an uncomfortable arrangement over the years. Not everyone has accepted the wisdom of it, and there have been resentments on both sides, but by and large it has held. Lady Coldwater gets all the resources of the Office to employ and we get the benefit of her knowledge and courage."

"And what is this work? What are these special circumstances?"

"As well as other things, the remnants of the Pale Sisters devote themselves to removing cursed objects and tomes of evil magic from the world; it is one reason they have so often become librarians over the years. That, and the fact that such a position allows them to operate without having to interact with the rest of us much."

"They are allowed to use magic to track down these forbidden items."

"And to stop anyone else gaining access to them, which explains their often frosty demeanour. The books are kept partly because some are almost impossible to destroy, and partly because much can be learned by studying them. Lady Coldwater's knowledge of the forbidden arts greatly surpasses my own. It is some measure of my trust in her that I allow this situation to continue."

"Are you telling me not to investigate her?"

"Not at all, Danesh. You must go where your investigation leads you. I might have missed something, and we must all be vigilant. I tell you all this because it might help you to understand the situation better, as well as to demonstrate how much I trust you. I simply ask you to be aware: the Lady might appear to have turned against us without having done so at all. Although she is technically a part of the Office, she finds it hard to trust the rest of us. As I say, the Sisters were once ruthlessly suppressed."

"Although her position would be perfect cover if she had succumbed."

Hardknott-Lewis considered the notion, then nodded his

head. "Quite so. It isn't always clear when someone has started using forbidden powers – or covering up their use."

Did he mean to imply anything by that? I chose to believe not. "How do you think the Pale Sisters would have felt about English Wizardry?"

"There has never been a united faction opposing English Wizardry; this is no simple case of two sides. But it's clear the Sisters would have seen the use of death magic as a great evil, an abomination. I haven't asked her, I confess, but I imagine Lady Coldwater views events around these deaths with extreme distaste."

My mind was starting to kick into life again. "And has anything happened while I've been out of it?" I asked. "Have the two individuals in the photograph been identified?"

"I believe not, although I have been somewhat distracted. Olwen has done what she can to keep a watchful eye on the case; she can brief you if you wish to continue with it."

"I do." The days I'd lost might be crucial; I needed to get back onto the case before there were more deaths.

"Are you able to stand?" he asked. "You suffered no physical injuries, just the spiritual wounds of having your soul assaulted by the malevolent. Forgive me, but partly I have come here today to assess whether you are, in fact, yourself."

"And am I?"

He held my gaze for a moment, his bird eyes considering me through his spectacles. "I believe so, yes. If you feel able to resume your work on the case, then you are free to do so. However, my warnings about the risks you face remain. If you were deliberately attacked right here in the centre of Cardiff, it's possible you are getting close to some answers, but you might also be getting close to someone pinning you down in a runic circle of your own. I do not wish to have to visit your mother's house in Dulwich burdened with the news that she has lost her other son."

I swung my legs around off the bed and, after a few moments, tried to stand. The room lurched to-and-fro a couple of times, then pulled itself together and resumed its usual square solidity.

"How do you feel?" asked the Crow.

"Fine. Good as ever."

"Very well. But if you're called out again, make sure you follow procedure. Don't attempt to approach a malevolent or any other sort of supernatural hostile without backup in place. I have your word?"

"Yes."

"Very well."

I spent thirty minutes at my desk catching up on events via MORIARTY and email. My phone had lost its charge some time back, and I plugged it in to my work computer to boot it up. Within a minute I was getting a series of notifications from Zubrasky, now back on duty. She started out saying she needed to speak to me urgently. Then, as I failed to reply, her messages became more and more concerned. The growing worry in her words was clear; she'd clearly heard what had taken place at in the churchyard. I felt bad at not replying – but also touched. She appeared to be genuinely troubled by my unresponsiveness. With no other contacts in the Office, she'd have no way of finding out the truth.

I pinged off a message immediately telling her not to worry. Her response came back quickly, asking to meet up as soon as possible. Her message included two exclamation marks and even one or two frivolous emojis, something she'd certainly never used before in our communications. I found myself smiling as I reread her words. We agreed to meet in an hour's time in the city centre café we usually used for our off-the-record assignations.

There were also several messages from Olwen providing me with updates on the case – which unfortunately contained very little of use. She'd been keeping an eye on Gilroy, and he hadn't left his dungeon since I'd returned him. There'd been no manifestations of the Librarian above ground. Olwen had requested CCTV footage from stores and the pedestrianised shopping street near St John's Churchyard, which she'd studied for suspicious characters lurking in the little park, or hurrying through carrying a likely-looking package. She'd found nothing of interest.

She *had* found me a copy of the relevant edition of the Mabinogion, which was in my drawer with a yellow post-it note stuck to it. I leafed through the book, but nothing leapt out at me. There was no handwritten inscription on the title page. I held the paper up to the light, hoping some clue might make itself apparent. I set the book aside to look at later. Perhaps reading through the wild and magical stories within it would lead me to some revelation I'd so far missed.

I took my time strolling into the city centre, past the decorated walls of Cardiff Castle and down to my flat. It was good to be out in the open air; I could feel a little of the cotton wool in my head dissipating. I hadn't been completely honest with Hardknott-Lewis, which was turning into something of a pattern: I felt pretty dreadful from my ordeal. My head throbbed and every movement was an effort. My limbs felt like they were made of lead, as if *I* were an animated statue. Perhaps not too surprisingly given what I'd been through, I felt like death. My hope was that a quick shower and a change of clothes would see me ready to meet Zubrasky.

She rose to meet me as I came to her table, and she embraced me with an unexpected warmth. For the briefest moment I felt the swell of her breasts pressed against my chest. I tried not to notice it.

"I thought we'd lost you," she said. "From what DI Robbins said, you appeared to be dead when they carried you out of the park."

"I was attacked and overwhelmed by a malevolent spirit. It knocked me out until this morning."

"Sounds like my typical Saturday night."

This time, I bought the coffees. I also treated myself to something sweet and sticky, thinking some blood sugar was probably a good idea. Perhaps it was the aroma of coffee, but I was suddenly starving. I bought a pastry for Zubrasky, too, but she only nibbled at it and I eventually ended up eating both.

"I don't have a lot of fresh intel to give you," I said, "what with my soul wandering the unmapped pathways of the shadow realms and all. I *can* tell you the Assay of Martha Ndidi revealed a similar pattern to that of Cornwallis: two unknown figures, probably one man and one woman. Only one was a user, as Ndidi was herself."

"No useful IDs?"

"Nope. I'm fairly sure Martha was killed in the room where

we found her and, for what it's worth, it looks like one of the two perpetrators can draw trees nicely. Other than that, we're no further forwards. The memories we recovered were indistinct."

"Okay, well, while you've been sleeping peacefully, I've been doing some work. There are things going on here I really need to understand."

"I'll do what I can."

She glanced around, making sure no one was eavesdropping, then leaned a little closer. The hubbub of voices and clatter of cups provided another good backdrop of white noise.

"Firstly," she said, "we managed to get into Cornwallis's phone."

"I didn't know you had his phone. The killers didn't take it? If they were looking for contacts, it would be the obvious thing to do."

"We found it down the back of his sofa. They didn't know it was there, although from what you've told me they'd have been able to find it easily enough if they'd tried. Perhaps they simply weren't interested; they had all they wanted with the eyes."

"And you managed to break into his phone using a special Police backdoor exploit?"

"There are no secret Police backdoors into modern phones. At least, if there are, they aren't available to a DI in the Welsh Police. We used his fingerprint to unlock the phone."

"Right, of course. Just as well he didn't secure his phone with a retina scan. What did you find?"

"Cornwallis was careful; it seems to me he thought his phone might be compromised. There were no contacts stored, and he'd either wiped his logs or had never made any calls or sent any texts. There were no photographs on the device and no social media apps."

"But you got something."

"He used the same secure messaging app we do, and there was a snatch of conversation there. A group conversation, with four participants."

"With names?"

"Sure." She took out her own phone and consulted a screenshot. "Pwyll, Branwen, Manawydan and Olwen.

Manawydan was Cornwallis. Do those names mean anything to you?"

Olwen obviously rang a bell. But it was a common enough name in the Principality, and surely if our Olwen were involved in this conspiracy, she wouldn't have used her real name. "They're Welsh names," I said, "but you probably know that."

"They are all also characters from the *Mabinogion*, as you'd know if you'd properly embraced the culture that has welcomed you to its bosom. Pwyll is the Prince of Dyfed, Branwen marries the King of Ireland, Manawydan is Branwen's brother and Olwen is the beautiful daughter of a giant. They got their code names from the book they were reading."

"Are all the women in the book defined by their relationship to men?"

"How dare you; this is one of the central artefacts of my cultural heritage."

"Okay, so there was a conversation recorded on the app?"

"A snatch of one. I'd guess all previous messages had been removed, but Manawydan – Cornwallis – didn't have time to tidy up this one."

She showed me the screen grab on her phone. The brief conversation went:

> Manawydan: They're here they've come for me. Get underground. Branwen, I'm so sorry, I think I saw you. May be traceable.

> Olwen: Get out of there.

> Pwyll: Make for safe house.

> Manawydan: No time. Protect Myrddin. Protect yourselves. Goodbye my friends.

> Olwen: No.

The chat app conversation ended there, I read it several times, making sense of it. "So, he'd met Branwen. I guess that must be Martha."

"That's how I see it. Cornwallis was apologising to her because he thought his recent visual impressions could lead them to her. You'll notice she doesn't reply."

I tried to fit these new fragments of information into the puzzle in my mind. "Assuming they used pseudonyms matching their identified genders, Pwyll and Olwen may be the two others in Martha's picture: Oliver Auchter and the unknown woman. Maybe Martha was offline or didn't pick up the message at the time. Mobile signals are pretty bad out there. This makes it seem like Auchter and the other woman are potential victims here, not the two we're seeking."

"I agree."

"No way of tracking down locations for Pwyll and Olwen from IP addresses?"

"Even if we could get injunctions for that data to be released, an IP address isn't going to tell us much. As well as anything else they were probably careful, used proxies."

I read through the messages again, looking for anything I'd missed. "Who do you figure this *Myrddin* is?"

"That is *so* not how that word is pronounced. He's the Welsh equivalent of Merlin."

"Okay, but whose code name is that?"

"I was hoping you'd be able to tell me," said Zubrasky. "Some kind of leader of their group, someone powerful but also someone they need to protect. Any idea who that might be?"

Once again, I had to disappoint her. "No, but I can tell you one interesting thing about the magic they use to steal visual memories: the recollections have to be relived in real time, going backwards from the point of death. You can't fast rewind them like a movie. So, the fact that the deaths of Cornwallis and Ndidi were three days apart suggests those two had met roughly three days prior to Cornwallis's murder. It took the killers that long to identify Martha's whereabouts."

Zubrasky absorbed that. "Cornwallis was at Martha's house three days prior to his death, or they met somewhere else and Cornwallis saw her address written down or a picture of her house or something."

"I think so. My guess is that it was pretty exceptional for

them to meet in the open. They knew they were being pursued, and they went to a lot of trouble to keep everything anonymous. When they met, supposedly for their reading group meetings, they probably kept their features hidden. Sat in the dark while they talked, wore masks or blindfolds."

"They knew about this visual impression magic you've described," said Zubrasky.

I nodded. "Which explains the lack of recent photographs, the code names, all the rest of it. From what I know of Cornwallis and Martha, the picture of all four of them together is several years old. My guess is that they learned about the risks of the optogram spell and stopped meeting openly, did what they could to keep each other's appearances out of their recent visual memories."

"Martha and Oliver couldn't do that. They lived together."

"It must have been hard for them," I said. "They knew they were endangering each other just by being together. They were links in a chain, and they knew that if one of them was found they could lead the killers onto the next person."

Something was troubling Zubrasky. "That doesn't make sense, though. Three days went by between Cornwallis sending his frantic message and Martha's murder. Why didn't she run for her safe house in all that time? If her net connection was that unreliable, they wouldn't have relied on it."

"There may have been a delay, but I think she did leave," I said. "I assume you noted the lack of a toothbrush in the bathroom, for instance. I think she did pack and go."

"Very good, Acolyte Shahzan, it's almost like you're doing police work. Why do you think she went back?"

"My guess is, she made the same calculation we have, and went to try and lay a trap for her pursuers."

"But it didn't work out; she underestimated them."

"That's my guess."

"Where was Auchter in all this? Surely he'd have tried to stop her."

"Maybe he tried. Maybe he was too far away to intervene. I don't know," I said. "We have to track Auchter and the other woman down, to protect them and to find out who they're protecting."

Zubrasky's frown made it clear she wasn't hopeful.

"Except now they've gone underground. If I were them, I'd have made sure we each had a safe house the others knew nothing about so they couldn't be traced. They could be anywhere, always assuming they haven't been killed already and we don't know about it yet."

She was right; finding two users who didn't want to be found wasn't going to be easy. "You got nothing from facial recognition of the woman?" I asked.

"Nothing useful. No close matches, too many distant ones."

"Anything else useful come to light on their computers?"

"Nothing. They covered their tracks well."

"There may be something at Ndidi and Auchter's house giving us a clue about where he might have gone."

"We'll look," said Zubrasky, "but I think it's unlikely; they knew they were a terrible risk to each other simply by being a couple. They'd have made damn sure they put each other in as little danger as possible."

"Do you think that was Cornwallis's safe house? The derelict building he was killed in?"

"Must have been," said Zubrasky. "He learned they were coming for him and ran to ground. Maybe they were tracking him and followed him there."

"I guess a derelict building makes sense for a safe house, but he would have needed a new place once it was demolished."

Zubrasky took a mouthful of her coffee. "There's another thing."

"This is the bit where you give me the good news, right?"

"More bad, I'm afraid. We recovered some DNA from both murder scenes."

A trickle of dread seeped through me. This was a subject she was reluctant to get to. "You identified someone?" I asked.

"No; none of it matched the DNA of any known suspect or criminal. The thing is, we obviously recorded all our findings very carefully, properly tagged and tracked in case they're needed in court. Yesterday, I happened to be looking at the results again, and I noticed a discrepancy."

"Someone has removed evidence?"

"It was subtler than that; someone has tampered with it, modifying DNA records in subtle but extensive ways so they would never match other samples from the same individuals. It was lucky I even noticed; whoever did it knew their way around the system, knew how to make it look like timestamps hadn't been altered and so on."

"You said *individuals*."

"Two individuals. We went back to the original lab results and confirmed they were very probably the same two people."

"The killers."

"Seems likely," said Zubrasky. "Certainly, one was female, and one was male, but we definitely have no matches on them in our database."

"But it's possible your existing records have been tampered with, which means there's no way of getting a reliable ID."

"And if evidence has been altered, it would never be admissible in court, anyway. Either the samples were tampered with because we already have DNA from the two suspects, or the killers calculated we might acquire identifiable DNA at some point and wanted to cover their tracks."

"Have you ever come across anything like this before? How is it even possible?"

"That's just it," said Zubrasky. "It isn't possible. Our records can't be tampered with. Which is why I'm here talking to you."

Her frank stare made it pretty clear what she was saying. She'd implied more than once in our time together she thought we had a backdoor into HOLMES, even if she'd never come out and said so. Now she was saying exactly that.

"You're suggesting someone from the Office has tampered with police evidence."

"I know I'm not going to get you to admit that the Office can access our systems, but I can see no other explanation for what's happened. I don't know whether they used magic or technology to do it, but that must be what's happened."

"*If* that's what's happened, it certainly wouldn't have been done by magical interference. I told you, we don't do things like that. That's the opposite of what we do."

"It doesn't matter much, does it? I'm sorry, Danesh, it's genuinely lovely to see you alive and well, but I think we've reached the point of declaring this case *ultra judice*. We get precious little cooperation from the Office as it is, and now it seems you're doing all you can to thwart our investigation." I'd never seen her angry; she was always the calm and resourceful police officer. Now her eyes flashed with controlled indignation.

"I'm honestly not doing anything to thwart your investigation," I said. "I'm doing all I can to help you."

She conceded the point with a nod of her head. "I truly believe you are. I don't think it's you, but I do think it's *someone* in the Office. Maybe several people. The problem is, I don't even know who your colleagues are, do I? I only know about you and Hardknott-Lewis and Kerrigan. How can I even begin to investigate you? How on earth can I trust you?"

"You can, I promise you, you can. We're on the same side here."

"I'm sorry, I don't see it. I realise you're just my point of contact in all this, but if you were an ordinary member of the public, I'd probably caution you for obstructing a police officer. Of course, I can't, because you have immunity. But I *can* wash my hands of the case, and that's what I've decided to do. I'll get the process kicked off today. Whatever's going on here, it's nothing I can help you with."

I made one desperate attempt to reason with her. I may even have unleashed what I fondly imagined was a winning smile. "We have to work together. Regular crimes have been committed here."

She was having none of it. My smile bounced off her shields. "Sorry, Danesh, I'm sure we'll work together on future cases, but until the Office sorts itself out, you're on your own."

16 – Pale Sisters

Rather than risk the escape of the sorcerer and his books of malign incantations, we burned the house to the ground with him inside it. By the morning, all that was left of the malefactor was dust and ash. All thought it a good night's work.

–Sister Agneish Faygold, *Accounts*, 1686

Olwen intercepted me on the way down through the Office's corridors to the Vault. From the folders she was carrying, it looked like she was hurrying off to some mission-planning meeting. The poor soul.

"It's good to see you back," she said. "How are you feeling?"

"I'm good. Thanks for covering for me."

"I didn't do much in the end. The phone lines have been pretty crazy in the aftermath of Hallowe'en."

"You've cut your hair," I said. Her locks normally flowed down to the small of her back; when she braided it into a ponytail, it lashed around like a striking serpent.

"It was getting in the way during combat; this is much more practical."

I thanked her for the copy of the *Mabinogion* she'd bought. "How much do I owe you?"

"Nothing. I let the Welsh taxpayer buy it."

"You knew I was looking for that particular edition?" I tried not to sound like I was questioning her; so far as I recalled, I hadn't asked her to get me a copy.

She didn't appear to notice my suspicion. "I read on MORIARTY that you thought it was significant; I thought a copy might be useful."

Was it possible there was some ulterior motive to her action? I dismissed the idea pretty quickly. She was trying to be helpful, that was all. She certainly looked nothing like the Olwen in the photograph. She went for innocent, smiling assassin rather than Queen of the Goths.

"Thanks," I said. "It could be."

"You think they were using it to communicate somehow? Or using it as a sign to identify themselves?"

"Most likely, it was just a cover story for their reading group."

Kerrigan pushed by and Olwen let him past before stepping closer to me. "They might be able to alter their appearances, change their faces. Some users can do that, right, even in photographs? Maybe that was why they needed the books as proof of who they were."

She was always intrigued by the details of the magical secrets kept from her – just as I was with the arcane knowledge kept from me. She was correct, too: some users could radically alter their features. It had made more than one case extremely tricky to solve. And she made a good point: could I rely on the appearance of Auchter and the unknown woman I'd seen in the photograph? Except, neither Cornwallis nor Ndidi had attempted to mask their true appearance. Such magic faded when the caster died and could no longer maintain the illusion.

"You figure the other two are users as well?" I asked the question even though I was already convinced they were.

"They must be a secretive cabal intent on doing *something* bad," said Olwen. "Don't you think?"

"Probably, yes. Which is going to make tracking them down all the harder."

She set off to leave, then turned back. "Oh, I looked into the Pale Sisters, too, but I couldn't find a whole lot on them. The odd mention here and there."

"I found out a few useful things from Hardknott-Lewis," I said. Something else occurred to me, then. "Tell me, did you mention to him I was looking into the Librarian and the Sisters? He seemed to know all about it."

Olwen shrugged. "I was getting nowhere, so I mentioned to him what you were researching. Is that a problem?"

"No, of course not. I appreciate the trouble you've gone to."

She flashed me a smile and hurried off to her meeting.

The LED blinked green as I swiped my card through the

reader. The lock clicked innocently, as if it had never dreamed of refusing me admission. The brand name on the lock system was, I noticed for the first time, *Cerberus*. It seemed apt. I had been admitted to the underworld.

This time I deliberately made as much noise as possible rather than creeping along. I did not want the Librarian to come leaping at me from one of the high bookshelves, blade first.

"Lady Coldwater. It's Danesh! Can we talk again?"

There was no answer. I kept walking and calling, working hard to keep any note of tension from my voice. I simply wanted to ask a colleague a question. There was no need for anyone to lose a limb.

"Lady Coldwater, I wanted to thank you for the optograms!"

A figure appeared at the far end of the bookshelf corridor, silhouetted against the light. From the deliberate way she drew a blade slung across her back and held it aside for me to see, I knew it had to be the Librarian. She stood for a moment more, considering, then stepped forwards.

I resisted the urge to flee and, instead, walked towards her, being sure to keep my hands visible. It was hard to escape the notion that we were Wild West gunfighters, except I wasn't armed, and my opponent was. I did what my training taught me to do: keep talking, sound reasonable and reassuring.

"Thank you for your note. It's been very useful."

She didn't reply but continued to stride towards me. So far as I knew, she'd never actually killed one of her colleagues for daring to enter her domain – but maybe they suppressed such stories to stop us from worrying.

The bookshelves on either side loomed larger and larger over me. I didn't fancy my chances of climbing up them to get away. I kept talking, kept moving. "We've had two victims now, both with their eyes surgically removed. I think you're right that visual memories are being magically harvested. It looks like a trail is being followed, a chain of contacts leading to someone who doesn't want to be found."

She stopped two yards short of me. I was momentarily relieved – until I grasped that was the perfect distance for her to lunge with the short Japanese sword she carried.

"So, I wanted to thank you," I finished lamely.

She finally spoke, her voice as hard as glass. "I heard you the first time. Why are you still here talking to me?"

"I wanted to discuss some other things. If you have the time."

"What other things?" The overtones of threat in her voice were very clear. She did not like to be questioned. She did not trust me at all. She was one of us, but she was also one of the Pale Sisters – which meant that on some level she considered me an enemy and an oppressor.

The temptation to mumble something incomprehensible and leave was strong. But I couldn't do that. "I want to know why you took Gilroy from his cell on Sunday."

Her hand flinched, as if she were having to make an effort to stop herself going for me. "That is no concern of yours."

With an effort I kept my voice level, my expression blank. "If it's relevant to my investigation, then it is my concern."

She took a final step closer, inside my reach. She could gut me with a single stabbing movement from her blade. The word was she spent an hour each day honing her weapons' edges to a razor perfection. "It is not your business. Turn around and leave."

"Where did you go with Gilroy? Where did you take him the other times?"

She moved closer still, putting her face close to mine. The breath through her nose tickled my chin. Her voice was almost a whisper when she replied. "You think Gilroy and I are your killers? Those two hooded and cloaked figures?"

"You know about the killers?"

"I have full access to MORIARTY just as you do, and I can read. Are you really accusing me of being one of them?"

Did I think she and Gilroy might be the killers? The timing was all wrong; Martha had been killed many hours before the Librarian had taken Gilroy out. Then there was the history of the Pale Sisters: the Crow had been very clear that they despised the use of such cruel magic.

"No," I said. "I do not think that."

"Then I've given you all the help I can."

She wasn't going to confide in me, and there was very little I could do to make her. She was hiding something; she hadn't attempted to deny the truth of her excursions with Gilroy, but probably not even Hardknott-Lewis could force her to explain what she was up to. She'd helped me with her single word clue, but it had been grudging, a bare minimum.

"Is there something else?" she asked. "Was there a forbidden book you wished to consult perhaps?"

She had to have answers to some of the questions whirling around in my head. As well as the case, there was the whole vexed question of my family history, and whether her records revealed anything about the deaths of my grandfather, father and brother. I didn't have many places left to go to find answers. In the dim light, her unblinking eyes were points of light, needle-sharp and implacable. They watched me to see what I would do.

I was about to turn and leave, defeated. But, instead, I heard myself saying, "There is one other thing. It's my mother. I think she might be the victim of a longstanding and potent magical curse."

The Librarian didn't move – but it was in the tense, ready-to-strike way that a fencer or a cobra didn't move. "Why are you telling me this?"

She thought I was testing her to gauge what her reaction would be. I said, "Because I know something of the history of the Pale Sisters. I thought you might know of ways to remove such a curse without risking anyone. There might be healing magic the Office doesn't approve of."

"Does the Lord High Witchfinder know you are here asking me about this?"

"Hardknott-Lewis knows I'm here to pursue my investigations into the eye killers; he doesn't know anything about my mother."

"You're sure about that are you?"

"If he knew I'd failed to report her, I wouldn't be walking around free."

"You are asking me to commit a severe magus law crime."

I had no way of knowing if I could trust her – there was every chance I could not – but I had nowhere else to go, no one else I could talk to. I should have reported my mother days ago and by not doing so I'd damned myself, committed a grave sin against the Office. "I'm committing a magus law crime by asking you. And – unless I'm wrong – this is what you do, isn't it? The Office turns a blind eye so long as you don't stray too far over the line."

She thought for a moment more, considering me. Then she turned on her heel and headed back between the high bookshelves. "Come with me," she called over her shoulder. Her blade was still in her hand, but at least she hadn't drawn my blood this time.

She led me to a hexagon of desks in the open space from which the bookshelves radiated in lines like the spokes of a wheel, allowing her to keep an eye on the whole floor. It was also clearly where she sat and worked: three books lay open on the desks, their contents illuminated by lamps. There was also a notepad, its top page half-filled with dense handwriting. I'd interrupted her in the act of some arcane research. Seeing my interest in the illustrations contained within the books, she slammed each volume shut with a deliberate thud.

"Come around here."

Inside the ring of desks there was a chair, and a low camp bed with a blue sleeping bag draped across it. She preferred to keep a watchful eye on the tomes in her protection than to sleep anywhere more comfortable. Some sort of weapon, a staff with a curved blade at one end, leaned against the bed. Underneath the single pillow peeped the handle of a dagger.

She said, "Sit, and tell me about this curse. Start at the beginning, and leave nothing out."

The wooden chair was uncomfortable to sit on, creaking as I shifted around. "Are you saying you can help me?"

"I'm not saying that at all. I want to know what I'm dealing with."

Now she was testing me. The problem was I didn't know if she was deciding whether she could trust me, or if she was extracting a confession to take to Hardknott-Lewis.

I could have said nothing, but then I'd be stuck in the same dead end. I didn't tell her everything, but I told her enough. My family history, the things my mother had written, the things Gilroy had said. Lady Coldwater sat impassively throughout, taking in every word.

When I'd finished, she said, "Do you have that notebook of your mother's here in the office?"

"It's at home."

"It needs to be in the Vault. Bring it to me when you can for safekeeping."

"Can you help her? Is there any hope?"

She thought for a moment longer, then, some decision reached, all wiry energy, flew into sudden activity. "Wait here."

She strode off, heading down one of the lines of bookcases. Maybe she was going to fetch Hardknott-Lewis and the others. She'd collected the evidence about me, recorded me for all I knew, and now they'd be coming for me to take me away for my Star Chamber hearing and my walk through the broom cupboard to Oblivion. Still, I didn't move, didn't attempt to make a run for it. If that was going to happen, there was nowhere I could run to.

Her footsteps faded away, and the Vault became a very quiet place: the watchful hush of so many books waiting for someone to read them. I sat in the bubble of light at the centre of the floor, a spider waiting on a web. Or, more accurately, a trapped fly. If I'd wanted, I could have leafed through the tomes the Librarian hadn't wanted me to see. I didn't move. Just possibly she'd decided she could trust me, a little, and I didn't want to do anything to jeopardise that.

A few minutes later, a door slammed somewhere, and I heard her returning. In the shadowy light I could see she was carrying something. She strode up to the desks and dropped her burden: a pile of tattered Manilla folders bound with string. She untied the knot on the top one with a practised flick of her hand.

"What do these have to do with my mother?" I asked.

"They are the private accounts of some of those involved in the battles with English Wizardry adepts, as well as one or two reports retrieved from those that fought on the other side. I want to see if there is any mention of your grandfather. I don't recall the name, but perhaps there's something." She'd lost some of her spikiness as she described the papers.

"There was an organised opposition to the group?"

She perched a pair of silver-framed reading glasses on her nose and began to study the papers. She'd set her blade down on the desk, but the act did little to put me at ease. She could grab it in a moment if she chose to. "There was not; there was a ragtag collection of individuals and groups who despised English Wizardry but who, unfortunately, found it hard to unite to form a coherent counterforce. The Office of the Witchfinder, for example, refused to cooperate with magic users on what you might, loosely, call the light side."

"Peter Warder said the opposition coalesced around Arthur Stonewall, the *Destroyer*, in the early days."

"Warder is correct."

"The Pale Sisters were involved in the struggle?"

Some of her former frostiness returned to her voice. "As you know, the Pale Sisters haven't existed for a long time. Those sympathetic to the tradition were involved, certainly. Many people were involved; there was much bloodshed."

I kept her talking. "Perhaps you could persuade Gilroy to tell you more. He must have been one of the English Wizardry adepts."

She regarded me for a moment over the top of her reading glasses. Her look bled from disapproval to something like sympathy. "You really don't know anything, do you? All of you upstairs are the same. Misguided at best, idiotic at worst. Gilroy wasn't on the side of English Wizardry; if he encountered your grandfather as he claimed, then it was because they were fighting on the same side."

"Gilroy?"

"Of course. Why not Gilroy?"

"But he just, I don't know, he just seemed the type to be into all that true British native shit."

"Did he ever give you any good reason to think that?"

"He laughed at the idea of me, a Shahzan, being a witchfinder."

"Because he was with your grandfather when the Office came hunting them, and the irony of that wasn't lost on him. And did you assume the same about me because Gilroy and I have worked together? Do you think I'm some kind of white supremacist, too?" Her stare was as sharp as one of her blades. All of her former antipathy was back in her features. There was anger there, too, anger someone might think that of her.

"No, I don't think that," I said, and not just because she was so well-armed. Her outrage at the suggestion was perfectly clear.

"I'm very pleased to hear it. For your information, Gilroy suffered a great deal at the hands of English Wizardry. He was only captured by the Office because he was at death's door and couldn't fight back when the witchfinders came for him. He had very little ability with magical combat, but still he fought, putting himself in danger again and again."

"I didn't know. He's always so angry with me."

"He's been locked in a dungeon for many years for no good reason. That might have something to do with it."

"He committed crimes under magus law. He was offered imprisonment as an alternative to Oblivion." My words sounded like those of a child to my ears.

"You think that's a choice, do you? You know nothing of what you're talking about. Now be quiet while I read."

I sat and said no more while she leafed through the papers. Occasionally, she made a little grunt of acknowledgement at something she read and scribbled a few words in her notebook. She read quickly, working her way through the pile of papers.

After maybe twenty minutes she closed the last file and removed her glasses to consider me. "There are several mentions of your grandfather. He was clearly active in the struggles against English Wizardry after the Second World War. I think it's highly likely they were responsible for his death. He was a non-white wizard from an overseas tradition, and he was implacable in his opposition to them. They hunted him down and murdered him. He had to know the risks, but he didn't let that stop him. I think he was a very brave man. You should be proud to be his grandson."

"I am."

"Good." She picked out one of the papers from the top binder. "Here, for instance, is a page from the diary of Edward Gravesend, an English Wizardry adept active before and after the war. Gravesend was notoriously brutal; he and his coterie pursued their enemies ruthlessly. The passage mentions a Shahzan briefly, and from the date it's very likely to be your grandfather. Would you like to hear?"

I nodded my assent and Lady Coldwater began to read. Her voice remained coolly impassive throughout.

In the East End of London, we were ambushed by a motley assortment of mongrel tricksters and mumblers who thought their degenerate practices would be a match for high English spellpower. They'd planned to kill us all, but we soon showed them the errors of their ways. Most we didn't know, although one or two we'd met before. The voodooist Okonkwo was there, as was the Hindoo, Shahzan. Shamefully there were also several white wizards among them, betraying their brethren by siding with the lesser races.

The fight was brief but decisive. We captured Okonkwo while the rest of his pack scuttled off like cockroaches. We received a few minor wounds, although Digbeth was briefly troubled by a nasty little animist curse that sent fire blazing through his nerves until Jansen dispelled it.

Later we had our fun with Okonkwo. Peeble held him within a powerful circle while I unleashed a swarm of Bloodcrawlers through the cavities of his body. He was soon reduced to his natural level: a screaming animal begging for release. We refused to give it to him. We kept him alive for the best part of an hour while the voracious imps ate away at him from the inside. His cries and sobs were most amusing to hear as we sampled some fine whisky Jansen had brought south from his travels in Scotland.

"I deliberately left out several regrettable words," said the Librarian when she'd finished. "No doubt you can work out what they might be."

I could, of course. "The summoning of Bloodcrawlers is dangerous magic," I said, "requiring great skill. They're vicious things, hard to control." I'd never seen them used, but my training had been very clear on them. The agonies they inflicted were like having your nerve pathways filled with sulphuric acid.

"Don't be fooled by English Wizardry's aristocratic associations," said the Librarian. "There were many powerful adepts within their ranks. Most of them were charlatans, there to be seen in the right circles, but some were genuinely fearsome. Family libraries dating back hundreds of years, and the time and resources to practise, account for that. One or two of them were graced with rare power."

"And my father? Is there any mention of him in the accounts?"

"No, but it's possible Gravesend's cabal or some other

group of English Wizardry adepts decided to wipe out your grandfather's entire line. Your father, your brother."

"Then why not me?"

"Perhaps your childish game did save you. Perhaps if it had been your brother's turn to hide that day then it might be him sitting here today, trying to discover how his long-lost twin Danesh died."

"Or they simply decided I wasn't worth killing as I have no magical potential."

She took that comment with a frown of contempt. "If you think that then you know nothing about them. It's more likely that particular cabal was wiped out by an opposing group before they could get to you. Or perhaps they've been biding their time, regrouping, waiting for the right moment. And here you are, investigating a case in which English Wizardry appear to be involved. The danger to you is extreme."

Now she sounded like Hardknott-Lewis. At least she appeared to have decided she could trust me. "Will you tell me now where you went with Gilroy on Sunday?"

She considered for a moment, then said, "First tell me where you are up to with your investigation."

"I'm searching for two individuals who I believe might be the next targets of the killers."

"And why do you wish to find them?"

That was a strange question. "To prevent further magus law crimes being committed. To stop and perhaps capture for trial the English Wizardry adepts responsible."

"And what of the two potential victims? You wish to put a stop to them, too? You must know they are also adepts."

"So far as I know, they haven't committed any crimes. I'm trying to protect them, not punish them. Even if they are users, there are… degrees of contravention. Some crimes are worse than others."

She looked amused at my comment. "Oh, they are? I don't recall it saying that anywhere in magus law statute."

"I'm concerned with preventing serious crimes here, not victim-blaming."

"But if you found these two potential victims, you would also have to arrest them, wouldn't you? See them tried?"

"I honestly haven't thought about it."

She considered me for a moment more. She stood. Her

hand went to the knife she'd left next to her notebook on the desk. Before I could react, she had the blade pointing towards me. Despite her years, she was whiplash fast when it came to combat.

"What are you doing?"

"Give me your hand."

"Why?"

"Just give it to me. You'll get it back."

Warily, I submitted. She grabbed my hand and turned my palm face upwards. "Stop struggling, boy. Let me work."

"What are you doing?" I repeated.

She jerked my hand to make me comply. "Do you want my help or don't you? Stop fussing; it won't hurt."

I forced myself to relax. When she drew the edge of her blade across my palm it did sting, despite her words. In fact, it stung like hell. I refused to let it show on my face. Blood welled from beneath the flap of skin she'd raised, purple-red on my skin. She lifted my hand to her face as if she were smelling me, then, before I could object, dipped the pink tip of her tongue into my blood.

"What the...?"

She shut her eyes, waved away my objection with her spare hand. She was tasting my blood, like she might a fine wine. The notes, the aftertaste. I come into contact with a lot of weird and disturbing things, but this was one of the weirdest. Drops of my blood tapped to the stone floor.

When she was done, she opened her eyes. "Interesting," she said.

"What's interesting? What was that all about?"

She passed me a tissue to staunch the flow of blood, then took a sip of water from the plastic bottle on her desk. "Well, we've learned a lot about you today, Danesh Shahzan."

"Like what?"

She looked amused. "For one thing, we've learned you were wrong when you said you had no magical potential. Whatever the reason was for you not being killed along with you brother, it wasn't that."

"That's not true."

"Of course it's true, as you must know deep down."

"No."

"Think what you like, you can't hide from reality. Now I

think there's someone you need to meet."

"Who?"

"Follow me."

She hared off between a different set of bookshelves while I sat unmoving for a moment, her words bouncing around in my brain. She couldn't be right. I wasn't a user. I was an acolyte in the Office of the Witchfinder General; I wasn't *allowed* to be a user. Hardknott-Lewis had claimed I had potential, but it had never manifested. She'd made a clear mistake. She'd been alone for too long, down in the dark of the Vault with her slumbering books and her delusions. For all I knew, she imagined them whispering to her, filling her mind with paranoid conspiracies.

Still, the wild conclusions she'd come to appeared to mean she did now trust me. I presumed she was now taking me to meet Gilroy once again. I hoped that this time the two of them would fill me in on what they'd been doing, what they really knew.

Sliding across the desk I set off after her, left fist clutching the tissue she'd given me to control the bleeding. I caught up with her as she was unlocking a door I'd never seen before, on the other side of the room to the entrance. It was a wooden door, heavy and old, and it also had an outer screen of criss-crossing iron bars, like something from a mediaeval castle or a dungeon, built to keep someone captive within. Which puzzled me: this couldn't be Gilroy, because there were no other entrances to his rooms, but I had no idea who else it might be. The Librarian was unlocking the inner door with an oversized key pulled from her pocket. The lock whined a complaint at the intrusion, then yielded.

She pushed the door open. I half expected her captive to come barrelling out, leaping to the attack, or to see a flight of stairs leading down to the unknown mysteries of the books on Level -2.

Neither of my guesses was correct. Instead, when she flicked on the light, there was a short corridor with three doors leading off it.

"It's okay, it's me," she called into the empty corridor, her voice bouncing off the stone walls. After a moment, the handle on one of the doors twisted and the door was pulled open. I caught a glimpse of a little cell, a bed and a chair, but also books and a television screen, and a red rug on the floor.

After a pause, a man stepped out of the room. I recognised who it was immediately. It wasn't Gilroy; it was the man I'd been pursuing. *Pwyll*. Oliver Auchter.

He regarded me warily, his features strained with his weariness and his loss.

17 – Safe Houses

Quis custodiet ipsos custodes – who watches the watchers? The question is as pertinent to the workings of the Office of the Witchfinder General as it is to any other powerful law-enforcement body. In the Office's case, the answer is that it watches itself – or at least that all factions and individuals within it must observe everyone around them, at all times. Our credo must be *semper vigilans*. Always vigilant.

–Earl Grey, Witchfinder General,
Office of the Witchfinder General Handbook, 1999

I didn't speak for a moment, my brain adjusting to the appearance of Oliver Auchter in the Book Vault of the Welsh Office of the Witchfinder General. It was just about the last place in the entire country I'd have thought to look for him – which perhaps explained why it was such a good place to hide. Cornwallis had told them to *get underground* in his last, desperate message, and Auchter had done just that – quite literally secreting himself underneath my own nose, when my nose happened to be in the office.

Auchter stepped closer, keeping his eyes on me, then spoke to Lady Coldwater, not caring that I could also hear. "I don't trust him; he's Hardknott-Lewis's man." His voice was strained to cracking point. He'd been through a lot in the past few days. His life had been turned upside-down: not only were a sect of magical killers trying to find him, they *had* found Martha, the woman he'd lived with and, presumably, loved: found her, and subjected her to a brutal end.

"Maybe he is, and maybe he isn't," the Librarian replied, "but we're going to need him for what is to come. They have to be stopped and there's not enough of us to do it. He has the resources of the Office behind him and that could make all the difference. And his position isn't anywhere near so simple. He's conflicted."

"I am here, you know," I said. "And I am not conflicted. My duty is perfectly clear. I should take this directly to Hardknott-Lewis."

"But you're not going to, are you?" said the Librarian, turning to me. The threat was clear in her voice, even though this time she wasn't relying on anything as obvious as a sharp knife.

"Why shouldn't I?"

"For many reasons. The fact is, you, Oliver and I are dispensable. There are greater events taking place; a long war for the soul of magic use in this country is being fought, and that is what matters. Sometimes you have to ignore personal animosities and pick a side, as I believe you will do. This war we're fighting is one that we thought we'd won, but suddenly our whole side is facing obliteration. That's what matters. You've seen what it's like out there. English Wizardry and people who think the same way are suddenly on the march: active, triumphant, marching to old drumbeats and turning back the tide of civilisation. We cannot let that happen."

"We have to maintain the rule of magus law," I said. "Without that, everything breaks down."

"But what if magus law is not enough? What if the Office is weak, out of touch and has been deliberately stretched too thin to handle what is coming?"

"We'll manage," I said. "We always have, through the darkest times. We draw the line and the demons can't cross it. Why do you keep saying *what is coming?* And what is Auchter doing here with you when the Office and the Welsh police have spent days looking for him? You must have known."

Auchter slumped against one of the walls. He looked too beaten down to object any further. "Tell him," he said. "It hardly makes much difference now."

The Librarian put an arm around him, a curiously tender act. She helped him to his feet, and we made our way back to the centre of the library where we could sit and talk. As we walked, after a few moments, Auchter touched my arm. His voice was cracked. "You saw her at the house? Martha?"

It was painful to look directly into his eyes. I was glad of the low light. "She was taken away before I got there."

"Gilroy told me how she died. How did she look? Was it a bad end?" He'd loved Martha, there could be no doubt. He'd loved her, but hadn't been there to help when the attackers came. He'd failed her.

"She looked peaceful," I said. It was a stupid cliché, but all I could think of to say. He must have known how grim it had really been. Still, he appeared to be grateful. He squeezed my arm and summoned a weak smile.

I said, "Do you know what Cornwallis meant when he said he thought he'd seen Martha? That she'd be traceable?"

Auchter nodded. "She mentioned it on the phone when I spoke to her the last time, two days before Evan sent his message. It was a stupid coincidence, sheer bad luck."

"What happened?"

"Martha was driving home on a narrow road through the Forest of Dean. She came around a corner and there was another car coming at her, no room to overtake. They both braked hard but couldn't avoid each other. In the end it was only a minor bump, but they had to get out, swap details, that sort of thing. Of course, she recognised him immediately, although they both tried to pretend they were strangers."

"Something gave them away."

"Martha did say she'd left her copy of a particular book on the front passenger seat as she drove. It slid into the footwell when she slammed the brakes on, and she had to ferret around to pick it up when she went to look for her insurance details. There's a good chance Evan, and therefore the killers, would have seen it."

"This book would be the edition of the *Mabinogion* you were all reading?"

I could tell from his reaction that he was surprised. "You know about that?"

"The four of you pretended to be in a reading group as cover for your meetings."

"It was Evan's idea; he was into all that fantasy stuff."

Things were starting to make sense to me. Presuming the killers didn't know about the reading group at that point, it meant that someone at Cornwallis's house had seen the book he was reading – as I had – and made the connection when they replayed Cornwallis's stored visual impressions. They'd spotted the same volume in Martha's car and calculated she wasn't just some random stranger. It was an impressive piece of detective work. Worthy of the police – or someone from the Office.

"So, when the killers gained access to Cornwallis's memories," I said, "they would have seen Martha's car number plate and traced it back to where you lived."

"That's my guess," said Auchter. "We all lived in roughly the same area, but it was such bad luck."

"When did this collision take place?"

"On Sunday evening, a week before she was killed."

I thought about that as we made our way down the canyon between the bookcases. The timing worked. Since visual memories could only be rewound in real time, that meant there were three days between the unfortunate collision and the murder of Cornwallis on the Wednesday morning. That gave them until mid-Saturday to step back in time to the collision and identify Martha. I'd been called in early on Sunday, but the date of death had been put at the day before, or very early on the Sunday morning.

We perched on the desks back in the centre of the floor, and the Librarian explained how Auchter had ended up there. "You already know most of what is going on. Our enemies have been tracking us down, one by one. They got to Cornwallis and from there Martha. Oliver was out of the country when Cornwallis sent his desperate message. By the time he returned, it was too late; they already had Martha."

"Why were you out of the country?" I asked.

"Occasionally, we get whispers that our enemies are onto us. In order to protect ourselves, either I or Martha would leave the country for a few weeks, stay out of sight."

"If they got one of you, then they wouldn't be able to quickly identify the other."

"Yes."

"But why did she go back to confront them?"

"It was typical of Martha; she didn't take any shit from anyone," said Auchter. "She resented a lot of the precautions we took. If I'd been there I might have been able to talk her out of it, but she wouldn't accept that they were any match for her. She wanted to fight them."

"In the end he came to find me," said the Librarian. "He was outside waiting for me on Sunday, just standing there near the door with his backpack. I didn't know who he was until he used a code word."

"This is his safe house?"

"It is. An old arrangement. His mother was a Sister."

"I assume Hardknott-Lewis knows nothing about his presence."

"He does not."

"So, you took Gilroy and went to Herefordshire to try and help Martha."

"No, we assumed that it would be too late by then. We went to learn what we could about our enemy. We wanted to perform an Assay of our own, but Hardknott-Lewis was already there, and then you turned up."

"You were watching?"

"From the woods," said Auchter. "There are paths invisible from the road."

"But why did you keep yourselves hidden? We're on the same side here. Why all this secrecy?"

A glance passed between Auchter and the Librarian. Auchter shrugged almost imperceptibly.

"Because," said the Librarian, "we don't know if we *are* on the same side."

"Of course we are. I get you're from a different tradition, but we agree on all the big things."

"And yet, again and again, we are thwarted. Again and again, someone in the Office – perhaps several people – get there ahead of us, or fail to catch the English Wizardry adept, or keep the rest of us in the dark. The Office has been infiltrated; the circle is broken. I don't know who among you I can trust, so I don't trust any of you."

"You don't trust Hardknott-Lewis?"

"I don't trust any of you."

"You trusted me enough to tell me about optograms."

"I gave you that single clue, no more. If I'd given you any less, it might have seemed suspicious. Plus, I wondered about you; I wanted to see what you were really about."

"But now you're confiding in me."

"Oh, I'm still not convinced. I trust you a little now, enough to tell you what I have, but that is all. If I'm wrong, then be very clear that I will use everything I know about you against you."

"I don't believe the Office has been infiltrated by English Wizardry," I said.

"Really? Then you're not looking hard enough. Did you think it was complete coincidence that you were nearly killed by that malevolent spirit?"

I shrugged. "It was bad luck. It happens."

"Don't be ridiculous, it was far too convenient. Someone familiar with Office rosters and agent availability planted that touchstone knowing you would be called out, knowing there was a very good chance it would overwhelm you there and then. It was a murder attempt, pure and simple, staged to look like an accident, using a weapon that the attacker knew would not trouble the regular police or the normal courts. You've been looking for the next potential victim without even realising it could be *you*. I told you, they want you dead, because of who you are and because of the threat you pose to them."

Auchter said, "It doesn't matter who trusts who. We have to get to Olwen before they do."

"Olwen is not *our* Olwen, right?" I said to the Librarian.

"Of course not. The other Olwen will have gone to ground; she needs our help if she's not to be the next victim. Oliver is safe enough here, but she's in all kinds of danger."

"What's her real name?" I asked.

The Librarian hesitated, threw a glance at Auchter. She knew Olwen's true identity, it was clear. But they hadn't decided if they trusted me that much yet.

"If you tell me it may help me to track her down. You've got nothing much to lose at this point."

Auchter visibly sagged, conceding the point, but he answered my question. "We aren't supposed to know each other's real names, but secrets get out. An overheard conversation, a glimpsed letter or word, and slowly you get to know each other. Over a period of several years, Martha and I managed to fall in love despite all our efforts to keep ourselves in the dark. Olwen's true name is Sally Spender."

"Has she ever been known by any other names?"

"Not that I'm aware of, but it's obviously a possibility."

"Did she ever have a thing with Cornwallis?"

"Very briefly. We used to meet under cover of gaming and fantasy conferences, and they had a brief fling at one of them, I believe. We avoided using our real names there as well, of course, went to great lengths to avoid revealing anything material about ourselves. But it became too risky, spending so much time together in the open. That was why we switched to the reading group."

"This mysterious fifth person you're all trying to protect," I said. "Myrddin. Who is he?"

"Truly, I don't know" said Auchter, "I can speculate, but I don't want to prejudice you. I don't know his real name, or what he looks like, or where he is, or whether he's even a *he* at all."

"You were in a chain of contacts. If you needed to pass a message to Myrddin, who was nearest to him?"

"Everything went through Sally; she's the most powerful adept of the four of us."

"Would she know who and where Myrddin is?"

"Maybe, but she'd guard the secret using every power available to her. All that really matters is that we stop English Wizardry reaching Myrddin."

"You all seem prepared to risk your lives to protect this person. Why? What is this all about?"

The Librarian said, "The person we know as Myrddin is a very significant threat to English Wizardry, someone they've battled and pursued for a long time. If they could kill Myrddin there might be no stopping them. The balance would tip. The Office thinks that it keeps the magical peace, but for a hundred years now it has simply benefitted from sitting idly by while the two warring factions cancel each other out. With that battle lost, we would be powerless to prevent the onslaught, the rise of magical fascism in England and the echoes of that in many other areas of national life. It would be like the worst excesses of the Crusades or the British Empire all over again."

Auchter was staring at the ground, his defeat clear in him. He'd been through too much. The Librarian's eyes, by contrast, blazed into me, waiting for me to decide what I would do next.

"So, you know Olwen's real name," I said. "Do you know where her safe house is? We know she saw Cornwallis's warning message and I assume she would have fled immediately."

"She would," said Auchter. "The problem is we were extremely careful not to tell each other where our retreats were. That had to remain a secret even if we let other details slip. Only the three of us in the whole world know I'm here. I didn't even know Martha's safe house; it was perhaps the only secret we kept from each other. It was what we had to do to protect each other. Or try to, at least."

"It's possible I'll be able to track down something about her," I said. "We have her name and her appearance."

"We can do better than searching for her by name," said Auchter.

"How so?"

"Because I know where she normally lives."

That threw me. "Surely you kept that a secret from each other as well?"

"I found out by accident at our last meeting. Actually, that was also because of that stupid book. It's like it's cursed or something."

"What happened?"

"When we met up to discuss current events, we were always very careful. We wore robes and hoods so there was no chance of us revealing each other's appearances. We kept the light low, too, and often sat round a candle while we conversed. We must have looked like full-on fantasy nuts to anyone looking in on us."

"You knew visual memories could be magically recovered from someone's eyes after death."

"We learned about it. We'd obviously all met at the conferences, but we calculated that would be too long ago for the images to be recoverable."

"Why not use sorcery to conceal your appearances? Or talk from afar and not have to meet up in the first place?"

"The use of magic attracts attention. You know that; it's a fact the Office relies on. A few disturbances in the aether and people come sniffing around. There are ways to conceal what you're doing, but it becomes an arms race, a risk, and we wanted to do nothing to attract the attention of our enemies. So long as we made sure we weren't being followed and met on neutral ground, the risk was minimal."

"You could have phoned each other, used your chat app."

"We decided we couldn't trust them. We couldn't be absolutely sure the messages weren't being intercepted, or that one of us hadn't been compromised."

"Where did you meet?"

"Upstairs in a Cardiff pub, a quiet private room where we could talk. Evan thought it made sense to hide in plain view rather than trying to look secretive. Actually, we did talk about books sometimes, too. We always picked good ones. And if anyone asked about the robes or the candle, we could just say it was for an RPG, a bit of cosplay, and they'd think nothing of it."

"Who chose the books you read?"

Auchter seemed puzzled I'd be interested. "It was a joint decision. To be honest, we got through books extremely slowly, because we spent most of our meetings discussing the threats we faced."

"And Evan suggested the *Mabinogion*?"

"He did. Martha wasn't really into fantasy – that was always pretty obvious when we met up at conventions – so it seemed like a way of combining Evan's thing with something, you know, more mainstream, more academic. It was the same with the next book we planned to read."

"Which was?"

"Oscar Wilde's *The Picture of Dorian Gray*. Evan called it a fantasy that respectable literary types could read without feeling guilty. He used to say things like that."

"Did you always buy paperbacks?"

"Always."

"Never ebooks?" I hadn't seen any ereader devices at either murder scene, which made me wonder if the killers had taken them for some reason.

"Not for the reading group. Partly that was because the paperbacks were sort of a sign between us, a passport to get into the group when, maybe, we'd changed our appearances. Also, they could act as a warning: that particular book left somewhere was a clear indication that something was wrong, that personal contact shouldn't be made."

"Do you have any idea how the killers tracked Cornwallis down?"

"There are groups like ours all over the country, trying to cooperate but keeping contact to a minimum at the same time. Between English Wizardry and you in the Office it's a marvel any of us survive. Someone in another group who knew about Evan must have been caught. It's been going on for years."

"Okay, so something happened at your meeting and you discovered where Olwen lived."

"It was her bookmark. Another stupid little thing. She put her copy of the Mabinogion down and I noticed she was using a letter, a water bill I think, to mark her page. When she opened her book, I saw the address. That damn book yet again."

"I wonder," said the Librarian. "There are wide-area misfortune curses. They may have worked one knowing they were closing in."

"So, you saw her address," I said. "Did Evan and Martha notice it too?"

"I don't know. I … oh. Shit."

He'd worked out the significance of my question. If Cornwallis or Martha had caught sight of the address, then the killers would also learn it.

I worked through the timeline in my head. "What day did you meet?"

"It was always a Monday evening thing."

"And what was the address?"

He gave me the number and street of a house in Cardiff. So, the reading group meeting had been – what – eighteen days previously. Cornwallis had been killed nine days ago and Martha six. The killers would have been sure to study the visual footage of the gathering very carefully. If Cornwallis had noticed the address and the fact was spotted in his memories, the murderers would just have had time to get to the address already. But if Cornwallis hadn't spotted it and Martha had, they wouldn't yet have had time to go back through her recollections to the reading group meeting. And if neither had noticed what Auchter had seen, we were still in the clear.

"I'll go there," I said. "Maybe there's some clue about her safe house."

Lady Coldwater narrowed her eyes as she made the same calculations I had. "It's a risk. They might be there waiting for you."

"There's a good chance they're not, in which case we can set a trap for them, try and capture them when they do show up."

"You can't trust anyone else upstairs to go with you. There's no knowing who is on their side."

She was the obvious one to accompany me; she was a

formidable fighter and she knew much more arcane lore than I did – including, no doubt, illegal curses and spells that could prove useful. Even so, I wanted to go alone. Partly it was because I still didn't completely trust *her*, even after all her revelations. She kept telling me to be wary of my colleagues in the Office, and for all I knew that was an elaborate way of distracting my attentions from herself.

There was another reason, too. "I think you should protect Oliver. I don't know who it is we're facing but one of them appears to be a powerful adept. If they come here it could be a battle. You need to stop them."

The Librarian's eyes glinted in the light from the desk lamps. She'd been preparing for just such an eventuality. Her gaze flicked to the books she'd been studying.

"You've been researching the magics required?" I asked.

She admitted it openly. "I have. I'm ready to complete the weaving of the protection spells around Oliver, as well as the warding incantations on the doors to the Vault."

"I assumed you had wards in place already, to keep us out."

"Oh, I do, but now they need strengthening."

"And my mother?" I asked. "Do you think you can help her?"

"There's every chance," said the Librarian.

"If I don't come back, you'll help her?"

"I'll do what I can for her, but it will have to wait until all this is resolved. By the sound of it, she's been struggling with this curse for years. A few more days won't make much difference."

I wanted to say it might make *all* the difference. She was suffering unnecessarily and, worse, if the Office did somehow find out the truth, it might be the end for her. But the Librarian was right; it would have to wait a little longer.

As Lady Coldwater led Auchter back to the relative safety of his refuge to work on weaving her highly illegal spells, I made my way back upstairs. I picked up a few items I thought I might need from my desk and from Supplies, then headed outside to make my way to Sally Spender's house before any of my colleagues could intercept me.

Hardknott-Lewis had instructed me not to enter dangerous situations alone, but it seemed that was exactly what I was going to do.

18 – Something in the Basement

But devils are subservient to certain influences of the stars, because magicians observe the course of certain stars in order to evoke the devils.
　　　　　–Henricus Institoris, *Malleus Maleficarum*, 1487

I strode back to my flat to pick up my car – a somewhat battered and weary Mini that would have been embarrassed to park next to Warder's neat BMW. I could easily have walked to Sally Spender's house, but I wanted to stake the place out first, see who came and went, find out if anyone else was watching it. You were a lot less conspicuous sitting in a car than loitering on the pavement.

Cathedral Road is a long, straight, tree-lined thoroughfare running alongside the parks and fields surrounding the River Taff: Cardiff's own Central Park. The houses are ornate, graceful villas, although many are now businesses rather than dwellings: the offices of dentists and architects, as well as some of the more alternative healing disciplines whose approach to medicine would have Hardknott-Lewis frowning.

The road is almost always lined with cars, especially when there's something on in the city centre, a match or a big concert at the Principality Stadium. It was no different today. Eventually, I managed to squeeze into a spot thirty yards or so up the road from the number Auchter had given me.

I sat for an hour or two, watching the house while also keeping an eye on the streets and cars to see if anyone else was sitting and watching. It was a grey autumnal afternoon, the low light leeching all colour from the world. The normal array of parents pushing buggies, strolling couples and joggers passed by – joined, after about half an hour, by schoolchildren racketing their way home. Everything looked utterly, utterly normal. I had walked and driven down the road a hundred times; strange to think I'd been passing by the house of a powerful adept, living there among us as if it was all perfectly normal. I felt uncomfortable at the notion of it, but it was a confused sense of disquiet. My own discomfort was, in itself, worrying. Perhaps it was some kind of suppressed guilt over my mother's long suffering, or over the way I hadn't reported her condition. Then, again, perhaps it was all to do with my complicity in the Librarian's illegal magic use. A sense of unease crept through my bones at what I was doing, although I couldn't see any better course to take. Doing the right thing sometimes means getting your hands dirty.

I put it all out of my mind and resumed my surveillance, taking care to glance at my phone occasionally so that anyone noticing me might think I was just sending texts or catching up on social media nonsense. I also studied the cars parked along the road to try and work out if any of them might be hers. Over time, cars came and went. Eventually, there were only three that hadn't moved and which were parked vaguely near the house. It might mean nothing, of course. She might not drive, or her car could be elsewhere. I noted down the possible registration numbers anyway, just in case.

I saw nothing suspicious or disturbing on the street, or at least nothing any more suspicious or disturbing than was usual on a damp Cardiff afternoon. No one entered or left Spender's house. The street was a stage, waiting for the action to begin. The day wore on, the road becoming busier as the working day ended. It was time to act, before there were too many people around. It looked like the shadowy killers hadn't yet tracked down the address, but the longer I waited, the greater the risk was of them doing so. I slipped on a pair of cotton gloves so that I wouldn't leave any fingerprints at the scene that the police could recover. I would be sloughing off plenty of DNA as I moved through the house, which I could do nothing about, but I wanted to avoid depositing any obvious identifying marks.

As agents of the Witchfinder General, we have, like the police, the power to enter buildings we consider to be suspicious or the possible scenes of a crime. Unlike the police, we can do so without approval or any kind of paperwork. It's probably a contravention of no end of human rights legislation, but many such noble efforts at social progress have passed us by, on account of the fact that so few people know we are even a thing. It often comes in useful.

Another advantage we have over the police is that we don't need to resort to battering rams and all that shouting to smash through a locked doorway. We have another piece of m/tech that makes the whole thing so much easier and less conspicuous: ensorcelled devices colloquially called *sesames*, capable of achieving the same thing much more discreetly. Essentially, they operate by persuading the lock – or any similar-sized mechanism – that they don't exist for a few moments. It makes the operation a simple matter of timing. Activate the stored magical power of the device and push the door open in the same smooth action. The lock mechanism winks out of and back into existence, and the door can be opened during the brief disappearance. In fact, as I understand it, the locks don't disappear so much as temporarily translocate to an alternative plane. Somewhere in another realm of reality there have to be some very confused denizens seeing unfathomable metal objects randomly appear and, moments later, vanish once more.

There was an alarm on the property, too, a high-end model with reliable motion detectors. It was probably rigged to send notifications through to a call centre when something was detected, as well as waking everyone up for half a mile around. The control box near the door gave me the usual few seconds to enter the deactivation code. Unfortunately, I had no idea what it was. Fortunately, I had brought another useful gizmo from Stores with me: a stasis propagator, or a *holdfast* as we call them. I have it on good authority that the devices employ a powerful circle of entrapment under the hood, but their official name sounds so much less troubling. Their effect is to freeze everything in a small area: not freeze as in *cold*, but freeze as in *pause all physical activity*. The spell can be used to lock demons in place mid-breath, but what works for summoned horrors also works for electrons flowing around a circuit. While the device was active – I'd have maybe thirty minutes – the alarm would do nothing as, for it, the flow of time had effectively stopped.

You just have to be damn careful when you set the devices off. If you're in range, you get held, too. There are plenty of stories in Office lore about operatives activating one of the devices only to get caught in the radius. They would then awake at precisely the same moment as the horror they were trying to capture did so, at which point everything tended to go downhill rapidly.

Fortunately, the devices had a timed activation. I had mine primed for two seconds. I slapped it on the alarm control box, activated the controlling rune (okay, pressed the *on* button) and ran down the hallway. Two seconds later there was a sound like the universe drawing a breath, and a one-metre diameter grey sphere sprang into existence, centred on the holdfast. The alarm control box was trapped in its own little pocket of non-time. Reality would catch up with it in half an hour and the alarm would sound. I had to make sure I was far away by then.

There was a small pile of mail on the ground behind the door. Taking great care not to touch the sphere, I retrieved them. Most were flyers for pizza joints and the like, but two were addressed to the occupant by name. Both referred to *Ms. Spender*. I was in the right place.

The house was attractive and well-maintained, its interior recently modernised and finished to a high specification. The kitchen was a thing of beauty, all cream and black marble. I had no idea what half of the gleaming silver contraptions on the worktops were even for. The house was clearly lived-in; there was clutter and things out of place. There was milk and juice in the fridge, along with tubs of yoghurt and cream and avocados and tomatoes. Everything was fresh. Recent newspapers were strewn on the coffee table next to an empty coffee mug. I was willing to bet that the house was owned, not rented. Landlords tend to paint their walls in neutral magnolias, the least offensive option, but here the occupant had gone to town, splashing bold colours, purples and reds, onto feature walls.

The significance of all that wasn't lost on me. A villa on Cathedral Road was not going to come cheaply, and clearly a great deal more cash had been lavished on the interior. Maybe Sally Spender earned good money, or maybe she'd inherited wealth. But it was also a possibility that she'd illegally used her magical abilities to enrich herself – and had perhaps even made up her surname as a joke.

She wouldn't have been the first to abuse her powers. It's a common theme in many of our cases: adepts cheating the system for their own personal gain. It's an area of activity that has consumed us more and more over the years. Some of it is low-level stuff: the use of clairvoyance to predict the lottery numbers, say, or the winner in the 2:30 at Chepstow. The dangers ran much further: the entire financial system could be brought crashing down if powerful adepts focussed their attentions upon the computers employed in microsecond trading. The rumour was that more than one of the recent banking failures were due to groups of organised users making a killing by shorting stocks on financial institutions that they then targeted and destroyed. It perhaps explained how the enemies we faced were often extremely well-resourced. It was just one more way in which magic use corrupted the normal functioning of society.

I stepped carefully about the house, taking in details. Like Cornwallis, it appeared Spender lived alone. She had a fine hi-fi system and an impressive array of CDs, including many of my favourite albums. She'd even gone retro and amassed a good selection of classic vinyl. I approved. It was hard to believe too much evil of someone with such good taste.

There were also shelves full of books – fiction and non-fiction. Spender appeared to have a wide array of interests: philosophy, archaeology, astrophysics, you name it. Her fiction tastes were satisfyingly eclectic too: she appeared to enjoy good books whether or not they involved alien life forms or magic. Again, like with the CDs, I had to approve.

On a high shelf I spotted the familiar spine of the edition of the *Mabinogion* that the supposed reading group were using. I pulled it down and leafed through it. By examining the spine, I could tell she'd read the entire book at least once and that there were no bookmarks left inside. The familiar inscription was there: *Borderland Reading Group*. A quick check against the handwriting on a kitchen noticeboard suggested Spender had written the words in each book. Next to the *Mabinogion* stood a copy of *Dorian Gray*: my guess was that she'd got ahead of the group and bought the relevant edition of their next study piece. She'd started reading it, too: there was a business card advertising *Mab's Cabs*, a local taxi firm, marking the start of Chapter 2.

I took out my phone and took pictures of the marked page. It had occurred to me that Spender might have left a trail for her friends to follow, in case things went badly wrong and she needed assistance. If she had, it would have to be a subtle one, so that the group's enemies would miss it. There was a good chance that the eye collectors wouldn't know about *Dorian Gray*, as neither of the two victims had bought their copy so far as I'd seen. I studied the words on the marked page, thinking they might contain some such clue, but I couldn't come up with much. The page mentioned *a club in Whitechapel* and also *Curzon Street*, but I couldn't discern anything more specific. Both were places in London and not, as far as I knew, Cardiff. I needed to talk to Warder again, see if they made any bells go off in his brain. Auchter, too, might recognise some code the group had used.

There didn't appear to be any pets at the house – which again could be relevant or utterly unimportant. Either she'd lived under the expectation she might have to flee at any moment – or she simply didn't like animals much. I didn't see any hidden cameras in any of the rooms, but of course that didn't mean they weren't there.

Upstairs, it was more of the same: the décor was quirky, bold, but professionally done. In the bedroom there was some suggestion that she'd packed and fled in a hurry: clean clothes were strewn around on the quilt as if she'd quickly tossed what she'd needed into a bag. There was more of the same in the bathroom: essentials like a toothbrush were missing while more esoteric makeup concoctions were scattered on the window ledge and even in the bath. It all suggested someone grabbing what they needed in a panic. I took pictures as I went: I'd seen no hint of magical symbolism, so there was no problem with magus law.

A small room at the back of the house had been turned into a study. The drawers were locked but a quick zap with the Sesame gave me access. There were papers and bank statements and letters within, but nothing that gave me a clue about any other address.

At the end of the landing corridor I discovered a curiously low and narrow doorway – so small that at first I assumed it was an airing cupboard. It turned out to lead to a cramped, steep set of steps winding upwards into the loft space. It was immediately intriguing: the doorway wasn't exactly hidden, but it could so easily have been larger, too. The stairs were scruffy, the edges scuffed from heavy use. The musty air within smelled of dust. I ascended warily, half-expecting to find the place where she carried out her incantations: a floor littered with forbidden sigils and the bloodstains from her sacrificial victims.

Once again, there was none of that. Spender was using the loft space for a different activity completely: painting. A flat, natural glow filtered down from two skylights in the roof. Her current piece stood on an easel, facing away from me, with numerous other pictures leaning against the walls all around. The floor was bare boards, worn by many footsteps and spattered with drops of paint. I walked around so I could see her current work. I half-expected to find a representation of an oak tree with a crown of stars, although that would have completely messed with the story I had in my head of Spender as victim, being pursued by English Wizardry.

For once the universe played along with my views on how it should work. The painting was a watercolour landscape, the Sugar Loaf above Abergavenny if I wasn't mistaken, the treatment slightly impressionistic and rain-washed. It was a long way from the stylised design and simple lines of the drawing in Martha's house.

I studied a few of the other canvasses stacked against the walls. Almost all were landscapes, although there were some cityscapes too: the skyline of Cardiff seen from various vantage points. One had the Black Tower clearly visible in the background, but it was hard to see anything illegal in the image. I snapped more photos, just in case.

I took one more quick look around the house, hoping for some clue about where she might have gone. I could see nothing. Downstairs, the holdfast's grey sphere looked hazier, as if it was on the point of winking out of existence. I had to get away soon. It was then that I trod on a patch of carpet in the hallway that creaked and gave slightly underfoot. I tried it a few times. The floor groaned each time. Maybe it was nothing more than a loose floorboard. I stamped harder, and the thud sounded hollow despite the muffling effect of the carpet.

I glanced at the sphere, thought about leaving, then decided that I needed to be sure. The carpet wasn't attached to grippers along the nearby walls: instead, a heavy iron ornament in the shape of a sleeping cat kept it in place. I lifted the cat aside and pulled the corner of the carpet away. Underneath, in the centre of the hallway floor, there was a hatch that perhaps led down into a cellar.

Was it possible that *this* was Sally Spender's safe house? That she'd hidden herself away in her own basement? But if she had, how had she replaced the carpet to cover the hatch, and slid the cat ornament back into place?

Magic use, I supposed.

I pulled open the hatchway to reveal a square of darkness. The air on my face smelled chill and slightly damp, faintly tinged with the aromas of chemicals. I felt around inside the hatch and found a switch screwed onto the underside of the floor. When I flicked it on, it revealed a flight of unpainted steps leading down and, dimly visible in the shadows, the sort of clutter you'd expect to find in a cellar: tins of paint; piles of old magazines; rusting garden contraptions that the owner didn't need but couldn't bring themselves to throw away, just in case they ever did.

It seemed an unlikely setting for a bolthole, which was maybe exactly the point. I crept down the steep flight of steps, conscious of every creak and groan underfoot. A single, unshaded bulb hung from the low ceiling, its wire tied in a loop to shorten it. It looked oddly like a noose for a toy or a doll. Shadows lurked behind the piles of clutter and rusting steel shelves. The floor was uneven concrete, but it didn't look as if it had been disturbed for a long time. The hum of the city traffic was hushed and distant.

A tang of something rotten, some corruption, crept into my nostrils, faint but repellent. Maybe some animal had become trapped down there and met its end. I hoped that was it. The other possibility was all-too-clear: that somewhere down there I would come across the mutilated remains of Sally Spender, cornered in her own safe place. A third victim, whose visual memories maybe held clues to the mysterious Myrddin.

I drew my handgun and pulled my clothcutter from its scabbard on my ankle. Neither action was particularly rational, but they made me feel a little safer. There was always the possibility I'd disturbed the killers in the act and that they were waiting for me somewhere in the shadows.

A brick wall reached halfway across the open space of the

cellar, supporting the walls of the rooms above me. The floor-space I could see was maybe two-thirds the size of the floors overhead, but the single light provided no illumination about what lay around the corner. I pulled a pencil torch from my pocket and held it – and the knife – aligned to the barrel of my gun. Keeping a clear exit path back to the stairs, I edged forwards.

The sight revealed was disappointing: a blank alcove containing nothing more than a rusting bicycle. Except that there was also a metal door at the far end, directly ahead of me. It was closed, but I could see no padlock. There was room for – what? – a six by ten-foot space behind the door. Maybe it had once been a coal cellar, but I could only guess what use it had been put to now. The stench of corruption grew unmistakably stronger; it was coming from behind the door, horribly sweet and sickening at the same time. I suppressed the instinctive urge to move back, get away.

Five paces, and I was at the door. I put my ear to its metal, frostbite cold on the side of my face. It vibrated quietly with the thrum of the city – or perhaps the noise was in my ears – but I couldn't pick out anything from within.

I placed my free hand on the cold brass of the handle. My plan was to pick a moment, wrench the door open and step rapidly backwards so that I had a clear shot at anyone coming out. But as my fingers wrapped around the knob, another attack, another of my episodes, hit me...

An episode, but this time it was different. In the past they'd always felt like an affliction, a bad thing happening *to* me. Now I felt like I was *inside* the vision. I was part of it, and it was part of me. It wasn't an attack or a fit; it was something to be welcomed, taken hold of. It was a flow and a rush, and instead of floundering I could flow right along with it. I wasn't rolling around groaning on the floor; I was standing, alert, clear-headed, my hand still on the door-handle, and the roar in my head was mine. All mine and all me. Mine to wield if I wanted.

I wanted. I had little time to understand what any of it meant, but I accepted it gratefully. It felt like the right thing to do. I accepted it, and a vision of a hideous presence came to me: the thing that stood quietly on the other side of Sally Spender's hidden basement door, maybe two inches from me, waiting so quietly.

I recognised the creature from hours of revision learning the hierarchies of Hell. A *Pestilential Presence*. I couldn't recall what circle it came from – Hardknott-Lewis could probably have provided its post code – but I didn't really need to. It was a creature to haunt humanity's nightmares: its body in perpetual decomposition, its misshapen form slumped in semi-liquefaction, held together by sagging tatters of flesh.

Despite all that, it was strong, powerful and unrelenting, with a demonic magic animating its disarticulated sinews. Its touch was death; within an hour, anyone coming into contact with one would become like it: no longer human, no longer alive. They'd once been common enough during plagues and epidemics – there were several reports of them wandering the streets of London during the Black Death – but these days they were rarely glimpsed, although there'd been a credible report of a sighting during one of the recent Ebola outbreaks in West Africa.

Only a powerful adept could summon and bind such a being to their will. Spender? Possibly. It seemed a strange horror to keep in your basement. No binding magic was absolute. This was a creature you really wouldn't want to break free of its shackles in the quiet of the night to come slithering and burbling up the stairs for you. It seemed more likely it was the work of the killers. They'd got there ahead of me after all, and left the writhing horror as a surprise for anyone daring to follow them.

Pure revulsion made me back-pedal rapidly from the door. Three, four steps. It was probably that instinct that saved me. The door burst open and the monstrosity was there, framed by the doorway, coming at me, a wordless animal shriek of fury bubbling from its ruined gash of a mouth.

The stench of decay made bitter bile rise into my mouth. Stepping backwards all the time, reversing to the stairs, I emptied my gun into the horror, the cracks ear-splittingly loud in the confined space.

Standard Office guns have six bullets. The rounds are all different and are loaded in a very specific order. Some are silver-tipped, others ensorcelled to deal with particular threats or dangers. In theory we're supposed to use the revolver mechanism built into the gun to choose the right round for the right target. There are little symbols on the barrel that can be used to select the right projectile in the darkness. I didn't bother with any of that. Six shots with varying kinetic, explosive and sorcerous power slammed into the slithering demon as it reached for me.

None of the shots stopped it, but each slowed it momentarily. Perhaps it registered pain on some level, although searing agony had to be its normal experience. Still, its stumbling gave me a moment to act. I turned and raced for the stairs, pounding up to ground-level, expecting some rotting tentacle to wrap around my ankle at every moment.

I had to get out of the house. Move. Think. The door onto the street was only yards away. I needed to stop the creature, contain it, but before I could do anything, I needed an escape route, a position of strength to establish a cordon, or I'd be dead. Worse than dead. It was possible the terms of its binding didn't allow it to step over the threshold of the house. If I could get outside, I could come up with a strategy, deploy what runes I could and hope they were enough.

I reached the door, and turned to see how long I had. Moments, only moments. The creature flowed up the basement steps quicker than I could run and was now filling the hallway, a pulsating mass of mismatched flesh. Its stench was overpowering. I was cornered, my back to the door. Releasing the lock, either magically or in the normal way, would take a few moments, but by then it would have me.

I turned to face the demon, clothcutter in my hand. A blow from that blade should suck it back to its own dimension, but how to strike such a blow? I could hurl the blade – it was balanced to work as a throwing knife – but that would give me only one chance, and there was every possibility the creature could deflect the blow in some way. Then I would be helpless. A stab into its flesh was the only sure way, but that meant getting inside *its* reach, with every likelihood of being infected by its corrupting grasp.

I stood waiting, blade in hand, my breathing panicky as I searched desperately for a way to strike the creature without letting it touch my skin.

Maybe I should have listened to Hardknott-Lewis.

19 – Signs

The greatest care must be taken when operatives of the Office of the Witchfinder General come into contact with members of the public. We do not only protect, we keep those we protect in the dark, oblivious to the true nature of the threats we all face. There is peace of mind in ignorance.

–Earl Grey, Witchfinder General,
Office of the Witchfinder General Handbook, 1999

A series of connected things happened in more or less the same moment. The sequence went like this:

To my right, the holdfast keeping the alarm in stasis winked out of existence, its magical battery – which, okay, probably wasn't how that actually worked – finally expiring.

The Pestilence saw the sphere vanish and paused, very briefly, in its onslaught. So far as I knew, they were mindless creatures, so it was probably assessing whether the disappearance of the grey sphere was some sort of threat. The point was, it stopped, just for a moment.

The frozen electrons in the alarm's circuits got up to an appreciable percentage of the speed of light again. All the movements registered in the house since my entry flooded in from the various sensors and were duly noted by the alarm's software.

The alarm blared into deafening life, its urgent wailing blasting into my ears from a few inches away.

The Pestilence, still unsure of what was going on, visibly flinched at the sound. I'd always thought there was something of the banshee in the cries of house and car alarms, some undertone of wanton savagery. To my twenty-first century ears they were maybe just more irritating alarms, this one punishingly loud, but the demon heard – what? – the attack cry of one of its superiors? Something terrifying on a bestial level. The demon cowered back, just for a moment.

Seeing my chance, I lunged with the clothcutter.

The demon, off-balance, reacted, but a beat too slowly.

My slim black blade, fizzing with malevolent energies, struck the demon's flesh. Immediately the ensorcelled blade burst into life, as if a circuit had been completed, or a long pent-up fury had finally been released.

The handle froze to ice in my hand. I let go before it welded itself to my skin, as I'd been trained to do.

My ears popped as something weird happened to the air pressure in the hallway.

A random thought about the bookmark in Sally Spender's copy of The Picture of Dorian Gray passed through my mind.

The demon screamed a terrified scream. There was a clear gash where the blade had struck its torso, but it wasn't a gash in the demon's flesh so much as a gash in the world. A gash between the worlds. The fabric cut by the clothcutter was the fabric of reality.

The black slit of darkness widened and began to pull the sinews of the creature inwards, like a black hole sucking in space/time.

I threw myself backwards until I was pressed up against the wooden door of the house and could go no farther.

There was a moment when the demon's malformed, dripping eyes looked into mine and I saw confusion, fury – and fear.

The circle widened rapidly to consume the creature. The demon lurched and spun, falling away from me to recede into the distances of its own dimension. In a moment it was nothing more than a black dot against a field of furious, burning redness.

The tear in the fabric of the worlds stitched itself back together with a blast of hot, sulphurous air, the planes of our reality becoming reassuringly whole again.

The blade, now just a short length of inert metal, fell softly to the carpeted floor.

All of that happened in the space of a couple of seconds. I slumped to the ground, leaning against the door, trying to take in everything that had occurred. My breathing was ragged. Sweat trickled down the small of my back.

The demon was gone, but the alarm was still blaring. I couldn't just sit there. I forced myself to stand and, picking up the blade, opened the front door and raced for my car before any neighbours or passers-by could stop me and difficult explanations became necessary. I made it to the car without anyone apprehending me, but there had to be a great chance someone would have spotted a young man – a young Asian man at that – fleeing the scene of a crime. So much for operatives of the Office working quietly in the shadows. I gunned the Mini's unimpressive engine into life and surged away from the scene.

I drove for a mile or so, mind spinning, letting the road signs and markings lead me where they would. After ten minutes, when I was far enough away, I pulled into a parking spot that was technically not a parking spot to make a call.

DI Zubrasky picked up after five rings. "Danesh. What a delight to hear from you again so soon." The tone of her voice suggested that, in fact, this wasn't the case at all.

"I'd like to report a crime," I said.

"If you've been the victim of a crime, we have a special number all set up for that, available for any member of the public to use. It's a great system. You don't need to call the private mobile of a police officer you happen to know."

"I haven't been the victim of a crime. I'm the perpetrator."

I was sure I could hear her sighing very quietly to herself on the other end. "Okay, what crime is it you've committed?"

"I suppose it would be breaking and entering." I gave her the address. "I fled the scene with the house alarm ringing."

"Have you decided to switch career and take up burglary or was this an Office thing?"

"All part of the Eye case. The house is perfectly safe to enter now. I did no damage and took nothing away."

"The house is perfectly safe to enter *now*?"

She didn't miss much. "There was an altercation with a supernatural entity, but it is no longer a problem. The thing is, if you search well enough you'll recover my DNA from the scene. I'd obviously like to make sure that doesn't happen."

"There are official channels for this sort of thing."

"Yes. I'm asking you as a favour."

There was the briefest pause. "I can make any

complications like that go away if I must."

"There are a couple of other favours I'd like to ask. Now that we're talking."

"You don't recall that little chat we had? The *ultra judice* thing?"

"Things are moving rapidly here and there's a lot at stake."

"A lot that you can't tell me about."

"I… yes."

"If it's information you need, then I think we've already established that you can get it just as easily as I can. You appear to have full access to our systems, and you can, of course, request an official co-option of a police officer to find out anything you need."

"I want to keep this off the books, out of sight of any of my colleagues."

That got her interest, at least. "So, either you've gone rogue or you suddenly don't trust your fellow officers."

"It's possible there may be a question mark over one or two of them. If the wrong ones know what I'm doing, it could turn out very badly."

"Badly for you?"

"For lots of people, but mainly for those the eye collectors are pursuing. I'm trying to prevent more deaths here."

She sighed. "Okay, Danesh, tell me what you need to know. And some day you must explain to me just what I'm getting out of this little arrangement we have."

I gave her the registration numbers of the cars that might have been Sally Spender's. We hit lucky on the second one: a bright red, sporty convertible that had been parked a short way up the road from her house was registered in her name.

"Can you tell me if she owns any other cars?"

"Not unless she has a fake ID."

Which of course she might, but I chose to ignore that possibility. Perhaps because it fitted the theory that had popped into my mind during the battle with the Pestilence.

"You believe she's one of the killers?" Zubrasky asked.

"The next potential victim. I think she's our Wood Elf. If I can get to her first, maybe I can catch the killers."

"Where is she?"

"I can tell you where she *isn't*. I'm hoping you can give me a clue about her current whereabouts, even though it might involve a little creative policing."

Zubrasky was, at heart, a good officer, for all the right reasons. Strictly speaking, she wasn't supposed to help me in the case, but I figured that she would because it was the right thing to do, even if that meant going beyond looking up a few DVLA records. Fortunately, she saw it the same way.

"What are you looking for?"

I gave her the name of the taxi firm whose card Sally Spender had been using as a bookmark in her copy of *Dorian Gray*. I'd taken a picture of it without even realising I was doing it: I'd imagined she'd been marking that particular page in the book as a subtle clue for anyone friendly coming to look for her, but I'd realised that wasn't it: she was using the book to draw attention to the card. She'd fled in a hurry but hadn't taken her own car, perhaps because it could be tracked. Instead, she'd used one of Cardiff's taxi firms for her getaway.

"They do not have to reveal information to the police just because we ask nicely."

"No. That's where I'm hoping you can be imaginative. Ask for a favour or apply a little pressure. I don't know, suggest you can get their licence withdrawn or something."

"Again, you watch too many TV police dramas. That isn't how it works."

"There has to be something you can do."

"I'll try, Danesh. I assume you're interested in journeys from the address you've given me some time after Cornwallis sent out his alert?"

"Within an hour of that, I'd say."

"Let me make a few calls. And the next time I'm stuck on a case you damn well better get your crystal ball out and show me the face of the person I'm pursuing, okay?"

"That isn't how it..." I started. But she'd already hung up.

It was tempting to drive home while I waited for her to call me back, but I decided against it. If there was a rogue element within the Office, they'd obviously know where I lived. In the end I took a circuitous route around Cardiff's one-way system and worked my way back to Cathedral Road. I squeezed into a spot fifty yards away from where I'd previously stopped, only a very small part of my tyre touching the zig-zag lines near a pedestrian crossing. I had a reasonable view of the house I'd run from half an hour earlier, using the pair of folding binoculars I kept in the car. My plan was to see who, if anyone, turned up next.

By now the alarm was reduced to sulking with an intermittent chirp rather than its original full-blown wail. A red light flashed on the wall, but no one was going near, and no one looked out from any of the windows. After twenty minutes, a police car drew up and double-parked right outside. I had no way of telling if it was responding to the alarm or if Zubrasky had sent it. Two officers climbed out, clad in all their bulky stab armour and utility belts. They approached the house with some caution judging by the glances passing between them. Fortunately, they didn't need to batter the door down, because in my haste I'd failed to lock up behind me. They went in one-by-one, signalling to each other as they went.

Ten minutes later they were out again, looking much more relaxed as they talked into their radios. Clearly, they'd encountered no more fiends summoned from the nether worlds. Someone was obviously in communication with the alarm company as the light on the outside of the house stopped flashing and the chirp cut out. The police officers shut the door behind them and drove off.

Zubrasky phoned back ten minutes later. No one else had arrived at the house in that time.

"There's good and bad news," she said. "The company was keen to be cooperative. They kindly put me onto the driver who took the fare, and he remembered it well because it was so odd. That's the good part."

"Odd how?"

"He said he drove the young woman down to the docks, but not to any specific destination. She just kept telling him to turn, sometimes abruptly, following a route that didn't make much sense."

"She was worried she was being followed."

"Taking precautions just in case, at least. The strange thing, though, was where they did end up."

"Where?"

"Within a few hundred yards of where they started."

"Damn."

"The whole thing was a ruse to put pursuers off her scent.

She had to have another escape method planned and used that once she was back home. Assuming she's not still in the house somewhere."

"I'm sure she's not."

"Okay, well, I don't see what more help I can give you. I need to get back to doing some proper police work anyway. Criminals to catch, crimes to prevent, that sort of thing."

"Thanks for what you've done. I really appreciate it."

I hung up and swore softly to myself. Sally had made a show of fleeing her house, then doubled back. It didn't make a whole lot of sense. Except... what if she hadn't been fleeing at all? An idea stepped out of the shadows into the light of my mind. Could that be it? Could it be that she'd intended to take the fight to her pursuers by doubling back to her own house to see who turned up in pursuit of her? That might be what I'd have done if I were a powerful adept. If it were true, it implied that she was somewhere nearby, watching even now. Maybe even watching me, as I sat in my car working out where she was.

I peered up and down the road, but I caught no glimpse of anyone observing me. I had no choice but to go and look for her, in plain sight of everyone. If she was watching her own house, she'd be in one of the properties on the other side of the road. Let's say, fifty or sixty yards in either direction for a good view. I took a few items I figured I might need from the car and began to check out each building. Most were, as elsewhere along the road, businesses: a chiropractor, a dentist, a couple of beauty salons. There was a private medical clinic that attracted my interest as the signage was deliberately vague about the nature of the medicine practised, but there were people – patients I assumed – going in and out. Then, next to that, at the far end of my range of possible vantage points, there was a villa that had been converted into flats: six of them, judging by the panel of buttons near the door.

Pretending to look at my phone, I studied the building for a moment. The upper floor would offer a good view of Spender's house, especially with the leaves gone from the branches of the trees. From the arrangement of windows, I guessed that there were probably two flats on that floor. I walked up to the main doorway. For some reason, I was absolutely sure it was the right thing to do. The six buttons had numbers on them, without names, but I figured the two at the top would be for the flats on the upper floor. I was about to press one of them when a disembodied voice spoke to me through the little grille above the buttons. A woman's voice.

"So, you've found me. The question is, why were you looking?" Through the slightly tinny speaker she didn't sounded hunted, or wary, or afraid. She sounded, if anything, *amused*.

20 – Olwen

Well, said Merlin, I know whom thou seekest, for thou
seekest Merlin; therefore seek no farther, for I am he.
　　　　　　–Sir Thomas Malory, *Le Morte d'Arthur*, c. 1469

I held one of the items I'd brought with me up to the little
camera built into the panel. The copy of the *Mabinogion* that
Acolyte Olwen had bought for me. "I'd like to discuss this
book with you."

There was a pause. Then, by way of a reply, the buzzer
buzzed and the lock on the door clicked.

I climbed the grand flight of stairs warily, peering upwards,
conscious that Spender was supposedly a magical adept of
some power. The décor around me was past its best, the
painted wooden banisters chipped, the carpet on the stairs
rubbed bare on the treads – as was normal enough for a
communal space. I passed four doors on my way up and
arrived on the top landing to be faced with flat numbers five
and six. The door to flat six was slightly ajar.

Resisting the urge to draw my handgun again – I'd
reloaded in the car but, somehow, I doubted it was going to
be much use – I pushed the door wide open and, when
nothing flew at me, stepped inside.

A low, pearly light glowed from around a corner, but I
could see no one. Feeling slightly weird I called out, "Hi! I'm
not from English Wizardry."

Still I hadn't been attacked. I approached the doorway that
the pearly light shone from and peered around the corner.
Spender stood in the middle of the floor. She'd worked a
glowing magical circle around herself: a wide one
encompassing most of the room, including the bay windows
overlooking the street. I couldn't tell the precise nature of the
warding spells that she'd employed, but I knew they were
potent, the air heavy with their thrumming buzz. Spender
herself was shorter than I'd imagined. Shorter and younger:

she appeared to be closer to my age than the others in her group. In the glow from her circle she looked slightly ethereal, her white face and arms almost translucent. Her black hair, by contrast, was pure shadow.

"Yes," she said. "I worked that one out. English Wizardry killers generally don't ring the bell and ask to come up."

"I didn't ring the bell, either," I said.

"No, but you would have done. If you're not English Wizardry, then I guess you must be a witchfinder, yes?"

"I am."

The revelation didn't appear to trouble her in any way. That was a little disappointing, frankly.

"I watched you go into my house," she said. "Then you fled a short while afterwards with the alarm ringing. I'm assuming the other two left some sort of nasty surprise in there for whoever came after them?"

"A Pestilential Presence. Which other two?"

A look of distaste twisted her features briefly at the mention of the demon, and I knew for sure that she hadn't summoned it. "I couldn't see who they were; they both shadowed their appearance. A man and a woman."

"When was this?"

"Maybe four hours before you showed up. They were in there for a good hour. I thought that they were probably setting up some sort of surprise welcome. Then you came."

"You haven't seen any sign of them since they left?"

"Nothing. I assume they missed the thing with the bookmark that I left in case friends came looking for me."

She must have seen the look passing across my face at that. "You know something, don't you? Something's happened. Tell me. And tell me where you got that book from."

We were both still standing, she in her glowing circle, me hovering by the doorway. Hovering in a socially awkward way, that is, not literally. It was pretty clear she wasn't going to let her guard down and talk to me normally.

"It's not good news, I'm afraid," I said. "This particular copy of the book I got from the bookshop, but I've seen three others in the past few days. The last was at your house, but the first I came across was at Manawydan's and the second at the house Branwen and Pwyll shared. I'm afraid that, of those three, only Pwyll is still alive. English Wizardry – or at least those two individuals you saw – got to both Manawydan and Branwen. That was how they learned your address." I used her colleagues' agreed code names, partly to let her know I knew about their group, and partly because I wasn't sure she would know all of their real names – although it was highly likely she was aware Manawydan was Cornwallis, given their fling.

At my words, Sally sank to her knees as if she were inflatable and all the air had gone out of her. The light in the room noticeably dimmed. "No, no. It can't be."

She hadn't known, then. Perhaps she'd hoped they'd all managed to escape, even Cornwallis. She'd have heard nothing from any of them since the alarm went out.

"I'm sorry," I said. It was a pretty useless thing to come out with. "I came here to try and stop the killers before they got to you, too."

She looked up at me from her collapsed heap on the floor, her face etched with raw pain. Her voice was little more than a whisper. "They got to Martha from Evan?"

"I believe so. You knew their real names, then?"

"Yes, Evan's especially, of course. We tried to protect each other, keep our identities a secret, but inevitably we found out things. We've been playing this game for years, now."

"I'm sorry," I said again. It didn't sound any less lame the second time.

She pushed back her raven hair from her eyes with a practised sweep of her hand. "We knew the risks; we accepted them. We'd been so careful, though, staying in the shadows for such a long time, one step ahead of English Wizardry *and* the Office."

It troubled me more than I could say to be lumped together with English Wizardry. From her perspective, I guessed there wasn't too much difference between us.

"You got unlucky," I said. "Somehow they found out about Cornwallis. Chances are you did nothing wrong."

"A witchfinder is telling me I've done nothing wrong? You can see the warding circles I've woven, can't you? You must know how frequently I've contravened your damn' magus law over the years."

"You know what I mean. It isn't your fault they found you."

"No, but it might be yours. I mean, if not you personally,

then some element in the Office sympathetic to English Wizardry. Or are you going to deny that's possible?"

She was angry with the universe and I was a convenient target. I wanted to deny her accusation, but I couldn't. "There's a chance that might be true. It's something I'm pursuing."

"Well make sure you do, witchfinder. We've been victimised by the Office too often." She looked down, as if there were answers written on the floor, then back up at me. "Tell me, how is Oliver coping?"

"He's struggling, I'd say. Fortunately, he's with a friend who's looking out for him."

I could tell from her face that that was a surprise. She had no idea where Auchter's safe house was. She didn't ask me for any details.

"Tell me everything that's happened," she said. "How you got involved, how you found me, all of it. Please, give me as much as you can."

Although it was against all the rules to divulge the details of a case to a non-witchfinder – especially one who was also a magus law criminal – I did more or less exactly that. I sat down in a scruffy and randomly-sprung armchair near the door and gave her a summary of the facts of the case since the discovery of Cornwallis's body – leaving out the names and details of Office and police operations that she didn't need to know. I also didn't delve into my family history. But I figured she had a right to know the fate of her friends.

After I'd finished, she didn't move for some time. I thought maybe it was going to be too much for her, this unravelling of her long plans, this loss of loved ones; she'd remain collapsed on the floor, beaten. Instead, she stood and forced a deep breath into her lungs. As she did, the nacreous light glowed brighter around her.

"We have to stop them," she said, an edge of steel in her voice. "We have to stop the bastards *now*."

"To protect Myrddin."

"Yes, to protect Myrddin. That's what really matters."

"You know who he is?"

"I know who he *or she* is; I was the only one in the group who did. But, no, I'm not going to tell you Myrddin's true name."

"Why is this Myrddin such a threat to English Wizardry? Why are you going to such extreme lengths to protect this person?"

She more or less confirmed everything the Librarian had told me. "Because Myrddin is the best weapon we have against English Wizardry. Myrddin knows secrets about them, knows their weaknesses and their flaws. Knows who they are. Which I'd say is a really, really good reason for you not to stop us protecting him."

"How does Myrddin know these things?"

She weighed up whether to tell me, then appeared to decide that she could trust me that far. "Because, once, Myrddin was one of them. Then she or he turned against them, betrayed them as they would see it, and they've been pursuing Myrddin ever since. Partly they want retribution, and partly they do so out of fear. With what Myrddin knows, there's a chance we could destroy English Wizardry once and for all."

"Then perhaps it would be best to lead them to Myrddin."

"That time may come, but if it does it will be at a moment of our choosing."

Interesting. I was beginning to get an image of Myrddin in my mind. Someone old, maybe, because how else could this person have known secrets from English Wizardry's early days? Perhaps someone not in the best of health. "If they know that you know who Myrddin is, they'll keep coming after you. They won't ever stop."

A wicked smile crept across her features. "Yes," she said. "They can try to do that."

Some semblance of her former humour returned to her features. On better days she had to have a warm and mischievous smile. It was strange: I'd been trained to think of users as dangerous and disruptive individuals, and most of those I'd encountered had been just that. But Auchter had been broken and sad, and Sally Spender was, now that she'd recovered herself, full of light. It seemed to shine from her. The look in her eye made me think of warm summer evenings and the laughter of loved ones and the aromas of all my favourite foods. A thrill of something went through me, a dizziness that felt something like my episodes of nausea – but also something like their exact opposite. It wasn't terror or fear, it was excitement.

Bloody hell. The timing was hopeless and the fact that we were on opposite sides of the war against the unnatural was doubly hopeless, but it was clear: I fell a little bit in love with Sally Spender in that moment. Something to do with the way she laughed – literally laughed – in the face of adversity and horror. A witch and a witchfinder: what could possibly go wrong with that?

"You weren't running from them, were you?" I said. "You don't seem like someone facing death. You want them to come, don't you?"

"They were supposed to think I was fleeing. The idea was they'd track me down here thinking they had me cornered and walk into my trap. I'm a spider waiting patiently in her web. A beautiful, deadly spider."

"But I got here first."

"They'll be here soon enough; one way or another they'll find me. The trick was not making the deception too obvious."

"And when they come?"

"Then I'll kill them, or they'll kill me. You say there are only two of them?"

"So far as I know. Only one a user."

"They've been weakened over the years, just as we've been. We've had our victories as well as our defeats. If I can destroy the two who've pursued us, Myrddin might be safe for a time. The question is, where do you fit into this? And the deeper question is, why haven't you arrested me? And the deepest question of the lot is this: why the hell are you wasting your life working for those puritanical fascists in the Office?"

That was hardly fair; I'd tracked her down to prevent her from becoming the next victim, even if she didn't appear to want my help. "Without us puritanical fascists, everything would break down; the social order would be corrupted by random magic use. Those lucky enough to have powers would be unstoppable. Who knows what horrors would be unleashed upon the world?"

She shook her head, as if pitying me. "That's Office bullshit, and I suspect you know it. The world isn't so black and white. Magic use is one of our greatest gifts; it gives us the ability to work wonders and conjure marvels. It's the colour in life, the joy. Why suppress that?"

"The temptations of its power are too great. People abuse it, abuse others with it."

"So, what, we should stop using technology because it can be put to destructive ends? Your problem is that you only see the bad stuff and you extrapolate from there. You've been brainwashed by the Office to deny your own nature."

"I have not. I have no idea what you mean."

"Come on, you as good as told me yourself. You can't be so far in denial; it was perfectly obvious to me the moment I saw you."

Her words sent an unpleasant jolt of anxiety through me. "I truly have no idea what you are talking about."

"Of course you do. You're one of us. You're a magic user, I can see it in you. You're suppressing it, but it will come out eventually, one way or another. Let it come, embrace it, or it will force itself into the light, not caring if it rips you in two to do it. You can't deny your true nature and you shouldn't try. You'll make yourself ill if you attempt it."

"I don't… that's simply not true."

"Don't be ridiculous, of course it is. You told me you sensed the presence of that demon before you opened the door. You attempted to rationalise it, but the truth is obvious. I'm willing to bet there have been similar episodes in the past: moments when you saw visions of something about to happen to you, when you sensed threats before you had any logical way of knowing they were coming at you. What did you decide they were, bouts of some mental illness? Fits of some sort?"

"No." But, even as I denied it, I thought about my episode in Cornwallis's house, and then again in the London office. There had been many other such moments, too. I thought about my family background, and the warnings of Hardknott-Lewis. I thought about the fact that the Librarian had told me more-or-less exactly the same thing.

Sally saw it all in my face. Her look wasn't one of triumph, but sympathy. "It's a hard thing to come to terms with, I know. It shakes your whole world view, changes everything, especially for someone like you. I mean, for a witchfinder. But the truth is the truth. I wish we had more time to talk about it and what it means for you. You need guidance, just as anyone would. The good news is, there are lots of us here to help you. Despite the best efforts of you and your colleagues, we're here. Not trying to destroy and pervert, but living our lives, doing no one any harm. Or, should I say, not doing *too* many people *too* much harm."

I thought about Gilroy, imprisoned in our basement, bitter and raging at the world. Had he been like her once: filled with the possibilities and the positives? Had we done that to him? So far as I knew, all he'd done was work spells to fight English Wizardry.

"Join us," she said. "A double-agent inside the Office could make all the difference."

I wasn't having it. There were grey areas, yes, but the rules had to be upheld or everything fell down. Hardknott-Lewis was a stern master, but he was fair. "No, you've got it all wrong about me. I'm not going to do anything to undermine the Office. I'm not one of you."

"And yet here you are, still not arresting me."

"We simply have similar objectives at this moment. We both want to stop this killing spree, stop the killers getting to anyone else. That doesn't mean we'll be on the same side permanently."

"Seems to me it does, but it's your choice. Think on what I've said, though, won't you? It's a shame to live a lie."

I shook my head, trying to dislodge the notion she'd planted there. For one thing, there was no time for it. "Tell me your plan. Perhaps two of us will have more chance than one. Two of us against two of them."

She couldn't resist. "You mean, two free magic users fighting two English Wizardry soldiers."

"Whatever you say. You meant to fight them here? One of them's clearly powerful; there's every chance they'll destroy you."

"I'm not so weak myself. But you're right, it would be stupid to let myself be cornered here. Which is why I'm actually several miles away, projecting myself across the aether. But thanks for not noticing; it's been a useful test of the illusion."

I'd never heard of such magic, but then there was clearly a lot that had been kept from me. "This isn't just a circle of protection you're inside?"

"Oh no, it's a lot more. The plan was simple: lead our hunters here and then start hunting *them*. Turn the tables. They might see the deception quickly enough, but by then it'll be too late. I can unleash a bit of pain upon them. Unless they find where I really am, I'm safe enough."

It was a clever ruse, and one I'd utterly fallen for. "Then I'll help. When they come here and discover the truth, I'll track them, see where they go. Once we've found out who they are we can take the fight to them."

She considered. "I can track them magically, but it is possible they'll be able to block that. They might not even think I'd use *technology*. But what happens if we prevail: you arrest me and haul me off to Hardknott-Lewis?"

"You have my word, at this point I'm only interested in capturing or stopping the killers."

She didn't look concerned. In truth, she still looked amused. "Okay, witchfinder, I'll take the risk. Let's see who comes knocking on my door next."

"How will I get in touch with you?"

She waved a hand in what might have been an overdramatic way. "I've put my contact details into your phone."

"You can do that?"

"Of course I can. You'll find me under *Goddess*."

21 – Faebrook Folly

> The Office of the Witchfinder General makes use of its
> *Assizes powers* only when there is truly no alternative.
> A growing range of scientific and technological tools is
> – thankfully – slowly making the use of supernatural
> objects and vile incantations obsolete.
>
> –Earl Grey, Witchfinder General,
> *Office of the Witchfinder General Handbook*, 1999

I watched Sally Spender's safe house from the relative discomfort of my car for an hour, waiting for the arrival of the killers. Precisely no one turned up. However good they were at sorcerous murder and necromancy, it was clear they had so far missed the clues that should have led them to Sally's safe house.

Her words kept replaying in my head. I did my best to ignore them: she'd been trying to put me off my guard; she was playing tricks with me so I wouldn't arrest her or raise the alarm about her; she was manipulating me, and I needed to focus on the case. I thought about contacting the office to arrange for someone to take over the stake-out when I needed a break, but I couldn't be absolutely sure who I could trust. Probably Lady Coldwater, and I found it impossible to doubt Hardknott-Lewis, but I couldn't imagine either of them sitting in a car for twelve hours monitoring a house. It occurred to me that it would be interesting to know who was and who wasn't in the office at that moment, but I decided not to ask. Better to let the trap shut on the killers quietly.

In the end, I decided to commit a serious breach of Office rules and falsify some records on MORIARTY in an attempt to flush out the killers. If my contravention of magus law ever came up at a Star Chamber hearing, I figured I could justify my actions with my suspicions about my colleagues. Maybe that would even work.

Once again, Office technology came to my rescue: I could

VPN into the system from the aforementioned discomfort and write up my notes without having to be at my desk and risk missing the killers. Sometimes it seemed like our tech was an overcompensation for all the antimagical gadgetry that we couldn't get to function very well. I worked my way through the two-factor authentication and brought up my notes on the Eye case. Then I appended:

> Tracked probable victim by the name of Sally Spender to an address in Abergavenny. Entered property with caution but Spender absent. No sign of magical activity. A thorough search revealed some utility bills, one of which mentioned a third address back in Cardiff. Possible chain of safe houses? New address very close to her original house: possibly she intends to stake out herself to see who turns up? Returning to Cardiff to attempt to track her down.

I provided the real address of the Cathedral Road house I was currently watching but not an Abergavenny address. Hopefully the killers – assuming they were monitoring my activity on MORIARTY – would think I was just being slightly less than rigorously professional. I didn't want them charging off to Abergavenny; I wanted them here.

I only had to wait another ten minutes. Clearly someone was looking for my activity, ready to act. Furthermore, they were nearby. They'd obviously calculated they could get to Spender before I returned from Abergavenny. A large black four-wheel drive car crept along the road, in the way cars do when their drivers are looking for a particular address. It slowed to a halt outside Spender's flat, seemingly unconcerned about blocking the road. A minute later a man emerged from one of the other properties – by his suit I guessed he was a lawyer or an accountant at work – and walked to his own parked car. There was something in his glazed expression that I recognised: the man was under a *glamour*, his mind magically controlled to make him act against his will. It was hard sorcery to work, the harder when someone was being forced to do something strongly against their nature. This, however, was only a minor intervention:

the beguiled man was being made to move his car to make a space for the killers. It was a small but telling way in which users abused their power to the detriment of normal people.

The black car parked in the space made for it, and two individuals climbed out: a man and a woman. Although the light was good, and I wasn't too far away, I couldn't see their faces: once again they'd worked some shadowing magic that made their features blurry however hard I tried to concentrate on them. It was like looking at a news report with the faces pixelated out, or the briefly glimpsed features of people passed in a crowd. My concentration kept slipping off them. The man, I thought, was someone I recognised, someone I'd met. The way he walked and held his body was familiar. The woman I didn't recognise at all. She, clearly, was in charge. The man held her door open for her as she descended from the car, then walked a step behind her as the two approached Spender's. The man carried a leather case like those doctors had supposedly once used on their house visits. No doubt it contained all the implements they planned to use to extract Sally Spender's eyes. Perhaps it also contained their cloaks and hoods, neatly folded up in preparation.

Whether they used magic or made the same calculation I had, I couldn't tell, but they soon disappeared inside. The moment they were gone, I acted. I picked up the tracking device I'd brought with me, then climbed from my car. Trying to look like any bored pedestrian, I crossed the road to wander aimlessly past the four-wheel drive. When I reached it, I made a little play of noticing my shoelace had come undone and bent to retie it. While I was there, I slipped the magnetic tracker onto the underside of their car. Then I carried on walking, checking on my phone that the device was broadcasting and giving me a good location. Fifty yards up the road, I crossed the road again and returned to my own car.

I was just in time to see that the killers had reached Spender's top-floor flat. White lights arced suddenly out from the windows, bright even in daylight, as if someone were taking a series of flash photographs. A rumble shook through the car, like an earth tremor had chosen that moment to strike Cardiff. More than one car alarm on the road began to wail. I thought I heard someone scream. Impossible to say who.

I resisted the urge to rush in and confront the killers.

They'd have come fully prepared for confrontation; much better to take them when they weren't expecting it. I also didn't fancy my chances of tackling the two of them alone.

Another explosion of white brightness blasted out from the windows, as if the Cardiff villa had been turned briefly into a lighthouse. This time there was definitely a cry from someone. Thirty seconds later the man and the woman emerged. The man had come off worse. The woman supported him, almost dragging him along as if he were semiconscious or had lost the use of his limbs. His legs flexed at awkward angles as if his bones no longer connected properly. Spender's magical attack had struck home. I could only hope the killers hadn't had some means of reaching Spender through the aether, of inflicting some injury on her. If they had, it might be me facing the two of them alone.

The woman poured the weakened man into the passenger seat of the four-wheel drive car, then got into the driver's seat. A moment later they surged away from the pavement. Once again it appeared they used magic, influencing the minds of the drivers around them to leave gaps or slow down so that the killers had a clear path through the traffic. A set of traffic-lights a short way up the road inexplicably turned momentarily green to let them speed through. A white van actually swerved out of their way as it might an ambulance to let them blast by. A shocking abuse of magic, sure, but I had to admit the ability to cut through traffic jams was pretty appealing.

I resisted the urge to pursue them closely. On the screen of my phone the blue flashing dot slid along the road on the map of Cardiff city centre, following their progress perfectly. They turned left a few hundred yards away and the dot dutifully followed. They appeared to have no idea they were being tracked.

Content that the technology would lead me to their evil lair, I pulled into the side of the road to make a call. Just as Sally had promised, there was an entry for *Goddess* in my contacts list that hadn't been there before. She picked up after a few moments.

"Hi, Danesh." I could hear the weariness in her voice. The fight had taken its toll on her.

"How do you know my name?" I asked.

"You'd be surprised what a skilled adept can learn from someone's phone. I probably shouldn't tell you that."

"It looked like you injured one of them."

"I caught the man with a bone dislocation curse. Pretty grim magic, but I decided they'd earned it. The backwash hit the woman, too, but she was able to deflect it."

Such abusive magic was way, way up the banned list, inflicting severe physical damage upon its victim as well as terrible, incapacitating agonies. It would be enough to assure her of a long stay in Oblivion. An *until the end of time* sort of stay.

I chose to skim over all of that. "Did you see his face?"

"I did. It was no one I'd met before."

"Young or old?"

"He was about our age, but he may have been masking. I was a little too distracted to check. Are you tracking them? The fight didn't go quite as well as I'd planned."

"I've got them on the screen. You're hurt too?"

"They were fooled completely at first, but they reacted so quickly. They very nearly got to me across the aether despite all the warding circles I'd woven. She's powerful that one, terribly powerful. This may not be as easy as I'd thought."

"You know the woman?"

"Oh yes, everyone knows her. The funny thing is, I could have sworn that you lot had her locked away in your damned Oblivion."

"Who?"

"Who do you think?"

"You're talking about the *Sorceress*?"

"As large as life, no doubt about it. One of the killers is Evangelina Mormont. Care to explain to me how that's possible?"

"I can't, I truly can't." My thoughts raced. What Sally was saying was impossible; everyone knew that Mormont was safely locked away. "It can't have been her. It had to be someone pretending to be her, or who looked like her."

"Trust me, Danesh, if you'd been on the end of the hexes she threw at me, you'd know. That was Evangelina Mormont, and I very much hope I never have to fight her again. She's fucking *evil*. And I imagine I've just made her a little bit angry, too."

Okay. If Mormont was free that explained many things, but Sally was right, it also raised a whole bunch of other questions. Troubling questions. But now wasn't the time. The killers were wounded, fleeing for their lair. Now was the time to press the attack.

"I'm going to follow them, but I'll keep a few miles back."

"Where are they heading?"

"Looks like they're getting out of the city, up to the M4".

"East or West?"

"East."

"I'll follow, too. Keep me posted on their direction."

"You'll be using magic to follow them? Like, flying through the air or something?"

I could hear the amusement in her voice. "No, Danesh. I'm going to drive in my car, just like you."

A wary game of cat and mouse went on for an hour and a half as I shadowed the two killers without ever getting close enough to see them – or to be seen by them. The urge to catch up and check I was still pursuing the right car niggled at me. The killers might have discovered the tracker and attached it so some other vehicle to lead me astray. I suppressed the itch and held back – and, besides, my Mini was struggling to keep up with their bigger and faster car. No doubt they were using magic to clear a path through the traffic and fox the speed cameras. I would have to bide my time. If I did have them on my line, this might be my only chance to reel them in. At least I knew Sally was safe: I kept her appraised of my position and she assured me she was somewhere nearby, shadowing me as I shadowed the killers.

My thoughts kept turning to her claim that I was a user. I couldn't get it out of my mind. Past events kept returning to me, slotting into place as if they suddenly made sense. Hardknott-Lewis had said I had potential, and the Librarian had clearly also thought the same after the weird blood-tasting session. Maybe my magical powers had been manifesting all along, and I'd been suppressing them. The thought was terrible – but also kind of thrilling. I had to push it aside and concentrate on the job in hand, even though that was proving difficult.

We sped past Newport, over the Prince of Wales Bridge and into England, past the *Croeso i LOEGR* sign than meant I was leaving the land of my adopted fathers and returning to the land of, well, my mothers at least. Gloucestershire and then Wiltshire drifted by. By the time we hit Berkshire I was maybe five miles behind my quarry and beginning to think they were heading for London, but then they slowed, leaving the motorway at Junction 14 to turn north into the rolling rural vistas and tree-lined avenues of Oxfordshire.

They turned onto smaller and smaller roads until they hit a track that, on the screen of my phone, looked to be nothing more than a farm lane. It snaked across three fields and then stopped abruptly. By the time I reached the turning there was no sign of the killers – or, apart from the occasional car whooshing by, anyone else. A weather-faded wooden sign attached to a low stone wall read *Faebrook Folly*. The track leading away around a copse of trees was rutted mud, flecked with loose stones – terrain for which their four-wheel drive was clearly much better suited than my Mini. The weird thing – the latest weird thing in the list of weird things – was that the blue dot representing the killers on my map that I'd so carefully pursued had suddenly winked out of existence. But, by the look of it, there was nowhere else they could have gone than along the lane; there were no junctions or ways back out onto the road proper. So far as I could see from the map there were also no buildings. The worry was they'd used magic in some way to fool the technology and lead me miles and miles astray into the middle of nowhere.

From the copse of trees, a flock of black birds, crows or rooks maybe, boiled from the branches with angry grating calls before settling back down again to let the rural silence resume.

Five minutes later, a yellow VW Beetle rattled to a halt behind my car. The door opened, and Sally Spender appeared. Apparently, she did have other cars besides the sporty red number parked outside her house – which maybe meant she had fake IDs, too. How far had her abuse of her powers gone? She limped slightly as she walked towards me, although whether that was the result of an injury sustained in her long-distance battle with the killers, I couldn't tell. She was definitely there in person this time: there was a solidity to her, with no halo of mysterious lustre. She wore a floaty white dress and black leather boots as if she'd simply come out into the countryside for a walk, but there was a determination in her eyes suggesting she was ready for a fight. There's a feeling you often get with powerful adepts: a field they give off, as if the air around them is charged. I got that strongly now, sending a shudder up my spine. At the same time, weirdly, incongruously, I found myself wondering if she'd get on with my mother.

"Hey, Danesh," she said.

"Hey."

"They're down there?" She indicated the track to Faebrook Folly with a nod of her head.

I explained about the blue dot. She didn't seem too frustrated or even surprised. "If they have some lair up there, they probably have shielding and magical spheres around it."

"There are no buildings, though," I said. "See." I showed her a satellite view of the terrain. The track was clearly visible winding between fields, stopping abruptly at precisely nowhere half a mile away.

"They maybe hexed the satellites, too, wiped themselves from the captured images."

"They can do that?"

"Sure."

"So, you're saying the fact that they appear to have completely disappeared is actually a good sign?"

"I'm saying it might be. I guess we have to go and see."

"Is that wise? Wise that you go, I mean?"

She looked me in the eye, and it felt a little like a knife was being waved in my face. "*You're* trying to protect *me*?" She appeared to find the notion amusing.

"What I meant was, there's a risk that they'll capture you and gain access to your memories. If we're trying to protect this Myrddin, then walking into their lair is the last thing we should do. They could track him down from your recollections, right? Then, yes, there's the risk to you. They want you dead and I'm supposed to be preventing crimes like that taking place."

"So far as I can tell, they want us both dead."

"I'm not posing any risk to Myrddin, only myself."

She considered, then shrugged. "Yeah, you're probably right. But I'm going to go anyway; it's time we brought the fight to those cunts. And, let's face it, you don't stand much chance alone against Mormont, even with all your Office gizmos. Your powers are real, but you have no control over them. They won't threaten her in the slightest."

They were all good arguments. In truth, I was extremely glad to have her with me. We decided that her car was possibly slightly better suited to traversing a farm track, so I parked the Mini in a lay-by fifty yards up the road and we set off to lurch and bounce our way up the lane.

"What do we know about Faebrook Folly?" she asked, her eyes clamped on the road ahead as she tried to manoeuvre around the worst of the gaping chasms in the road.

"There's not a lot on the interwebs," I said. "It is, or was, a folly, built by a local landowner in the eighteenth century."

"What does that even mean?"

"It's like a fantasy tower or mini castle that doesn't serve any purpose other than looking good in the landscape. Except, this one doesn't look good because it's no longer there. According to the page I found, it burned down early in the twentieth century and the ruins were demolished."

"How convenient. Or maybe it's still standing and we're just not seeing it," she said.

"Or that, yes."

After half a mile we reached the end of the road. It simply stopped, as if the people who'd built it had become suddenly bored with the whole venture one afternoon and gone home. Beyond where the lane petered out there was only field and wood, and certainly no car or folly. A hill rose beyond it, green and dotted with sheep, but there were no buildings or towers on top. I counted very carefully, just to be sure, and definitely got zero.

"It has to be there," said Sally. "No one would go to the trouble of building a track like this that goes nowhere."

We stopped the car and went to investigate. The world was quiet, the familiar hum of the city utterly absent. High overhead, an invisible bird twittered away a constant stream of notes like an ancient fax machine. I couldn't help thinking it was watching us, reporting back.

Stepping off the road we ascended the slopes of the hill to where the theoretical folly might be. After three minutes of this, Sally said. "Interesting. We seem to be angling around the hill rather than up it."

"The countryside can be confusing."

"Or it's deliberately pushing us away."

We tried again, concentrating on the crown of the hill. Once again, we found ourselves slipping aside, edging diagonally up the slope and then sideways along it. The hem of her dress turned damp from the longer grass we found ourselves straying into.

"Cool," she said. "The landscape is definitely doing it to us. Pretty neat magic." She stopped and placed her hands out in front of her, pushing them outwards like a bad mime artist. She closed her eyes for a moment. "It's there. Subtle but strong, enough to disorientate anyone wandering across these fields."

"Can you dispel it?"

"Will you immediately arrest me if I do?"

"I imagine I'll happen to be looking the other way."

She leaned into the invisible barrier, muttering syllables I probably didn't need to hear under her breath. After a few moments she grunted with effort and began to move her hands slowly away from each other, palms facing outwards as if she were pushing two columns of stone aside.

A pulsing circle of light appeared in the air between her hands, something like the tear in the fabric of reality the clothcutter had opened up. It widened as Sally stretched it open. The physical effort of it was clear in the bunching of her arm muscles, her gasps. It took her maybe three minutes, but eventually there was a circle wide enough for us to step through. Clearly visible through it was a version of the rolling countryside we were already familiar with – except that, sitting quietly atop the hill stood a four-storey stone tower. Parked outside its front door was a black four-wheel drive car.

Directly in front of us there was also a high mesh fence that appeared to track the line of the magical barrier. It fizzed with electrical energy, making the hairs on the back of my neck stand up. I stepped through the portal Sally was maintaining, taking pains not to touch the fence. With the help of a holdfast on a junction box I deactivated a section of it, then cut out a hole with the help of the folding bolt cutters I carried in my field kit. I crawled through warily, and Sally followed. No alarms either of us could hear sounded.

"Sorcery and technology combined," she said. "Definitely looks like the work of the Office to me."

I ignored her comments and looked back at the fence. From inside, the shimmering curve of the magical sphere was clearly visible, like looking through the turbulent air above a log fire.

"Yeah," I said, "and now we're trapped inside with them."

The spiky glint came back into Sally's eye. "That depends on your perspective. Seems to me they're trapped inside with *us*."

22 – The Eye Collectors

Although I was one of the first officers on the scene, I did not witness the moment of Evangelina Mormont's capture. As we moved to surround her, she unleashed a blast of radiant magical energy from her hand, engulfing me and three other officers in its sphere. I knew nothing about it, but I must have been thrown backwards out of the worst of the fighting. From what I have been told, it was another twenty minutes before enough Office resources were brought to bear on Mormont to finally subdue her. The effect on my health of these experiences has been grave: I was in a coma for thirteen days, and I still suffer from epileptic seizures. I have yet to return to my duties. I was the lucky one: the other three officers were killed instantly. By the time I regained consciousness, they had already been buried.

–Acolyte Li Nang, Office of the Witchfinder General, *MORIARTY case notes*, 1997

We set off up the hill for the folly. A sheep eyed us with frank puzzlement on her face, as if she had never seen creatures like us before. When we got to within a few yards, her nerve gave out and she darted away in search of her sisters.

The tower was clearly inhabited: through the leaded windows I could see curtains and furniture. An array of satellite dishes clustered upon the spire like an outcrop of fungi. The four-wheel drive stood slewed at an angle near the front door, and the tyre marks in the gravel suggested the driver had sped up to the tower and braked hard. When we got nearer, I could see the passenger-side door had been left wide open.

I spoke in hushed tones. "Looks like they were in a hurry."

Sally seemed less concerned to keep her voice low. "Maybe some vital organ got pushed out of line, too; it's hard to control strong magic across the aether. They should be grateful I didn't treat them the way they treated Evan and Martha."

It wasn't the time for an ethical debate about magic use. "If they're preoccupied dealing with their injuries, we might have a chance. I'd like to arrest them rather than kill them; they might provide useful information about others."

She shrugged, as if that was a luxury she didn't think we could afford. "Better we kill them than they kill us."

The tower's arched wooden door was ajar. It swung inwards without resistance, not even creaking in the prescribed manner. The non-existent building was well-maintained. There were still no alarms, or at least none that I could hear. My guess was the occupants were used to being safe within their magical bubble.

Inside, it took a few moments for my eyes to adjust to the lower light. The place smelled old and dusty, the sort of aroma that takes decades and decades and proper aristocratic money to build up. But the building was also lived-in: someone had a log fire burning, the tang of smoke and ash lingering in the air. A clock ticked thoughtfully from somewhere in the shadows. The tower was larger on the inside than it appeared from without – which I assumed was a simple optical illusion. The ground floor was given over to a grand entranceway, the floor tiled with some old English family crest. A flight of wooden stairs curved off to the upper floors, passing beneath an impressive stained-glass window depicting some knightly figure having a few difficulties with a fire-breathing dragon.

A doorway off to the right led into a second room, also deserted. The walls there were lined with wooden bookcases, shelves filled with leather-bound volumes. A system of cast iron stepladders on runners provided access to the highest shelves. I was willing to bet Lady Coldwater would give anything to check out the books there so she could seize any that spelled out illegal magics. Perhaps there are old libraries like that all across Britain, rooms full of tomes that have lain quietly for decades or centuries, harbouring their forbidden secrets.

From somewhere up above, a full-throated cry of anguish cut through the still air, then ended abruptly. Someone was in genuine torment. I saw the look of wariness in Sally's eye, but there was no other way to go. Taking care to step on the sides of the stairs, where there was less chance of creaking floorboards announcing our presence, we began the ascent.

A flickering blue light filtered down as we approached the next level. It felt magical in nature, something I'd seen before, but I couldn't put my finger on it. Another magic above my paygrade. The agonised cry rang out again, rising to a ragged crescendo. There was terror in it, the raw fear of looking over a cliff edge of pain. It was followed by a woman's voice, commanding in tone, angry. "Lie still while I work! There's no time for this; we're too close."

There was a sharp *crack*, like the sound of some heavy stick being broken across a knee, and another bestial cry coloured the air. Something like regret flashed across Sally's face, a moment of doubt at what she had done. It passed and was gone.

We paused at the top of the stairs, wary of being seen. A short passageway led off to a series of doors, from one of which the screams were coming. The light was low in the hall, but a mirror or perhaps a glass-covered painting on one of the walls gave me a darkened reflection of what was going on in the room. It looked like the sorcerous equivalent of an operating theatre: the man on some sort of stone altar, the woman standing over him, weaving her spells while trying to hold him down with her spare hand. Open flames flickered in a circle around the dais, and by the look of it there were runes daubed all over the walls.

The man cried out a half-formed word, but it degenerated into another full-throated scream as one of his bones was forced back into place. The shrieks at least did a good job of covering our movements.

The blue light came from above, up another flight of stairs. The top floor, I reckoned. I paused, trying to decide the best approach to take. This might be a good time to tackle Mormont: she was preoccupied and on her own. On the other hand, I really needed to know who or what was waiting for us up above. We'd been lucky so far, our pursuit unexpected, but there might be all manner of ineffable horror waiting to be unleashed if intruders were detected. We could rapidly reconnoitre the next storey, make sure we weren't going to get surrounded, then come back to take on the two killers before Mormont finished her brutal surgery. With the repeated howls of agony, we at least knew where they were at any moment.

I pointed upwards. Sally, after a moment's consideration, nodded her assent.

The grand staircase ended at the next floor, and from the angled roof it did indeed look like we were at the top of the tower. The scene was illuminated by a column of wavering blue incandescence in the centre of the space. It was maybe six feet tall, plasma lines of energy whipping off it. It illuminated clearly the runic circle containing it. Now it made sense: I'd been shown something like it once before, the day Hardknott-Lewis first showed me around the Office. The portal to Oblivion we kept in the broom cupboard glowed with the same unearthly luminescence when the relevant magics were worked to open the doors to the endless frozen lake of the Oblivion dimension.

Sally was also clearly aware of what it was. "This is how Mormont escaped her prison."

"An unregistered portal," I agreed. "She still would have needed help, the intervention from someone outside. Not even she could escape Oblivion by herself."

I could feel the raw energy of the rift crackling in the air as I stepped nearer. I made what sense I could of the runes inscribed upon the floor around it; they looked more complex than those I'd seen on gateways before. So far as I could tell, this wasn't only a door through to Oblivion but, potentially, to many different dimensions. The right incantation and endless planes of existence were available for the knowledgeable adept to visit – or to summon creatures from. I wondered how long it had stood there and what had come through it over the years. I wanted to deactivate it immediately, so that nothing could pass into the room while we were there, but I lacked the magical knowledge.

"Do you know how to turn it off?" I asked.

Sally didn't reply.

"Sally?"

"Hmm?"

She was standing in the far corner of the room, staring into a cupboard she'd opened. "You should see this."

"What is it?"

"Best you see."

I trod carefully, fearful of being heard in the rooms below. The cupboard was divided into a matrix of small pigeonholes, containing a collection of what looked like precious gems or birds' eggs. Except, as I drew nearer, I could see they weren't either of those things. They were eyes. Each little square contained a glass beaker, and within each beaker was pair of human eyes, held in suspension within some liquid. There were twenty-three pairs of them, with only one empty space. The forty-six eyes stared out in frank astonishment.

Sickness rose within me at the sight of them. "My god. Are they alive? Can they see?"

Sally's voice was quiet. "They still function, I think. They still see. But they're not connected to anything, so I suppose there's no one really there."

She had to be right, but it was hard to believe looking into the wide-open gaze of so many sets of eyes. Thin streams of bubbles rose through each beaker, making some of the veined white globes bob around. Beneath each pair someone had written, in purple ink, a label containing a set of initials. Beneath the last occupied slot, it said *MN*. Martha Ndidi. The eyes they'd cut from her head upon the stone-flagged floor in the house in Herefordshire. The space before that was labelled *EC*. Evan Cornwallis: the eyes whose removal had brought me to the condemned Cardiff house at the start of the case. Sally reached out to touch the last space, the empty one where Oliver Auchter's or her own eyes might have ended up. Might still, if things went badly.

"So many," she said. "They've been pursuing us for so long. I had no idea."

"Who are they all?"

"I don't know. People."

"We should destroy them," I said, "put an end to this sorcery."

"This is hardly the time."

"If we don't come out of this, then at least Mormont won't be able to use the eyes to pursue others."

Sally hesitated, then nodded. "We need to be quick. Help me do it."

I took a picture of the display case first, making sure to capture each set of initials. They could be material evidence in a bunch of old cases. Then I lifted the beakers down, one by one. With her pointed finger, Sally burned a small circle onto the wooden floor in lines of fire. We poured away the liquid from each beaker into a stoppered flask of spare fluid, then made a flopping, slipping pile of the stolen organs in the middle of the circle. With a frown of concentration on her face, Sally worked further magic. An angry red fire consumed the eyes. Flesh sizzled and the liquid in the eyeballs fizzed and popped.

After a few minutes, the magical flames guttered low and died out, leaving only grey ash on the floor and a foul smell I wasn't going to forget in a hurry.

"It's done," she said. "For what it's worth, it's done."

Neither of us spoke for a moment. Then we both noticed the silence that had taken over the room at the same instant. Our gazes met, seeing the realisation on each other's face.

The screaming from downstairs had stopped.

Before either of us could take a step, a voice cut through the silence. A woman's voice, stern and loud. "It hardly matters now we have you, does it, Sally? You know where he is. Even if you won't tell us, your eyes will. We will find him and end him."

Evangelina Mormont stood at the top of the stairs, calmly watching us. Her proud stare was familiar from photographs: there was something regal about her, an assumption of superiority. She'd worked strong magics over the past couple of hours but looked calm, unruffled. She stood tall, her red hair flowing over her shoulders, one hand held forwards, finger pointing at us like the barrel of a gun.

She was joined by the other killer, the man whose bones she'd just forced back into alignment. His face was ghostly pale, and he was breathing heavily from the effort of labouring up the stairs, but I knew him immediately. Here was the Office traitor. Clutching onto the bannister for support, limbs wobbling, stood Peter Warder.

His voice was a hoarse croak. "I tried to warn you off, Danesh, make you see the bigger picture, show you we weren't a threat worth fighting, but you wouldn't listen, would you? You kept coming back. What happens now is your fault. All your fault."

"Let's talk about this," I said. "It's not too late." Standard operational procedure: try to talk your attacker round, establish a rapport. It didn't usually work. "Tell me why you're doing this. For money? Does she have some hold over you?"

Warder shook his head in forced amusement. "You know nothing, half-breed. I have all the money I need. I'm a free Englishman. This is about something much more important. History. Civilisation. We turned from the old ways and everything fell apart. We're degenerate, tainted. Except now we're putting it all back together."

He pushed himself off from the bannister, making his way towards me like he was wading through deep water. His face was a grimace of pain. "Of course, you can never understand. This isn't your history. This isn't your country."

I'd heard it all before, it and worse. Warder wasn't going to be talked around, he was too far gone. How long had this shit been worming its way through his mind? Years, maybe.

I glanced at the other two. Mormont had clearly concluded Sally was the greater threat and was focusing all her attention on her. Sally stepped away from me so the blue flame of the rift was between her and Mormont, forcing the Sorceress to step sideways to keep her in view. Warder took his chance and went for his Office gun. Of all the ways I thought I might be killed in my duties, I hadn't thought that one likely. I went for my own weapon, but I was too slow. Warder had raised his aim, pointing his weapon at my torso. His hand shook but he had a pretty good chance of hitting me at such close range.

"Peter, please," I said. "You don't need to do this."

But I saw in his eyes that he did. His grip tightened on his weapon as he selected the bullet he wanted to pump into me. It didn't really matter which one he went for; they were all going to be fatal if they hit a vital organ.

There was only one thing I could do. I had no time to raise and fire, but there was time to attack in another way. My other hand was raised, as if I'd intended to shield myself against his shot. Opening my hand so my palm faced outwards, not thinking how I was doing it, I threw all my anger and fear at Warder. It manifested as heat – a searing heat, raging within me. But I wasn't in control of it; I lacked the skill to channel it, stop it consuming my tissues before I could expel it. Once, when I was a boy, helping my mother cook the rice, I managed to pour boiling water over my hand. I screamed the kitchen down while she held my hand under the cold water with a strength of grip I didn't know she possessed. The pain was like that now. Or worse: it felt like my blood was boiling in my veins.

With a scream, frantic, I forced the magical power at Warder. It emerged from my palm in a boiling red line, hitting him squarely in the chest, throwing him backwards. He discharged his weapon, but too late. The bullet cracked into the wall to the side of me.

He landed in the far corner of the room, screaming from the pain of the impact on his already-tortured tissues. From the shock in his eyes I guessed he'd had no idea about me; his researches genuinely hadn't unearthed the truth about my family. But then, I'd barely known the reality of it myself. I'd unleashed a bolt of seething magic without understanding how I was doing it.

No time to think about it now. Unleashing the blast, directing it at Warder, had felt good, though. Possibly, a small part of my brain said, too good. Also, my hand and wrist stung like hell.

Warder tried to rise, and a jolt of panic went through me. He now knew the truth about me. Maybe no one would believe him and maybe they would, but I couldn't afford to take the risk. Telling Hardknott-Lewis the truth might not save Warder, but it would condemn me.

I lifted my hand again, palm towards Warder. He saw what I was doing, what my intention was, and tried uselessly to scramble away. I thought he was going to beg for his life, but instead he said, "We'll get you in the end. Mormont and the others will get you all."

I hesitated. Then I thought about Az, and my father, and my grandfather, and the two victims I'd seen as well as the twenty-one others I hadn't. I thought about all the victims of English Wizardry over the years. *Ultra judice*. And perhaps this was kinder than an eternity in Oblivion. With a snarl I unleashed another uncontrolled magical attack, burning myself again in the process but catching Warder square in the belly. His scream was cut off as he slumped to the ground, eyes closed.

This time, he didn't move.

On the other side of the room, Sally and Mormont were circling the blue column of fire, preoccupied, stalking each other, casting hexes the other dodged or deflected. I crossed the room to check on Warder. A hand on his chest soon confirmed the truth. He wasn't going to endanger anyone anymore. He'd attacked me and I'd killed him. Maybe I'd had a choice and maybe I hadn't. Again, there was no time to think about it.

Mormont saw what I'd done and reassessed the danger I posed. Her gaze darted between Sally and me. She still looked calm, though, bored even. I edged towards her, positioning myself so she couldn't hit both of us at the same time. Mormont regarded me with her dazzling blue eyes, tilting her head on one side as if deciding which torment to inflict upon me first.

Behind her, Sally, seeing that Mormont was momentarily distracted, knelt down to one of the runes in the circle surrounding the portal. She did something I didn't follow, a rapid flick of her fingers as if drawing a new sigil there. A spark of green shot through the flame before the bright blue returned.

I had no time to consider her actions any further. I still held my gun. Under my finger, the marking on the barrel told me a standard round was lined up. It would do. I aimed and fired at the Sorceress. Warder had been expecting a bullet and had been surprised by magic. Perhaps the opposite would work on Mormont.

It didn't. Mormont waved the shot casually aside, as she might an irritating fly. Casually, she threw a spell at me, her gaze always on Sally. I had time to raise my arms to protect my face, little more. A solid weight thudded into me, sweeping me off my feet and hurling me backwards. At the same time, an acid pain burned through my nerves, lighting me up. I heard myself scream from the agony of it, even as I crashed painfully into the wall, jarring my spine against the sharp edge of a bookshelf.

I lay there at a broken angle, limbs shaking, body convulsing. I'd bitten my tongue in the impact, the blood coppery in my mouth. My body didn't work at all: my limbs ignored me as I tried to control them. The fire in my nerves raged and there was nothing I could do. I'd been incapacitated so she could have her fun with me later.

Mormont returned to stalking Sally as they circled the portal, and I could only look on helplessly. They continued to fling sorcerous death at each other, deflecting each other's attack again and again. But Sally was being worn down, gasping from the effort of the magic she was working.

Mormont, meanwhile, remained as impassive as ever. The slight smile that crept across her beautiful face suggested she was enjoying herself, savouring a duel that she knew well she would win.

"Tell me his hiding place, and I'll let you live," she said. "Give me Stonewall, and you can keep your eyes, keep your little life."

Some part of my brain leapt onto her words like a wounded wolf pouncing upon its tormentor. *Stonewall*. Arthur Stonewall, the Destroyer, was Myrddin. The man was still alive, still at the heart of the fight against English Wizardry. So that was it. The man had to be pushing one hundred and fifty years old by now, and perhaps he was weakened by age, but he was the one Sally and the rest of them had been protecting. Despite my agonies, there was a satisfying sense of things slotting into place, like a dislocated shoulder being pushed back into its socket. Stonewall. Not, as some part of my brain had wondered, Hardknott-Lewis. Not one of the Pale Sisters, not Earl Grey. Instead, it was the supposedly long-dead Arthur Stonewall. A man Peter had known all about, as his history lesson had revealed.

Sally, meanwhile, ignored Mormont's command, not taking her eyes off the Sorceress's moves. She continued to hurl magical attacks, block those thrown at her. The wary dance went on for a minute more before Sally made her mistake. She was a step too slow to move around the flame and Mormont suddenly had a clear line of sight. I saw the moment of triumph on Mormont's face, the instant she knew she'd won her long pursuit. She had Sally in her power, and now she would kill her and Assay the knowledge from her head to discover the answers she needed. Mormont's expression wasn't one of triumph so much as satisfaction; she'd always known she would prevail and now the universe had simply caught up with her preferences. Maybe this had been her plan all along: to escape her confinement at the Aldwych ghost station by forcing them to move her to Oblivion, knowing that minions like Warder would rescue her and let her walk free once more.

The Sorceress acted, throwing some tar-black gout of darkness at Sally, a patch of night like a swarm of bats boiling from some underground cave.

It hit Sally... but something about her shifted and the blast passed right through. Then Sally wasn't there anymore, and I saw her mistake wasn't a mistake at all. It was a feint. She reappeared directly behind Mormont, who was caught for an instant still watching to see what effect her magic would have on her target. Sally charged, throwing her arms around Mormont, thrusting her forwards. It wasn't magic; it was a matter of simple strength and momentum – an inelegant attack that Mormont, perhaps, simply considered beneath her. Mormont twisted to free herself, but she couldn't reach Sally, couldn't break her grip in time. The amused look on her face was finally gone, replaced, if not by alarm, then at least by irritation.

Together, the two users fell into the raging blue flame of the portal and were gone.

I still lay slumped on the floor, immobilised, my agonies burning through me. My arm had fallen in such a way that my new watch was visible. Two minutes, then three, ticked off while I waited for Mormont to reappear: victorious, angry, ready to exact her revenge upon me. Or while I waited for Sally to emerge, Mormont conquered, everything in the world back into some sort of order, the enemies we both sought defeated.

Neither thing happened. Wherever the two adepts had gone, they didn't return. Warder was dead and I lay alone, twitching, drool running down my chin. For the best part of an hour I lay there, the second hand on the expensive watch creeping slowly around, until I was finally able to coax my fingers into reaching my phone and fumbling off a distress call to the Office. It took long minutes for the SMS to send, but eventually – maybe the shielding around the building was fading with Mormont's disappearance – it went off.

23 – Spelling It Out

The only way to get rid of a temptation is to yield to it.
–Oscar Wilde, *The Picture of Dorian Gray*, 1890

A week later, I finished filing my report on the events of the Eye Collectors case. I'd been allowed a few days off after the fight at Faebrook to get over my injuries. It had taken me three hours to regain the use of my limbs in that room at the top of Faebrook Folly, three hours of squirming agony. Hardknott-Lewis and two other officers had found me there: me barely able to stand, Warder dead. Neither Sally not Mormont had reappeared, and there'd been no sighting of either since.

I'd barely clicked *Save* on the final version of my report when the summons came from Hardknott-Lewis. It was given in his usual polite, restrained tones: *Could you possibly spare a moment to discuss matters arising from your recent investigation?* The subtext was clear: I had absolutely no choice but to comply.

A low drizzle-filled cloud had descended upon Cardiff, scribbling grey pencil lines over the hard outlines of the buildings, veils of rain slanting down as if curtains were being drawn across the city. I shrugged my way into my waterproof and set off for the Castle. It was still painful to walk, my muscles bruised, my *bones* bruised, but I'd been assured it would wear off. The burning sensation in my hand had subsided into a background throb that I was able to ignore most of the time. As I hobbled along, elation and relief at having successfully concluded the case jousted with a set of more troubling thoughts. How much did the Crow know of what had happened? The fact I had kept the truth of my mother's condition from him was bad enough. That I had been complicit in the illegal use of banned magics was much worse. But both of those crimes paled into insignificance when compared to the fact that I, Danesh Shahzan, acolyte in the Office of the Witchfinder General, was guilty of the capital crime of Magery, in severe contravention of magus law. Not only that, but I had used sorcery to kill a suspect, and then concealed the truth of the situation.

I was one of the people I spent my days hunting down.

There'd been some talk of an Assay on Warder to establish details of events at Faebrook Folly. Fortunately, that prospect had receded, and it became less of a threat with each passing day. I still woke up in the dark of the night as my mind replayed events in the tower. What I'd done to Warder haunted me. It was a terrible thing. But, somehow, I also didn't feel like I'd done very much wrong.

I really needed to get away and think about where that left me. Despite what Sally and the others had said, there was a lot of good done by the Office. We did protect the public from the unnatural. We saved lives and we allowed people to go about their days happily oblivious to the horrors lurking around the corner of the building, or whispering into their dreams as they slept.

But also, I couldn't deny what I was. I was a user. And the thing was, I didn't feel bad or sullied by that. On the contrary, it filled me with an unexpected delight. Working magic had felt good. I felt like I'd been denying something within myself for a long, long time, and now my vision was clear. I felt weirdly light, somehow in tune with myself.

Which was all lovely, but it clearly brought with it huge danger. Sally had hinted that I should remain at the Office to act on behalf of those oppressed users who meant no great evil to the world, who simply wished to be themselves. The dangers of that filled me with alarm. If Hardknott-Lewis caught an inkling of any such thing, his punishment would be swift and terrible.

I really needed to sit down with someone I could trust and talk things through, but there simply weren't many candidates. Some days I felt the absence of Az in my life more strongly than I could say. Zubrasky, perhaps, might listen, and it would be good to see her again, but I needed to build bridges there, offer her something in return for all the help she'd given me. I'd thought about at least sending her a bunch of flowers, but, in truth, I wasn't at all sure if she'd appreciate the gesture.

My mother? I didn't want to load anything more onto her just then; she had enough to face as it was. The Lady had promised to do what she could for her, and perhaps after that was resolved – if it could be resolved – it might be time for a long and honest conversation. The Lady herself? She knew more than anyone else about me, but she wasn't exactly the warm, tell-me-your-problems type.

I reached the top of the Black Tower's flight of stairs with these thoughts chasing around in my brain. I half-expected a welcoming committee of officers to be up there, waiting to escort me to Oblivion. Instead, there was only Hardknott-Lewis, sitting behind his great desk, frowning at something he was reading on his screen.

A squall of rain hammered against the ancient windows of his office, cold air seething through the gaps in the ill-fitting metal frames. A single-bar electric fire glowed away in one corner, giving off an electrical smell of burning dust and very little in the way of heat. The Crow appeared not to notice. He probably found the autumnal chill pleasantly bracing.

He finished reading and looked up at me. "So, you survived the dangers and risks we discussed, Danesh."

I wasn't sure if that was a statement or a question. I was clearly still alive, but that may or may not have been what he meant. He'd warned me very clearly of the lure of magic use.

"Yes," I said.

He did that thing where he steepled his fingers together, as if in contemplation of difficult concepts. "This has been a troubling case, for many reasons."

Again, I kept my responses neutral. "It has."

"Have you found any evidence that anyone aside from Peter Warder and Evangelina Mormont were involved?"

"So far as I know, they acted alone."

"It is deeply concerning to find that a trusted agent of the Office has been involved in the use of such loathsome magics. If we can't trust ourselves then, really, what is the point of any of it?"

A little lump caught in my throat and I could only nod in agreement.

"If word gets around that we have succumbed, then we lose all authority among the supernaturalists. The monsters forget their fear of us, and everything starts to break down. It has happened before, more than once, in the Office's history."

Again, I nodded. As with the last interview I'd had with the Crow, I really didn't like the direction this was going in.

"It seems to me that Warder made the mistake of giving away a few genuine details about himself when he first talked to you."

Relief flooded through me like lights being switched on. Pretty, sparkly lights. He meant Warder, not me.

"He did?"

"His fascination with the history of English Wizardry and Mosley's fascists should have rung a few alarm bells. I've now looked into his history a little more. He did indeed give up on his PhD, but it wasn't because he lost interest in favour of working at the Office. In fact, it was because his supervisor became concerned about the direction of Warder's thinking. She refused to accept Warder's submitted manuscript without significant changes."

"What changes?"

"Officially it was because Warder's conclusions about the origins of English Wizardry were not adequately supported by the evidence he'd mustered. I suspect what that really means is that Warder began to express overt support for the English Wizardry version of history in his analysis. I think he was dazzled by them, became completely caught up in their world-view, and he lost all his objectivity as a result."

I tried to nod wisely, like I'd never been concerned about anything.

"There's more: Faebrook Folly belongs to a wing of his family in Oxfordshire. His background was wealthy. He had no powers, as you discovered, but it seems his maternal grandfather was active within English Wizardry in the early days. Then there was the fact of Warder's Art History degree; we perhaps should have spotted that. He was a talented artist, as his work at Martha Ndidi's house illustrated."

I wasn't sure if this was criticism of me, or of the Office generally.

"Yes," I said again.

"And, of course, it was Warder who tried to kill you using that malevolent spirit's touchstone in the centre of Cardiff. He brought it here from the warehouse, phoned you claiming to be in London. I checked the phone-mast logs. The lion was perhaps a warning shot when he learned you were investigating the case, but he quickly decided that he needed to be rid of you. He was using you to report his alibis, too, telling you he was in Richmond and on the Thames Estuary when he was actually involved in the ritual murders of Evan Cornwallis and Martha Ndidi."

It explained why Warder had needed his high-powered BMW: he'd killed Martha sometime early on Saturday morning, then sped down the M4 to be at the Possessed Statue Warehouse in time to arrange my welcoming committee.

"The Pestilence in Sally Spender's house might have been his doing, too," I said. "Some other cursed object he had access to from the London warehouse."

"I'd say that was Mormont's work, although whether it was specifically meant for you is open to debate. The fact we missed the signs about Warder isn't, however, the most troubling aspect of the affair. There's something here that concerns me very much more than one rogue operative succumbing to the temptations of the ineffable. You see what it is, of course?"

I took a wild stab in the dark at what was troubling him. "You believe that there is a resurgent English Wizardry, and that Warder was telling the truth when he hinted there are other members out there we don't know about."

"There's that, yes, but one aspect of it in particular. I mean the release of Mormont. Six days ago, I made an excursion into Oblivion through our own portal and confirmed the truth of it: she is no longer there. She most definitely *was*, but someone freed her, and I don't believe Warder would have had the knowledge or skill to do it alone. Similarly, as I believe you know, someone has been tampering with the records held within both MORIARTY and HOLMES, removing DNA evidence and the like. That could only be one of us, someone with specialised knowledge. My fear is this conspiracy goes both wider and higher than Peter Warder."

"How high?"

"That I don't know. I wish I did. I think we may be in for some interesting times in the months to come. The resurgence of English Wizardry has been checked for a time, I fancy, but with Mormont free – if she is still alive – and the

Office compromised, it's clear we haven't heard the last of this."

"You have no idea where they went?" I asked. "Mormont and Spender?" He'd spent many hours studying the runes at the portal.

"None. As you speculated in your report, Spender reworked the sigils binding the circle while Mormont was distracted and pushed her through to some unknown dimension."

I nodded. In truth, I wasn't really thinking about Mormont. "Do you think it's possible they survived?"

"I suspect they're both dead. Perhaps Spender deliberately took Mormont to some realm inimical to life. Sacrificed herself to be permanently rid of the Sorceress."

I nodded, but didn't reply. I'd come to the same conclusion myself.

"And you, Danesh," said Hardknott-Lewis, "if there is anyone surviving from English Wizardry, they'll really hate you now; you will have to be especially wary. The dangers to you have only increased, pressing in upon you from all sides."

Weirdly, the thought of that didn't trouble me too much. It seemed Hardknott-Lewis wasn't going to ruin my whole day by condemning *me* to Oblivion. The rest I could cope with.

"I'll be careful," I said.

"Very well," he said, and something in his tone told me I was dismissed. I was free, as easily as that. But as I reached the door he spoke again. "Oh, there is still the issue of the supernaturalists English Wizardry were hunting. If Spender is lost there are still the other two. Do you have any idea of the identity of this Myrddin?"

I'd neglected to mention that Mormont had revealed Myrddin's identity. Arthur Stonewall, English Wizardry's *Destroyer*, would undoubtedly be near the top of the Office's target list of powerful adepts, if they knew he was still alive.

"I don't," I said.

"Do you know the whereabouts of Oliver Auchter?"

Again, I hadn't mentioned my meeting with Auchter in my report. From a brief conversation with the Librarian, I knew he was still struggling to come to terms with the loss of Martha, but I hadn't actually seen him down in the Vault that time – which made my next statement at least technically true. "No."

"Is it your view we should pursue Auchter – or Spender if she ever turns up again?"

I tried to look like I was weighing up the notion carefully. "We've put them on a watch list. I think that's as far as we need to go for now."

"To your knowledge has either illegally employed magic?"

"No," I said, without hesitation. *Grey areas and white lies.* I'd stated in my report that Warder had been caught in the crossfire of one of Mormont's spells and that I'd only seen Sally use Mormont's portal against her – which was technically still a crime, but there were surely plenty of extenuating circumstances. Sometimes you had to do the right thing, not the legal thing. Worrying a little that I sounded like Warder, I said, "I think we have bigger targets to worry about."

He held me in his gaze for one more moment, considering my words. I couldn't read his expression at all. I had the troubling and familiar sensation that he was testing me, knew more than he was letting on. That he already knew the answers to his questions but was asking them anyway, to see what responses I gave.

Finally, he looked down, writing something on his pad with his gold fountain pen.

"Very good," he said. "Oh, and Danesh?"

"Sir?"

"Well done. You did good work."

"Thank you, sir."

Back at the office, I sat at my desk and closed my eyes for a moment, letting my racing heart calm. It had been an interesting couple of weeks, but it seemed I was in the clear. There was still English Wizardry to worry about, but Hardknott-Lewis had accepted my story. The only person who knew my secret – apart from Lady Coldwater, herself conflicted – was lost on some unknown plane of reality. Life could get back to normal.

"Hello, lovely, this came for you." Olwen stood by my desk holding a wrapped gift. By its shape and size, it looked like a DVD or a book.

"Who's it from?"

"You don't know? Get many gifts from secret admirers?"

"No. And no."

She shrugged. "She left it at the front office this morning."

"A woman?"

"Pronouns can be tricky these days, but that's why I said *she*. If you want to know who it's from, maybe you should open it and find out. I mean, that's just a random idea, you're the star investigator."

"Yes. I should do that."

I waited until she was gone, though, then tore the gift wrap off the present. It was, indeed, a book, an edition of *The Picture of Dorian Gray* I recognised very well. There was no card, but on the title page were the words *Borderland Reading Group*, handwritten in a familiar script.

It was – what? – a message, I guessed. Sally telling me she'd survived her fight with the Sorceress and was back in our world. Or it might have been a token of gratitude, a gift.

As well as that, it was also quite clearly an invitation. *Join us. A double-agent inside the Office could make all the difference.*

So much for life getting back to normal. I slipped the book into my desk, intending to look at it properly later.

The End

Acknowledgements

My eternal thanks to Elsewhen Press for believing in my book, and for producing it with such care, attention and good humour.

Thanks again to my good friend and Wales correspondent, Andrew Walton. Several of our trips into Cardiff to see bands show up as episodes in the book, including the night we drove up and down Cathedral Road – as Danesh does – looking for somewhere to park. In the end, we gave up. We wanted to see Public Image Ltd, but Cardiff was full because Ed Sheeran was also in town. Next time!

Thanks, also, to Peter Sheeran who provided invaluable input on earlier drafts of the book and to Christine Rains for her beta-reader input.

Writing can be a lonely business, and I'd like to thank the British Fantasy Society, the Untethered Realms collective and the British and Irish Writing community for their support and encouragement. Special mention, also, to the wonderful Project Gutenberg for making the texts of so many books available – several of which I drew on.

I'd like to thank my contacts in the magical and supernaturalist community, who obviously have to remain anonymous in the current circumstances. My thanks, also, to "The Whisperer", my contact in the Welsh Division of the Office of the Witchfinder General, who has also requested anonymity. Couldn't have done it without any of you.

Finally, thanks to my wonderful wife and my two daughters. All of this is for you. I couldn't have written the book without your tolerance, love, support and, obviously, all the cups of coffee.

Elsewhen Press

delivering outstanding new talents in speculative fiction

Visit the Elsewhen Press website at elsewhen.press for the latest information on all of our titles, authors and events; to read our blog; find out where to buy our books and ebooks; or to place an order.

Sign up for the Elsewhen Press InFlight Newsletter at elsewhen.press/newsletter

Supernatural Gothic by David Craig

David Craig's *Sooty Feathers* series is a masterful gothic tale about a supernatural war for control of the Second City of the British Empire, and the struggle of flawed characters of uncertain virtue who try to avert it. It is set in a late 19th century Glasgow ruled by undead – from the private clubs, town houses and country manors of the privileged to the dung-choked wynds and overcrowded slums of the poor. Undead unrest, a fallen angel, and religious zealots intent on driving out the forces of evil, set the stage for a diabolical conflict of biblical proportions.

Resurrection Men
The first book of the Sooty Feathers

Glasgow 1893.

Wilton Hunt, a student, and Tam Foley, a laudanum-addicted pharmacist, are pursuing extra-curricular careers as body snatchers, or 'resurrection men', under cover of darkness. They exhume a girl's corpse, only for it to disappear while their backs are turned. Confused and in need of the money the body would have earnt them, they investigate the corpse's disappearance. They discover that bodies have started to turn up in the area with ripped-out throats and severe loss of blood, although not the one they lost. The police are being encouraged by powerful people to look the other way, and the deaths are going unreported by the press. As Hunt and Foley delve beneath the veneer of respectable society, they find themselves entangled in a dangerous underworld that is protected from scrutiny by the rich and powerful members of the elite but secretive Sooty Feathers Club.

Meanwhile, a mysterious circus arrives in the middle of the night, summoned to help avenge a betrayal two centuries old…

ISBN: 9781911409366 (epub, kindle) / ISBN: 9781911409267 (400pp paperback)
Visit bit.ly/ResurrectionMen

Lord of the Hunt
The second book of the Sooty Feathers

June 1893.

Undead prowl the streets of Glasgow at night hunting for blood. They, in turn, are hunted by the formidable Lady Delaney and her apprentice Kerry Knox, whose fight against the secret society ruling Glasgow will lead them into the city's industrial heart where the poor toil in miserable conditions. Children have been exploited in mills and factories for decades, but the Sooty Feather Society has refined its cruel disregard in service to the undead.

Delaney and Knox are not the society's only problem. The elusive demon Arakiel employs murder and necromancy in his campaign to seize control of Glasgow, avenging betrayal and reclaiming what was once his.

Wilton Hunt and Tam Foley are lying low in the Highlands where Hunt's father has recently inherited title and estate. The blue skies and clear waters of Loch Aline may seem a tranquil sanctuary to the city men, but its forbidding forests and shadowed glens conceal dark secrets pertaining to Hunt's family, and a diabolical revelation will change Wilton's life forever.

Demons walk the crowded, cobbled streets of Glasgow, and a necromancer's debt is called in. Knox will learn what joining this war might cost her; Hunt and Foley will learn they can't escape it. Their diverged paths will meet again when dark magic unleashes a horror not everyone will survive…

ISBN: 9781911409762 (epub, kindle) / ISBN: 9781911409663 (416pp paperback)
Visit bit.ly/LordOfTheHunt

Urban fantasy by Tej Turner
The Janus Cycle

The Janus Cycle can best be described as gritty, surreal, urban fantasy. The over-arching story revolves around a nightclub called Janus, which is not merely a location but virtually a character in its own right. On the surface it appears to be a subcultural hub where the strange and disillusioned who feel alienated and oppressed by society escape to be free from convention; but underneath that façade is a surreal space in time where the very foundations of reality are twisted and distorted. But the special unique vibe of Janus is hijacked by a bandwagon of people who choose to conform to alternative lifestyles simply because it has become fashionable to be 'different', and this causes many of its original occupants to feel lost and disenchanted. We see the story of Janus unfold through the eyes of eight narrators, each with their own perspective and their own personal journey. A story in which the nightclub itself goes on a journey. But throughout, one character, a strange girl, briefly appears and reappears warning the narrators that their individual journeys are going to collide in a cataclysmic event. Is she just another one of the nightclub's denizens, a cynical mischief-maker out to create havoc or a time-traveller trying to prevent an impending disaster?

ISBN: 9781908168566 (epub, kindle) / ISBN: 9781908168467 (224pp paperback)
Visit bit.ly/JanusCycle

Dinnusos Rises

The vibe has soured somewhat after a violent clash in the Janus nightclub a few months ago, and since then Neal has opened a new establishment called 'Dinnusos'. Located on a derelict and forgotten side of town, it is not the sort of place you stumble upon by accident, but over time it enchants people, and soon becomes a nucleus for urban bohemians and a refuge for the city's lost souls. Rumour has it that it was once a grand hotel, many years ago, but no one is quite sure. Whilst mingling in the bar downstairs you might find yourself in the company of poets, dreamers, outsiders, and all manner of misfits and rebels. And if you're daring enough to explore its ghostly halls, there's a whole labyrinth of rooms on the upper floors to get lost in...

Now it seems that not just Neal's clientele, but the entire population of the city, begin to go crazy when beings, once thought mythological, enter the mortal realm to stir chaos as they sow the seeds of militancy.

Eight characters. Most of them friends, some of them strangers. Each with their own story to tell. All of them destined to cross paths in a surreal sequence of events which will change them forever.

ISBN: 9781911409137 (epub, kindle) / ISBN: 9781911409038 (280pp paperback)
visit bit.ly/DinnusosRises

ABOUT SIMON KEWIN

Simon Kewin is a pseudonym used by an infinite number of monkeys who operate from a secret location deep in the English countryside. Every now and then they produce a manuscript that reads as a complete novel with a beginning, a middle and an end. Sometimes even in that order.

The Simon Kewin persona devised by the monkeys was born on the misty Isle of Man in the middle of the Irish Sea, at around the time The Beatles were twisting and shouting. He moved to the UK as a teenager, where he still resides. He is the author of over a hundred published short stories and poems, as well as a growing number of novels. In addition to fiction, he also writes computer software. The key thing, he finds, is not to get the two mixed up.

He has a first class honours degree in English Literature, is married, and has two daughters.

9 781911 409649